Embers at Midnight

To Becky –
best wishes

Kate Lance

Kate Lance,
18 February 2022

SEA
BOOKS
PRESS
seabooks.net

Print ISBN: 978-0-6489851-3-6
Ebook ISBN: 978-0-6489851-4-3

Published by Seabooks Press
seabooks.net

A catalogue record for this
work is available from the
National Library of Australia

BY THE SAME AUTHOR

Fiction

Testing the Limits
Silver Highways
Atomic Sea (As CM Lance)
The Turning Tide (As CM Lance)

Non-Fiction

Alan Villiers: Voyager of the Winds
Redbill: From Pearls to Peace

To Alison Shields, Gillian Clarke and Ruth Carson

with love and gratitude

I caught this morning morning's minion, king-
   dom of daylight's dauphin, dapple-dawn-drawn Falcon, in his riding
   Of the rolling level underneath him steady air, and striding
High there, how he rung upon the rein of a wimpling wing
In his ecstasy! then off, off forth on swing,
   As a skate's heel sweeps smooth on a bow-bend: the hurl and gliding
   Rebuffed the big wind. My heart in hiding
Stirred for a bird, – the achieve of, the mastery of the thing!

Brute beauty and valour and act, oh, air, pride, plume, here
   Buckle! AND the fire that breaks from thee then, a billion
Times told lovelier, more dangerous, O my chevalier!

No wonder of it: shéer plód makes plough down sillion
Shine, and blue-bleak embers, ah my dear,
Fall, gall themselves, and gash gold-vermilion.

The Windhover – Gerard Manley Hopkins (1877)

CONTENTS

PART I. A SINKING SHIP

1. Eliza: A Confidential Path

Golden Charlotte always gets what she wants. In this case it's my brother Pete swearing his life unto hers, here at the Registry Office. (Even the bride's famous charm could not convince the local vicar to let a divorcée wed in his church.)

The bridal bouquet is heavy, a mass of lilies as lush as Charlotte herself, and I'm tired. Any day with Charlotte can seem long but this one started particularly early.

Yet Pete is so happy. My feckless baby brother is a man now, dark-haired, rangy, strong. He's a farmer at heart and an engineer by profession, although once, in another life with another woman, he was a pilot. But now he's landed his beloved Charlotte, and they kiss and turn to the wedding guests as the organ rings out in triumph.

Eight-month-old Vivian gurgles in the arms of the housekeeper and waves her small hands at her parents. The polite fiction has it she's from Charlotte's previous marriage, but those bright brown eyes mark her unmistakably as Pete's daughter. Vivian, laughing, flutters her hands at me too. I feel as if my heart is being squeezed and wave back to my tiny niece.

I hand the bouquet to Charlotte and follow the newlyweds along the aisle. Pete's best man, Toby, falls in beside me and we roll our eyes at each other in relief. He murmurs, 'Dear God, I need champagne.' He's had a long day too.

It's May 1937 and chilly in the spring sunlight. We arrange ourselves for photos, then climb into cars and return to Pete's farmhouse for a wedding breakfast. Toby delivers a witty speech, although twice he comes perilously close to mentioning Pete's previous love, Billie.

We toast the happy couple and eat. Seated to my right is Charlotte's father, Professor Otto Fischer, as burly, bearded and committed as Karl Marx. On my left is Harry, Charlotte's ex-husband, grey-eyed behind his gold-rimmed glasses. Now and then he strokes my thigh deliciously beneath the table.

As I argue with Toby about who's had the most exhausting day (I win), I notice Harry and Professor Fischer are deep in worried, private conversation. I know it's not about the wedding.

Once Charlotte was my friend, and I tried earnestly not to fall into Harry's arms. But a year ago I did, and high time too — Charlotte was already pregnant to Pete. But she was terrified of the scandal of divorce and refused to let her marriage go: until the birth of baby Vivian gave her the courage.

So Harry and I went to a hotel and expressed amazement when the detective burst into our unlocked room, and the divorce came through in six months. Since then Charlotte and I have rebuilt a wary friendship, based mainly upon my love for small Vivian and Charlotte's love of ordering me around.

That evening, when the newlyweds have retired and only a few close friends remain, we dance in the sitting room to the gramophone. It's great fun, especially when the avant-garde gang — Toby, Stefan, Klara and Sofia — do the Charleston, now absurdly outdated.

Then Stef and Toby sit down at the piano, their heads together, laughing and playing snippets of Noel Coward songs, and pale Klara waltzes, her eyes closed, in the arms of red-lipped Sofia.

Later, Stefan and I dance too, his slim body pleasingly familiar. We were lovers once, until he realised Toby meant more to him than any woman could. It was a painful time, eased now by new happiness: this marriage and baby Vivian and of course, Charlotte's ex-husband.

Stef goes to the kitchen for more champagne, refills our glasses, then stands at the gramophone chatting to Harry about the music. I gaze at them both, such fine-looking men, and smile to myself.

Harry and I survived these long years of believing we could never be together, and now at last we are. A waltz begins and we dance. He nuzzles my neck, and I caress his back in a place I know brings him particular pleasure. Then we go upstairs to bed.

Lying sated and content, Harry murmurs, 'Did you miss Billie today?'

I kiss his warm shoulder. 'Terribly. She should have been here despite everything.'

'Jealous of Charlotte, perhaps?'

'Doubt it,' I say. 'Remember it was Billie who left Pete.'

'Where did you say she was living now?'

'All over the place really, wherever the aerial circus is performing,' I say. 'Poor thing.'

'I suppose she'd still prefer to be teaching RAF recruits at Hamble aerodrome.'

I laugh. 'The "snotty-nosed, public-school types"? Don't think so.' I roll onto my other side and Harry cuddles me from behind.

'What were you and Otto Fischer talking about?' I say. 'You seemed rather intense.'

'The civil war in Spain. He's appalled at what's happening.'

'Oh, *matros*, surely it'll work out somehow. You mustn't worry.'

'I try not to, but really, it's unbelievable. A Fascist coup against an elected Republic, in *this* day and age?' Harry sighs. 'Otto wants Billie's opinion on some planes his group would like to send to the Spanish government.'

'Hope he doesn't expect her to *fly* them. Why not ask Stef or Pete, they're pilots too?'

'They don't have her experience with so many different old crates.'

I nod. 'Well, she might need the work, she said the aerial display could be closing down soon. No one wants to see planes for fun any more — just reminds them of the Guernica bombings.'

'And who could blame them?' says Harry. 'Anyway, I told Otto to speak to you in London. So sleep now, *jungman*. We've got cleaning up to do in the morning.'

'It's bloody Charlotte's home now. She can clean up.'

'Unlikely,' he says. 'Bet you she has a headache and everyone else has to do it.'

'You terrible cynic. Anyone would think you know her well.'

'Oh, far too well. I'd love to forget.'

I turn to face him, and stroke him slowly from nipple to belly to groin. 'Again? I can do my best.'

'Yes please, my darling.'

A week later I'm sitting on the small balcony of my flat in Bloomsbury, reading in the spring sunshine. I put the book down and gaze at the leafy garden square across the road, thinking about the wedding and my brother Pete.

He's resigned himself at last to his manager's job in an aircraft factory, and leaves his small plane stored at a nearby airfield. With all the demands of Charlotte and the baby he doesn't have time for flying.

I wonder how much he misses it. I wonder how much he misses Billie as well.

Of course he adores Charlotte, most men do. She's wry and seductive and restless, while fierce Billie couldn't be more different. Pete used to call her a red-haired Amelia Earhart — a sarcastic, scowling Earhart.

He and Billie had planned their own aviation business, but Pete sabotaged everything by getting thrown out of flying school and flinging himself into Charlotte's arms.

Billie picked herself up and tutored for a time at Hamble (which welcomed the air-mindedness of the fair sex they said, yet took forever to provide any women's bathrooms), but finally even she couldn't bear the casual, constant prejudice any longer.

'Everyone loves a girl flyer, Lizzie,' she told me. 'Except the boy flyers.'

Oh, *Billie.* I sigh.

Just then the bell rings, and standing at the door is Charlotte's father, Professor Fischer. Though he and Harry have been friends for a long time, we've never spoken much before. I make us coffee and we go to sit out on the balcony.

'Miss McKee,' he says formally, 'Harry Bell has mentioned to you my request regarding Miss Quinn?'

'Yes, he did. But Professor Fischer, surely you don't expect Billie to fly aeroplanes in Spain?'

'No, not at all! And please call me Otto. I will take the liberty of addressing you as Eliza, since that is how Harry has spoken of you from his heart these many years.'

'Of course.' I'm amused at the Professor's old-fashioned charm.

'I must ask you, Eliza, do you understand what has been happening in Spain?'

I sip my coffee. 'Not much. I know civil war broke out last year after General Franco's right-wing rebels staged a coup against the Republican government, but it's all been a bit confusing ever since.'

Otto leans forward, his eyebrows drawn. 'Then you should know, Eliza, if the rebels do defeat the Republic, Fascists all over Europe will believe they are invincible. Another war will almost certainly begin.'

'Oh, surely not, Otto.' I smile. 'This isn't the Middle Ages. An elected government should be able to crush some raggle-taggle rebels.'

'Eliza, those rebels are very powerful. They are supported by the richest landowners, the Catholic Church, the Italian Fascist and German Nazi governments. Even our own conservative British rulers wish them well.'

'But aren't the Republicans supported too? I thought volunteers from around the world were helping them.'

'Indeed, but they *must* be volunteers — their own conservative countries loudly proclaim neutrality. Eliza, the rebels are powerful and wish us all to return to the Middle Ages. We must stop them now. Or soon it may be the Nazis we have to stop.'

'Oh.' My chest feels tight. 'I've read about them doing terrible things to their Jewish people.'

'*Ja.* Even my own family —' He swallows. 'Now. I work with a committee that wishes to send old aircraft to Spain for the air force. They are loyal to the Republic but do not have enough planes to fight the Condor Legion. You have heard of the Condor Legion?'

I nod. 'The German pilots who bombed Guernica.'

'Indeed. War should take place on battlefields, or so civilised people have always assumed. It should not descend from the sky onto market-towns full of innocent people. Now there is nothing to stop such a thing happening everywhere. Even here in quiet London.'

Bombs here? I gaze at the sunny garden square and shiver.

'Our committee has located some unregistered planes, but we have no idea if they are airworthy, and their owners would like a great deal of money for them. So Miss Quinn could help us decide if we should buy them.'

'But how would you get them to Spain?' I say. 'Aren't all the ports blockaded?'

'We can ferry them legally to France, then,' Otto shrugs, 'not quite so legally into Spain. The Republican pilots would do the fighting and your friend would not be involved in the slightest. Of course we would pay for her advice.'

'Well, Billie's still touring, but I'll give you the number for head office. After that it's her you'll have to convince, and she has no interest in politics.'

'Ah, but she has interest in flying, and we all know the aerial circuses are finished. I doubt anyone needs persuading today what extraordinary inventions aeroplanes have become,' he says drily.

He leans back and stretches a little. 'A good wedding last week, *ja*?'

I'm relieved to change to easier topics. 'You must be pleased Charlotte is so happy. And baby Vivian too —' I smile to myself.

'What joy she brings. The image of Charlotte's mother Ilse, gone these two years now,' he says, his eyes suddenly bright with tears. He clears his throat. 'Still, my work is a consolation.'

He looks around and sees my book on the table. He picks it up, puzzled, stroking his beard, and gazes at me from under his eyebrows. '*The American Black Chamber*?'

I laugh, a little shyly. 'I read anything that interests me.'

'Indeed. Cryptography interests you?'

'I've always loved mathematics — and in operation like that it's fascinating.'

'For me too, of course,' he says slowly.

'But aren't you a professor of philosophy?'

'My philosophical research is based upon the concepts of the Vienna Circle, now of course devastated by the Nazis.' He sighs. 'But mathematics is essential to that work. Connected, in unexpected ways, to cryptography.'

He gazes at me for a moment and I think he's seeing me properly for the first time. He carefully puts down the book. 'When you have read this, Eliza — and only if you are interested of course — I have one or two introductory papers you might enjoy. I would be happy to discuss them, but they are highly confidential. Still, perhaps that is too much of an undertaking.'

'No, *no!*' I say. 'I'd love to see your papers, I'd *love* to talk about this, it's always fascinated me. But as a woman I've been told pretty often that such things are not open to me.'

'But now at this time, in this place,' he says, 'everything is open — *must* be open — to all.'

We walk to the door and he shakes my hand. 'I will send you the paper, Eliza, then let us talk. But please remember they are secret, for you only.'

'Thank you. I'll look forward to it, Otto.'

'Of course, this is unconnected to your friend Billie Quinn, quite a different matter.' He shrugs. 'But perhaps not. Many things may help preserve civilisation in this increasingly gloomy world.' Then he laughs sadly. 'I am a romantic fool. Civilisation is already lost.'

I'm curious to see Otto's papers, because lately I've been at rather a loose end. Harry is a doctor, a researcher in malaria, so the many and varied species of *Plasmodium* parasite are a common topic at our dining table.

My own interests are odd too, but they don't occupy me in the same way. I run a small company for my grandmother in Australia, importing pearlshell from Broome for the jewellery trade. But in recent years overfishing has damaged the market, so business is quiet.

The other interest doesn't demand much of my time either. It's a shareholding in a cargo ship, *Inverley*, left to me by my late grandfather, Freddy. But *Inverley* isn't the usual sort of ship with an engine — she's a great steel windjammer, a four-masted barque.

There are very few of her kind left afloat nowadays, and if I mention them most people are puzzled. '*Steel* sailing ships?' they say. 'But aren't those clippers or galleons or whatever, made out of wood and they race to China and back with tea ... or something?'

'No,' I say, 'these are modern vessels, well, modern forty years ago —

and they're gigantic, hundreds of feet long. Only a dozen or so still exist and every year they bring the grain harvest from Australia to Europe. They're owned and sailed mostly by the Finns.'

Usually at this stage, say at a party, people give me a look as if I'm teasing them and go to talk to somebody else. But I'm not teasing. Square-rigged *Inverley* may be an anachronism in this era of engine-driven vessels, yet she certainly exists. And I love her.

Eight years ago she brought me from Australia to England, and on our four-month passage I was grudgingly permitted to work with the crew. They rechristened me Elias, and under their rough tutelage I grew strong and confident and a little wiser in the ways of the world.

All the square-riggers are growing old now, and one by one going to the breakers, so I'm lucky to have known such a life. *Inverley* is the wellspring of my happiest memories.

And of course I love her most of all because Harry and I first became friends upon her deck.

True to his word, Otto sends me a large envelope by first class mail with three of his papers. The formal language is intimidating but, little by little, the logic unfolds, along with a surprising sense of beauty. I also buy a textbook he suggests will help, and slowly this new world draws me in.

We meet every few weeks for a chat over coffee, and Otto guides me towards what he calls the wider view. Not only of the work itself but how it's applied in real life: especially in the intelligence services, about which he seems to know a surprising amount as well.

Conversations with Harry at our dining table about *Plasmodium* research are now interspersed with my excited insights into the realm of codes and cryptography. I read at my desk when it rains and out on my balcony in good weather, and sometimes I look across to the trees in the garden square and feel utterly content and absorbed.

It never occurs to me to wonder where this fascination will lead.

I don't ask myself why Otto is being so helpful, why he is clearing a path before me, a confidential path, one I would never have discovered for myself.

I don't question what it might mean for me, or Billie, or Harry.

The Great War passed so long ago it's easy to assume today's peace will last forever. I cannot for a moment imagine these sunny days will pass, and soon an eyewall of thunderclouds will slowly engulf the sky.

I cannot imagine, either, how carelessly I will stray into that stormfront.

Perhaps some things are beyond imagination.

2. Billie: Kites in Spain

Miami, Saturday, 31 May 1937: Mrs. Amelia Earhart Putnam announced tonight she hopes to restart her world flight tomorrow. Noonan, who will act as navigator, will accompany her on the entire journey. She will fly to South America and then across the Atlantic and the Channel to Aden, Karachi, Darwin, Lae, Howland, Honolulu and from thence to Oakland, California.

I put down the newspaper and sigh. Lucky cow, wish it were me instead. Pete always said I was like Earhart, but she's calm and patient and good natured — I'm just a cranky bitch, as Pete wasn't too slow to point out, either.

I look up and realise there's someone hovering at the opening to my tent. Wilfred Bettany. I really don't want to deal with his anxious politeness — polite anxiety? — this afternoon. Sometimes I think I should take out a newspaper advertisement: *Miss Billie Quinn would like to apologise to all the men of Planet Earth for making them nervous because she can fly aeroplanes better than they can.*

'Ahem, Miss Quinn?' he says, taking off his hat.

'Hello, Wilf. What's up?'

'The meeting, Miss Quinn. Remember? Major Stott's come from London to address us.'

'Reckon he's got good news, Wilf?'

'Doubt it.'

We walk together to the large tent where everyone else is assembling. Wilf's not that bad really, but I've told him often enough not to call me Miss Quinn. If he didn't annoy me so much, he'd be almost attractive in a puppy-dog sort of way.

We move towards the rear of the tent as the Major stands up to speak. He took over the business a couple of years ago, but unfortunately it was when the novelty of human flight was wearing off and the unpleasant reality of aerial warfare was emerging. Not a good time to try to charm the paying public with a flying circus.

At least he doesn't beat around the bush. Tight economic conditions, blah blah, poor weather, blah blah, reduced takings, blah blah. Terribly sorry, old chaps. When you finish today it's for good. Thank you.

'Do you think we'll get paid out for the month?' says Wilf as we leave the tent, everyone murmuring around us.

'I'll be surprised if we get paid out for the week.'

'Will you be all right, Miss Quinn? What will you do?'

'No idea, Wilf. And for Christ's sake call me Billie. What about you?'

He shakes his head. 'Family's disowned me and I never finished my studies. Not many civilian aviation jobs around now.'

'Air Force?'

'Well, it's a pay-packet. And they're desperate for men —'

'Not much use to me, then.'

He grins. 'Suppose not. Couldn't have girls —' He goes red. 'Sorry.'

Something simmers over, as it does all too often nowadays. 'You know how many women hold pilot's licences in England now, Wilf? Close to *two hundred*. You don't reckon there's a few of them might be some use in the air? Especially if ... when ...'

I run out of steam.

Wilf gazes at me. 'I'll be sorry not to see you every day, Billie.'

'Yeah.' I'm surprised to find myself thinking *me too*.

'Will you come to the pub with us later? I know you usually don't, but it's the last night.'

I shrug. 'Maybe.' He smiles and I think, okay. Nice skin, broad shoulders, slim hips. And I'll never see him again after this. Why not?

Wilf goes to check his plane. I can see people already lining up for tickets at the gate, even though the afternoon show doesn't start for an hour. Maybe they've heard this is going to be the last one.

As I get to my tent I'm surprised to see a large bearded man in an overcoat waiting by the entry. He takes off his hat as I approach, and steps forward.

'Miss Quinn?'

'No, Queen of bloody Sheba.'

He smiles politely. What an utter shit I've become.

'Sorry. Force of habit. And you are —?'

'Professor Fischer, Otto. You would know of me as Charlotte's father.'

'Oh, okay. How did the wedding go?'

'It was very pleasant. I was sorry not to see you there, but I was able to prevail upon Miss Eliza McKee to help me track you down.'

To my amusement I'd been sent an invitation to the wedding. I'd ripped it up, not out of pique, I just couldn't be bothered to go. After all, Pete didn't dump me for Charlotte — it was me left him after he stupidly threw away all our years of hard work.

I don't even hate Charlotte either, although I'm perfectly aware of the barbed steel spine beneath all that sweet lushness. At my kindest, which isn't very often, I sometimes pity her, though could never have said why.

She has Pete, she has their child, she apparently has everything she ever wanted. But I'll be mildly curious to see if that's enough for her in the years ahead.

And Charlotte did one good thing at least: she released poor Harry Bell from their bitter shell of a marriage and made Lizzie's life complete. My dear friend Lizzie, who has her own spine of steel, but hers is flexible and far from barbed.

'Miss Quinn?'

'Sorry. Just thinking how delightful the wedding must have been.'

To my surprise he says wryly, 'I rather doubt that,' and I can't help but grin.

We sit on folding stools in my tent and he says, 'As I explained to Eliza, we hope to buy several aircraft to send to the Republicans in Spain, but we need a professional opinion on their airworthiness. It must be confidential of course, as it is technically against the law. The Non-Intervention Committee has some very peculiar ideas, and we prefer not to attract their attention.'

'The Non-who?'

'A government body preventing anyone sending arms to Spain, but in reality stopping only those who would aid the Republicans. No such restrictions hinder the Germans and Italians in their support of the

Nationalists.'

'Okay. And the Nationalists would be —?'

He smiles kindly. 'The rebels who carried out a military coup against the elected Republican government.'

'Oh, the baddies.'

He stops smiling. 'In any war both sides may behave culpably, but yes, there have been extraordinary barbarities ...' His jaw clenches. 'Yes, the baddies. And if they win, German aggression will be unstoppable. You would know that many British volunteers — soldiers, nurses, drivers — have already joined the International Brigades to support the Republicans.'

'Not really, I only read the aviation news. So why do the Republicans want these old kites?'

'The Spanish air force is loyal, but the pilots are poorly-trained and have few working planes.'

'Poorly-trained?' I say slowly. 'Well, I need a job and I'm a qualified instructor.'

'Spain is a *war* front, Miss Quinn, not suitable for —'

'I think that's for me to decide, Otto.'

'Ah.' He hesitates. 'Certainly, a number of foreign airmen were hired last year to help protect Madrid. They did well, although most have now left, forbidden by their own countries to take part.'

'Hired? What were they paid?'

'I believe it was something like two hundred pounds a month.'

'That's pretty good. What would they pay for a flight instructor, do you reckon?'

'I do not know.' He frowns in concern. 'Miss Quinn —'

'Call me Billie, for Christ's sake.'

'Billie, please understand that half the country is now held by the Nationalists, and they are ruthless and very well armed. And by 'ruthless' I mean they visit atrocities upon civilians on an almost inconceivable scale. Women especially are targeted for —'

He stops and rubs his face with both hands, his eyes sad. 'Spain is not a place for innocents of any kind, Billie. Political or personal.'

'I'm thirty years old, Otto, and I've worked with men as an equal since I was seventeen.' I shrug. 'Okay, maybe I'm a political innocent but I'm not interested in all that argy-bargy.' I lean forward. 'I just need *work*, this job's finished. Why shouldn't I train Republican flyers?'

'The Russians are setting up a school at the moment to instruct Spanish pilots, so the job would not last for long — months at most.'

'Any paid work suits me. Those Russian planes are mainly Polikarpov I-15s and I-16s, aren't they? I've flown an I-5, it's a good bird.'

'I have no idea at all about those machines. It is why I am here in the first place.'

'Come on, Otto, I need a job. Do it for the Revolution.'

He closes his eyes. 'Billie, it is the legally elected *government* we are supporting.'

'Oh that's right, it's the baddies who are doing the revolution.'

'Indeed it is.' He sighs. 'Very well. I will enquire.'

'Great. Now, those planes you wanted me to check, what are they?'

He gets a notebook out of his coat and shows me a list of names, and I have to smile.

'Sorry, Otto, I don't need to see any of these. If even one of them could get off the ground I'd be surprised. They were slow and obsolete twenty years ago. You'd be wasting your money.'

One of the assistant riggers calls from outside the tent, 'Final checks, Miss Quinn. Don't be late.'

'All right,' I say, scribbling on a page of the notebook. 'Here's my phone number in London. Ring me when you know more.'

Miss Billie's Daredevil Handkerchief Stunt goes off as usual, but I can't say I'm sorry it's for the last time. Swooping past the crowd in a Tiger Moth and hooking a hanky off the ground with one wing may not be quite as terrifying as it looks, but getting it wrong would leave a large and bloody hole in the ground.

Afterwards I help strip down the planes and load them into the trucks. Everyone's subdued but careful, as always. There'll be plenty of work ahead for the mechanics and riggers and pilots — the Royal Air Force can't get enough men — but the women who sell the tickets and cook and keep the whole shebang ticking over don't have any such guarantees, and I see a few red eyes.

By evening it's all over. The sleeping and mess tents will stay till tomorrow but everything else is packed. I go to my tent, have a quick wash and change, then head along the path through the wheatfield to the pub. The other pilots are already sitting around a table in the courtyard, so I get half a pint and sit beside Wilf, who goes red.

The pilots are pretty easy company. They gave me some shit at first but we've learnt to get along. There was one creep who thought I'd fall into his bed with a sob of gratitude, but I enlightened him. He departed a few months ago, still sulking, but at least he never touched me again.

Night falls and most people leave for their tents — it'll be an early day tomorrow. Finally it's just me and dear old Wilf, who's run out of conversational gambits and has a faint air of desperation.

'Would you mind escorting me back through the field?' I ask, as if I haven't safely negotiated paths through fields and lanes to our campsites for months. He nods, speechless.

We set off in the dark but luckily he's brought a torch. Half-way back I stop and look up to the sky. It was hazy earlier, but now there's a quarter-moon and the stars are brilliant in the mild night air. I love them, even though these northern skies aren't nearly as beautiful as those of my Western Australian childhood.

'Switch off the torch, Wilf. I can't see properly.'

He does so, and after a time gazing upwards I turn to him, and step close and put my hands on his shoulders. I rest my head lightly on his shoulder too, surprised at how tired — of just about everything — I suddenly feel.

But he smells of young, healthy male and I nuzzle his cheek and nibble my way to his nicely-shaped mouth, and he obliges me with a kiss that's rather more pleasingly experienced than I'd expected. I tilt my head back and smile at him in the faint moonlight.

'Billie,' he says, breathing deeply. 'God, that's ...'

I take his hand and draw him away from the path and we sit down among the soft green wheat. He puts his arms around me and kisses me again, as delightfully as the first time.

I suddenly regret I didn't try this with him before, but it wouldn't have been wise in the gossipy world of the aerial circus. But tomorrow we're going in different directions.

He leans over me, and I reach up to his amazed face and bring his mouth to mine again. I guide his fingers to my buttons and he opens them and I shrug off my shirt. I'm so slim I usually wear just a camisole beneath and, as he pulls it off and his tongue finds my aching nipples, that seems a particularly good idea.

I groan and his mouth comes back to mine and his hands are doing marvellous things — everywhere — but the rest of my bloody clothes are getting in the way.

I undo my trousers and kick them off, along with my knickers and shoes, and don't even have to suggest to Wilf he does the same. Efficient lad, I think, as the stars waver above us and stalks of wheat slide smooth against my back.

Exquisitely, wickedly naked to the air, I wrap my thighs around his hips and pull him deep into me: then I don't notice the stars above or anything else. I haven't had a man in quite a while, so it's not very long before I'm arching in pleasure, waves throbbing through me, softening and glowing and easing away.

Wilf comes too, hot on my belly, then we doze for a few moments.

He wakes, cups my face and whispers, 'Oh, *Billie* —'

I put my hand on his mouth. 'Shh. We'd better get back before anyone notices.'

We dress, Wilf finds his torch, and we walk calmly back to the camp. No one is about so I kiss him quickly and push him towards his tent. He goes to say something and I shake my head.

'Night, Wilf.'

Next morning he's shy and pleased, but I'm glad to see there's no swaggering or significant looks.

At the breakfast table the chat is of future prospects. Ours was the last of the civilian flying displays and now only the RAF, with its promises of power and protection, draws the crowds.

'What you going to do then, Billie?' asks one of the mechanics.

I shrug. 'Might be getting work in Spain, training pilots for the

Republicans.'

'Who, the *Reds*?' says a man named Jones. 'Better get paid in advance. Haven't got a hope — the Krauts and Wops are walloping them.'

'They're not Reds,' says Wilf, surprising me. 'They're the government, elected to modernise the place and bring in some of the freedoms we all take for granted.'

'Ha! Fellow traveller over here, boys,' says Jones. 'Give it up, Wilf, they're just Commies, and the Krauts'll show 'em what for.'

'And then?' asks Wilf. 'They'll try to show us what for as well.'

'Doesn't matter — we've got the RAF,' says another pilot proudly.

The head mechanic says, 'Don't be so confident, laddie. The Germans are miles ahead of us, *miles*. Christ, what I'd give to get my hands on one of those Messerschmidts.' He grimaces. 'But Jones is right, the Republicans don't stand a chance. Trying to take on the Condor Legion with a few old kites?'

'Well, not me personally,' I say. 'But if they'll pay me to teach them flying, why would I turn down the job? Not much else available.'

'Maybe they'll start up a women's RAF just for you, Billie,' says someone, snorting with laughter and the others join in.

I grin, but oh, how sick I am of the same old jokes.

I know I can outfly any of these smug bastards, and I know they'll never acknowledge it. And they'll always have work handed to them on a plate, they'll always get the newest, sleekest birds.

And me? Clapped out old kites in Spain.

3. Toby: Whitfield Street

Stefan drives us back to London. I'm tired, but mainly glad that ghastly wedding's over. Poor old Pete was terrified something would go wrong at the last minute (which it has fairly often in the dear boy's life), but now at last he's happy. Even the terrifying Charlotte seemed content, and she's never been what you'd call a serene soul.

Klara is beside me in the rear seat and she dozes, her head on my shoulder. I gaze at Stef and Sofia in the front.

They're cousins, two peas in a pod as they say, both dark-haired and green-eyed; although Sofia is buxom while my love is slim and entirely beautiful under his well-cut clothes. Their mothers were the Naughty Diamant Twins, dancers who came from Poland at the turn of the century and found themselves generous and compliant husbands.

I suppose we're really rather a mixed bunch. Klara, slight and fair, is from Finland — I believe there was a brief marriage to some oaf in Cambridge, then she met Sofia and that was that. Me? I'm the mundane one. Tall, blond, English, and my accent as anonymous as I can make it.

I watch the trees flickering past the window and return to thinking, what *will* I do about that bloody house? My darling old aunt Maude died recently and bequeathed me her London terrace in the bohemian district of Fitzrovia. Some might rejoice at their good fortune, but I used to visit her in the ghastly old pile and my heart sinks.

The Depression may be easing off but it's left a lot of good property going for pennies. It would be hard to even give the house away right now, let alone find a willing purchaser — it's shabby and Victorian and hopelessly unfashionable.

In any case I know Maude wanted it to stay in the family. She was always kind to me, even paid for my education, so I do owe her that.

It's not as if Stef and I couldn't do with a bit more space. My desk is in a corner of the sitting room in our small flat and, although he says it doesn't bother him, my tapping on the typewriter must be irritating. But I've got to get a manuscript to the publishers in the next few weeks so I simply can't avoid it.

Maude's place has four storeys plus an attic and cellar. It might be possible for us to live on a couple of floors, but the cold, decrepit remainder? Rent it out perhaps? That could be tricky. I'd have to do it up and I'm not very handy that way.

Tricky in other ways too — who would we share the house with? There are rather a lot of loud and unpleasant individuals out there who'd love to see me and Stef in gaol simply for being who we are. Even at our current lodgings we have to be ludicrously discreet, yet the landlord is still spitefully watchful.

I say lightly, 'Sofia, want to live in my rotting inheritance?'

'What would the rent be, dear one?'

'Only joking, blossom. I wouldn't impose that slum on anyone.'

Sofia turns around. 'No, honestly, Toby. I've been to your aunt's — remember when we took her a hamper last Christmas? It's not that bad. And our landlady has just given me and Klara notice.'

'Why?'

'You know why. For being us, despite always paying our rent on time and putting up for years with her ghastly cats.'

Beside me Klara murmurs, 'And the minister wants my printing press out of the church cellar. Your new house has a cellar?'

'It's not a *new* house, Klara, it's a horrible, disgusting old one. And you'd have to clean it and paint it and repair it —'

'We could do that,' says Sofia.

She's correct. Unlike me, they both maintain their surroundings simply and competently.

'Tell you what, old chums,' I say, laughing. 'You do the repairs around the place and you can have a floor to yourselves for free.'

'I want the cellar for my press,' says Klara sleepily. 'And an attic room for a study.'

'You drive a hard bargain, darling. God knows, I had plans to bury bodies in that cellar, but if it's what you want —'

Klara sits up and claps her hands. 'Toby, that would be excellent indeed.'

'Are you serious? Stef, what do you think?'

He keeps his gaze on the road and nods. 'It's rather a good idea, Toby — could protect all of us.'

Sofia says, 'Of *course*. Two men, two women. As far as the busybodies are concerned that's how it's supposed to be. Our real lives can remain our own business.'

'I suppose it *could* be something of a haven,' I say doubtfully.

'Plenty of space, too,' says Sofia. 'I desperately need a rehearsal studio with good acoustics. One of those big empty rooms would be perfect.'

'Are you sure?' I say. 'You do realise how much work it needs?'

'Ha!' says Klara confidently.

She's rather less confident the day we go to see the house in Whitfield Street: a vulgar Victorian interloper in a row of elegant Georgian residences. The rain doesn't help much, but even a sunny day wouldn't flatter the garish red bricks beneath their layers of London soot.

I unlock the front door and a dreadful smell hits us in the face.

'Just needs an airing,' says Sofia briskly. She looks into the front room and says less briskly, 'Oh God, poor decomposing beastie. Those rugs'll have to go, *then* an airing will work wonders.'

Downstairs the walls of the two reception rooms are covered in acres of printed brown agapanthus, and at the rear is an old-fashioned kitchen and bathroom. Being careful not to catch our feet in the worn runner, we climb the staircase to the first floor. It has a sitting room, two bedrooms and its own small kitchen and bathroom.

'This was where my aunt lived,' I say. 'She was converting the upstairs floors into flats to rent out, but became unwell and stopped. So they weren't finished off, although the basics are there.'

'It might do us rather nicely, Toby,' says Stef. 'What do you think?'

I have to agree. Maude's rooms are musty-smelling but not in bad condition, and they also have a few good sticks of antique furniture. We climb the next flight to the second storey, laid out like the first, but needing a little more work to make it livable.

'One of these rooms would make a good music studio,' says Sofia.

Klara says, 'I like this place, Toby, but I still want a study in the attic to look out at the sky.'

'Let's hope the roof is sound, poppet, or you'll be closer to the sky than you might prefer.'

'Really, the whole place does have potential,' says Stefan slowly.

'If you overlook the squalor,' I say as we reach the third floor, where we stand, astonished at the mess. I shudder and say, 'Beyond redemption,' and the others murmur in agreement.

Klara dashes up the last flight of stairs to the attic. She calls out, 'There is a very good view over the rooftops and I do not see the sky through the ceiling. I think I will have my attic, Toby.'

'It's not bad, you know,' says Stefan. 'The mould is only superficial.'

'Hopefully.' I shrug. 'All right, let's have a think about how on earth we might do this.'

Aunt Maude left me some money and I have a small income from my books, Stefan is gainfully employed, and Sofia plays her cello in elegant hotels. Klara is perhaps the least prosperous, but still manages to get by, selling her hand-printed volumes of poetry to devotees and bookshops.

None of us is as poor as perhaps it sounds, but we're all in our late twenties and certainly don't want to ask our parents for help. And while Stefan and Sofia's families are well off, Klara's are rather less so.

And mine, I always fib, are long since departed.

Sofia and Klara start on the house immediately and we hire a man to help them. They labour happily at Whitfield Street throughout the rest of that long summer, while I argue with my publisher's copy-editor and wrestle with successive drafts of my manuscript.

This is my first novel, a light-hearted detective story. My two earlier works were non-fiction, based upon my travels in the Middle East as a wide-eyed innocent. They were well-received, even garnered small literary prizes, but I'm finding fiction rather harder to write.

It's a relief to be able to skip the reference lists, but I'm not a slap-dash author and even fiction, no matter how light-hearted, still needs research. I sometimes discuss my female characters with Eliza, although she's such an odd little thing I'm not certain she's a reliable exemplar of womanhood.

She laughs when I say that, and insists females are very different from each other, and most of them want more than marriage and babies in their lives. That's not what the ladies' journals tell me and Eliza herself can hardly talk: she's absurdly fond of babies, and marriage to gorgeous Harry is certainly on the cards.

But her women friends certainly sound like a rum lot, especially Billie, the girl flyer. I'd love to meet her one day, although she does sound rather fearsome.

Stefan is a pilot too, and an engineer at an aircraft factory. He's also a member of the RAF Reserve, but I'm not quite certain what that entails, apart from him having to attend dull lectures or go away on aviation courses.

Lately he's been bored with his work, and speaks longingly of the Supermarine works at Southampton where they turn out those new Spitfire planes. That's where Eliza's brother Pete works too, and when they get together it's as if they're speaking a foreign language.

Pete used to share my flat. I took him in when flygirl Billie decided she'd had enough of him, and it was there he finally fell prey to Charlotte's sheathed claws.

Pete used to feel sorry for me because I'd never bring girls home, but I didn't have the faintest idea how innocent he was until he tried to pair me off with Sofia and/or Klara.

I had to break it to him gently they had no interest in me and equally, I had no interest in anyone but the man I'd loved hopelessly for a decade. At that, he nearly ran terrified for the hills. But then he decided being part of our little avant-garde gang made him a sophisticated chappie of the world: dear old Farmer Pete.

By then I'd long given up any hope of Stefan. I still had lovers of course, I won't pretend that men don't find me attractive. And I'd go cottaging when lust became too much, despite the astonishing hypocrisy of the law — peers of the realm soliciting in dark corners, judges taking their pleasures in parks, and most infuriating, members of Parliament condemning us all as monsters then creeping out at night for blow-jobs.

Of course it's part of everyday life for a queer man in modern

England: terror that the next moment of joy might also mean the pantomime of arrest for *persistently importuning*, the condemnation of court, the brute violence of prison. I know poor chaps who've been flung into gaol, and afterwards were denied jobs or places to live.

Still, there's nothing I can do to change society or myself. I've loved Stef since we were at school, and when he fell for other boys I accepted it, and when he experimented with women I pretended not to care.

In fact I like women, but to me they're an interesting, separate species — I could no more want to make love to one than, say, to a friendly zebra.

Yet Stef has always yearned to fit in, and when he began a relationship with Eliza a few years ago I truly hoped he'd be happy. In the end he couldn't keep pretending to an orthodoxy he didn't feel, and he turned, thank God, to me at last.

The house at Whitfield Street is livable by November 1937, the agapanthus wallpaper gone, the ceilings painted and floors waxed, the lights repaired and chimneys swept.

By some miracle of modern plumbing we have working kitchens and bathrooms on each floor (except the third, which is still a shambles). We fit a new runner to the staircase and Stef's parents give us a few old Turkish rugs for the living areas.

Moving in is hard work, but Pete drives to London with his farm truck and, with Eliza and Harry's help, we manage to shift all our books and clothes and beds and desks and wardrobes, even Sofia's fragile cello and Klara's *infernally* heavy printing-press.

At the end of that long day I'm in Aunt Maude's old bedroom unpacking some of our things, and notice an object wrapped in brown paper at the back of the wardrobe.

I undo it and discover a framed oil painting, a portrait of Maude as a young woman, her blue eyes brimming with laughter, blonde hair in a loose knot, a gauzy wrap around her bare shoulders.

Until I was eleven I didn't know my aunt very well, but then she'd visit me at my boarding school, a quiet presence overshadowed by her glum banker husband.

When the husband died a few years later Maude blossomed in an endearingly eccentric way and I became very fond of her. I can barely recall my own mother, so Maude was always the most important female in my life. I'm gazing, charmed, at the portrait when Stef comes in with another suitcase.

'Remember Aunt Maude?' I say. 'She'd visit our school on open days.'

'Vaguely. That's rather a good painting though, isn't it?'

We take the canvas downstairs and hang it above the fireplace in the sitting room. Klara says solemnly, 'To have Aunt Maude up there is like thanking her for this house.'

'It's *perfect*, Toby,' says Sofia, stepping forward to level the frame slightly. 'She's so like you, especially around the eyes.'

'Well, my mother's sister, after all.'

'Did your mother look like Maude?' asks Klara.

'No idea, poppet. She died when I was very young.'

'But don't you have a photograph?'

'Sorry, no.' I quickly change the subject. 'Who's for a cup of tea?'

By Sunday evening the move is done and Stef and I return to our old lodgings to give the nasty little landlord his key. We wait in the hall until he shuffles to his door, then he rudely snatches the key from my hand. I'm tired and have had more than enough by then.

'By the way, you old bastard,' I say. 'Here's what you've been hoping to see all these years.' I kiss Stefan slowly and pleasurably.

The landlord's eyes bulge. He says, 'You *perverts*, how dare you?'

'Oh, we dare, and I bet you wish you did too, darling. Can't keep it hidden forever, you know.'

As we leave Stef murmurs, 'You don't really think he's secretly queer, do you?'

'I always thought he was just a little *too* fascinated by our every move. I expect we've just made his day.'

Laughing, we saunter down the road to catch the underground back to our new home. Our haven. Whitfield Street.

4. Eliza: Man's Work

Toby and the avant-garde gang's new place isn't far from my flat in Bloomsbury, so Harry and I walk over to Whitfield Street for the house-warming party. It's a crisp winter evening in late 1937, and under my coat I'm wearing the crimson velvet dress I bought when my aunt Izabel had her big break playing the lead in *West End Winnie*, seven years ago.

Reminded, I say, 'Oh, I had a letter from Izabel today.'

'Is she finding Hong Kong any easier now?' asks Harry.

'At last, yes. She's teaching dramatic arts to the English children, and there's less talk about the disgusting streets and more about the kids she likes.' I think for a moment. 'That's interesting — one of them's named Nancy Kuan. Perhaps she's teaching Chinese children too.'

'Can't imagine the British — or Felix — being too happy about that.'

'I doubt that would bother Izabel.'

We smile. Izabel is my father's much younger half-sibling. She's only seven years older than me so she's more of a melodramatic big sister than an aunt. Her own father was Portuguese and her mother Min-lu — my grandmother — is Chinese.

Nanna is an educated, perfectly-spoken businesswoman, but in the eyes of the world my small clever grandmother is just a Chink. This of course means that my father and Izabel are what used to be called half-caste: today, more politely termed Eurasian.

When Izabel was a famous actress she told everyone her mother was dead, while her real mother was forced to play the role of her faithful old nanny. That was cruel to Min-lu but, when the deception was revealed, it was cruellest of all to Izabel.

We arrive at Whitfield Street and Sofia flings open the door. A rose is tucked into her dark curls and she's wearing a red flounced Spanish dress and dance shoes.

She clatters her heels noisily and says, 'Welcome, you two — *olé*!'

Harry says, laughing, 'I didn't realise it was a costume party.'

'It's not, dear one, I just felt like dressing up,' says Sofia, kissing us. 'Come and get a drink.'

We move through the crowded hall, greeting friends. In the sitting room a fire is blazing in the hearth and Klara is passing around a tray of drinks. She's dressed in pale blue chiffon fluttering in layers to the floor, her silver-fair hair loose down her back.

Harry says, 'Come on, Klara, it really is a costume party isn't it? You're the fairy at the bottom of the garden!'

She laughs. 'Harry, I will have you know this was my mother's wedding dress. Now, let me show you all the wonderful things we have done here.'

Manoeuvring around groups of people, she leads us up the stairs. On the first level, Stef and Toby are chatting to friends by the fire in their sitting room. After more greetings we admire the antique furniture, their prints of Venice, and Toby's new study, with his typewriter on the desk. 'Blessed peace at last,' says Stef, and he and Toby grin.

We follow Klara up another flight to the flat she shares with Sofia. Their sitting room has plump couches and bowls of flowers, and Sofia's cello rests beside a music stand. The fire here is banked, the air warm.

'Oh, how pretty,' I say. 'You must be so comfortable here, Klara.'

'We are indeed. But come now — there is someone in my study you will wish to greet.'

'Is that the study all the way up in the attic?' says Harry. 'Two more flights?'

'Come on, you poor old man,' Klara says. 'You can do it.'

Harry laughs and we keep going. At the top of the house we find an attic room with another cosy fire and Professor Otto Fischer seated in an armchair.

'Here is *Otto*!' announces Klara. 'He came upstairs to see my study and then he had to sit down for a very long time to get his breath back.'

Old friends Otto and Harry shake hands, and Otto says, 'Eliza, I must thank you for your assistance — I have spoken to Billie. Unfortunately our conversation did not go quite as I planned.'

'Wasn't she able to identify the planes for you?' asks Harry.

'Oh, in that she was most helpful.' He laughs ruefully. 'But after we discussed Spain, Billie decided she would take a job over there training Republican pilots.'

I sit down. 'Otto, how could you let her *do* that!'

'You know Billie well, Eliza. How could I possibly *stop* her?'

'Will she be in any danger?' says Harry.

'The training airfield is at Albacete, south-east of Madrid, and well behind the lines. It is the headquarters of the International Brigades and as safe as anywhere in the country.' Otto sighs. 'At least the work will not last long and she will be paid well. I think she should be safe.'

I nod. 'Heavens, I hope so.' I look around, and the window shows the night sky over the London rooftops, lights gleaming in the distance, outlining ranks of chimneys. Neat piles of paper sit on a desk and two full bookcases line the wall.

'My goodness, Klara, what a lovely place to work.'

'I am writing well here,' she says. 'I like it very much.'

'But I didn't know you and Otto were friends,' I say. 'Did you meet at Charlotte's wedding?'

'For the first time, but we have known of each other for years,' she says. 'We are distant cousins.'

'*Cousins?*' I laugh. 'You're not much alike.' Large Otto is bearish and dark-bearded, while Klara is slight and the fairest of blondes.

'I resemble my Finnish father,' says Klara, 'but my mother was German, from Otto's family.'

'Ah, we have confused you, Eliza,' says Otto lightly. 'Not all Jews are swarthy with hooked noses, you know.' There's understandable pain in his voice too: anti-Semitic venom is everywhere now, not just in Germany.

I say wryly, 'Is that the same way not all part-Chinese wear cheongsams, Otto?'

'Precisely,' he says, smiling. 'But you would still look most becoming in a cheongsam, Eliza.'

'You see, I do not practise religion,' says Klara, 'but I am Jewish nonetheless. In Germany I would no longer be a citizen or allowed to work in a profession.'

'My God, has it gone *that* far?' asks Harry.

'Worse, my friend,' says Otto. 'It is now beyond my comprehension, and I could never be termed politically naive.'

'But what are German Jews supposed to do?' I say. 'They can't just leave — their homes and schools and jobs are in Germany.'

'Many have fled, but many more remain. They simply cannot believe their dearest friends and trusted colleagues would ...' Otto smiles sadly and shakes his head.

'Some try to come here,' says Klara, 'but only the wealthiest and most educated are permitted entry. The poor have nowhere to go.'

Harry says, 'Wasn't a boat-load of children from Spain welcomed here a few months ago?'

'The Basque refugees were permitted entry on a temporary basis, but I doubt you would call it welcomed,' says Otto. 'However, this sad talk is most unsuitable for a party — we should drink and be merry. I am rested now, Klara, so let us go downstairs and join the others.'

'I've been meaning to ask, blossom,' Toby says, refilling my glass. 'Is your fabulous aunt Izabel making any films at the moment?'

'No, she hasn't done anything since *The Bride's Secret* a few years ago.'

'I simply don't understand why that didn't win her an Oscar. Of course Garbo's wonderful, but Izabel *Malory*? There's never been anyone like her. But why on earth isn't she working?'

'You know why, Toby. The scandal, remember?'

'Oh, vaguely — something about her mother, wasn't it? Surely quite forgotten by now.'

'Newspapers never forget and never forgive. Remember those dreadful headlines about her Half-Caste Roots, her Tainted Blood, her Lewd Oriental Attractions?'

'Oh, yes! The Depravity no Respectable Paper Could Bring Itself to Print? What *was* that?'

I laugh. 'Probably the sin of keeping something a secret from them. But those hypocrites made a mint out of Izabel for years, especially when she married her "Barrister Beau".'

'So how *did* they find out in the end?' says Toby.

'Some gossip columnist did a hatchet job.'

'Can't have been a very well-hidden secret, then.'

'No, Izabel had covered her tracks. She told everyone Min-lu was her old nanny and her real mother was dead. She'd also had some tiny, perfect touches of surgery on her eyes and nose. It was very plausible.'

'So what went wrong?'

'She was betrayed, Toby. By the Barrister Beau.'

'Her *husband*?'

I nod. 'Felix had the offer of a high-level job in Hong Kong but Izabel refused to go. He decided that sabotaging her career on the quiet would make her want to run away, and he was quite correct.'

'But how on earth do you *know* all this, Eliza?'

'She told me. Remember, her mother is my grandmother. We don't have many secrets.'

'Yet she still went to Hong Kong with that swine?'

'Izabel is capable of a certain — self-persuasion. She thought she'd get over it.'

'Did she?' says Toby.

I sigh. 'I don't know.'

I remember Izabel, tears on her cheeks, saying, 'Felix is my husband, Eliza. I love him and I know he loves me, despite all this. Indeed, I *shall* go to Hong Kong. I'll have a *marvellous* time, I'll make certain I do. Goodness, one day we'll even be able to laugh about all this.'

'*Laugh*?'

'Of course, darling. Got to send the audience away with a smile.'

Brave, blinkered, actress Izabel. Always playing a role.

Towards the end of the party I sip a cup of tea in the sitting room and gaze at the portrait above the fireplace, a sweet-faced blonde woman from the turn of the century.

Klara told me earlier, 'She is Toby's Aunt Maude and the benefactor of us all. I believe she is the guiding spirit of this house.' (I think at that point she'd had a bit too much to drink.)

Otto sits down beside me on the sofa. 'Did you get the paper I sent last week, Eliza? An early work of Schlick, most influential. Poor man.'

'I think I grasp it, but I need to read it again,' I say. 'Why is he a poor man?'

'He was murdered last year, shot by a student who claimed his philosophy had undermined his *moral restraints.* In other words, Schlick was Jewish and he was a good Aryan. Then he said it was over a woman. All nonsense, but the Fascists loved it. The student was gaoled with a slap on the wrist and will soon be out.' Otto smiles bitterly. 'And poor old Schlick wasn't even Jewish.'

'How *terrible*! Did you work together?'

'By correspondence. But my direction is more mathematical than the Vienna Circle's, although their studies have been an invaluable foundation.' He gazes at me. 'You are truly enjoying those papers, Eliza? Most people would find them dull.'

'Oh, never dull, Otto. Sometimes difficult but never dull.'

He says, in an offhand way, 'Well, I suppose your great sailing ship and your grandmother's company keep you busy and contented.'

'Oddly, Min-lu has just decided to start winding up the company,' I say. 'The bottom's fallen out of the pearlshell trade and it's not worth holding on.'

'And your ship?'

'Things are only busy with *Inverley* when she's laid-up for repairs in the summer. In fact, my life is surprisingly quiet at the moment.'

'Ah.' Otto changes the subject. 'Of course you know your grandfather Freddy and I were once close friends, and Min-lu and I have kept up a correspondence ever since.'

'Have you? I didn't realise.'

'Indeed. She wishes you to keep busy.'

'I know that well enough,' I say, laughing.

'She says I should find you another job.'

'Doing what?' I say. 'I hardly think philosophy's my calling in life.'

'Eliza, you have experience with languages and a great facility for mathematics, puzzles and patterns. Min-lu told me it was so and now I have seen it for myself.'

'Honestly, Otto, what on earth would *that* make me useful for?'

'GC&CS.'

I stare at him. 'GC&CS? But — they don't employ women.'

Four years ago, when Izabel's husband Felix was recruited into the Government Code and Cipher School, he told me: *Dear child, this is man's work and they only hire ex-military or boffins. Girls'd be too busy filing their nails! But I'll keep you in mind if they need a typist.*

'Remember I said, Eliza, at this time, in this place, everything must be open to all. Yes, today GC&CS employ women. They employ anyone with true skills.'

Otto's bearded cheeks dimple. 'That, of course, is why your uncle Felix is in Hong Kong with a listening post, and not here in London.'

After we stop laughing he says, 'Shall I set up an interview for you?'

5. Izabel: Happy New Year

My God, Nancy Kuan's extraordinary — at eight I was a fat little thing who cried all the time, but this girl's got poise and beautiful extension. And that intense reserve: it's not shyness at all as I'd first thought.

When she lifts her eyes and starts speaking her lines I can feel her control and power and the hair on my neck lifts — and that doesn't happen very often with adult performers, let alone an eight-year old Eurasian in the dripping humidity of Hong Kong.

I wonder what her background is? Brown hair, straight nose, fair-skinned freckles. Some of the boys try to bully her but I've made my displeasure clear and they've stopped. I notice she's always accompanied by an old amah, with no European parent in evidence.

I light a cigarette while the little girls and boys squeal and chatter, putting on their shoes and street clothes in the dressing room. Amid the market clamour of vendors outside, and the many passers-by who would rather yell when they could simply speak, I hear someone clear his throat and spit luxuriously and I barely even shudder. Must be getting used to the place at last.

I go to the outer door as the amahs and mothers arrive to pick up their darlings. I see the English women glance shrewishly at Nancy Kuan and Elsie Chau and Eddie Tsang and think, Oh, you'd like your talentless spawn to attend the famous Malory Studio, would you? Then I'll teach whoever I want, you mean-minded bitches.

Felix hates it of course, says it hinders his career. I feel a pang of rage. A few little Chinese kids are hindering your career, darling? Try your own mulish stupidity for a start, or your petty bullying of the nice young soldiers who have to call you *sir*.

I wave at the departing spawn, and smile at the few children who make it worthwhile. Of course I'd love to be back in movies or on the stage, but I do like teaching. And sometimes I wonder: I'm thirty-seven now and perhaps it would have been harder than I ever imagined to stay at the top.

I hear a string of small fireworks go off in the street, crackle-crackle-crackle, as I close the door. Today is the thirtieth of January 1938, and tomorrow the Chinese New Year begins. An unsettling year of the Tiger is ahead of us — bold, aggressive, stubborn, unpredictable.

I shiver. God knows enough unsettling things are happening already.

Six years ago the Japanese invaded Chinese Manchuria to the north, and step by step they've encroached southwards. They took historic Peking last August, then the Chinese section of Shanghai fell in November after months of fighting — the International Quarter, of course, was allowed to remain untouched.

When they attacked the capital of Nanking, the spineless government of Chiang Kai-shek was forced to flee. Since then, the Japanese have been visiting atrocities on poor Nanking that beggar belief, yet Generalissimo Chiang, a strutting little dictator, still prefers to direct his enmity towards his fellow Chinese. He tells everyone the Americans will one day fight the Japanese and the true battle is with the Communists.

In fact, my uncle Bao-lim says, quietly and in private, the Reds have been the only forces resisting the invaders for years, and the Americans are still perfectly happy to keep selling arms to Japan in copious quantities.

He thinks I should know the truth because many people are deceiving themselves. When he says 'many people' he means Felix and the British, but he's too polite to say so — and cautious as well: Chiang's murderous spy network is everywhere.

I return to my office, reassuring myself that Nanking and Shanghai are eight hundred miles away, and Hong Kong, a neutral British possession, is perfectly safe.

But then, who knows what could happen in a Tiger year? So says Mrs Lau the cleaner, clever and cynical, who tells me often of her forebodings, interlaced with acid observations on some of the pupils' mothers that make me laugh.

I can hear her sweeping in the next room and call 'Mrs Lau?' She comes to the door, a thin widow in her fifties. I hand her a red envelope containing money to celebrate the New Year, and tell her to go home to her family to prepare for tonight.

I lie in my bath and idly soap my arms. On New Year's Eve all families come together for a special meal and tonight I'm going to Bao-lim's house. Tonight will be special for another reason: my mother Min-lu, Bao-lim's sister, will be here. I'm so happy at the thought of seeing her again — it must be a year since she last visited.

Her ship arrived from Perth earlier today and she's gone straight to Bao-lim's great house, half-way up the side of a mountain in an area they call the Mid-Levels. It's where the wealthier Chinese went to live after cool Victoria Peak itself was reserved for Europeans only.

I love going to Bao-lim's house and have suggested we rent somewhere nearby, but Felix refuses to consider it, claiming he must stay in the city, close to his office in the Naval Dockyard. For him, no matter how pleasant the Mid-Levels, it's not European enough, and God forbid he be accused of going native.

I wonder if he'll put in an appearance tonight? He says he will but I doubt it: in the past the numbers of Felix's 'gyppy tummies' or 'security emergencies' that happen to coincide with events at Bao-lim's house would astonish any statistically inclined doctors. Or spies.

The Schiaparelli, I decide. It's a silk-satin gown in russet that flatters me — tonight is a special occasion after all. It's odd, but I rarely wear my most attractive dresses any more. I suppose that's because, amazingly, I've lost my sense of desire, once such a fiercely pleasurable drive in my life.

Now I feel dry and uninterested and wonder what all the fuss was about. I remember when I told Eliza I'd go to Hong Kong with Felix, despite what he did, and make certain I had a wonderful time.

She was astonished, and rightly so. But I told myself I'd hit my mark: I'd play the happy, supportive, passionate wife until we returned to our old selves and I could feel my love for Felix again.

Of course, taking on the essence of a role is second nature to me. Even when bored or sad or unwell I can play any face, any posture, any mood, and be utterly convincing to the world. But it never occurred to me it would be myself I had to convince.

The first time Felix made love to me, the first time after I understood he'd betrayed me and destroyed everything in the world I valued, my body shuddered with loathing at his touch. Felix chose to interpret it as passion and plunged on regardless.

Now I shamelessly trot out all the shabby evasions — it's that time, darling; such a headache, darling; a bit sozzled, darling. He complies because he knows what a wound he inflicted — or some part of him knows, the clever mind, the charm I once loved: surely it *must*.

But how can I tell? It's gone, hidden beneath layers of smug certainty: the hallmark of the minor British official.

And now my body feels nothing for Felix. Nothing for any man.

In my russet silk, my hair a tumble of brunette waves to my shoulders, my face so perfectly made up there's no telling where the artifice begins, I gaze in the mirror and can almost believe my smile is real.

As a taxi carries me in the dark up the steep mountain road to Bao-lim's house I think, of course I'm happy. I'm comfortable enough playing Mrs Malory. I wake, I eat, I work, I sleep (I avoid my husband). A good life really, and better than most of those around me. At least I get enough to eat.

And tonight I'll see my loved ones, the people I used to deny. Eliza once said, 'What about *you*, Izabel, the real you? Min-lu's daughter — '

'She's Chinese,' I told her flatly. 'And I'm not. That's the real me.'

How wrong I was, Eliza, how absurdly wrong. Then I smile and think, don't take yourself so *seriously*, darling. It's a new year after all, and we're going to have a wonderful evening.

The car turns off the road down a driveway to the front of the house. The hillside falls away steeply here so the house's ornate swallowtail roof is almost level with the road above.

There are red celebration lanterns around the massive carved timber door where Bao-lim is standing, smiling, and we bow to each other. Beside him is my mother, a familiar neat figure in a cheongsam, and we greet and kiss and move into the house.

While Bao-lim's politics have always been a little radical, his house is in the traditional style. It's laid out around courtyards although, unusually, he put the great reception room at the rear, not the centre.

Its tall windows look north over the flickering lights of Victoria City, across the harbour to Kowloon and the Nine Dragons mountains beyond, a spectacular view.

I've arrived a little early to have time to talk to my mother. We sit down while Bao-lim goes to check what's happening in the kitchen, and a servant brings us fragrant tea.

'Darling child,' Min-lu says. 'How good to see you.'

'Oh, Mummy, you're looking wonderful,' I say, and it's true. She's just turned seventy-seven but her brown eyes are clear, her skin smooth, her white-streaked hair thick and swept up with the solid gold combs she always wears.

My father, Leo Peres, a Portuguese man from Macau, gave Min-lu those combs when my older sister Filipa and I were born. She'd been apart from my brother Sam's father for many years by then, and the marriage to Leo Peres was very happy, although sadly too brief.

He died when I was two and I can't remember him, although throughout my childhood (to bossy Filipa's scorn) I always pretended I could. Perhaps that's how my acting career began.

'Tell me everything, how *is* everyone?' I ask.

'Where do I begin?' Min-lu says laughing. 'Well, Filipa's bought a new stable just outside Perth for her horse-training business, and one of her mares won a big race recently.'

'How nice,' I say politely. Filipa and her silly nags!

'Lucy and Danny are marvellous — I had a holiday with them in Broome.' (My mother is very close to Eliza's aunt Lucy.) 'But Michael is off to university in Melbourne next year!'

'My God, it's been *that* long since Lucy had little Mikey?'

'And *you*, darling, how is it with you?'

I take a sip of tea. 'Well, the Malory Studio is doing very well — I'll have to get larger premises soon. I've got some good students too — one's a Eurasian girl, Nancy Kuan, who's simply compelling. I'm enjoying it so much.'

She lifts an eyebrow. 'Felix?'

'Puffed up with importance, running around telling people what to do. What can I say?'

'Oh, *Izabel*.' She squeezes my hand — she knows what Felix did. I told her and Eliza, no one else. Harry knows too of course, Eliza would never keep it from him, but I don't mind that. He's a kind man who tried to warn me about unreliable Felix long ago.

We look up as Bao lim leads five elderly cousins from the mainland into the room, and we begin the polite rounds of family chit-chat required at New Year.

I'm glad my Hakka and Cantonese — both of which I refused to speak as a child — have improved so much with Bao-lim's tutoring. He glances at me, proud of his Second Niece.

There'll only be a few relatives here tonight, although Min-lu and Bao-lim were once part of a large family. My mother was the eldest, followed by four boys. She was unusually lucky because her father (a great admirer of Queen Victoria) allowed her a good education.

There is much I've come to love about the Chinese, but rather a lot to deplore in their treatment of women. Then again, life is fairly short and brutish for most Chinese men as well.

Three of my four uncles are dead — one who joined the Reds a decade ago, one who died of plague (yes, the medieval sort), and one, the youngest and quite apolitical, who was taken in Shanghai by Generalissimo Chiang's secret police and never seen again.

Bao-lim leans towards me — I may be looking a little distracted — and says, 'I have several other guests coming tonight, Second Niece, men from the university who have nowhere to go to for the new year. One of them has a child whom I believe attends your acting classes.'

Oh God, that could be awkward. Still, it's kind of Bao-lim to open his house to people without family on this special night.

Just then a servant ushers in three men who gaze shyly around until my uncle jumps up and introduces them.

Two are students, unmemorable. The third, about my own age and wearing the sombre robes of an academic, teaches history says Bao-lim, but he doesn't have to tell me his name.

I can see her face in his: the direct eyes, the well-formed bones, the long sensitive mouth, the poise, the power, the reserve.

'Professor Laurence Kuan,' says Bao-lim.

He is seated to my left at the table, an elderly cousin to the right. I ask my cousin about the harvest, the latest diseases of pigs, the need for rain, the many refugees fleeing from the Japanese; although I'm not quite certain what he says in return. I've often eaten here so I know the food must be delicious, but I can barely taste it.

Finally I can't avoid him. A new course is brought in and I turn politely and take a breath.

He forestalls me. 'I must thank you for being so kind to Nancy, Mrs Malory.'

'Kind? I'm not kind, Professor Kuan — most of the parents could tell you that.'

'Those with the talented children?'

'Those with the talentless, as I expect you know. No, I'm not kind to Nancy, she's just an extraordinary child. I've rarely seen such finely-controlled intensity. Has she always been like that?'

'Since she was small. I'd see her watching people, then later she'd copy their postures and gestures, emotions flitting across her face. She was mesmerising.'

I smile. 'I'm told I did that as a child too, but my sister says it was because I was a half-wit.'

'Clearly not.' He reaches out for his jasmine tea. His hand is golden and sinewy and male.

After a moment I say, 'You teach history, is that correct?'

He nods. 'I used to specialise in European history, but that can be unwise, especially when ... *some* are not happy with the British or Americans.' He means the Generalissimo, of course.

'What about Chinese history?'

He smiles. His teeth are even and beautiful. 'A minefield. Who knows if an emperor's tribulation of the past might unwisely predict a setback for a leader today? So now I research an obscure corner of Dutch exploration in the seventeenth century and hope that nobody notices.'

I laugh, but he's making light of something serious. Those in power dislike those who seek the truth, and many academics as apolitical as my mother's poor young brother have lost their careers, their health, their lives.

'How did you meet Bao-lim?' I ask.

A slight hesitation. 'At a meeting,' he says. The line of his jaw curves as sweetly as a seashell.

'Ah.' Not a wise course of enquiry. 'Is Nancy's mother here in Hong Kong?' Oh dear, untactful too. 'I'm sorry —'

'No, she died at Nancy's birth. She was French: of course you will have noticed Nancy has European blood.' His face changes. 'She died in agony because, as the wife of a Chinese man, there was no care for her. The British doctor refused to attend, saying she'd *made her bed*.'

After a moment he clears his throat. 'Perhaps, one day, things will be different and China will have medical facilities, good ones, for everybody. We can only look towards the future.'

'That may be a dangerous thing to look towards,' I say quietly. '*Some* might think you were criticising the current arrangements.'

He smiles with his eyes, glancing at me. His mouth, the upper lip winged like a bird, is still. 'Heaven forbid,' he says.

So he's a Red, I think, my heart thumping. And although I've long tried to avoid acknowledging it, so of course is Bao-lim. Still, I've been here long enough to know that a Communist in China is a very different creature from the spectre that haunts Western conservatives.

Here the Reds want people to have jobs and doctors and unbombed towns, to be safe from Chiang's thugs and Japanese invaders. I may be politically naive, but that doesn't actually seem a lot to ask of life.

Laurence Kuan is watching me and says, 'Emotions flit across your face too, just like Nancy.'

'I keep my emotions under complete control, I'll have you know,' I say lightly. 'What sort of an actress would I be otherwise?'

'I've seen your films. You're a peerless actress.'

I almost gasp at the stab of grief. 'I was peerless once. Now I teach in a Hong Kong slum.'

'Now you teach a lonely, bullied child she has her own strengths. Still peerless.'

I return his poised, velvet-brown gaze for an instant — it's all I can bear — then turn at the cries of admiration, smiling as if I haven't a care in the world, to see what magnificent new dish is being brought to the table.

The streets are crowded with people lighting fireworks and screaming and laughing as they explode, and it takes the taxi some time to push through. When I get home Felix is slouched in his armchair with a brandy.

Padded by alcohol, the line of his jaw does not curve as sweetly as a seashell, although perhaps once it did. I put down my purse with a small sigh.

'Good night, then?' Felix says.

'Lovely, you'd have enjoyed it. Mummy sends her regards.' (She hadn't.)

'Sorry I missed it. Bit of a flap on, needed to get some cables away to London on the double.'

'Really. Oh well, Happy New Year, anyway.'

He gives a contemptuous snort and finishes his drink. 'New Year's supposed to be the first of January, not whenever the locals feel like holding a party.'

I say nothing, and sit down to read a letter from Eliza I didn't have time to open earlier. Somewhere outside there's the screeching whoosh of a skyrocket followed by a cluster of explosions. For a moment I think, is that what it's like in wartime? In Peking or Shanghai or Nanking?

Then I scold myself, don't be so *gloomy*, darling, and open the letter. Eliza's words are always a pleasure to read. They take me back to a civilised place that's now a distant dream, where the streets are not scattered with human waste, where I don't sweat like a pig, where my career is not a public humiliation.

A place where I'm a peerless actress.

I read quickly and say, 'Oh, how lovely! Eliza and Harry are getting married!'

Felix grunts. 'About time. He's been screwing her for, what, a couple of years?'

'I recall we were lovers for that long too before we made it legal.'

'I wasn't a married man then, though,' he says pompously. 'No, not quite the done thing.'

I think of Felix's friends, their unhappy wives and hard-faced mistresses.

'You *are* joking, aren't you?' I stop myself.

He grunts again and gets up, walks out and down the hall to the lavatory. He pees loudly with the door open, concluding with a familiar blurting sound that's thankfully drowned out by the crackle of a string of bangers exploding in the street.

I put my hands over my eyes and think, *honestly*, what with the hawking and spitting and shitting in the streets all around us, how can the odd fart make me want to kill my husband?

6. Eliza: 54 Broadway

A few weeks after speaking to Otto I receive a letter requesting my attendance at 54 Broadway Mansions, a block of offices near St James underground station. Despite Otto's confident assertion that the Government Code and Cipher School now employs anyone with genuine skills — even, heaven forbid, women — I expect the job won't involve much more than typing and filing.

Years ago my grandparents were good friends with the head of the Secret Intelligence Service, a man Nanna called *dashing*. When I'm shown into Admiral Sinclair's office I can see what she meant. He asks me to sit down and gazes at me for a few moments.

'My goodness, Freddy and Min-lu's granddaughter. Marvellous man, Freddy, such interests. And Min-lu — what a woman.' He smiles with a far-away look. 'Is she well?'

'Very well. Retired to Western Australia now.'

'Excellent. Please send her my heartfelt regards.'

He asks about my academic achievements at school — great for Mathematics, reasonable for Geography, dire for Domestic Science — then checks some papers on his desk.

'Now, Miss McKee, Professor Fischer assures me you have a range of talents we might find useful in these rather bleak times — some Japanese language and a facility for numbers. As it turns out, keeping tabs on Japan is but a minor, although essential, aspect of our work. Germany is obviously our most important target, followed closely by the Russians, then those rather unreliable Americans.'

I'm secretly amused as I've heard Min-lu use the same phrase.

'Still, if you feel you might be interested in working for us, before we go any further I'll need you to sign this copy of the Official Secrets Act. I'll go through it first, as you must be exceedingly conscious of what His Majesty's Government will expect of you, now and in the future.'

He does, and the penalties for failing the expectations of His Majesty are sobering, but I take a breath and sign.

'Excellent. Now we'll go downstairs and I'll introduce you to the head of GC&CS, Alastair Denniston. Lovely chap.'

Mr Denniston is indeed a lovely chap. He's Scottish, with shrewd blue eyes, and as his secretary brings in a tray with tea and biscuits he makes me feel welcome. Once we're settled he says, 'I'm told you have some skills in Japanese, Miss McKee. Spoken, not written?'

'Yes, only spoken. I learnt it as a child in Broome — my father ran a pearlshell business with Japanese divers, and some of my playmates were Japanese too. I'm told I was quite fluent as a child. We left Broome when I was six but went back often for holidays.'

'So were the Japanese themselves city or country people?'

'Very much country, and of course all they talked about was diving and sailing and shell-fishing. So probably not very helpful,' I say, feeling embarrassed. How on earth could my childish remnants of Broome patois be of use to anyone?

'We shall see. Of course, this is quite outside my sphere of expertise, but we only have a few dedicated Japanese scholars in GC&CS and I think they'd rather welcome any contribution, no matter how small. You don't perhaps have any Chinese as well, do you?'

'No. My grandmother always spoke English with us.'

'Indeed. Now, I believe Felix Malory is a relative of yours?'

'My uncle by marriage.'

'Our recruits are usually family or university connections, makes it easier to check out. Of course the Foreign Office would rather this be a strictly Services matter, but I believe we must use whatever talent we find, even civilians. Or women. I won't insult you with claptrap about intuition, but women do seem to pick up patterns in code that go right over the heads of most chaps.'

He gazes at the ceiling for a moment then says, 'As you know, we did find Malory more useful on the, ah, administrative side of things. His smattering of Japanese was helpful, but our experts and he didn't quite — get on. We always need people who have not just a little language but, shall I say, enough humility to be willing to fill in the gaps in their knowledge.'

I try not to smile.

'Now. In terms of employment I'd think of starting you as a clerk, then a traffic sorter, get an idea of how the place works. If your skills mature as they should, then a position as a Junior Assistant may become available. Does that sound at all acceptable?'

'That sounds wonderful, Mr Denniston.'

'Good. Now do tell me, what *is* this remarkable story of you sailing on a windjammer? I've worked for the Admiralty, of course, but never had my time before the mast. How I envy you.'

A short time after starting at 54 Broadway I receive a letter from my old friend Captain Nilsen, master of *Inverley*, the sailing ship in which I have a share. *Inverley* is coming to London for a dry-docking and *Kapten* asks if Harry and I might meet him at Millwall Dock. Even better, *Kapten*'s wife Maria will be with him, a dear friend to us both, although I haven't seen her for six years.

The last time was on a trip to the Ålands, the Finnish province of thousands of islands in the Baltic Sea, whose capital Mariehamn is the unlikely home port of the few four-masters still in trade.

Harry and I take a taxi to the East End, drizzle floating past the street lamps, puddles glittering on the streets. At least it's not as cold as the Åland Islands, I think, remembering Granddad's wry voice, 'Knew a chap who touched a ship's rail in winter in Mariehamn and left a chunk of his hand behind.' Darling Freddy.

It was Captain Nilsen who had sold Granddad the share in *Inverley* that is now mine, despite the steely disapproval of Gustaf Erikson — known to all as Gusta' — the greatest sailing-ship owner in the Ålands. But nowadays even Gusta' is buying steamers. I sigh. Fortunately we arrive before I descend too far into gloom.

The taxi halts, and while Harry pays the driver I gaze at the familiar sight of *Inverley* riding high in the water, her soaring masts and spiky spars delightfully incongruous in a dock full of modern vessels.

I smile. I always forget how enormous she is, how massive and solid and *true*.

'Eliza, Harry!' calls Maria from the gangway and we wave and hurry towards her. We sit around the table in the barque's saloon, a stove keeping us cosy. Captain Nilsen refills our wine-glasses, laughing at

one of his own jokes. He's a handsome man in his late forties, running
to stoutness, his face and hands weatherbeaten. Maria is fair and fine-
boned, younger than her husband. She has a motherly air and was
enormously kind to me on our passage together.

'You know, Eliza, Mattias and I just spend our *first* Christmas
together in twenty years,' Maria says. 'It was very nice.'

Kapten smiles at her. 'Good to sit by the fire for a change and not be
fighting the Roaring Forties. I must be getting old.' He takes a drink
and says ruefully, 'Indeed, I am getting old. I intend to retire next year
— the 1939 season will be my last.'

'What will you do then?' asks Harry.

'Well, *matros*, I have a farm to look after.'

'And a wife,' says Maria, mock-scolding.

He chuckles. 'And a wife, indeed. A good Ålands wife, who has sent
me away to sea for twenty years to earn a living.'

'As if anyone could have kept you at home,' Maria says. 'But now, we
are not talking about the most important thing!'

'What is that?' asks Captain Nilsen, surprised.

'Oh, Mattias. Look at Eliza's hand!'

A ruby ring Harry gave me many years ago is now glimmering on my
engagement finger. 'Next month, in late March,' I say. 'Are you able to
come to the wedding?'

'Oh,' says Maria, 'of course! Yes, yes, we will be here until then.' Her
eyes fill with tears. 'Oh, Eliza, Harry, how happy I am for you both.'

'Where will you honeymoon?' asks *Kapten*. 'You can always come to
Mariehamn, you know.'

'In winter?' Harry laughs. 'No, Eliza's just started a new job. We'll go
to a nice hotel for a weekend, then in summer we'll take time off.'

'Ah, so romantic,' says Maria. 'And goodness, a new job, Eliza — what
do you do?'

'Oh,' I shrug. 'Office work. Typing, you know.'

Captain Nilsen clears his throat. 'There is something we must
discuss. When I retire I shall sell my share in *Inverley* and Gusta' wishes
to buy it. He concentrates on steamers now of course, but he still
appreciates good sailing vessels.'

'But that means he'll become the majority shareholder,' I say. 'And he's never wanted foreigners as part-owners, either Granddad or me.'

Kapten nods. 'Perhaps, *jungman*, the time has come for you too.'

I smile — he always calls me *jungman*, deckboy, from my days on the ship, and Harry *matros*, able seaman. Then I realise what he's saying.

'Oh,' I say. 'Do you think I should also sell?'

He shrugs. 'It is a good time. The ship is wearing out, and the price for grain is lower this year than ever before.'

'But if war comes the price will go up,' I say.

'If war comes what sort of future will square-riggers have? Merchant vessels will be at great risk, no matter whether sail or steam.'

'Then why would Gusta' buy into another four-master?'

'As you say, the price of grain will go up,' says Captain Nilsen. 'Also, Finland will remain neutral in any conflict, so that may offer protection also. But I am sorry, *jungman*, I know you care greatly for this ship, but she is no longer a wise investment.'

'It was Freddy's bequest to me,' I say, my throat tight.

'We do not need to discuss this tonight,' says Maria firmly, glancing at her husband. 'We have many things to celebrate, and who knows, perhaps there will be no war at all.'

'And we are speaking of my retirement, eighteen months away. Let us worry about it then,' he says. 'To happier things. Our dry-docking! We may be able to mend that leak in the forward hold at last — it ruined two hundred tons of grain last voyage. And we will raise a new steel foremast too. Will you climb it to test it for me?'

I laugh. 'Oh, *Kapten*, I'm thirty years old and climbing masts is quite beyond me now!'

He nods philosophically. 'Beyond us all.'

After an intense introduction to a variety of techniques at 54 Broadway — and, it must be said, a certain amount of typing, filing and tea-making — I begin to comprehend the network of skills involved in deciphering secret signals.

'Intelligence work is part-translation, part-poetry and part-crossword puzzle,' Mr Denniston says, and I can only agree.

Where the Japanese are concerned, everything starts at the Hong

Kong headquarters of the Far East Combined Bureau, the spy centre where Felix works. While it may be 'Combined', it's mainly an Admiralty operation, and runs from the Naval Base in Victoria City.

Thirty-odd Intercept operators are based on small Stonecutters Island in Hong Kong harbour. They listen for radio signals sent in Kana, a complex Japanese morse code of nearly seventy letters and characters. The messages are not in the clear either: they've been enciphered, put into secret codes in different ways.

The intercepts are sent to the codebreakers at the Naval Base, who use all sorts of sophisticated means to break them down and rebuild the original Japanese. After that they go to the translators, who render them into English, and then copies are flown to us in London to assemble and analyse the overall picture.

Some of our staff concentrate on a single area of expertise, such as decryption or translation, while others, like fellow Australian Commander Nave, have multiple skills — mathematical insight as well as great fluency in languages. And some are better at the broader scope of intelligence: interpreting scraps of information to deduce military or political developments.

That's where the art of seeing patterns comes into its own — Mr Denniston's translation-poetry-crossword puzzles. Although I work on improving my Japanese it turns out my true skills lie in this kind of intelligence gathering.

After a time, when my apprenticeship is complete, I am promoted to Junior Assistant. Then begins the more sobering process of uncovering the secrets His Majesty expects me to keep for the rest of my life, the secrets I'm not allowed to talk about to anyone — not even Harry.

Several fascinating months pass by, then one day Mr Denniston asks me into his office.

'As you know, Miss McKee, Japanese military codes change frequently, and breaking them always takes time, time we may not have in an emergency. As a supplementary measure we thought perhaps the suppliers and shippers, the actual *businesses* keeping the Japanese forces running, might be a little more usefully careless. Would you be at all interested in joining our new commercial intelligence section?'

I certainly would. The Commercial Section is a group of only five people (including me), but we get along well and I soon feel as if I've found my own small, happy niche.

And Mr Denniston is perfectly correct. The lower-grade codes of Japanese businesses reveal far more than their senders could ever imagine. It's surprising how much information may be gleaned from orders for items such as tropical uniforms, or Burmese maps, or cold-weather kits.

My wedding to Harry is rapidly approaching. I'm planning to buy a new outfit today, and this morning Charlotte drops by. She seems subdued so I ask her to come along with me.

By midday her spirits have revived and I've found myself an elegant pale blue suit that fits me like a glove. We stop for a well-earned lunch: new shoes can wait till this afternoon.

I ask if she wants a drink and, unusually, she shakes her head. 'Off the booze for a bit, sweetie.'

I can't recall a time she didn't drink at lunch. 'Are you all right, Charlotte?'

'Oh — making me a little bad-tempered, that's all. Want a break.'

The waiter takes our orders, then I ask, 'Where's Vivian today?'

'With the housekeeper — Mrs Spencer, remember?' she says pointedly.

Of course I remember. It was at the Spencers' wedding Harry kissed me for the first time, only for us to be discovered moments later by a furious Charlotte.

'Don't look so guilty, Eliza,' she laughs. 'Dear God, it was five years ago and you weren't the only one being naughty — I was playing around with Pete then too.'

'True.' I laugh ruefully. 'Anyway, I'm just glad it finally worked out for us all.'

She's silent. 'Charlotte?'

She looks up, her cornflower blue eyes remote. 'Think I will have a drop, after all.' She beckons to the waiter and orders a gin. I get water because I need my wits about me when buying shoes.

After a few mouthfuls of her drink, Charlotte says, 'Truth is, sweetie, I'm going bonkers at the farm. I've decorated every room. I've taken an interest in the garden and the crops and those bloody sheep. I've learnt recipes and cooked them to Mrs Spencer's exacting standards. Dear God, I even went flying with Pete in his little plane, but once is certainly enough for this girl's lifetime.'

Our lunches arrive and we eat, then Charlotte orders another gin and lights a cigarette.

'It's almost hilarious, Eliza. I'm at such a loose end I even offered to help my father with his silly refugee organisation — my German's as good as his and my French even better. But he keeps saying I should stay at home with Vivian.'

'But Vivy probably wants you with her.' I say. 'She's not even eighteen months old yet, after all. Perhaps when she's bigger —'

Charlotte ashes her cigarette with an audible flick. 'Perhaps it's better I'm not with her.' She glances at me, her face pale. 'It's just — you see, I'm not very good at being a mother, Eliza. I love her, I've never loved anyone so much in my life, but I can't *show* it. And I'm afraid ...'

There's a long silence.

She rubs her forehead. 'You remember my late mother, Ilse?'

'Of course. She was — not very kind to you.'

Charlotte laughs bitterly. 'Quite the understatement, sweetie. What's that gorgeous expression of Harry's — mad as a cut snake? She certainly was, especially about sex. She kept a cane especially for hitting me. And the names she'd call me, dear God, even when I grew up. The *names*.'

Her head is down. 'The only time Ilse was kind was when I cleaned and cooked and said yes, *Mutti*, you're right, I'm a whore. Christ, I was a child, I didn't even know what a whore *was*! But still she'd beat me. How I hated her.' Her mouth twists. 'How I wanted to please her.'

Her face is stricken. 'The other night I was hung-over. Vivian was being a bother, a tooth coming in, and for an instant she looked like my mother. I wanted to grab something and *strike* —'

She covers her eyes.

The waiter comes to clear the table and I get the bill. We walk outside and find a small park and sit on a bench in the cold. I hold her hand while she sobs.

After a time she wipes her face and says, 'Pete and I have been talking for ages about having another baby. But what if I'm not very good at being that one's mother either?'

'Charlotte, I'm certain you would be,' I say. 'But, look — I know a psychiatrist, a lovely man who helped me years ago when I was very unhappy. Perhaps you could talk to him about it?'

She's silent for a time, then nods.

Harry and I were no more than friends when I first met his dazzling Charlotte. I knew she had an odd fondness for gambling, but she was so wry and warm and charming I adored her. But I found out she deceived Harry into marriage, and she lied to me, and her gambling became a lust for risk, especially with other men.

Then she fell in love with my brother Pete but, oddly, when she became pregnant to him with Vivian, she insisted she could never seek a 'shameful' divorce from Harry. I couldn't understand why, but at last those contradictions make a kind of sense.

The birth of the little girl brought a wary truce between us, and Charlotte finally let Harry go and married Pete. Over time we've developed a certain fondness, but she's never before revealed herself to me this way.

Yet I've never forgotten Min-lu saying, 'She's not your friend, Eliza. She's not anyone's friend, not even her own.'

7. Billie: Not Yet

Wilf and I left for Spain eight months ago, but today we're back in London watching Eliza McKee and Harry Bell recite their vows at the Registry Office.

Eliza's brother Pete is seated a few rows ahead, not much different from the eager young man I trained seven years ago at my Perth flying school. That was before I had to close it down: the costs were too high, the students too few.

Pete went away to sulk, the returned from his sulk with news about a company called Air Services Training at Hamble, near Southampton in England. He thought we should go to Hamble and learn everything possible, then set up our own flying school in England.

We even had a name: QM Air (Quinn-McKee of course — he certainly wasn't going first on the letterhead), and I remember our hope and excitement, planning by the fire with rain pouring down outside.

We sailed on the *Oronsay* in September 1932. Trouble was, Pete imagined he was in love with me. He was twenty-one, I was twenty-five. Love? More like raging hormones and too many stories from *Boy's Own Paper*.

Of course he was tempting, but I believe in free love; love without the restriction of marriage or monogamy. But to Pete (and most men) that means having lots of boyfriends without caring for anyone.

But oh, Pete, when we finally became lovers I cared for you. We were so happy for a time. Until you threw it all away, then topped it off by falling for Charlotte. She may be attractive, Pete, but she's not kind and she won't let you do whatever you need to do with your life.

I sigh and Wilf, beside me, touches my hand and smiles. Perhaps he thinks I'm sentimental about weddings.

Eliza and Harry kiss. All right, marriage is probably going to be good for these two. They suit each other and they've waited long enough. Everyone stands and follows the newlyweds out. It's not a large crowd, just old friends and family. I probably know most people, apart from a few of Harry's boffin mates and one or two obviously maritime types.

We cluster at the top of the Registry Office stairs while someone take photos. I catch Charlotte's eye and she gives me a cool smile — typically, she's wearing one of those fashionable fur stoles made out of a poor dead fox chewing on its own poor dead tail.

Pete comes over and kisses me on the cheek in a brotherly manner, and says my name as if we've only ever been acquaintances. But after I first took him flying — in a series of loops and rolls and plunges that left even my hair on end — he took to calling me *crazy lady*. Affectionately too, sometimes.

He's carrying Vivian, who waves at me. She's getting big, must be a year and a half by now. I can't stand kids normally, but I gave her a wooden Tiger Moth which she loves, so I wave back. Got to encourage her and anyway, her fondness for me annoys Charlotte.

Wilf is hovering at my elbow, so I introduce him to Pete and they shake hands, perfect gentlemen. Wilf knows Pete and I used to be together but doesn't understand how intense it was. They chat about flying and I see Pete is envious of Wilf's life, as he doesn't get to use his own plane as much as he'd like.

They're both tall men, but fair Wilf is more conventionally handsome than my old love, I think, a little unkindly. I've dressed up today for the wedding and am perfectly aware Wilf and I make a good-looking couple.

Eliza comes towards me and I hug her in delight. She's a tiny thing — I'm a head taller, and we've known each other since our schooldays in Perth. She says she used to be terrified of me, but I think there's not much in this world terrifies my friend Lizzie, not even her ridiculous ship. (Whenever I tease her about the risks of ancient vessels, she just recites grim aviation statistics back at me.)

'Congratulations, Mrs Bell!' I say. 'You look beautiful. Any second thoughts?'

'About marrying *Harry*? Are you crazy, Bill?' she asks, laughing. 'I'm so happy.'

'Lizzie, this is Wilf Bettany — Wilf, the happy bride.'

'*This* is Wilf?' she asks, her eyes amused as she kisses him on the cheek. 'Hello, Wilf. Lovely to meet you at long last.'

'Sorry, we've been pretty busy. Here just a couple of weeks,' I say. 'Things to arrange for Spain.'

'Oh, Bill — you're not going *back*, surely? Must be so dangerous.'

That's a sore point, so I change the subject. 'Otto says you're a working woman now! Is it fun?'

'Mmm, interesting,' she says.

'What's your new job?' asks Wilf innocently.

'Oh, Civil Service sort of thing. Typing, documents, you know,' Eliza says. 'Anyway, must go! Harry's waving frantically. See you at the wedding breakfast.'

After she leaves Wilf murmurs, 'Intelligence, do you think?'

I nod. 'Probably. Dear old Otto has some very strange friends.'

I remember telling Otto I wasn't interested in all that political *argy-bargy*. Well, I've learnt a lot since then. I turn on my back and stare at the ceiling, the ornate plaster outlined by a streetlight. I'm finding it hard to sleep even now, and we've been home for weeks.

We're staying with Toby and the avant-garde gang. They cleared a room for us on the third floor of their house, apologising for the mess, but it's the Ritz compared to where we've been.

The rain is bucketing down outside and I can hear the occasional car swishing along the street in the cold. It makes me shiver and I turn and nestle into Wilf's large warm back. He murmurs and pulls my arm over his waist and goes back to sleep, softly snoring.

Wilf. Hell.

He was the last person I'd expected to see at that tiny airport at five in the morning. It was summer but I was in my leather coat, helmet and boots. It's always freezing in the air and we had a long haul ahead to Toulouse, another to Barcelona, then a train or truck to Madrid — Otto was a little vague on the details.

I wasn't so naive as to imagine the big kite on the runway was for my benefit, though. For half-an-hour three men had been loading it up with some very heavy-looking crates. I was keeping my head down reading the paper, but it had a story I didn't much want to see either.

PUTNAM SEARCH HOPES FADE, Honolulu, 12th July 1937: Although holding out little hope for a rescue of Mrs. Amelia Earhart Putnam and Captain Noonan, naval flyers from the battleship Colorado scoured the Phoenix Islands, while the aircraft carrier Lexington, carrying 300 aviators, is hurrying for a survey of the South Pacific area.

Amelia Earhart was gone, poor cow. She'd almost done it too, three-quarters of the way round the world, just that final Pacific leg to do.

I looked up and a familiar figure was walking into the shed.

'What the hell are you doing here?' I said.

'Going to Spain,' said Wilf, grinning.

'But you're not a qualified instructor.'

'I'm going to fight,' he said calmly.

I stared. Pilots from all over the world had gone to fight for the Republicans — but Wilf, the most gentle-natured man I'd ever met?

Out on the runway they were closing down the tanker and it looked as if we'd soon be leaving.

'You're insane,' I said. 'Go home. You won't last five minutes.'

He said, 'Want a hand with that bag?' I said no and refused to speak to him again.

After two long, cold flights and a halting train journey we finally got to Madrid late that night. It was stinking hot and I'd already shed layers of clothes in a shattered bathroom in Barcelona. At Madrid we were given a couple of oranges for sustenance, then loaded into the back of a lorry beside the mysterious crates.

At dawn, sleepless after hours of pot-holed roads, we arrived at the town of Albacete, 160 miles from Madrid and the headquarters of the volunteer International Brigades.

I knew so little about where we were, and even less about why.

I'm bleary and bad-tempered the morning after the wedding. Wilf gets up first and cooks sausages and toast — the kitchen is basic but at least it's got running water, another improvement over the last few months. We were so hungry in Spain that everything now tastes wonderful, but this is particularly good. I'm still bad-tempered, though.

Wilf pours us both mugs of strong tea. He's looking at me but I refuse to meet his eyes. After a time he says gently, 'Billie.'

'Mmm?' I say, gazing down.

'I've got to go back to Spain. The French have just opened their border, but who knows for how long? If I don't leave soon I may have a problem getting through.'

'Then don't go, mate. Problem solved.'

He laughs. 'We've been over this already. You know I must.'

'I don't know that at all, Wilf. In fact I can't quite figure out why you imagine you can do a fucking thing over there. Not after Teruel.'

Teruel. Last December the recapture of the strategic town had looked like a Christmas gift to the Republicans: Ernest Hemingway himself turned up for the celebrations. Then the Fascists counter-attacked in the freezing cold. By January the place was a disaster, by February a bloodbath.

So many of our planes were lost, so many pilots we knew, stoic Russians and gallant Spaniards, killed or wounded or captured. One of our friends was returned to us in a box dropped from a Junker: he'd been butchered into chunks.

'Look, it's obvious *you* shouldn't go back, Billie. They don't need trainers at Albacete any more, not with all the Russian-trained pilots — but it's different for me.'

'No, Wilf. There's no need for naive fools like you, either. Everyone says if the volunteers like you are sent home then the Germans and Italians will leave too. The Republicans'll go along with it, they're desperate — so even if you return you'll soon be sent packing.'

'If I don't go I'll be betraying all our friends who've ...'

'Who've gone down screaming in flames, you mean?'

He nods.

'Pathetic schoolboy fantasies,' I say viciously.

'It's not that, love.' Wilf shrugs carefully — his right shoulder will probably never move smoothly again. 'The Republicans might be crazy Reds, but at least they're not Fascist rapists and torturers. And if we don't stop those bastards in Spain, God knows where we'll be fighting them next.'

'Who cares! This is *now* and you've done what you could. Remember when you were limping home, fuselage shot up, tail practically off? Jesus. A few little holes, you said. Wilf, your shoulder's still oozing *blood!*'

Gazing at me with that infuriating sweetness, he says, 'I'm flying out to Toulouse tomorrow to join a convoy crossing the border in a couple of days. Don't worry. I'll be fine.'

I stare in disbelief. It took me time to let down my defences, to lean on him a little, to allow us a few happy moments in that nightmare of madness and death and bright-eyed boys pitting hopeless Great War relics against Messerschmidts.

But I've come to trust Wilf body and soul, even to love him.

The stupid fucking idiot.

He leaves anyway. I don't expect letters, the post in Spain barely operates. In fact the odds of knowing what happens to him aren't high, though word usually gets back to Otto's group and then they have to break the news of a shooting or a crash or a dismemberment. Sometimes the word is of prison camp, and that particular detour through the torture-chambers is never good news either.

At first, those bright-eyed boy flyers were shocked at the idea of me teaching them, but came to accept it because freedom for women is a Republican ideal. I'd see posters of female fighters on walls and lamp-posts; I'd even see real women carrying their own rifles.

But that was then. Now the anarchists and socialists and communists — usually at each other's throats — are united in insisting that women go back to the kitchen. General Franco must be laughing his head off.

I'd often wonder why he didn't just roll over us and slaughter us with his superior forces. But he's boasted openly he wants to wage a war of attrition. A war of slow blood sacrifice. Franco wants to kill — one by one — every single person in Spain who has ever held a thought that might have displeased the medieval Inquisition.

I light a cigarette. I'm sitting at the kitchen table beside the open window, looking out over the neighbours' rear courtyards, all concrete and pipes and struggling weeds. I hear the doorbell ring but don't move. I know Klara is downstairs to answer it.

I'm so tired. I rub my eyes. Last night I woke yelling again, but this time Klara and Sofia didn't burst in thinking I was being murdered, they just tapped on the door and asked if I wanted company. I said no. What good would company do?

Anyway, it wasn't clean old-fashioned murder making me scream. I've tried to talk about it to Eliza, hardly a naive woman, but her horror is such an innocent horror. It doesn't compare, for instance, to the faces of the women in a town we passed through.

An interpreter told me that all the males that once lived there were now dead. Every grandfather and father and husband and brother had been shot by Franco's thugs, while every infant with barely a bud of manhood at his soft round thighs had been bludgeoned to death by the Fascists, who don't, of course, waste bullets upon the young.

Although the agony in the women's eyes may also have been for themselves, set upon after that orgy of murder. Orgy. Blood-lust. Rape and pillage. Just words, tossed around until you find out what they really mean.

Of course the Republicans shoot the Nationalists too, it's a fucking war after all. But they don't *obliterate* with such visceral, animal hatred. They don't do what the Fascists do to women and children and, believe me, if I could I'd shoot them myself.

I think I hear Otto's rumbling voice speaking to Klara downstairs.

Not yet.

It's also quite hard — well, impossible, really — to talk about the smells. Broken sewage pipes and open cesspits of course, although they seem almost clean compared to the other stench: familiar as fly-blown meat, but on such a scale it's like a screaming that won't stop. It didn't leave my nose, my lungs, my very skin, until we'd been back in England for a week.

So I don't talk much, although the news — the political argy-bargy — leaves me pretty shaken. In March, the Germans invaded poor old Austria. The politicians squeaked in dismay, although in April they were happy enough to recognise the Italian violation of Ethiopia. In May, the good Christian Pope acclaimed the Nationalists as God's own Spanish government, while Hitler pondered an invasion of

Czechoslovakia. The politicians emitted more squeaks of dismay.

The sound of Klara's light voice drifts up the stairwell but I can't make out what she's saying.

Not yet.

In July — oh thank God! In July, the Non-Intervention Committee and the Republicans agreed at last to the foreign volunteers being sent home, and perhaps, perhaps ...

In August, the Japanese forced the Chinese government to retreat to Chungking. I wonder how close Chungking is to Hong Kong and whether Eliza's aunt Izabel is safe. (See, Otto, I follow *all* the political argy-bargy now.)

Lately there's been further chit-chat about Czechoslovakia. Hitler's still champing at the bit, and Britain and France are supposed to dash in to help if it's invaded. But I can't stomach the thought, and anyway, the International Brigades — and Wilf — may soon be coming home. Otto will be sad, but it's obvious the Republican cause is lost.

I hear Klara's voice again. They're an odd pair, Otto and Klara — cousins, I think. They talk about the Jewish refugees and tell us hair-raising things about what's happening in Germany, things the avant-garde gang find hard to believe.

I don't.

Otto says he's a secular Jew, but lately he's returned to observing the Sabbath. That's why it's strange he's downstairs. Must be something important to bring him out on a Saturday.

Not yet.

I draw on my cigarette and gaze up to the blue sky — just a few clouds, good flying weather — and two swallows swoop and turn in a sweep that makes me want to applaud. Pete and I used to lie on the grass watching the birds fly and say how we'd perform such aerobatics, given throttle and aileron and rudder: still, we'd never have matched such mastery.

When my plane crashed five years ago I bailed out safely, but poor old Pete didn't realise and mourned beside the embers for a day. He said he cried when he saw swallows flying because they reminded him of me. That was when I let down my defences and we became lovers.

I let down my defences with Wilf too. Even in Spain it's not war all the time. There are moments of peace and gatherings for the exhausted, with cheap wine and guitars and defiant songs. The landscape reminds me of Australia too, rocky hills, scrubby bushes, endless heat. Some evenings Wilf and I would lie in a quiet place by a stream, and he'd murmur poems he loved by some priest.

Not yet.

There was one about a falcon — *in his riding of the rolling level underneath him steady air* — and I said, oh come on, a pilot wrote that, not a priest, and Wilf laughed and kissed me. The poem ended: *blue-bleak embers, ah my dear, fall, gall themselves, and gash gold-vermillion* — but I never much liked that bit about falling.

After we'd made love in his room Wilf would play me old gramophone records, intricate, sombre pieces on cello, and a violin piece called *Lark Ascending.* The birds outside soar and soar like music themselves into the sky until they've disappeared. *My heart in hiding Stirred for a bird.*

I stub out my cigarette. Flying was once such an innocent joy: how did it bring me to this?

I can hear Otto and Klara coming up the stairs to my rooms on the third floor, Klara's steps light and precise, Otto's heavy and mournful. They stop outside my door and I know Otto is taking a breath, steeling himself. Then he knocks, very gently, and says my name.

Please, not yet.

8. Izabel: Shanghai

I stand at the door of my new, large Malory Studio and watch young Nancy Kuan, her brown hair in a braid, walking away with her amah. As they reach the corner she turns and waves, and I wave back. Her amah was late picking her up today, so we amused ourselves imitating people we know, then experimented more seriously with the gaits and gestures that mark the races here.

With a shift of her shoulder, a glance of her eyes, Nancy can switch in an instant from being one of the spoilt English boys in my classes to one of the shy, clever Indian girls. She watches and ponders, and she's the first person I've met who notices the same small revealing things I do, another of her chameleon skills.

I collect a list of measurements from my desk and take a taxi to the narrow, noisy streets of downtown. Bao-lim has recommended a tailor who'll make curtains for our small theatre. The man shows me swathes of fabric and I choose a dark red velvet, and agree to come back in a few days to pick them up.

Once a week I go to my uncle's house to have a language lesson, so at home I get ready a little earlier than usual — I don't want to see Felix. Most evenings we end up arguing about where I'm going and where he's going, and it's rarely the same place.

I take off the tight stockings and girdle and formal dress I wear at work and with relief put on a Chinese cotton top and loose trousers. I hear the front door slam and a moment later Felix comes into the bedroom. I once adored his rakish black eyebrows and blue eyes, but now those eyes are narrow with dislike as he stares at my clothes.

'You can't wear *that* to the club — it's Binkie's birthday, for God's sake.'

'I'm not going to the club, I've got a lesson with my uncle.'

He sneers. 'Skating on thin ice, that one. Be careful you don't fall through, Izabel.'

'Bao-lim's a respected businessman, Felix. What specific thin ice did you have in mind?'

'Got a few dodgy pals of the Bolshevik persuasion, so I'm told.'

'I imagine most people here have met a Red or two over the years,' I say. 'It means nothing.'

'Not to the secret police.'

'Felix, do you *know* something? This is my uncle you're talking about.'

'Just rumours,' he says resentfully. 'He's probably safe enough in a British colony. Still, I wish to God you'd stop acting like one of the bloody locals.'

How ironic. If Felix had escorted the famous actress Izabel Malory to Hong Kong he'd probably be an intimate of the Governor by now, but the Felix who betrayed me ended up with just a disgraced Eurasian on his arm.

His superiors mistrust my Chinese relatives and his friends think I'm a stuck-up bitch. To my own small pleasure I'm of no advantage to my husband in any way.

Despite the argument with Felix I'm still early for my lesson with Bao-lim, and when I'm shown into the reception room it's clear I've arrived unexpectedly early.

I calmly greet my uncle and his companion, who moves a newspaper to cover something on the table.

'Lovely to see you again, Professor Kuan,' I say. 'I had such a nice time today with Nancy.'

'She tells me you'll be working on *Midsummer Night's Dream* soon.'

'In the autumn, when the weather's milder.'

I look pointedly at my uncle and he sighs.

'Second Niece, Professor Kuan and I are planning a trip to Shanghai. We are taking — resources — for friends who are fighting the Japanese.'

I nod. It was money Laurence Kuan had covered with the newspaper and a lot of it. 'How will you get there, Uncle?'

'By coastal steamer,' says Bao-lim. 'The Japanese destroyers don't bother them.'

'But will you be *safe* in Shanghai?'

'We will stay at a hotel in the International Quarter,' says Professor Kuan. 'The Japanese invaded only the Chinese part of the city, after all. They are more cautious with foreign territory — they do not want war with Britain or America, or at least not yet.'

'I've heard the International Quarter is terribly glamorous,' I say wistfully, reminded of my own lost days of dressing up and dancing and laughing. 'Jazz, cocktails, White Russian exiles, exotic Eurasians — it all sounds rather thrilling.'

'Thrilling, dear Niece, if you disregard the Chinese starving in the streets,' says my uncle gently. 'And while the peasants must eat mud, the Shanghai papers lament only that the quality of champagne in the International Quarter has plummeted.'

Professor Kuan gazes at me. 'Mrs Malory, you appreciate this is confidential. There are many, including the British, who prefer to offer little resistance to the Japanese.'

'I understand perfectly, Professor Kuan. Perhaps they hope the invaders will be too busy in China to bother anyone else.'

'A foolish hope,' says my uncle. 'The Japanese have never hidden what they want and how they plan to get it, yet those most at risk simply close their ears.'

I gaze at them curiously. 'But won't you two be implausibly *obvious* — an academic and a retired businessman heading for the bright lights of Shanghai?'

Professor Kuan nods. 'We will simply have to make ourselves inconspicuous.'

I stop myself saying, 'Don't be absurd.' Does he not understand how striking a man he is?

I turn to Bao-lim. 'First Uncle, remember your dead brother was a Red — perhaps Chiang's spies are still watching you.'

'Ah. Poor Yun-sen, lost to us on the Long March. No my dear, many families have someone with the Reds, and Chiang's spies cannot watch everybody all the time. We shall be safe.'

We decide to postpone the language lesson and take a small meal together. My uncle's household is modest for a man of his means — his wife and child died many years ago in one of the summer epidemics, but he did not take another wife, or even an official concubine. Despite his secret political life, he's a meditative man who loves to write poetry.

Servants are present so we simply make light, civilised conversation as we eat. I try not to watch Laurence Kuan's long thighs beneath his robe, or his strong brown hands, or the elegant line of his neck as he turns his gaze on me, his eyes smiling.

I try not to smile in return.

A few days later I go to check on the new red velvet curtains. They're just as I wanted, and I arrange for them to be delivered to my studio. It's stifling hot in the noisy, narrow streets and I look around for somewhere to get a cool drink. Not far away is a British hotel, so I go to the lounge and sit down in an armchair and order a lemon squash.

I think about my uncle and Laurence Kuan trooping innocently off to Shanghai without the slightest thought of disguise. Yet it's surprisingly easy to go unnoticed with the right posture and props, especially if you provide something else to divert attention.

As I'm musing I hear a familiar voice. Beyond some parlour palms I see Felix, his back to me, and across from him a blonde I recognise, the wife of one of his co-workers, a nice woman — Barbara something-or-other. I always liked her and certainly don't dislike her now.

Felix is holding her hand and she's gazing into his eyes. Poor cow, she probably believes every word. He leans towards her and she shyly nods. They stand and leave, heading for the stairs to the hotel rooms.

I've known through the years there have been other women — the memory of a hairpin I once found in our bathroom still makes me wince — but I've never had my face rubbed in it like this.

Ah, Felix. Blondes have always been your weakness.

I stand abruptly and go to find a taxi to take me to my uncle's house. I walk in as he and Professor Kuan are checking documents for their trip, and sit down on the sofa.

'I'm coming with you,' I say before I even know I'm going to say it. 'The two of you trotting off to Shanghai, lambs to the slaughter? You'll be outrageously obvious and attract the attention of the secret police in moments. But I can change all that.'

'How, Second Niece?' asks Bao-lim.

'Look at me! A glamorous Eurasian is *exactly* the sort of woman to be going to Shanghai to have fun! I'd draw every eye — charming, delightful, imperious me! And my dull escorts, who'd even notice them? It's a classic stage trick of misdirection.'

Bao-lim sits beside me, concern on his face. 'A clever plan, my dear, but you would be taking yourself into danger.'

'I'm coming, Uncle. I *must* get away from Hong Kong for a week or two. I cannot bear my situation a moment longer.'

Bao-lim nods. We've never discussed it, but I think he understands a great deal about Felix.

'What's more,' I say, 'I can show you simple tricks to make you as uninteresting as possible. Ugly glasses, unstylish clothes, poor grooming — by the time I'm done you'll bore even yourselves.' I stand up. 'Will you organise my ticket while I pack?'

Professor Kuan takes a breath. 'Yes. We leave at eleven tonight from the main wharf. Are you certain you should do this, Mrs Malory?'

'Have my ticket ready.'

When I get home Felix isn't there. He's probably still screwing poor Barbara — or snoring beside her as she realises he's not quite the great lover she'd dreamt of.

When I started my new studio I promoted clever Mrs Lau from cleaner to assistant, so I ring and ask her to close my classes for two weeks due to 'illness'. Then I quickly pack my makeup, jewellery and most sumptuous clothes.

I dash off a note to Felix saying I'm going to visit relatives in the country with Bao-lim, then call for a taxi and get to the wharf just before eleven.

My uncle and Professor Kuan are waiting for me at the foot of the gangway to the *Yunnan*. We rush aboard, the ship's horn sounds, the engines rumble and we ease away from the wharf. I gaze back at the lights of Victoria City as we move out into the harbour.

Felix is far behind me and I feel light-headed with joy.

The *Yunnan* will take three days to reach Shanghai. It's a small but comfortable ship and I sleep well in my cabin. Next day is warm and humid, and I wear a fashionable outfit of shorts and a top designed to attract attention. I play shuffleboard and deck tennis, laughing and flirting with businessmen and bored husbands and retired soldiers.

By the afternoon I know most of the ships' officers, and that evening, dressed in satin, I'm the centre of attention at the captain's table. (Next day he tries to kiss me in a corridor.)

I dance and dazzle and draw all eyes. Ignored and irrelevant, Bao-lim plays my absent-minded relative and Laurence Kuan a bespectacled swain shuffling cards in the corner.

At midnight the ship berths at Amoy, then the following morning we leave and I continue the demanding performance. We know there are informers aboard for any or all of the Kuomintang, the Japanese or the British, and I flirt with the obvious spies with gratifying success.

Another dizzy evening passes by of dancing and champagne and squeals of laughter, but that humid night I can't sleep.

I put on my light Chinese clothes and go up to the slowly rolling deck in the anonymous dark. I watch the waves glimmering in our passing lights and take deep breaths of cool air to clear my lungs.

A man comes to stand beside me and I turn to him with my Izabel Malory face, ready to work once more, then realise it's Laurence Kuan.

'Oh, thank God, it's just you,' I say. 'I can't laugh any more this evening, my cheeks hurt.'

He smiles — always with his eyes, the winged lines of his mouth quite still. 'Nancy has told me how exhausting it is to sustain a performance over a long time, yet you never flag.'

'Surely most would assume this glittering fool is the real me.'

'Some might,' he says. 'I think instead you are wise and courageous.'

I take a painful breath, gripping the rail. I can't say anything, I simply gaze at the dark sea. After a time I realise tears are flowing down my face.

Laurence Kuan wipes my tears with a handkerchief, then stands quietly beside me holding the rail. With the rolling of the ship the edge of his hand touches mine and we pass the moment we might have moved apart with a polite 'sorry.'

The universe contracts to that warm, light pressure, conveying all that is kind and understood between us. He gazes at me, light glancing off the swooping line of his cheek.

I have known male beauty in my life — and sometimes male integrity — but never, never, a man such as this.

The ship approaches Shanghai the following evening. We stand near the bow watching, and as we enter the Whangpoo river I comment on the vast amount of floating garbage.

Bao-lim murmurs, 'It is worse further north, where the Yellow River enters the sea. It is still full of bodies. Thousands of bodies.'

'From a battle?'

'From Chiang's flood, in June. You did not know?'

Laurence Kuan, on my other side, says quietly, 'In a bizarre gesture aimed at the Japanese — who were not anywhere in range — Chiang ordered the upriver dikes destroyed. Half a million of his own people drowned in the floods that followed.'

'Dear God, *why*?'

'No one can comprehend,' says Laurence. 'Incompetence? Malice? Insanity?'

'China has always been a place of corruption,' Bao-lim says sadly. 'But there must be wisdom too, the parasite should not kill the host. No wonder so many seek an alternative.'

We are dressed in Western clothes, ready to stay at the famous Cathay Hotel. The captain kisses my fingers lingeringly as we leave, and all eyes are on me still, none on my dull companions.

Our taxi takes us along the riverside thoroughfare of the International Quarter, the famous Bund. The road is slow, busy with trams, rickshaws, straggling crowds and stick-thin beggars.

I notice a doll on the road and think for a moment of my own favourite childhood toy. Then a rickshaw wheel strikes it and I see, sickeningly, it's a baby's corpse.

The occasional body falls on the streets of Hong Kong too, but the British clean it away — not for the sake of the dead Chinese of course, just so the English ladies won't be perturbed. But I've never seen …

and then there's another, an old woman. *How?*

Bao-lim touches my hand. 'Try not to look, Second Niece. There is no kindness during wartime.'

'But this part of Shanghai is supposed to be at peace!'

Laurence says gently, 'They are refugees, Izabel. No one cares what happens to them.'

We arrive at the hotel and again I adopt my glittering persona as we sweep through the equally glittering marble foyer, its great glass cupola above us. With bows and politeness we are welcomed to the most glamorous place in Shanghai: the most glamorous place in the entire Far East.

As the hotel manager shakes Bao-lim's hand a short man in uniform stands nearby staring at me. The manager introduces him — Colonel Huang. His clothing is perfectly tailored and he has a thin moustache above his thin smile.

He clearly inspires fear. I see the tiny flexing of muscles in the smiling manager's hands no one else would notice. But of course Huang inspires fear, he's an officer of the Kuomintang, Generalissimo Chiang's corrupt, vicious army.

We take the lift to the seventh floor, to a suite of bedrooms with a luxurious sitting room. A man brings us tea then thankfully leaves us alone. I collapse onto a sofa, exhausted.

Bao-lim, apparently tireless, says quietly, 'I must go to see someone now and will return at midnight. Both of you, eat in the dining room and keep up our masquerade, but then rest. Laurence, we may be going out in the early hours.'

'Be careful,' I say, suddenly realising we've reached a point of no return. 'Be *careful*, Uncle.'

He smiles and touches my face for a moment. 'Dear Niece.'

After he leaves, Laurence Kuan and I take our baths and dress in evening clothes. I wear an emerald silk gown that brings copper glints to my hair, and in the dining room we eat and drink and chat.

When we leave, I see cold-eyed Colonel Huang near the lifts. I smile prettily and he nods.

'My magic doesn't appear to work on him,' I murmur in the lift.

Laurence's fingers curl around mine for a moment. 'Then he clearly has no sight or sanity or wisdom.'

We enter the suite in silence, my heart thumping, and I walk to the window. Shanghai's streetlights and cooking fires and flickering lamps shimmer along the river and away into the distance. Laurence comes to stand beside me. I turn to face him and take his hands, and at last, my true self, I can return his calm gaze.

'So little time until midnight,' I say quietly.

He draws me close and kisses my hair. 'Then every instant is precious.'

In the lamplight the gown on my bedroom floor becomes a pool of emerald. Laurence is warm and silk-smooth, his muscles and sinews close to the skin. The black hair of his body is fine and straight, musky and intoxicating as incense. His mouth tastes of spices and his hands are supple and strong.

The first time I weep for both joy and sorrow, but the second time I do not weep. I lie in peace, joined to him, knowing I will never again be as complete as I am at that moment.

Before midnight we rise and wash and dress, then sit side by side on the lounge, waiting for Bao-lim to return.

'How — how will you deliver the money tonight?' I say.

'We'll carry it under our clothes to the meeting-place. Bao-lim will bring the guide here.' He hesitates. 'Izabel, I do not know what we must face and it is possible I may not return. I wish to ask a favour.'

'Anything.'

'My daughter Nancy — I have no family to care for her. Might you, if necessary, find her a home with someone who will treat her with kindness?'

My throat hurts. 'Her home would be with me, Laurence. Always.'

'And should the Japanese come, will you keep her safe and take her away, even from China?'

'She'll be safe with me forever, I swear it.'

'Tell her I was thinking of her now, at the last moment.' Laurence smiles fleetingly. 'Although I suspect the last few hours will also be much on my mind.'

I smile a little too. 'You'll be able to tell her yourself when you're back.'

He wears an old Buddhist mala beneath his clothes (I have so recently discovered) and now he lifts it over his head and puts it in my hand. 'Give her this, with my love.'

The beads are of turquoise, warm from his body, and I tuck them into my handbag. I remove a long, fine gold chain I always wear and place it around his neck, saying, 'Take this, with mine.'

He kisses me, then we sit holding hands, overwhelmed, our heads together, murmuring to each other now and then.

After a time we hear a key in the door. We glance up and move apart. Bao-lim enters with a stranger, wary and whip-thin, a scar on the side of his neck. As I look, his face seems to leap into focus: unknown yet eerily familiar.

'Izabel, Laurence,' says my uncle. 'May I introduce my brother, Yun-sen? Third Brother, this is Second Niece and my friend Professor Kuan.'

'Your brother is *alive*?' I say.

Bao-lim smiles. 'I found out only a few weeks ago, and I must say it has been very difficult keeping such wonderful news a secret.'

'Oh, Min-lu will be so happy!' I say.

'Please, no — you must tell my sister only in person,' says Third Uncle urgently. 'Never in writing. It could mean death, yours or hers. A letter of mine to Fourth Brother led him to the torture of the secret police. Do you understand me?' His voice is ragged with regret.

'Yes, yes, I promise, truly,' I say. 'Only in person.'

Bao-lim is sombre again. 'Laurence, we must prepare.' They go into my uncle's room.

Yun-sen sits down in an armchair and takes a deep breath.

'How good to see you alive, Third Uncle,' I say. 'We thought you were dead, fighting with the Reds.'

He shrugs and smiles bleakly. 'I thought I was dead too. But I survived and kept fighting.'

'And where have you been all these years?'

'In the mountains. It is better you know only that.' He sighs. 'It is very good to see you too, Niece, you were tiny when we last met. You are much like your mother — as children we were very close. Please tell her I miss her and hope we may meet again.'

My uncle and Laurence return, both a little bulkier under their clothes than before.

Yun-sen looks at Bao-lim and stands. 'We must go.'

The three of them move to the door and Bao-lim says calmly, 'We shall be back by morning.'

I hug my uncle the poet, and my uncle the revolutionary.

Then I hold Laurence close and he whispers, '*My love, my love.*'

And they leave.

I try to sleep but wake up every half hour, seeing grey light growing brighter at the edges of the opulent curtains. I rise and dress and send for tea — I can't eat.

I smoke and sip the tea, pacing around the sitting room, gazing out at the busy river with its junks and motor boats and dinghies and steamers buzzing back and forth. The trams on the Bund below clatter and ding their bells, motor cars stop and go, horns toot, streams of rickshaws pass, people stride busily.

By nine o'clock I'm desperate, but suddenly there's a knock at the door. Oh, dear God, they're back! Then a cold sweat forms down my spine. They have keys, they don't need to knock.

I open the door to hard-faced Colonel Huang. I turn on the charm just a little too late, but in any case it's a waste of time.

'Mrs Malory. Come.'

He walks away, two thugs shadowing him. I take my key and follow, my mouth dry. He says nothing as the lift descends. He walks through the lobby to a side corridor, past a kitchen to an outer door. I'm trembling. Outside is an alley, and a crumpled heap of clothes.

Not clothes.

Colonel Huang kicks hard with his shiny boot, but Bao-lim cannot respond. He's riddled with wounds. Wounds that no longer bleed because his heart has stopped beating.

I clasp my hands over my mouth to stifle my scream.

'Of course, you will need a coffin to take your uncle home to perform the funeral rites.' The Colonel smirks. 'I am a compassionate man and will see one is delivered immediately. However my compassion has its limits, so your uncle's accomplices must rot where they lie, enriching the soil for the peasants they loved so much.'

A whimper escapes my throat.

'Do not blame yourself. Your whorish performance was perfect. They were betrayed by simple coincidence — a patrol in the area, an unshielded light. Naturally, we have confiscated the money we found on their bodies, to pay for my time and the bullets of my men — and the coffin, of course.'

He walks away, his thugs following like curs, then he turns.

'Did you not know, Mrs Malory? This is how it happens in war. Suddenly. Shockingly. Finally.'

I stand at the bow of *Yunnan* as we approach Hong Kong harbour. Bao-lim's coffin lies in a refrigerated section of the hold. In recent years the shipping lines have made excellent profits transporting bodies from here to there, so families may fulfil their funerary obligations.

I am not wearing my Izabel Malory face, I am my new nondescript self. Although we travelled to Shanghai on this very ship two weeks ago, the officers don't notice me and only the captain peers at me occasionally in a puzzled sort of way.

I gaze at lofty Victoria Peak and wonder if I will ever breathe freely again.

My love, my love.

9. Toby: The Human Condition

Look, I'm a writer. I stand back and observe. People tell me their tales and I nod sympathetically and then, if intrigued or inspired, I use what I've learnt to enhance what I do. Never directly, of course. I doubt my confidants would ever recognise themselves or their dilemmas, but I know their lived experience is what pulses beneath my words.

Still, I can't conceive how I'd use what's happened lately.

When Wilf Bettany came home from Spain in an ambulance he was so damaged no one expected him to live. But he did, and after months in hospital he was discharged on crutches. Billie was still staying with us at Whitfield Street, but it was obvious they'd have to find a place to live without stairs.

To my amazement it was the terrifying Charlotte who offered them somewhere to go: the farmhouse near Southampton she shares with Pete and baby Vivian. It's certainly large enough, with a rarely-used room on the ground floor for a bedroom, but Charlotte's untypical act of generosity puzzles us all.

Yet we're happy to help move Wilf and Billie and their few possessions to the country. Wilf reassures us that the rural life will mend all that ails him, although Billie doesn't say much.

She's changed a great deal. Bizarrely calm and patient now, despite all the intimate and menial tasks she must perform for her lover. They're almost broke as well, but when I suggest they contact his parents and get them to pay for a nurse, she smiles.

'Toby, he's estranged from them. They were furious about him leaving Oxford and learning to fly, let alone going to Spain. I'm happy to do whatever he needs.'

'As far as I can see, my dear, you're barely getting by on coffee and cigarettes and no sleep.'

She shrugs. 'I'm all right. I'm just grateful Charlotte's offered him somewhere to go.'

'That's certainly wonderful, but *why?*'

'She's sad and lonely, Toby.'

'*Charlotte*? She could have any man in London, and half the women too. How could she be sad and lonely?'

'I don't know, but she seems desperate for company.' Billie says drily. 'Christ, she's even putting up with me just for the novelty of it.'

'She's not bothered about your previous passionate connection to dear old Farmer Pete?'

Billie shakes her head. 'Why? I'm no threat.'

Oddly, Billie and Wilf's move to the farm near Southampton coincides with a similar shift in my own life too. Stefan takes up a long-desired position at the place where Pete works, the Supermarine aircraft factory. He leases a flat in Southampton and we spend alternate weekends there and in London.

It's not an onerous trip to Hampshire, less than two hours, and I quite enjoy the train. I can gaze peacefully and think about writing without any interruptions. Of course I love our house in London, but people do come and go, and play music and chatter and trot up and down the stairs, and it's always too tempting to stop and join in.

Autumn this year is lovely too, made even more precious by September's worrying near-stumble into war over Czechoslovakia, averted at the last moment by funny little Mr Chamberlain with some sort of messing about with borders. I believe it was a bit rough on the Czechs, but at least Europe has *peace for our time*. (Not a bad way with words for a politician, either.)

Stef and Pete say it means we've bought time to build more planes and ships before war comes. Billie and Wilf also insist war is coming, but maybe they're bitter because it was a German plane that shot down poor old Wilf — although I still don't quite follow why the Germans were fighting in Spain.

I'm fairly certain there's no common border, but then, Europe does seem to keep changing around every five minutes. Really, I just hate the thought of war and hope we can avoid it. But when Harry and Eliza visit, even she says it will probably come. Her Civil Service department is already moving its files to some little country town, just in case.

Seems a bit extreme, but that's bureaucracy for you.

We often get together at the farm — it amuses Wilf and gives Billie a little time off. Only Sofia and Klara stay in London most of the time, because Klara's become absurdly involved with Otto's organisation, dealing with an endless stream of refugees from Europe.

But honestly, I don't know why these people feel they must leave their countries in the first place. Perhaps they think they can get some sort of advantage by coming here?

Klara gets furious if I say anything like that, and tells me dreadful stories about what they're fleeing from, but I don't know — wouldn't there be more of an outcry in the newspapers if it were all true?

And a lot of people admire what the Fascists have done for Italy and Germany — it seems to be just the Communist sympathisers who complain. Still, I know I'm pretty naive about this stuff, and I'm willing to believe things are serious. I trust Stef's judgement, if nothing else.

But you see, I'm a writer. I stand back and observe the human condition and rework it into words, and to me that's all that matters.

At the end of 1938, Eliza, Harry, Stef and I go to spend Christmas at the farm. The housekeeper, Mrs Spencer, produces feast after feast, while the snow drifts down as if in a story-book. It sheds that strange pale light you sense before you even look outside, and clings to branches and softens the hills; just right for making snowmen too. Little Vivian is enchanted. We all are.

Billie and Wilf don't come out of course, but the rest of us put on rubber boots and take a crunchy tramp in the snow after lunch on Christmas Day. The air is like champagne and the sky absurdly blue, and even Charlotte is surprisingly sweet-tempered.

When we get back we drink mulled wine and sit watching the fire, dozy and content. Charlotte takes Vivian for a rest and Harry has a nap in an armchair, while Stef, Pete, Billie and Wilf gossip about aeronautical matters.

Sometimes I'm amazed at how many pilots I seem to know, although I've never much wanted to leave the ground myself, despite Stef's kind invitations.

Comfortable on the sofa, I turn to Eliza. 'How's your famous boat going?'

She laughs. 'My far from famous *ship* has just reached Australia, Toby. We had the telegram the other day. She'll be back by June next year, full of the grain to make your daily bread.'

'In six months? Not very efficient, blossom.'

'No fuel costs, powered by God's winds alone,' says Eliza. 'What could be more efficient?'

'A little hurry-on wouldn't hurt, but I suppose you're correct. And what about your gorgeous aunt Izabel — how's she getting on in the wicked Orient?'

Eliza turns and folds her knees up on the sofa. 'Actually, a rather awful thing happened a few months ago. She was visiting Shanghai with her uncle and a friend of his, and both men died in a traffic accident. She had to escort her uncle's coffin back to Hong Kong.'

'Good God, how gruesome! Did you know him?'

'He was my grandmother's brother, but we'd never met.' Eliza sips her wine. 'Anyway, Izabel is going to adopt the dead friend's young daughter — she's eight years old and has no other family. It's a sort of informal Chinese adoption.'

'What about the stiff-upper-lip husband? Is he happy to adopt a Chinese child?'

'The girl's actually Eurasian, like Izabel. Reading between the lines Felix is furious, but I doubt that will stop her. She could never have children, you see, and she always wanted to.'

A sadness flits over Eliza's face.

I take her hand. 'And you, poppet?'

She shakes her head. 'It's just not happening, Toby. I don't understand why.'

'You *have* been indulging in frequent marital conjunction, I take it?'

'Look at him,' she says, smiling at the sight of rather dishy Harry, asleep in the armchair. 'Could you doubt it?'

Next morning everyone else stays in bed, but despite yesterday's excesses I get up early, leaving Stef snoring quietly. Billie is awake before me, sitting at the kitchen table, smoking as usual.

'For God's sake, woman. You need food, not cigarettes. I'll make us bacon and eggs.'

She stubs out the cigarette. 'I'm always happy to accept food somebody else cooks, Toby.'

'How have you been, anyway?' I say, opening the refrigerator. 'I suppose Wilf keeps you busy.'

'Not by any choice of his, but yes, there's a lot to do.'

I start the bacon frying, add a couple of eggs, and say hesitantly, 'Last night I heard someone calling out — sounded rather distressed.'

'Wilf often remembers the crash in his dreams.'

'It was your voice, my dear.'

Billie shrugs and runs her fingers through her short auburn hair. 'When I was living at Whitfield Street I used to wake the girls up sometimes.'

'Sofia and Klara mentioned your nightmares, but I didn't realise ...'

'If it's anything like Wilf —' she shrugs. 'I can only apologise.'

'Billie, don't *apologise*! My God, shouldn't you be seeing a doctor or something?'

'A psychiatrist, you mean?'

'Well, yes.' I flip the bacon.

'Charlotte sees a psychiatrist.'

'*Charlotte* does?'

'Mmm,' says Billie. 'Goes up to London every couple of weeks.'

'My God, why?'

'Depressed, I believe.'

'Shouldn't she just — buck up — or something?'

Billie gives a tired laugh. 'Toby, it's serious. I thought you said you were an observer of the bloody human condition.'

I'm a little stung. 'Well, I do try, but don't really know about that sort of thing. Does she lie back on a couch and tell her innermost secrets to Dr Freud?'

I slide the food onto plates and we start eating.

'I suppose it's something like that,' says Billie. 'Charlotte was just — withdrawing — from Pete and Vivian, it was awful. I don't know if the psychiatrist has helped but at least she seems happier lately.' She looks up and smiles a little. 'Thanks, Toby. Nice breakfast.'

'Oh, darling, no one's looking after *you*, are they? Charlotte's unwell, Pete's busy, Wilf ...' I shake myself. 'Well, it's me who should buck up, I expect.' I glance at her. 'He's getting better, though, isn't he?'

There's a long silence, then Billie says, 'Wilf has internal damage, it's not just his legs. No, he's not getting better. You must have noticed how thin he is now.'

'But what can we do? Surely someone can help. Otherwise, Christ —'

She gazes at me with pity. 'Dear Toby. There is no *otherwise*. He's going to die soon. That's the human condition.'

In spring, Wilf reconciles at last with his parents, who are withered with sorrow. They are there at his bedside when he and Billie are married, they are there when he dies, and they are there when he's buried in the churchyard of a village near the farm.

We attend the funeral, shocked and confused. After the wake Billie rests by the fire in the kitchen, wrapped in a shawl, her eyes tired.

I take a cup of tea into the living room and sit on the sofa. Charlotte, in the armchair, is gazing at nothing. Through a part-open door I can see the bed where Wilf slept, Billie beside him, right to the end.

Charlotte sighs. 'What a bloody nightmare. What a bloody, bloody, nightmare.'

I haven't given her much thought these last few intense months. I glance at her — she's as striking as ever (if you fancy lush blondes) but her eyes are shadowed and the good humour she displayed at Christmas is conspicuously lacking.

'How's Vivian taking it?' I ask.

'Half understands, half-doesn't. Wilf did his best to prepare her, but she misses him.'

'I suppose it'll take a while to get back to normal.'

'Sweetie, we'll never get back to normal,' says Charlotte.

After a silence I say, 'Must have been a strain with Wilf living here.'

'A bit.' She glances at me. 'Look, Toby, I know you've never been fond of me. But I've always tried to make things work for Pete and me and the baby.'

'As I recall, Charlotte, you've been pretty damned brutal towards Pete at times.'

She stares at her hands. 'Sometimes I become ... confused. Trying so hard to be a *good girl*, trying to make everyone happy. Failing completely, of course.'

'But when you had Vivian you made everyone happy — including yourself, I thought.'

'She's the best thing I've ever done, but I thought after we married I'd have a new life.' Charlotte smiles bitterly. 'So I'm still confused.'

'About Pete or the child?'

'God, no, they're everything to me. But I'm not. I'm not anything.'

'I don't understand —'

'Neither do I, Toby. Neither do I.' She laughs a little wildly and puts her hand over her eyes.

'Oh, *Charlotte*,' I say. 'Wilf wouldn't want you to mourn like this.'

'I know. But I'm such a bitch, you see — I'm not weeping for Wilf.'

Billie stays on at the farm. She seems fond of Vivian, and I don't think she wants to leave while Wilf's death is still raw to the child. That's intriguing, because she's always made it clear she dislikes kids and intends to have none herself.

But Vivian, it must be said, is rather a nice child — surprisingly level-headed for someone not yet three. Stef and I visit them all as often as we can during the beautiful summer that follows.

One day we go for a walk in the afternoon and I catch up to Pete for a chat. The talk of war never stops now and I'm curious about what it might mean for him.

'Who, me?' says Pete, grinning. 'Just more bloody work with the Spitfire program, I reckon.'

'What, are you a test pilot?'

'Nah, mate, they wouldn't let me near one. I'm just the paper-pusher, the manager. I help keep development ticking over, making the Spit better and better. Mind you, it's already a pretty amazing bird.' After a pause he says, 'Truth is, I'm too old, Toby.'

'You're only twenty-eight, Pete! How can that be too old to fly?'

'Too old for the test program — or even the Air Force. The pilots they're bringing on now are under twenty, that's what they want. And I haven't got the years in the Reserve behind me, not like Stef.'

I don't quite catch what he means. 'Oh good. You're both safe from aerial dogfights with the Red Baron, then.'

He laughs. 'No, they'll put men like Stef in command roles, but he'll still be up there fighting, of course.' His voice trails off as he sees my face. 'Didn't you know, Toby?'

'I've been so busy with a deadline. Don't like to think about it really, and Stef always downplays it, says it'll be a long time, if ever, before — before …'

My love is striding ahead of us, dark, slim, quick; chatting to Billie and making her briefly smile.

'Are you saying it *won't* be a long time?' It's hard to breathe.

'Oh, look, Toby, maybe it'll never even happen.'

'Pete?'

He's silent.

And it's only then I realise the human condition includes me as well.

10. Eliza: The Approaching Eyewall

After the joy of marriage surrounded by our dearest friends, Harry and I settle into the calm of safe harbour after a long, hard voyage.

Perhaps I imagine the world is becoming as content as we are, because it comes as a shock to hear that our head, the dashing Admiral Sinclair, has quietly acquired an estate in the country town of Bletchley for the use of the Intelligence Service.

'What do you mean, he paid for it himself?' I ask Mr Davis, one of my colleagues in the Commercial Section.

'Exactly what I said, Mrs Bell. Admiral Sinclair paid for Bletchley Park out of his own pocket. He couldn't wait for the budgetary wheels of the Civil Service to grind slow, or probably not grind at all, so he bought it himself.'

'That's dedicated. Do you think we'll have to go and work there?'

'I've heard our people have started setting up archives and organising accommodation and offices, so yes, should war come, we'll probably be expected to move.'

I sigh. I love working at 54 Broadway and don't want to leave London. Harry is here, his work is here, our home is here, and Bletchley is fifty miles away. It might be on the railway line but would we even be allowed to travel in wartime?

Don't worry, I tell myself. It might never happen.

Despite my daily overview of the secrets of a number of countries lusting for conflict, the prospect is still unthinkable. It's been barely twenty years since the Great War ended and since then, despite the Depression, the world has flourished with advances in learning, science and international cooperation.

Still, I sometimes recall the tropical cyclones of Broome I knew as a child. They'd build up over the summer, then usually brush us with a drenching or wander away into the Indian Ocean.

But once we watched from Cable Beach as looming charcoal clouds gathered out at sea, the wind whipping sand into our faces. Mama was busy in Perth with an art exhibition, so Pete and I were having a holiday with our aunt and uncle, Lucy and Danny. I was afraid and tugged at Lucy's hand, wanting to return to the safety of the house.

The grown-ups glanced at each other with worried eyes, and men spoke in low voices of sheltering the luggers among the mangroves of Dampier Creek. That night we gathered in the central room of Lucy's well-built house to wait out the storm.

Cyclones don't 'hit', they build up. Drumbeats of thunder and crackles of lightning grow louder and more terrifying, rain falls like an increasingly solid thing yet is blasted sideways, and the wind shreds trees and flicks iron sheets off roofs like playing cards.

Just when I though I could not endure my fear for a moment longer the cacophony calmed, the rain stopped, the wind eased. Cautiously I looked outside to see stars wavering above in patches of sky, the thunderclouds drawing away to the east. I sighed with relief.

Then Danny said gently, 'It's not over, child. This is the eye, the quiet part of the storm. It'll all begin again soon, and everything will be the weaker for the first battering we took.'

He was right.

And now I cannot stop wondering: have these two decades of peace been nothing more than the eye of a cyclone, a calm between the eyewalls of a great global insanity?

Billie's lovely man Wilf Bettany has returned to Spain, but I can't understand it, they seemed so good together. Billie says bitterly the Republican cause is lost — worse than lost, trapped in a nightmare spiral of violence — and she'll have nothing more to do with it.

'Fucking public-school fantasies,' she says, waiting, growing thin.

The reality of war takes a step closer in mid-1938, when Wilf comes home in an ambulance. Our joy at his survival slowly fades as we realise how damaged he is.

When he leaves hospital he stays for a time at Toby's house in Whitfield Street, but the stairs are too much for him. So Charlotte and Pete comes to the rescue, offering him refuge at their farmhouse outside Southampton.

After helping Wilf and Billie settle at the farm in September, I've barely had time to think before the Czechoslovakia crisis erupts, and that breathtaking fool Chamberlain acquiesces to an entire country's dismemberment.

Without hesitation Germany engulfs the Sudetenland, Poland rips off a chunk of Zaolzie, and Hungary swallows gobbets of Slovakia and Ruthenia. *Peace for our bloody time?*

At 54 Broadway, stunned at the hypocrisy, we look aghast at each other. 'We've just lost the Russians,' Mr Baxter says, shaking his head. 'They'll never trust us again. They'll make their own accommodation with the Nazis and to hell with us.'

A few weeks after the fiasco of Czechoslovakia, I receive a restrained letter from Izabel telling me about the sad deaths of her uncle and his friend in a car accident in Shanghai, and her adoption of the friend's orphaned daughter, Nancy.

Something doesn't ring true and I go to see one of the China intelligence specialists. When I tell him their names he's startled to hear of my family connection.

'Can't say too much, Mrs Bell, but we heard they died in a Kuomintang attack on some Reds near Shanghai. Well, that's par for the course, except a large sum of money fell into the hands of one Colonel Huang, a nasty piece of work we like to keep tabs on.'

'And Izabel's uncle and his friend were actually killed?' I say.

'Dead as dodos. It was a massacre.' He gazes at me. 'So this aunt of yours is a Red sympathiser?'

'Oh, certainly not. Just taking pity on a young orphan.'

'Mrs Bell, she was related to a Communist and she's married to one of our own men. I'm sorry, but we'll have to put a note in Felix Malory's file. And yours too, of course.'

Hardly reassuring, but at least I know a little more. I reply carefully to Izabel but her response is so bland it's obvious she doesn't want to put anything into writing.

Christmas 1938 is beautiful, snowy and crisp, so Toby, Stef, Harry and I spend days at Pete and Charlotte's farm. I'm shocked to see Wilf's decline and touched, too, at Billie's fierce calm.

But Charlotte at least is happier than I've ever seen her, and easier as well with young Vivian. This year she's been seeing a psychiatrist, at last coming to terms with her cruel upbringing and her fears of motherhood, and it certainly seems to have helped.

One evening, flushed and happy, she tells me she's pregnant again, although she doesn't want to mention it to anyone else until more time has passed.

I'm delighted for her, although I have to suppress a small pang of my own. It will soon be a year since Harry and I were married, with no sign yet of the baby we yearn to have.

But some weeks later, in February 1939, Charlotte rings me, sobbing so desperately it takes me moments to understand that her pregnancy has ended in a prolonged and agonising miscarriage.

When I call her back next day she's calmer.

'Not too much pain, sweetie. I'm in a cottage hospital and they give me lots of lovely drugs. But look, Pete's told Billie and Wilf I'm here for some minor dental surgery and I'd prefer you and Harry to say nothing either.'

'But why don't you want them to find out?'

'Oh God, I don't know. Yes, this is a ghastly loss, Eliza, but Billie's about to lose so much more. I just don't ...'

'Understood. But do you think he's that close to the end?'

'Perhaps. He's reconciled with his parents. And,' she laughs weakly, 'inconceivable I know, but Billie's agreed to marry him.'

'But she always *swore* —'

'Yes,' says Charlotte. 'That's why I think it'll be soon.'

I can't get away to see Billy and Wilf marry a few weeks later, but Charlotte phones me.

'It was at his bedside, he was too weak to get up. They held hands and that brave cow Billie never wavered, said her vows in such a steady voice.' Charlotte swallows. 'His hand was so thin.'

'Has she told him the Spanish war is over, that bloody Franco won?'

'She doesn't want him to know. A kindness, I think.'

Wilf dies soon afterwards but I still can't get away, even for a funeral. We're on high alert because Germany is invading the shattered remnants of Czechoslovakia. In tardy response, Britain and France bizarrely guarantee to support Poland if it's attacked.

At 54 Broadway, Mr Davis says, 'But that's *insanity!* Poland can't help us and they're just sitting ducks for the Nazis. For God's sake, *why?*'

Mr Baxter looks up and said, 'It's only for show, Davy — Poland's a bargaining counter. The Germans and the Soviet Union both want it, so that'll put them at each other's throats.'

'But what if they come to some agreement?' says Mr Davis, frowning. 'They'd be unstoppable together, they'd carve up Europe like a corpse. I've heard rumblings, Quentin —'

'Bet you five pounds it never happens. You're always hearing rumblings. Probably your lunch,' says Mr Baxter, and Mr Davis snorts.

By May, Mr Baxter's bet seems a sure thing.

The Tripartite negotiations begin in earnest, setting up a protection treaty between the Soviets, Britain and France (although it does seem odd to be making common cause with the Bolsheviks). Yet the mutual mistrust proves to be too great, and in August the Tripartite negotiations fade away.

By then it becomes clear that all this time the Soviets and Nazis have been discussing raw materials and lucrative loans and the distribution of spoils. On 24th August 1939, they sign a non-aggression pact, which defines German and Soviet 'spheres of influence.'

Like the tolling of a great bell, war comes one step closer.

Mr Baxter bets Mr Davis five pounds this means Germany will invade Poland by the weekend, which also seems a pretty sure thing, until something unexpected happens. Britain and Poland formalise an agreement on 25th August, offering assistance if either is attacked by some unnamed 'European country'.

The German army, slavering at the leash, is momentarily restrained.

That night Harry and I sit on the sofa, listening to the BBC report on the pact with Poland.

'Won't stop bloody Hitler for long and it'll probably just drag us into the fight,' I say, and rest my head on Harry's shoulder.

'Apart from the general mayhem in Europe, is anything else wrong, *jungman*?'

'Yes. I'm more and more worried I'll have to move to bloody Bletchley if war breaks out. I won't be able to live here with you.'

Harry nods. 'Funny thing, moving has been on my mind too — but a little further than the countryside. Today I was asked if I'd like to go to Singapore to become head of a new malaria unit.'

'What did you say?'

'No.'

'But love, it's what you've always wanted!'

'Not at the cost of leaving you in England,' he says.

I kiss him. 'Dearest *matros*. Still, I had one piece of good news — a telegram from Captain Nilsen. *Inverley*'s arrived, unloading at Cardiff. Let's go down tomorrow and get away from all this awful gloom.'

Next day, as the train clickety-clacks towards Wales, I think of the time three years ago, when Harry and I finally escaped the constraints keeping us apart and took a train together to see the great four-masted barque *Herzogin Cecilie*, stranded on the Devon coast.

He's clearly recalling the same thing and says, 'Remember when we last saw the Duchess? She was rusting away in Starehole Bay and I said, As *long as sailing ships are loved no one will forget this summer of Herzogin Cecilie*.' He shakes his head. 'How wrong can a man be? Now she's as forgotten as all the others.'

I smile ruefully, and kiss him.

At Cardiff we book into a hotel, then catch a taxi to Barry Docks, and at last I see a sight that makes me happy.

'Oh, Harry, isn't there something so *hopeful* about a sailing ship?'

He laughs. 'There certainly is — and not just *Inverley* either. Look, *Olivebank*'s over there too.' He calls her Oh-leever-bahnk, the soft way the Finns do.

Cranes are lifting bags of grain in slings out of the holds and lowering them into railway trucks, supervised by an old friend, Artur, second mate on *Inverley*. He beckons us aboard and tells us proudly he has just become a father.

'Your wife will need you at home now, Artur,' I tease him.

'But no, Elias! I am having a promotion and she wants me at sea.'

'Promotion?' says Harry. 'Which ship?'

'My friends, when *Olivebank* sails I will be first mate,' Artur says happily.

What good news! We shake his hand and congratulate him until he turns pink with joy.

Captain Nilsen comes to take us below to the familiar saloon, where he pours us glasses of sherry.

'To your retirement and a new life,' says Harry, lifting his drink.

'A new life? I am not sure how that will feel,' *Kapten* says. 'And if the Russians come ...'

'Do you think they will?' asks Harry.

'Their troops have been massing on the Finnish border for a year, demanding the Karelian Isthmus. Yes, *matros*, they will come.'

I say, 'What do you think the pact between the Russians and Nazis will mean?'

'You may fear the Germans, but we fear the Soviets far more.' *Kapten* laughs sadly. 'We threw them out twenty-two years ago, and now they want our land again. I expect the pact means we will stand alone, *jungman*. As always.'

After we bid Captain Nilsen farewell, Harry and I stroll past *Inverley* and *Olivebank*, their towering masts silhouetted against the golden twilight.

'Have you seen that photo of *Olivebank* taken from a plane?' I say. 'Pressing forward with sails round and full, casting long shadows on the glittering sea. Looks absurdly glamorous.'

Harry smiles. 'Yes, it's beautiful. You'd never imagine how grim the reality can be.'

We gaze at the two old ships. I think we're both wondering what will become of them in a world of modern warfare. They may not be fast or famous, but they've laboured faithfully for nearly half a century. What will happen to *Olivebank*? And to my own dear *Inverley*?

After we return to the hotel we take dinner in a restaurant, then go to our room. I sit at the dressing-table brushing my hair and say, 'Remember when my grandparent held a party here just after we landed from Australia?'

'My God, I'll never forget,' says Harry laughing, getting into bed. 'You were wearing a green gown with glittery bits, extremely low-cut. I had to keep pretending to be looking somewhere else.'

'*Did* you? I never suspected. I thought of you then as simply my shipmate.'

'Well so did I. You were only a kid and I was off to do research in London.'

'I was twenty-one, for heaven's sake.'

'You looked like a twelve-year-old in your shipboard dungarees. But certainly not in that gown.'

I get into bed.

'Interesting,' Harry says. 'A new negligee? It's extremely low-cut too.' He runs his fingers slowly, deliciously, beneath the silk neckline. 'Am I detecting a pattern here?'

'You're the scientist, my love. You tell me.'

Harry and I return to London, and *Inverley* sets sail for the Baltic Sea. On 29th August, *Olivebank* follows her, our friend Artur proud as her first mate. Of course, weeks will pass before we hear if they've arrived safely at Mariehamn: but suddenly we have far more to worry about than old sailing ships.

At dawn on 1st September, the Nazis explode across the borders of Poland, with two thousand tanks, thirteen hundred planes and over a million men, viciously crushing all resistance before them.

Two days later, on a bright Sunday morning, Mr Chamberlain announces his government's ultimatum: by 11.00 o'clock, Germany must agree to withdraw from Poland.

Silent, desperately hoping, we wait beside the radio, hearts pounding, mouths dry. But no agreement comes and, like myself and Harry, people all over the country gaze at each other in despair.

At 11.15 a.m. on 3rd September 1939, Britain is once again at war with Germany. We have passed out of the cyclone's calm eye, and now the stormclouds stretch to the horizon.

Next day at 54 Broadway, my section is told we are leaving immediately for Bletchley Park. As I'm gloomily packing files into boxes, Mr Denniston stops by my desk.

'Might I have a word, Mrs Bell?' I follow him into his office.

'Please have a seat,' he says. 'Now I do appreciate that the prospect of Bletchley leaves you a little less than enthusiastic, so I'd like to propose an alternative.'

'Alternative?'

'You see, Mrs Bell, there are changes in the wind at the Far East Combined Bureau. Given Germany's closeness to Japan we've decided to shift the headquarters from Hong Kong to Singapore.'

'Yes?' I say uncertainly.

'We urgently need more people at the Bureau. So would you be at all interested in a Singapore posting? With a promotion to Senior Assistant as well, of course. I believe your husband was recently offered a job in Singapore too so you must discuss this with him, but I need your decision quickly.'

'They're moving us around like pieces on a chessboard,' I say to Harry that night. 'They already know about your offer — don't we have any privacy at all?'

'Not in wartime, I expect.'

'Well, what do you think, love? Do we leave our life here and go to Singapore?'

'It's probably safer than London right now,' Harry says. 'The Japanese might want it but they're tied down in China. And I doubt your people would move the Bureau to Singapore if they thought it was too dangerous.'

I shrug. 'It's a promotion. And there's a steamer run to Perth, so we could visit my family. You'd have the job you've always wanted, and perhaps we could see your people in New South Wales too.'

He nods, smiling. 'That would all be very pleasant. Shall we?'

'Let's. It'll be our grand Singapore adventure.'

And with that, Harry and I make the most momentous decision of our lives.

I go to Bletchley for several weeks to help set up the Commercial Section in an empty school beside the manor, and rush around unpacking and briefing another Junior Assistant on my work.

Apart from a quick farewell over morning tea, I leave the Commercial Section without ceremony, but Mr Denniston says, 'Should you return to Britain in the future, Mrs Bell, please feel free to look us up. I'm sure we could always find a desk for you.'

I'm rather touched: that's the equivalent of a hug from this quiet, careful man.

On my last day, Mr Baxter, scanning the newspaper, says, 'Mrs Bell, here's something about one of those boats you're so interested in.'

'Ships, Mr Baxter, *ships*.'

He grins and hands me the paper. The small article reads:

> *The Finnish windjammer Olivebank struck a mine on 8th September, 105 miles south-west of Bovbjerg, Denmark, and fourteen lives were lost. Seven members of the crew have been brought to Esbjerg by a cutter which found them clinging to the rigging. They had been without food and water for three days.*

'*No!* I've got a friend aboard ... fourteen men *killed*? But the war's barely begun!'

'The Germans have been lobbing mines all over the North Sea, and a couple of merchant ships have already been sunk,' Mr Baxter says gently. 'Your *Olivebank* probably gets the glory of being the first neutral vessel lost in the war. First windjammer, that's for sure.'

Within days, more dreadful sinkings follow — a crowded passenger liner, a gigantic aircraft carrier. The loss of an old square-rigger fades before the greater tragedy; although at night, haunted, I cannot stop wondering about Artur's fate.

It's a relief, a few weeks later, to get Captain Nilsen's telegram reporting *Inverley*'s safe homecoming at Mariehamn. However the question of selling my share in a Finnish ship becomes suddenly irrelevant. Because of the war, says *Kapten*, none of the four-masters at all will sail this year.

It takes time to organise our trip to Singapore, so Harry and I stay in London for some weeks more. Still thinking about Artur, I ring Mr Weatherall, *Inverley*'s helpful agent at Clarksons the shipbrokers.

'Ah, Mrs Bell,' he says. 'I was just about to get in touch. A few of the *Olivebank* survivors have been brought to London and the first mate was hoping to contact you.'

'Artur's *alive*? Thank God! Yes, please, give him our phone number, we'd love to see him.'

Next evening Artur arrives at our flat for dinner. His arm is bandaged, he's thin and his smile is unsure. Over brandies he tells us what happened.

'Elias,' he says gazing at me, using my old shipboard name. 'You know of course we are always careful. In the North Sea we already passed much floating wreckage. Then in the afternoon the lookout yelled "Mine ahead!" We quickly turned the rudder, but I could see so many, just rising and falling in the waves.'

He clears his throat.

'Suddenly, there was a great explosion. My arm was hurt. *Olivebank* listed, we could not launch lifeboats. The ship sank in minutes, my friends, just *minutes*. I jumped with the others and swam like a madman to escape the suction. Then she was gone.'

Artur takes a drink from his glass, and grimaces.

'As you know, Elias, the North Sea is very shallow. When the ship settled the fore-upper-topsail yard was left sticking out of the water: it seemed a *miracle*. We swam to it, the water like ice. There, finally — we were just seven men. We lashed ourselves to the yard and waited. The waves broke over us. We had no food, no water. The sun set. The night was very, very long.'

Artur swallows and Harry quietly refills his glass.

'In the morning we saw a steamer far away, but it did not see us. A deckboy sobbed and tried to kill himself but we twisted his knife from his hand. I was rigid with cold, my arm so painful, and over that slow, grey day I lost all hope. Then the night surrounded us again.'

Artur looks up. 'Harry, did you know such cold brings drowsiness, but there is no true sleep?'

He slowly rubs his bandaged arm. 'In the dark we saw the lights of a fishing boat and we yelled, but they did not hear us At dawn, half-conscious now, we waved our shirts, but the boat turned away. That was a moment of ... blackness more than despair. And *then* —' he shakes his head in disbelief. 'They saw us and returned, and gave us warmth and water and food.'

Artur stares at the fire. 'On *Olivebank* we had three boys from my town, but now I must go home by myself.' He sighs. 'How strange it is to be at the topmast yet also to be in the water. I cannot stop dreaming of it, you know, not even in the daytime.'

Harry takes Artur back to his lodgings, and afterwards we sit in silence by the fire.

I finally say, 'Those sharp little work knives we all carried, I was so foolishly proud of mine — a boy tried to *kill* himself with one?'

Harry nods. 'We had it pretty tough on *Inverley* sometimes, but thank Christ we never had to face anything like that.'

'I keep remembering the feeling of ropes and steel cables in my hands — and being so bitterly, achingly cold.' I sigh. 'Oh, poor Artur. Poor *Olivebank*.'

After a moment I say, 'Harry, remember the old farewell?'

He takes my hand, holds it against his cheek and kisses it. '*Goodbye, shipmate. Fair winds and following seas.*'

Tears sting my eyes. 'Oh, love, what will happen to us all?'

PART II. A FRAGILE FORTRESS

11. Izabel: Final Hope

My family are from the migratory, hard-working Hakka people, who never sold their girl children or bound their feet. The cousin I sat with on the night I first met Laurence is now the most senior male of the family. First Cousin's farmhouse is on the mainland beyond Kowloon, built in the old Hakka style, round and solid.

We bury Bao-lim nearby in an auspicious place, and set his memorial in a shrine beside the other ancestral tablets. I tell everyone he died in a car accident, horribly burnt, so there is no question of his coffin being opened.

I say also that his friend Professor Kuan was incinerated in the accident, and not even his body remains for burial. Since only a child is left to mourn him, I have a memorial tablet made for Laurence (also a Hakka man). Nancy and I set it with those of my family, and say prayers to honour him. I know Bao-lim would have approved.

My mother arrives and takes part in the important forty-nine days of ceremony that follow the interment. She stays at Bao-lim's house and when we are alone I explain what really happened in Shanghai.

She gasps with joy when I tell her about her brother Yun-sen, then I crush that joy and explain what followed, for him and Bao-lim and Laurence Kuan.

'I'm so glad you met, even briefly,' Min-lu says, wiping her eyes. 'Yun-sen was a dear boy and I never quite believed he was dead. And Bao-lim — what a terrible ending! But what will happen to the Professor's child?'

'I'm adopting her,' I say. 'I promised Laurence, and I would anyway.'

My mother soon befriends Nancy, while I organise the simple, profound ceremonies that bring her into our family. In a country where it is regarded as the greatest tragedy possible to be left without descendants, the informal adoption of children is common. The relationships that follow have recognised rights and obligations, and even the British accept it. Not Felix, of course.

'Adopt? Are you joking, Izabel?'

'I've always wanted a child, Felix. And she has no one.'

'But she's *Chinese*.'

'She's Eurasian, like me. You were happy enough to marry me. Why not adopt Nancy?'

'Nobody *knew* about you then, but here everyone knows she's not white!'

I cannot stop myself. 'Nobody *knew*? That's right, Felix, nobody fucking knew until *you* made certain of it.'

He stares at me, his face suddenly pale. Did he imagine I would never learn of his betrayal?

He turns away and blusters, 'Maybe if you'd spent a bit more time in my bed we could have had our own child.'

'But I miscarried, Felix. I can't become pregnant any more, remember?'

'Probably something to do with that little *procedure* you had to save your reputation so long ago, the one you never actually mentioned to me.' He's smug now. 'Had a shufti at your medical notes while you were in hospital. Damned indiscreet doctor, Izabel.'

'Really. Then why don't you take a concubine to give you a child, Felix? You're in China after all. Maybe Barbara would like the job.'

'*Barbara*? What's she got to do with anything?'

I gaze at him steadily. He clears his throat and says, 'She's just a friend — I needed a friend when my wife ran off with her uncle and some strange man. Going to the country to see *relatives* was it? Funny how you ended up in Shanghai, Izabel.' He crosses his arms, triumphant.

I bluff shamelessly. 'It's where the relatives *live*. You don't know much about Chinese geography, do you, Felix?' This is a sore point, a shortcoming his superiors often mention. He's silent.

'In any case,' I say, 'I owe this to my uncle *and* his friend who, never forget, was the famous academic Professor Kuan. And everyone will praise your kindness to a poor orphan.'

As Felix ponders that possibility I force myself into my 'dear wife' role. 'Such a silly tiff, when Binkie and Maggie are about to arrive. We can chat later.'

'Oh God, here any minute. Izzy, can we just let this drop? Nothing's set in stone, after all, is it?'

I smile dazzlingly. 'We'll work it out, don't worry.'

But oh yes, my darling, it most certainly is set in stone.

My mother returns to Australia and I placate Felix. Nancy starts calling me *Ah-me*, the affectionate Hakka word for Mummy. She's shy, not from loyalty to a mother she never knew, but because I've been Mrs Malory for so long.

When she says it I feel as if my heart is turning over.

She calls her father Laurence *Ah-ba*, and when we speak of him she touches the turquoise mala she always wears. And we do speak of him, quietly, together: we both know how much we love him.

And I wait and I wait.

I am certain, I am convinced, I'll get a letter to tell me he's safe. Not with a perilous written message, but perhaps with just a few links of the gold chain I gave him. I don't believe what Colonel Huang said, or the police said, or the British authorities said — I know he's not dead, I know he'll contact me.

But a year passes and he doesn't.

'Have you lost your mind entirely?' says Felix, his eyes slitted with rage. 'I thought this was settled. Of course she's not coming to bloody Singapore with us. For God's sake, Izabel!'

'But I've got her a British identity document. I went to see the Governor and —'

'You went to see the Governor? That's why you were so tarted up the other day, you were going to see the bloody *Governor*?'

He sits down on the bed. 'You've made a mockery of me, I hope you realise that.'

'It's nothing to do with you, Felix —'

He stands up suddenly. 'You bitch. You yellow *bitch*.' He slams the door as he leaves, and I'm glad Nancy is still at school.

And now suddenly there's this. Within days the Far East Combined Bureau is moving from Hong Kong to Singapore, sixteen hundred miles away. How can a letter possibly find me *there*?

That afternoon I go to the market. I'm buying silk for a dress for Nancy, when I realise someone is gazing at me: a Chinese man, tanned, wary, thin, faintly familiar.

He sees me notice him and walks away. My heart thudding, I follow him into a narrow alley and catch his sleeve. He turns, not angry or curious, but oddly calm.

'You were at Bao-lim's funeral but I'd never seen you before, and then you were gone,' I whisper desperately. 'But you look like my uncle, my uncle from the *mountains*.'

For a moment I think, dear God, Felix is right, I've lost my mind. Then I see the man's arm is scarred and suddenly I'm certain.

'It was *you* who brought Bao-lim the news his brother was alive! It was you, wasn't it?'

He nods almost imperceptibly.

'Tell me, tell me — did Third Uncle survive the battle? Did Laurence Kuan? *Tell me*.'

He shakes his head. 'No. I am sorry. All was lost.'

He glances over my shoulder, then quickly the other way, biting his lip. 'Never speak to me again. If we pass in the street do not look, do not greet. You could kill us both.'

He drags his sleeve from my hand and walks quickly down the alley. I stand there helpless, sobbing, my final hope gone. Of course a letter will never come. All was lost.

All is lost.

Our time of mourning is done. I take off the blue garments marking the death of my uncle, and Nancy will no longer wear the black of an orphan. I ask the house-boy to get our trunks out of storage, and go through my cupboards, selecting clothes suitable for Singapore.

I discard most of my Izabel Malory outfits, but keep the russet silk I wore the night I met Laurence, and the emerald green of our last evening together; the gown that fell rippling to my feet as he kissed my breasts in the lamplight.

Felix comes home with a bunch of drooping roses. 'God, I'm so sorry, Izzy,' he says, with a sincerity that might once have touched me. 'You know I'm under such pressure with this move. Don't know what came over me. Are you all right, old girl?'

'I'm fine, Felix, I've even started packing. I suppose you'll want your evening clothes?'

'Thank you, darling. Look, I'm sorry I got a little over-excited about the child — of course she can come. The Governor, eh? You're a cheeky devil! I'd never dare speak to the man. Did he ... mind? About a British passport for a —'

'He was delighted to help, Felix. He knows how important you are to the war effort, after all.'

It was a little more difficult than that. But charm, appeal to venerable Oriental custom, and the stark urgency of the Bureau's relocation won the day. (I also had a pinch of blackmail in reserve, but in the end didn't need it.)

'Excellent, excellent. And there's no need to mention our argument, old girl?'

'Between us, Felix, and forgotten.'

'God, you're a *brick*, Izzy,' he says, overcome. 'In Singapore I'll treat you like a queen. We'll have a wonderful time once all this pressure is behind us.'

'Of course we will, darling.'

I'd have left him long ago if not for the protection of the marriage. My father was Portuguese so my claim on Britain is tenuous and, although my mother has residency rights in Australia, I have none.

So English Felix is Nancy's lifeline. I don't know what would happen to us if I divorced him, but I'm certainly not putting it to the test.

I smile. 'Why don't you go and relax, darling, and have a snifter before dinner?'

The university gives Nancy her father's papers, so I wrap them in silk inside a sandalwood chest, and leave them stored in Bao-lim's cellar. I now own half of that beautiful house on the Mid-Levels (my uncle left it to me and my sister Filipa), but Felix wouldn't let us live there.

Now my studio has closed, Mrs Lau is out of a job so she's happy to become the caretaker until I return to the house one day. And I will.

I take Nancy to visit First Cousin. She is now part of his family too, so we say our farewells to the living and our prayers to the dead. She stands in the dim temple beside me, incense curling around her head, chanting a soft prayer for Laurence.

It's a Buddhist prayer recited in a Taoist shrine to Confucian ancestral tablets, but that's how things are in this complicated country.

Light falls on Nancy's smooth cheeks. She's so brave and funny, and delights me in every way, this child of my mind and my heart. She's absurdly fond of all creatures too — even the slimy, scaled and multi-legged — and must leave behind her cat, a monkey and two parrots. She's begged (and I've bribed) Mrs Lau to care for them until ... until?

Then the move to Singapore is upon us.

One hot sticky night in August 1939 we're hurried up the gangway of *HMS Birmingham*, a long, grey vessel bristling with armaments. Oily water laps around the hull and reflects the shipyard lights in dirty rainbow ripples.

Nancy and I watch from the deck. She has ribbons in her brown hair and a pretty skirt: tonight we're both being as *English* as possible (tight shoulders and barely perceptible sneer — she does it remarkably well). Soldiers run about on the floodlit dock as lorries unload an extraordinary number of crates and filing cabinets.

'Hullo, Barbara,' I say to the woman beside me. 'How on earth can they need so many *files*?'

She smiles. 'I've been counting the lorries, trying to keep calm. Eighteen so far — they must have everything in triplicate. Is that your little girl?'

'Yes. Nancy, this is Barbara, a friend of —' I go to say *Felix's*, then simply finish, 'ours.'

Barbara glances at me, then speaks to Nancy.

'And this is my daughter, Tessie. She's a year older than you, I think. We've got dolls and books in our cabin. Tessie, why don't you take Nancy for a play?'

Nancy and Tessie gaze shyly at each other, then giggle and disappear together down a stairway.

Barbara and I watch the dock in silence, then she says, 'Twenty lorries now. Christ.'

'Why do you need to keep calm?' I say. 'Don't men always have everything under control?' A filing cabinet tips over and spills its contents everywhere. Soldiers swear and run about catching loose papers and we laugh, quietly and unkindly.

'I'm absolutely terrified of the sea,' Barbara says. 'Rather pathetic since I'm married to a naval officer, so I pretend I'm not. But I hate ships.'

'I don't like them much either.' I think of the passage home from Shanghai, and I suppose Barbara does too.

'I was sorry to hear about your uncle, it must have been *awful*. Felix said —' she stops. 'Well, what do you think Singapore will be like?'

'Hot, humid. The Japanese waiting to pounce. The Chinese laughing at us. Much the same as here, I suppose.'

Barbara smiles. After a pause she says quietly, 'Izabel, I *honestly* never meant —'

'It doesn't matter, just be careful,' I say. 'He's not all charm all the time, you know. He bullies people weaker than him, so you'd better be strong.'

She gasps, stepping back. On the dock, men release cables, the engines start up and we slowly move out and away. Away from my home of four years.

Away from my empty house, halfway up a mountain.

Away from my final hope.

12. Billie: Consolation

Six months after I bury Wilf, I leave the farm and go back to our old room in London on the third floor of Toby's house. I need a change, and Vivian seems to be over the loss of Wilf. Three-year-olds are lucky to have short memories.

I haven't recovered of course, and go to see a few doctors for my own specific reasons. But I seem to have used up every reserve I once had and now I'm simply worn out. Every day I wake and feel relief for a single breath, then greyness slowly fills me again.

Charlotte is spending time here in London too, while Mrs Spencer minds Vivian at the farm. Turns out that Charlie grew up speaking German, so she's helping her father Otto with the children saved from the Nazis by the *Kindertransport* trains.

She was endlessly kind to Wilf and I'll always owe her for that and, although we'll never be best mates, we get along well enough now. On my last visit to the farm I brought back a few things she wanted and this morning she's dropped by to pick them up.

'Tea, Charlie?' I ask.

'No thanks. Can't stay, must hurry to the office.'

'Gotta say I'm surprised to see you so gung-ho nowadays.'

'Sweetie,' she says drily, 'I'm probably the most surprised of all.'

'Probably a good thing. You seemed a bit under the weather there for a while.'

Charlotte nods. 'I would have told you before, Billie, but couldn't really talk about it.' She takes a breath. 'Actually … earlier this year I miscarried a child.'

'Jesus. Sorry, Charlie, had no idea.'

'Didn't want to mention it before, you had enough on your plate with Wilf.'

I nod. 'Thanks. So things are easier now?'

She shrugs. 'After years of ignoring my father's good causes, I suddenly wanted to help him. Help someone. Dear God, help *anyone*.

And the refugee children — they'd try to smile, but their eyes were so bleak. Rather how I felt.' She sighs. 'Ten thousand kids were rescued, but half of them still need foster homes, so I look for places and nag people for money. Every child needs a guaranteed fifty pounds for transport home after the war.'

'But why can't their families pay?' I say.

'Most of their families are Jews or anti-Nazis, so they're probably in prison camps by now.' Charlie takes a breath. 'What must they have *felt* putting their kids on our trains, not knowing when ... if ...' She laughs shortly. 'You know, Billie, I used to think you were exaggerating about Spain.'

'Yeah. Most people did.'

She clears her throat. 'Anyway, I brought you this, thought it might interest you.' She hands me a newspaper clipping.

Women in Britain's Air Service

Women are now recognised in aviation. The fact that Miss Pauline Gower has been appointed as a Commissioner of the Civil Air Guard speaks for itself. The expansion of the Royal Air Force has made a great shortage of men instructors, and women are proving very good instructors. There will be many more now that an air wing of the Women's Legion has been formed. It has as a nucleus 30 expert women pilots, with Pauline Gower as Commandant, and Dorothy Spicer, said to be the finest woman engineer in England, in charge of the ground work.

'Doesn't that sound like something you could do, Billie, instead of sitting at home all day?'

'I'm not sitting at home all day,' I say. 'I'm just — tired.'

'As it happens I know Pauline, we were at school together. Her father's a Member of Parliament and she rather enjoyed irritating him by learning to fly. Perhaps I could put in a word?'

'Read this bit, Charlie. Being a woman in the Air Service certainly does speak for itself.'

Pauline Gower's duty as Commissioner of the Civil Air Guard for London and the Eastern Area is to inspect training records.

I'm lying down on a cold wet afternoon and hear a distinct phrase of music — deep, familiar, mysterious. The hair on my neck prickles. I'm suddenly back in the refuge of Wilf's arms in hot, dusty Spain, the gramophone playing one of his precious classical records.

Sofia is practising her cello, and the door to their flat must be open. Without thinking I get up and go downstairs. I enter the room where Sofia is playing, her back to me, and sit down on a sofa. She sees me and quickly smiles, then concentrates again on the music.

The room is cosy, a fire in the grate. I listen and gaze at the flames and my eyes grow heavy. There's a blanket on the sofa and I pull it over me and lie down. Music flows around me and the rain pours down outside and I feel safe. For the first time in fucking years I feel safe.

I listen, utterly at peace.

Sofia stops every now and then, repeating a phrase, then continues. Slowly the music wends its way to a gentle closing.

After a pause I say, 'Thanks Sofe, I really liked that.'

'I'm going to be playing it next year with an orchestra.' She smiles. 'Imagine it, a real orchestra letting female musicians into their august company!'

'But a cello's hardly a four-engine heavy bomber. Why shouldn't females be allowed?'

'Oh, all the usual excuses. I only get work with female string quartets as a sort of genteel novelty. But with so many men going into the services, the administrators have suddenly realised they need women to keep the orchestras going. It's been *delicious* watching their horror.'

'I'm glad you'll get the chance, anyway.'

'It's a special tour, the conductor is a visiting American,' she says. 'I'm hoping to learn — well, everything, especially about composition.'

'You write music too, Sofe?'

She nods shyly. 'Another thing women aren't supposed to be capable of, but I rather enjoy it.'

'Play me something.'

'You mightn't like it. Most people find it a little odd for their taste.'

'Try me.'

Sofia is hesitant at first, and the music is certainly unusual — mellow, slow and sparse. It makes me think of flying over misty hills in the early morning, or still water stretching to the horizon, or the rhythmic flow of hedgerows across green fields.

Of course: the landscapes of Hamble from the air, the landscapes Pete and I used to love. I sigh. I haven't told anyone yet, but I've decided I don't want to fly, not ever again.

The music circles around and comes in for the gentlest of landings. After a moment I say, 'Sofe, that was amazing.'

'A little too much stopping and starting, dear one.'

'But I liked it stopping and starting. I liked it not coming to an end.'

In November, I visit the docks to see Eliza and Harry off to Singapore. Most of the gang are away or working, but Toby and Sofia come along. Eliza and Harry themselves are tired but happy at finally getting everything packed. Their flat is let and four crates of belongings are stored in Toby's cellar.

Eliza has given away some of her best clothes too, an elegant fur wrap for Sofia, and a crimson silk-velvet gown for Klara.

'Mementos of my days of glamour,' she said. 'Totally unsuitable for the tropics.'

While Toby and Sofia chat to Harry, Eliza takes me down to their cabin. I'm surprised when she hands me a soft parcel and says, 'Something for you too, Bill.'

She's slight and small, so I say, 'Thanks, Lizzie, but are you sure it's going to fit me?'

'Had it made especially for you. We're practically the same size on top, anyway — you've just got those giraffe-like legs.'

I open the parcel and inside is an evening gown in jade-green silk jersey. I hold it up. It has the new wide shoulders and three-quarter-length sleeves, and will fit me like flowing water.

'Oh, *Lizzie*, how beautiful.' There's a lump in my throat. 'Can't imagine where I'd wear anything as nice as that, though.'

'You'll be going out again one day, Bill,' she says gently.

'Nah, not interested in a new man. Seem a bit unlucky in love.'

'But aren't you attending Sofia's concert soon? You'll need an evening gown for that.'

I laugh a little tearfully. 'Suppose I will.' I hug her. 'God, I'll miss you, Lizzie. I reckon you'll both have a wonderful time in Singapore.'

'Hope you'll be fine here too, darling. Maybe the war will go on just being a phoney one, and they'll never drop anything at all on dear old London.'

'Yes,' I say. 'Such strange times.'

On the night of Sofia's concert, early in the wintry new year of 1940, I put on the jade-green dress and a warm coat, pick up the obligatory gas-mask and go downstairs.

'Almost ready, dear one,' Sofia calls out as I get to the door. 'Taxi will be here in an instant.'

Juggling her instrument case, handbag and gas-mask, she leads the way down to the ground floor, where Toby is waiting. He never bothers with his own gas-mask, so Sofia and I both give him ours and insist he carry them for us.

'Where's Klara?' I ask. 'Are we meeting her there?'

Sofia glances at me. 'She can't come tonight, too busy with work. Doesn't matter, of course. Heavens, she's heard me playing often enough, poor thing.'

We step outside. I'm still not used to the charcoal murk of the blackout. The streetlights are off and every window has thick curtains: even a glimmer at the edges brings rebukes from the air-raid wardens.

And cars must cover their headlights so only a tiny beam emerges, which means a lot of pedestrians have been run over in recent months. More people than Hitler's ever managed to kill, goes the joke in the pubs.

The taxi emerges from the darkness and we get in. Sofia cradles the cello case in her arms.

'Are you excited or taking it all in your stride?' I ask her.

'Oh, *thrilled*, of course. Evan's been an absolute darling in rehearsals.

Having women in orchestras is old hat for American conductors, so he's calm and disciplined and helpful. Although, really, he's like that with everyone.'

'Have you had a chance to talk to him about composing?'

'No, but I did meet his wife, also an absolute darling and a composer herself — somewhat overshadowed by the famous husband, but her work is good. We've chatted and plan to spend more time together during the tour.'

'How long did you say you'd be away, blossom?' asks Toby.

'Five weeks, travelling absolutely everywhere. Something of an endurance test, but the concerts are for servicemen, so all in a good cause.'

We stop at the theatre and wish Sofia luck as she leaves for the stage door. Toby and I stroll inside and find our seats in the dress circle.

'You're looking remarkably civilised tonight, Miss Billie,' says Toby.

'All credit to Eliza. I'd be wearing my dungarees otherwise.'

He laughs. 'Next time, please do. I'd be charmed to see the reaction.'

'I expect we'll all end up in uniforms or work-clothes soon.'

'Impossible. Anyway, nothing's happening with this ludicrous war. I hear half the evacuees came home for Christmas and don't want to leave again. It's been — what, five months? Where are all those bombs that were supposed to rain down upon our heads?'

My gut lurches with memory. Mud and blood and fire.

'They'll come fucking soon enough, Toby,' I say bitterly.

'No need to be rude, dear,' says Toby, oblivious. 'No, the only thing happening is gallant little Finland and those awful Russians. Klara was beside herself when they bombed Helsinki.'

'Well, she's got family there.' I change the subject. 'Anyway, why isn't she here? I know Klara's dedicated to her refugees but surely she could take one night off.'

Toby frowns but, unusually for him, says nothing.

The lights go down and the chat fade. Curtains draw back to show the orchestra, instruments gleaming, men in evening suits and three women in black gowns that cover them neck to ankle. 'Can't even show a wrist,' Sofia told me, laughing, 'might drive the chaps crazy with lust.'

The music is a joy, a very different experience from listening to records. I hear phrases familiar from Sofia's rehearsals, but the entire orchestra turns them into a great rounded sound, the music reverberating through my body.

The final piece, fierce and thrilling, ends so triumphantly the audience stands roaring at the end, and I do too.

'What on earth was that, Toby?' I say, breathless.

'*Finlandia*, by Sibelius. Most appropriate.'

'Oh, I wish Klara could have heard it!'

'So do I.'

Afterwards we meet an excited Sofia at the stage door. She says, 'We're going on to the Criterion for a meal now, *do* come along!'

Toby and I look at each other and nod.

Sofia says, 'Marvellous! Now, let me think — cello stays here, got my handbag, gas-mask — oh, there they are.'

Three people are coming towards us along the corridor. A dark-eyed man who was playing cello beside Sofia, a stylish redhead in a fur coat, and the conductor, long silver hair brushed back from his forehead.

Sofia introduces us. The cellist is Raymond something, the conductor the famous Evan Whittier, and the woman his wife Teresa, the composer who's going to work with Sofia during the tour.

'Just call me *Terry*, honey,' she says. 'No standing on ceremony here.'

It's only a short walk to the magnificent Criterion. Food rationing has just been introduced but fortunately restaurants are exempt. Although the place is busy, the head waiter recognises Evan and Terry and shows us to a very good table.

As Terry slips the fur coat off her shoulders I hear gasps from nearby diners. She's wearing trousers — flowing black trousers, sequinned and high-waisted.

Women in extremes of fashion are usually refused entry to posh restaurants, but here the head waiter smiles adoringly and takes her coat, while a lesser waiter takes everyone else's.

'Such a *sweetheart*,' says Terry, sitting down. 'We were here last night too. Couldn't do enough.'

Evan deliberates with the sommelier, and after the wine is poured and we toast the successful concert I agree it was well worth the deliberation.

Terry is opposite me, and in the chatter of menus and ordering and bowing waiters, I get a good look at her. She's wearing a simple cream blouse with her sequinned trousers, a crepe with beautifully cut square shoulders and a draped neckline.

I was never much interested in fashion when I was young. Pete would tease me if I ever wore a skirt instead of my dungarees, and I'd get cranky at him. Still, Eliza loves clothes, and over the years she's taught me a little.

And after Spain too, I'm often almost mesmerised by anything beautiful, anything that's uniquely, essentially itself. Wilf used to call that feeling *inscape*, a concept from his beloved poet-priest, Manley Hopkins. I didn't understand it at all until he was gone, but now I seem to sense it everywhere.

Terry murmurs in Sofia's ear, and throws her head back with laughter. She has full cheekbones, a long narrow nose and a trim, rather severe mouth. Her hair is to one side and wavy to her shoulders, sort of reddish-brown. In fact, I muse (after my first glass of wine) she's rather like a fox.

What would Evan be? He's a bit doggish too. Something all flowing hair and noble nose. And Toby, discussing the concert with Evan, would have to be a noble guard dog.

'Why are you smiling?' asks Raymond the cellist.

'Oh, just imagining everyone here as some sort of canine.' I'm well into my second glass by now.

'Well, Terry is clearly a vixen. What about Sofia?'

'Oh, something rather pretty with lots of black curly hair,' I say.

'A spaniel, perhaps? A very nice one, of course. And Evan — Afghan hound, do you think?'

'Oh, *exactly*! And Toby — German Shepherd?'

'Perfect.' He gazes at me. 'What about you? I'd say a whippet, a copper-coloured one.'

'Do they come copper-coloured?'

'They certainly do, my favourite sort. But rarely with green eyes.'

I glance at him. Fine-boned face, strong shoulders from playing cello (Sofia's are surprisingly muscular). Greyhound?

'You? Poodle, I reckon,' I say insolently.

'Brilliantly clever water-game retriever? Oh, a compliment indeed.'

I laugh despite myself. 'All right — a greyhound, then.'

'No, no! I much prefer poodle. You've perceived the essential me.'

Our dinners arrive and the chit-chat back and forth across the table becomes louder and more general. Afterwards we dance, something I've always loved.

Whenever I used to fly it would make me feel as if I were swooping across a dance floor. And vice versa.

I take a turn with Evan and tell him how much I enjoyed the concert.

'Fine bunch of musicians,' he says. 'Hard to go wrong with 'em. And Sofia's something else, a true talent. Terry's really looking forward to working with her.' He smiles, a little oddly.

Then I stand up with Raymond. He moves easily, thoughtfully, an attractive skill in a man. An attractive man overall, in fact.

Christ, what am I *thinking*? I plead a headache and leave.

Next morning I wake up feeling pleased with myself. I don't know why, then see my jade-green gown draped over a chair and think, oh *yes*. A good night after all, not just the concert but the civilised evening too.

What an idiot I was to run away. I've been waiting so anxiously for bombs to fall, I'd forgotten what a consolation food and wine and dancing could be.

Especially dancing.

13. Toby: Southampton

'*Passé?*' I clench my jaw. What would this old fool know? This old fool being my publisher, Alastair Jenkins (yes, *that* Alastair Jenkins *and* his bloody Associates, whoever they are).

He's just said he won't publish my latest novel, the third in my *Sophisticated Sleuth* series, the adventures of Baronet Jamie, his daredevil fiancée Lady Clare, and Jamie's sidekick, boy genius Steven.

The first book (1938) sold extremely well, the second (1939) less well, but that was probably because of the looming war. But now this?

First Jenkins tries fobbing me off: paper rationing, delayed print runs, lack of manpower at the printeries. That I can understand, although how paper is supposed to win a war rather escapes me. But, honestly — *passé?*

'Readers want *real* characters today, Toby. Ordinary people can't identify with a wealthy, bumbling aristocrat, not with the blackout, the rationing, the anxiety, the dreadful news. Charming little Toby Fenn mysteries seem horribly old-fashioned nowadays.'

'But people want to *escape.*'

'Of course, but not to the kind of world that dragged us into this appalling situation in the first place. Readers want honesty, not caricature. I'm sorry, Toby. You've a fine talent but this isn't any sort of expression of it.'

The rain is dripping down the train window as I watch the appropriately gloomy landscape. I couldn't bear Whitfield Street a moment longer — the echoing, empty house — so I'm going away to Southampton for a time.

Stefan still holds the lease on a flat there and it's where I always feel a little closer to him. Although I'm not. As soon as the war started they sent him off to a squadron in Yorkshire, which soon moved to somewhere near Edinburgh. *Edinburgh!*

The squadron has a gaggle of Spitfires from the factory where Stef used to be an engineer, so I suppose to the pen-pushers it was a logical posting, but I just don't understand why the squadron isn't here protecting London.

Lately there's a lot of things I don't understand.

Oh God, I miss him so much. Occasionally he gets a day or two off, but by the time he's here he has to turn around and go back. Once I took a train north to visit him but it was a furtive, anxious time.

Without the anonymity of London the risk of us being seen together is too high. Frankly, I wouldn't mind in the slightest if they kicked Stef out for "unnatural offences" but he would. Obviously. All he wants to do in life is fly and fight the Boche.

Boche? Christ, haven't heard that since my childhood and what we naively called *the* World War. Now they're calling it the *First* World War. How many more of the bloody things do they plan to hold?

Everyone's gone insane. At that eventful concert a few months ago I watched Sofia sleepwalking into disaster with vixen Terry and couldn't do a thing about it (I was too busy fending off the advances of the old roué beside me, the versatile husband of said vixen).

After Sofia returned incandescent from their tour, she started writing and rehearsing at all hours, and now she's been given a place for the duration with a symphony orchestra. Of course they'll kick her to the kerb when the boys come marching home.

'Toby, nothing actually *happened*,' she says. 'Anyway, Terry's already back in New York. It was just wonderful to be with someone I could communicate with.'

'Even if you didn't dive ecstatic beneath the sheets, blossom, there's still a lot can happen without a finger being laid.'

'But I've been so *lonely*, Toby. Klara's rarely at home and she's always too busy working to have time for me. I know I shouldn't, but I feel absurdly abandoned.'

'I'm sure she loves you, and her work does seem awfully important.'

'I don't *care*. It's utterly unfair of me, but all I want to think about right now is music and Terry.'

It's true Klara isn't at home much and her mind is certainly elsewhere. No longer the fey poetess, she cut off her waterfall of silvery hair and now it's as short as a boy's.

'Good heavens, Klara. You've become a little Nordic pixie!'

'Actually, Toby, it is because of lice.'

'*Lice?*'

'Not from the refugee children, but from some of the homes they go to. Kind homes but poor, and now with the war, getting poorer. Lice are not so bad. You just need to run a fine-tooth comb through your wet hair. The lice cannot move in the water so you just wash them down the plughole.'

'And you *have* done that recently, dear, haven't you?'

'Yes, Toby, I do not have lice now. But I do agree with Billie, short hair is easier to look after.'

I now fear the worst every time I feel the slightest itch anywhere.

Billie is also a concern. Emerged at last from her shell, she's seeing that good-looking cello player who was at at dinner with us, Raymond something-or-other. Not matter what sardonic mask she wears I know she's not over Wilf, and I worry for her.

'It's all right, Toby,' she says. 'Raymond's in love with someone else.'

'How precisely is that all right, Miss Billie?'

'We just have fun and we're both perfectly safe from falling in love.'

'Am I the *only* sane person here? No one's safe from falling in love!'

At first Billie made me nervous. She's certainly plain-speaking — well, swears like a trooper — but she's a darling really, and I based my daredevil Lady Clare on our wild colonial lass.

Oh God. Lady Clare. *That*'s what I don't want to think about: my bloody novel. What a fool I am, of course it's antiquated nonsense. Silly Lady Clare and pompous Sir Jamie and dark-haired sidekick Steven.

And thank you, Doctor Freud, I'm perfectly aware Steven is remarkably like the young Stefan I loved so hopelessly at school. Loved; lost; loved. And once more appear to be losing.

What with the lice I'm being unkind to Klara. The poor girl is so sad.

Last March the poor old Finns had to capitulate, and the Russians started pillaging the place. She tells me bitterly her homeland (which even *I* know gallantly fought off the Soviets in the Winter War) was left in the lurch by its allies — that is, us.

In April, the Nazis take Denmark and Norway with contemptuous ease, and Klara's eyes are dark with anxiety. In May they stroll into Holland, Belgium and France, and she disappears for days.

One morning I find her slumped on the sofa in the sitting room. Her face pale, Klara says, 'We did it. We got them out.'

I sit and take her hand. 'Who, my dear?'

'The final *Kindertransport* out of Holland, Toby. The last trainload of children we can save from the Nazis. There will be no more.'

She turns her head away and weeps.

In late May, our armies in France seething like ants before the implacable Germans, there's so much to mourn it's beyond tears. Still, every vessel afloat sets off for Dunkirk and ferries thousands of poor souls to the safety of troopships, a great-hearted deed that will never be forgotten.

But that's probably not why my own heart is in such a parlous state.

In June, Stef's squadron finally moves closer to London, but he might as well have moved to the moon — there's no possibility of seeing each other.

Every day I pick up the paper and read of our valiant Spitfires fighting so nobly in the skies above. Fighting, burning, and crashing.

Our Spitfires. Stef's squadron.

Another reason to leave London behind. I don't want to be at home if a telegram comes.

All men aged from eighteen to forty-one are being conscripted, starting with the youngest. It's a slow process: I hear they may get to the thirty-one-year-olds sometime next year. But by then I'll be thirty-two. Perhaps I can always stay one step ahead in sort of a Zeno's Paradox of war service.

I *should* volunteer, but the options are so limited. I could be an air-raid warden and build bomb shelters and nag people about the blackout. Or join the Home Guard and march about with a broom on my shoulder because they haven't got enough weapons.

The emergency services perhaps? Not ambulances, I don't know London streets very well. The Observer Corps, counting enemy planes and watching our fighters bravely engage them? (I don't think so.)

That just leaves the volunteer firefighters, who've been sitting around for ages being criticised because they don't have much to do. Still, the barbaric Germans bombed Paris, so perhaps even mighty London could be next. All right. If I'm *pushed* to it, the auxiliary fire service will do.

Luckily I'm not yet pushed.

As the train enters the outskirts of Southampton, as always I gaze at the large houses and imagine the lives of the people living there. But soon we approach the suburbs I never like to contemplate at all: where the fine gardens turn into squalid backyards of concrete, ragged clotheslines and outdoor privies.

But after we leave St Denys today, I keep watching as we run beside the River Itchen and, where the track turns west towards the town centre, I glimpse Stef and Pete's beloved aeroplane factory on the far side of the water.

Then the grim slum houses of Northam crowd the tracks, and I look for the shop I usually ignore. To my surprise it's boarded up, but the old sign is still there.

Fenn's Fine Meats.

At the pub they always called my father Chopper Fenn — he lacked two fingers, probably through a moment of sottish carelessness — and we haven't spoken in a decade. When Stef came to work in Southampton I told everyone how much I loved visiting the town. And I did and still do, certain parts of it at least.

But I've never mentioned to a soul this is where I grew up.

Stef's flat is in Bedford Place. It's half a mile's easy walk from the central railway station, past the Civic Centre and green Watt Park. The flat is the top floor of a small house in a street of little shops.

The landlady, Miss Mathison, lives on the ground floor, a retired teacher whose kindness is apparent in her polite lack of curiosity about Stef and me.

Once I've cleaned up and had a cup of tea I ring Pete at the factory, and discover that our Mr McKee is now important enough to have his own telephone line. When I'm through I say, 'Was that your secretary? My God, you *have* become eminent.'

'Just the switch, mate,' says Pete. 'Not that posh yet. Here for long?'

'Not certain. A bit browned off with London, it's too quiet.'

'Why don't I come down your way after work?' he says. 'Olde Blue Kitten or whatever it is.'

'Ye Red Lion Hotel, cheeky lad, and I'll meet you in the lounge at six.'

The twilight is golden as I walk the block or so to the hotel, but I'd know the way even in a blackout. Often Stef and I would drink here then wander unsteadily home: although never so unsteadily we couldn't make love when we got there.

I take a painful breath. Christ, that was a while ago now.

After I order a gin and sit down, Pete arrives. He gets a beer and joins me, grinning.

'Too quiet in London for *you*, Toby? That'd be a first.'

'Well, Stef's away flying, Sofia's on tour, Klara's at work and Billie's out all the time.'

'Oh,' he says. 'She seeing someone?'

'Not seriously. What, jealous?'

'Nah.' Pete's laugh lacks sincerity. 'What about Charlotte?'

'Drops in on Billie now and then, that's all. But doesn't your own wife keep in touch with you?'

'Of course, yeah,' he says. 'Rings every few days. It's just — you never know with Charlotte, what she's really feeling.' He pauses.

'And why *does* she spend so much time in London?' I say.

'Oh, doing her part, self-sacrifice, the war effort, you know.'

I almost spill my drink laughing. 'Self-*sacrifice*? Pull the other one.'

Pete smiles sheepishly. 'Look, she hit a pretty low point last year and I'm just grateful she's a bit happier now.'

'Certainly a rough time, wasn't it? Poor old Wilf.'

'Not just that, Toby.' He sits forward. 'Actually — Charlotte was pregnant then, but she lost the baby. Didn't want to say anything at the time, Wilf and Billie were in such horrible straits, but she was pretty knocked about. Body and soul, you might say.'

'Oh, *Pete*.' My eyes sting. 'Must have been rough on you both.'

'No picnic, I'll tell you that.' He hesitates. 'She's terrified of getting pregnant again. So the marriage is a bit rocky right now, you might say.' He clears his throat. 'Ready for another?'

'That was fast, but yes, please.'

He goes to the bar and I gaze at him. Lanky, nicely-built, dark eyes and hair (from the fabled Chinese grandmother I expect), but Farmer Pete's not really my type.

Still, I don't actually have a type — there's Stef and then there's the rest of the world. And what would I do, if ... *if*? Thank God Pete returns before I become too maudlin.

'How's the farm going?' I say.

'I'd be there all the time if I could, Toby,' he says wistfully. 'But they won't let me out of aircraft fabrication for the duration, that's for bloody sure.'

'You must be doing a good job.'

He shrugs. 'We've ramped up production like nobody's business. Hiring all sorts of people, young girls, grandmothers, old sods who haven't had a job since the Depression. There's plenty to do, even if it's just sorting out screws or doping wings.'

'Good God, you put opium on aeroplanes?'

He laughs. 'Dope's a varnish mix for canvas on older planes, Toby. The Spits are aluminium, of course.'

'Of course, silly me.' There's a silence, and I sigh. 'Sorry, Pete, I'm a little grumpy. Heard from Eliza and Harry lately?'

'Yeah, happy as larks. Singapore's exotic, food's delicious. Harry's work is good, so's Eliza's. They're planning a visit to the family in Perth.' He smiles. 'It'd be good to see them again — Mum, Anton, Min-lu. Been a while.'

'Would you ever go back to Australia to live?'

'Yeah, maybe. Some great farming land east of Perth. Very different though, drought, bushfires. Still beautiful.' Pete sighs. 'But Charlotte and Vivy are here, so out of the question really.'

He's already finished his beer so I go to get more, even though I'm well behind. When I sit with the drinks I say, 'And how's young Vivian?'

'Vivy? Ah, she makes me so happy — and *smart*? Only four but she's reading already.'

'A dear little thing,' I say, not fibbing at all.

'But ... I don't know, Toby.' He rubs his jaw, gazing remotely. 'The other day I asked her if she misses Mummy. She said she knows Mummy loves her but she needs to stay away for a while.'

'Oh?'

'I asked her why, and she said — sometimes Mummy starts crying and hitting her own legs. So she had to go away because she doesn't want to hurt me.' Pete swallows.

'My *God*. That's — well, I'm not sure *what* it is.'

'Charlotte saw a head-doctor a few years ago, and now she is again. Might help. Maybe Vivy's right, Charlotte needs to keep her distance for a while.'

'She might need a little distance from you too,' I say. 'But come on Pete, don't look so glum. You're the love of each other's lives, we all know that.'

He hesitates. 'She's always chosen what's best for her. We both know that, Toby.'

I suddenly remember the night Charlotte told Pete she was having his child but still going back to Harry. Not sure I've ever seen a man so heart-broken.

I try reassurance. 'Can't believe what I'm hearing!' I say. 'My God, what you two went through to be together.'

'Yeah, was crazy for her. But now — 'specially after having Vivy — I want more than Charlotte wants to give. Need more.'

His voice is slurred: I don't think I've ever seen him get drunk so quickly. He drains his glass and puts it on the table, staring.

'Reckon she's gone for good, Toby, not coming back. But I want someone to *live* with, rely on. Love.' He sighs. 'Nah, had that once. Had everything. But I fucked it up completely.'

An elderly man at a nearby table glances at him, amazed, and I whisper, 'Don't swear so loudly, you're nearly as bad as —'

Billie?

I stay on in Southampton. Everyone's convinced we'll soon be invaded but honestly, I don't want to know, and I certainly don't want to care. The Germans bomb the port in June (they mostly miss), and in August they try again, causing a handful of casualties, a derailed train and a sunken dredger. Memorably, they also hit the Cold Storage Depot, and thousands of pounds of butter burn deliciously for days.

But lately the air raids are increasing. Miss Mathison has a bomb shelter in her back garden, so a few times I go down there with her and a couple of the neighbours to wait for the All Clear; a damp, cold, tedious business.

Of course our raids are nothing much compared to other places. The Nazis have been destroying ports and airfields on a dreadful scale, and day after terrible day the Spitfires must go up to fight them.

The papers are calling it the Battle of Britain, and Churchill, the old ham, declaims in Parliament: *Never in the field of human conflict was so much owed by so many to so few.*

Towards the end of August, Central London is bombed for the first time. It's just a couple of miles from my house so I ring Sofia, but she reassures me everyone is safe.

When I tell Pete he frowns. 'Bit of a worry, that. Bombers usually go after military targets, not cities.'

The next night the papers say we've attacked Berlin in retaliation.

Then London is bombed again.

Then Berlin.

Pete looks even more worried. 'Targeting civilians is a whole new tactic. Remember Billie telling us how the cities in Spain were training grounds for the Luftwaffe? This could get out of hand.'

He is correct. The Blitz begins, and *out of hand* absurdly understates the horror that ratchets up in London, night after murderous night. I'm glad I'm living in Southampton's relative calm.

Stefan rings me occasionally but he's always in a hurry, always tired, his voice flat. Our paths have become unimaginably separate and there's nothing to say.

At least he's alive, I tell myself.

14. Eliza: Singapore Adventure

Harry and I leave grey, frightened London for Singapore on *SS Narkunda*, a fast P&O liner, which zig-zags to confuse submarines and drops depth charges from the stern. Every day we attend lifeboat drills and at night there's complete blackout.

But enemy planes or submarines don't find us and the tension eases once we're into the Mediterranean. Then we stop at Port Said, Aden, Bombay, Colombo and the sleepy green island of Penang.

In January 1940 we arrive at dazzling Singapore, and watch from the deck as *Narkunda* berths at Keppel Harbour, tied up by small brown men wearing not much more than rags. Dozens of other ships are nearby and hundreds of junks cluster along the shore.

The smells are appalling and the heat like a steaming blanket. The bright light hurts my eyes and sweat trickles down my spine. Thankfully we pass quickly through Customs, then I see Izabel waving, standing beside a girl with brown plaits. We hug Izabel, while Nancy smiles and shakes our hands.

'Over here,' says Izabel. 'The car's in the shade, though that doesn't make much difference.' She speaks to a man in Chinese, who nods. 'He'll bring your luggage later.'

'Are you sure?' I say.

'He's one of our servants.'

'One of? Goodness, how many do you have?'

'Too many. They come with the house.'

The road is full of muddy puddles. An Indian chauffeur in white clothes opens the doors. As he drives away the seat leather almost burns my thighs. We head down narrow streets full of strolling black-haired people, and shops with red lanterns and signs in Chinese characters.

'Now — let me look at you,' Izabel says. 'You seem well, darling.'

'Heavens, I'm so *hot*, Izabel.'

'I won't even pretend you'll enjoy the climate. You won't, but you'll cope eventually.'

She's browner and thinner than I remember, her eyes shadowed. Nancy leans forward and says shyly, 'We've got some cool drinks at home, Mrs Bell. You'll feel much better then.'

'That sounds lovely, Nancy. I must say I'm a little dazed —'

I gasp as we drive ruthlessly, horn blaring, towards rickshaws and people on bicycles. They scatter and Izabel says, 'You'll get used to that too.'

I can smell cooking, flowers, spices, fish, incense, sewage. There's a sudden, rattling downpour of rain, so noisy on the car roof we can't hear each other speak.

It just as suddenly stops and the sun comes out again, the roadways steaming. We turn onto a larger street with more shops and some official-looking buildings.

'Raffles Hotel is just down there,' says Izabel. 'This is Orchard Road, and if you go north for fifteen miles or so you get to the Causeway, which crosses over to the Malaya Peninsula. We live in Tanglin near the Botanic Gardens. It's only a few miles out and very convenient.'

'Look, Mrs Bell,' says Nancy. 'There's Mummy's studio.'

I see *The Peres Academy* on a sign as we pass a white building.

'Peres? Your maiden name?'

Izabel nods. 'To save Felix the embarrassment of being associated with the place.'

'Embarrassment?' asks Harry in surprise.

'Too many non-European children attend, of course. He calls it the bloody League of Nations. But really, I prefer my own name now.' She gazes out the car window.

'Izabel, I'm sorry. I didn't realise —'

'No, no, things are fine. We carry on, as they say.' She smiles quickly. 'And there's the Cathay, all sixteen stories of it, with the most heavenly air-conditioned cinema.'

'Do you like going to the pictures, Nancy?' I ask.

'Yes, Mrs Bell, but the amusement parks are more fun, especially the New World. It's got ferris wheels and a ghost train, and a dance floor where men waltz with ladies in silk cheongsams. I've got a cheongsam too, but the slits don't go so far up my legs.'

'Ah. No need to call me Mrs Bell. Would Aunt Eliza do?'

She nods, pleased, and the car turns into a street of scarlet-flowered trees. We pass through wrought-iron gates onto a drive lined with palms and orchids, and stop outside a mansion as ornate as a wedding-cake, with a shady colonnade around the ground floor.

'Home,' says Izabel drily.

'For a Maharajah, perhaps!' says Harry, laughing.

Inside, Izabel takes us up a marble staircase to an airy bedroom. 'Have a cool drink and rest now, and come down to dinner in an hour or so. One of the maids will bring you lemonade.'

The windows have white muslin curtains and the bed is wide and soft, with a cloud of mosquito nets caught up at the sides.

'Glad to see that netting,' says Harry, taking off his coat. 'I've come to study malaria, not get it.'

There's a knock at the door and a smiling Malay girl brings in a tray, ice clinking in a pitcher. She pours out lemon drinks then leaves.

'God, that's good,' says Harry, swallowing, and I murmur in agreement.

We lie down but it's too hot to cuddle.

'Regretting our grand Singapore adventure yet?' he asks, stroking my hair off my damp forehead with his fine, square hands.

'No, just dozy ...' I drift into sleep.

Dinner is delicious — three curries followed by fresh, sweet fruit. Afterwards we sit in the living room and sip brandy beneath slowly turning fans. Felix hasn't made an appearance yet.

'He's probably still at Far East Combined Bureau headquarters, out at the Naval Base,' says Izabel. 'That's where you'll be working too, I expect. When do you start with the Bureau?'

'Once we settle in.'

'You know you're welcome to stay here, darling, plenty of room.'

'That's kind, Izabel, but a place has already been arranged for us near the General Hospital.'

'Not far from Chinatown, so you'll find it interesting.' She sighs. 'I'd live there too if I could.'

I hear a car stop, and footsteps, and finally Felix makes an entrance.

'Awfully sorry, couldn't get here earlier. Bit of a flap on.'

I see Nancy mouth the words 'Bit of a flap on,' to herself, her shoulder shifting so they're suddenly Felix's rounded, tense shoulders, her face fretful and disappointed like his. I blink and suddenly she's a young girl again, shyly glancing at me.

Izabel smiles. 'I'm sure the cook has kept you some dinner, dear.'

'No need, had something earlier with the lads.'

Felix's face is flushed, so the something was probably liquid. He sits down, calls out *Boy*, and tells the elderly Chinese man who enters to bring him a gin.

Izabel says, 'Could we have coffee for everyone too please, Cho-lin?'

'You're settling in?' my uncle says to Harry, ignoring me. 'Comfy?'

'Very much so,' says Harry. 'Well, after five months how do you find it, Felix?'

He grimaces. 'Well, it's the Far bloody *East*, isn't it! Nothing but obstruction, corruption and unhelpful natives. Mind you, Izabel loves it, don't you, darling?'

She smiles again with that forced brightness. 'Goodness, yes. Every whim catered to, servants as far as the eye can see.' Her eyes are suddenly remote. 'Although the postal service —'

'Always on about the bloody *postal* service,' says Felix. 'Anyone'd think you're waiting for something special. What the hell does it matter?'

'Of course it doesn't, silly me,' says Izabel. 'Yes, the place is marvellous. Nancy's school is excellent, and my studio's doing well. We're very content.'

'My God, she's so *unhappy*,' I say to Harry as we get ready for bed.

'Poor woman,' says Harry. 'Suppose it's because of whatever *really* occurred in Shanghai.'

'Perhaps, now I'm here, she'll tell me more about it.'

'She certainly needs to talk to somebody.' Harry arranges the mosquito netting then gets into bed. 'Hasn't Felix changed? Drink?'

'Probably,' I say. 'Still good-looking, but he's aged ten years.'

'I noticed he didn't once acknowledge you'll be working in his section.'

'Hardly spoke to me,' I say, plumping my pillow and lying down. 'But perhaps he shouldn't talk about work for security's sake.'

'True. And young Nancy — rum one, isn't she?'

'Seems such a little English miss, then did you see her imitating Felix? I nearly laughed aloud. What a sweetheart.'

I don't mean to, but I sigh.

Harry hugs me. 'We'll have a child one day, love. But even if we don't, it doesn't matter —'

I turn my face into his shoulder. 'Matters to me.'

He strokes my back. 'Remember, the specialist said there's nothing wrong with either of us, we just have to be patient.'

'*Patient*? I'll soon be an old woman.'

Harry laughs. 'Lucky I like old women then.'

'Do you?'

'But I must say thirty-two-year-olds are my absolute favourite.'

I gaze at his dear, clever face, and kiss him. 'Good.'

The hospital has found us a small two-storied house, clean and comfortable. Upstairs has two bedrooms, a sitting room and a bathroom with Western facilities, still a rare thing in Singapore.

Downstairs are the reception and dining rooms, kitchen and servant's rooms — the house comes, inescapably, with a cook and a boy. The 'boy' is a middle-aged Chinese man named Ong-lee, the cook a cheerful Malay woman, Nilam.

Harry starts work immediately. He's head of a new malaria unit that's both treating patients and researching the still-mysterious disease: it's his dream job and I'm so happy for him. After a week or so settling in I report to my own new position as well.

The hospital has provided us with a car, so Ong-lee drives me to Sembawang, the big new naval base. It's twenty miles to the north through lush green palm trees and tea plantations.

I decide once I know the roads I'll drive myself, because Ong-lee sails along with the same careless flair as Izabel's chauffeur and I doubt his luck will hold forever. At the guardhouse the soldier checks my name on a list and tells us where to find the headquarters of the Far East Combined Bureau.

The staff residences we pass are white and modern, gardeners sweeping leaves or mowing the grass beneath splashy red-flowered trees. There must be dozens of the bungalows the locals call black-and-whites, with their elegant pale facades and dark window-frames.

Headquarters itself is a handsome two-storied building. I ask Ong-lee to pick me up this evening, and go inside, where a young man shows me to Felix's office. My uncle is sitting behind a large desk. He closes a file with a thump and looks up at me in disapproval.

'Never thought I'd see the day. *Girls* dabbling in national security.'

He's never seen me at work since I joined the department after he went to Hong Kong, so I smile as politely as I can. 'Felix, I've been analysing intelligence to Mr Denniston's complete satisfaction for two years. It's hardly dabbling.'

He harrumphs and stands. 'Better get you started then, but I'll just say this, Eliza. You make an almighty stuff-up don't expect *me* to come running to save your bacon.'

I'm saddened. In the past we had an easy friendship and, although I hate his unkindness to Izabel, it's a pity to see dashing Felix turned into this pinch-faced, unpleasant man.

We leave the office and walk along a warren of corridors. The smothering hot air makes me breathe deeply and wipe my forehead.

'Yes,' say my uncle loftily, 'in my experience, white women simply can't stand the tropics.'

I grit my teeth and luckily we soon reach the offices of the Bureau. The first person I see is one of the analysts I knew at 54 Broadway.

'Good heavens!' he says. 'Mrs Bell! Excellent. I *did* want that reference from you on the Taishō poem. You know the one.'

'I'll find it for you, Mr Kingsley,' I say, smiling. Dear man, it must have been well over a year ago we'd discussed the poem, which had given him a small, surprising insight into a translation.

'Well, I'm sure you'll be perfectly fine here in the hands of ...' Felix harrumphs and leaves.

'Who *is* that unpleasant fellow?' says Mr Kingsley.

'An administrator,' I say. 'Now, is there a desk for me anywhere? This is the oddest place.'

'Come this way, Mrs Bell. It certainly is odd. They hardly notice there's a war on for a start, and simply refuse to believe *anything* we tell them about the Japanese! Terrifyingly blinkered.'

He takes me to a room with desks, shows me to an empty one, then wanders away, preoccupied. I look around and see a grinning face from my old section in London.

'Mr *Baxter*! How did you get here?'

'Same as you, Mrs Bell — they're desperate for personnel. But I took a plane, no messing about on the high seas, thank you very much.'

'Thank God, someone to show me the ropes at last. I'm feeling rather confused.'

'Join the club. But look, we're not in stuffy London any more — do call me Quentin.'

'And I'm Eliza, of course. Now tell me what on earth's happening.'

'Let's see. Well, keeping strictly to form, the powers-that-be have set up a stunningly inept operation. Analysts and codebreakers are here at Sembawang, while the intercept operators are over at Kranji, twelve miles away.'

'Not very efficient.'

'So we have to depend on the incredibly unreliable teleprinter lines, or else someone has to jump on a motorcycle and bring the papers over here.'

'Absurd.'

'Ludicrous.' Quentin grins. 'But I hear Kranji's soon getting some women trained in Kana morse — Naval popsies and WRENs, though I fear we won't be allowed near the place.'

I laugh. 'We must be getting useful data.'

'We certainly are. While you were enjoying your leisure cruise, the boffins installed some whiz-bang antennae that can locate the *directions* of transmissions. When we analyse that traffic we can see where the messages originated — even identify the hands of the operators who sent them!'

'Goodness, that *is* interesting. So we can work out ship locations and directions?'

'Indeed we can,' says Quentin happily. 'Which means the Imperial Japanese Navy's intentions as they potter around the Pacific Ocean may not be quite as well-disguised as they imagine. Want a crash course in traffic analysis, Eliza?'

Outside my work, Singaporean life for Europeans and the richer Asians seems to be made up of dinners and dances, sports and swimming, cocktail parties and raucous outings. I meet Izabel fairly often in company but weeks pass before I have the chance to see her alone.

I park the car at the white wedding-cake house and the maid shows me into the drawing room. Izabel is gazing at nothing, waving her face slowly with a fan.

'Wonderful you're here, darling,' she says in a remote tone. 'The Academy's closed for holidays and I'm so bored.'

The maid sets out an elaborate high tea, then leaves. Izabel hands me a dainty cup and saucer.

'Lovely,' I say, sipping. 'Where's Nancy today?'

'Staying with her best friend Tessie at that big house down the road. They go to the convent school together.'

'But isn't Nancy a Buddhist?'

'Not much choice here for education, so it's the nuns or nothing. But I fear Nancy's picking up some *extremely* odd ideas about biology and theology, while young Tessie appears to be an even greater fount of misinformation.'

She smiles and fleetingly she's her old self. 'You'll meet Tessie's mother Barbara sooner or later. Her father Fred's also in the Bureau but he's stationed on a ship. Convenient for Felix, of course: Barbara's his mistress.'

I stare. 'Honestly?'

'Some cake? It's very nice,' she says. 'Yes, honestly. It's all right — we're good friends.'

'Izabel, what's on earth's going *on*? It's as if you're away in another world.'

After a moment she says helplessly, 'Am I?'

'If you can, *tell* me, darling — what really happened to you in

Shanghai? One of our analysts told me that Nancy's father and Bao-lim died in a *battle*, not a traffic accident.'

Izabel goes to the door, closes it and sits again, her hands clenched.

'Yes, they were killed by Kuomintang forces. They were taking funds to the Communists. It turned out my Third Uncle, the one we'd believed for years was dead, was actually fighting as a Red guerilla all that time.' She looks at me in desperation. 'For God's sake, Eliza, they're the only Chinese forces *resisting* the Japanese!'

'I understand,' I say gently. 'Remember, I get to hear a lot about the true state of the world, not the propaganda.'

Izabel rubs her face. 'I'm so sick of the jingoistic slogans that pass for thought around here. Everyone wants to pretend the Japanese are poor fighters because the mere *Chinese* have kept them at bay for years. They cannot imagine how fierce and battle-hardened both sides have become by now.'

I nod. 'And your Third Uncle?'

After a pause she say, 'I lost him. I lost them all. He died beside Bao-lim and Laurence Kuan.' She takes a shuddering breath. 'You see, Eliza, what *really* happened in Shanghai was that Laurence and I fell in love, utterly in love.' Her voice catches. 'And I will never recover.'

'Oh, *Izabel*.' I sit beside her and hug her. 'You'll recover, for Nancy if no one else. But you're not alone, you have me as well.'

After a time she wipes her eyes. 'Thank you, darling. I haven't been able to tell anyone of course, apart from Min-lu when she came for Bao-lim's funeral.'

I nod. 'Izabel, I know what might offer you a small comfort. I plan to visit Perth as soon as work allows it. Why don't you and Nancy come too, and see Min-lu and the family again?'

She sighs and says, 'Oh, I think I'd like that. Haven't been home for twenty-one years. Though it's not exactly home, is it? Nowhere is.'

At work I discover something rather sobering: nobody takes our intelligence reports very seriously.

'The military imagines it'll be fighting the Great War again, so Singapore's great coastal guns and the spanking new Naval Base will save us,' says Quentin.

'But aren't they reasonable defences?'

'Eliza, the munitions of those guns are calibrated for penetrating ships, not shelling armies, while the Navy's too busy in Europe to help out much here. And should the Japanese decide to saunter through undefended Malaya, we'll find ourselves in hot water very quickly.'

'Undefended?' I say. 'But aren't there bases and airfields on the Peninsula?'

'Dear, deluded Eliza. A smattering of untrained soldiers and a few planes that were barely adequate a decade ago. Basically bugger-all.'

'But surely the government is building up local defences?' I say, appalled. 'They *must* be.'

'Sadly, no. You see, it might perturb the populace, and our masters are none too certain which side the populace actually prefers. The prospect of independence within a Japanese *co-prosperity sphere* sounds rather enticing to some of the Indians.'

'But what about the Chinese? They've been fighting the Japanese for years.'

'Most of the Chinese here are immigrants. Unlike the motherland, this isn't their soil. No — Singapore's just a crossroads, an emporium, a big bloody *shop*.' He shrugs. 'Who'd die for that?'

Although everyone else at the Bureau seems frantically busy, less and less work comes my way. After a while I realise what's happening, and go to see Felix. He glances at me, then puts his head down again. 'Sorry, too busy to talk, bit of a flap on.'

I sit and wait. He looks up irritably. 'Didn't you *hear* me, Eliza? Haven't you got better things to do than loll around gossiping?'

'That's precisely the problem, Felix. I don't. Files aren't coming to my desk and the work is going to people already overburdened.'

He controls a smirk. 'Well, you're a very *junior* Junior Assistant, Eliza. Perhaps you don't have the security clearance for the level of intelligence coming through.'

'No, Felix. I was promoted to Senior Assistant for this job.' I feel myself flushing with anger.

He shrugs. 'A lot of paperwork gets mislaid around here, so I'm afraid I have only your word for that. Naturally, I'll write to London to clarify the situation and we'll know in a few months.'

'*Months*? It might be faster to telegraph Mr Denniston directly.'

'Good God, waste His Majesty's precious resources on such a trivial matter? That would be quite irresponsible of me, Eliza. And of course, while you're under this cloud —'

'Under a *cloud*? Are you serious?'

'It's security we must be serious about, young lady. You may be my niece, but you can't just swan in here and claim the sort of skills a girl, after all, would be *highly* unlikely to have.'

I force myself to be calm. 'Ask Mr Baxter or Mr Kingsley, then.'

'They can only recall that in London you were a Junior Assistant.'

'In London I *was*. But for this job I was promoted.'

Felix shrugs. 'Sadly your co-workers cannot vouch for that.'

'It was hardly advertised in the *Times*, Felix. But the letter of offer —'

I stop. The letter of offer is packed away with my papers in Toby's cellar in London. I can't let anyone without a clearance go through them, and in any case it would still take months to get here.

Felix smirks again. 'I think we'll just have to wait for the official word, don't you? Of course you can do some typing but really, Eliza, you'd be better off taking a nice little holiday.'

'But I'm going so well at traffic analysis, Felix, and we're getting excellent results —'

'Oh, really? Mumbo-jumbo I call it. Honestly, the boffins must think we're all fools.'

'Just because you don't understand the science ... Felix, we *need* that information!'

'I understand enough to know that tested methods — and tested men — provide exactly what we need, Eliza. Not claptrap about antennas. Not algebra, for God's sake. And *certainly* not girls.'

15. Toby: The Civic Centre

I remain in Southampton throughout that summer of 1940, marred only by numerous air raid warnings, mostly false alarms. Although I've been doing a little writing, it's dry and dull. But today I'm off to have lunch with Pete. He's going to show me over his beloved factory, right down to the doped wings, he says.

I take the train rather than the floating bridge, the ferry that runs from Northam over the river to Woolston. I don't want to run the risk of meeting anyone I knew in my youth — or worse, my father — on those mean Northam streets.

As the train crosses the river, I see the barrage balloons tethered in great glinting clouds above the factories. They say they make attacks from dive bombers more difficult, and they do look appropriately awesome.

The leaves of the trees are edged with gold, and a cool autumn breeze blows as I walk from the station to the factory. In mid-September — a week ago — the Germans bombed this area. They hurt a dozen people, but luckily missed the two Supermarine factories.

At the sandbagged front gate a warden checks my identity card and sends a boy to get Pete. I gaze up at the administration building, its stylishly curved windows criss-crossed with blast tape.

Pete comes down the staircase grinning, and vouches for me. He takes me past the large drawing office, where I see a surprising scatter of draughts-women among the men.

Then we reach the factory's vast assembly floor. I'm shocked into silence as I stare at the rows and rows of half-finished fuselages.

I finally say, 'But they're so *small*, Pete. How can a man fit? What about his parachute — pilots *do* have parachutes don't they? They don't just ... go up there without a ...'

Pete pats my shoulder. 'Of course they have parachutes, old mate.'

'Where are the wings?' I say.

'They'll be attached at final assembly. Pretty wide, you know, not enough room for them here.'

'Oh. Rather sculptural, aren't they? Almost beautiful.'

'Most beautiful plane ever made, Toby. Most responsive and well-behaved too. Don't worry. We're doing everything we can to make the best possible aircraft for Stef and his friends.'

I take a deep breath. 'Heavens, you've got a lot on the go, Pete.'

He laughs. 'This is just the old factory, you should see the new one up the road. Bloody amazing.'

I gaze the length of the shed, surprised to see exactly what Pete had told me: young girls, grandmothers and old sods, busily working away. The old sods look so much like my father's drinking mates I can almost imagine him there, half-way along the floor.

'Anyway, I'm starving,' says Pete. 'Let's go to lunch.'

He gets his bicycle and borrows one for me, and we pedal down the road half a mile to the hotel.

'Why exactly do I have to cycle everywhere?' I say over our sandwiches. 'I thought a manager of your eminence would have a chauffeured limousine at least.'

'Nah, with rationing I hardly get even enough petrol for my little car. The farm's about eight miles from here so it's pretty tight.'

'Well, we've got a spare room at the flat. You can use that as a bolthole if you need to.'

'Thanks, Toby, that'd be a help,' says Pete, finishing his lemonade. 'Ah well, almost time to get back to the treadmill.'

We're saying farewell at the factory gate when I hear the drone of planes and look up. They're swooping towards us along the river, evading the barrage balloons and dropping things.

Egg-like things.

The air-raid sirens start up with a horrible rising moan, then the anti-aircraft guns begin a fast blat-blat-blat-blat-blat. (Oh, *that's* why they call them ack-ack guns.)

In the distance I see the trails of RAF fighters attacking the bombers, but there don't seem to be very many of them.

'Come on Toby — *shelter!*' Pete yanks my arm. 'Railway embankment, *come on.*'

The embankment, near the other factory, seems a long way away.

People dash beside us, panting. With the roar of the bombers, the ack-ack guns, the wailing sirens, it's like one of those nightmares where you're running and running, going nowhere at all.

Suddenly everything shudders and a noise envelops us, so vast and rumbling it's quite beyond noise. Pete shoves me to the ground and falls down himself. I fling my arms over my head but it doesn't blot out the thundering through my body, the earth leaping at me.

In disbelief I count the explosions: ten, eleven ... twenty-five, twenty-six ... forty-eight, *forty-nine* ... I lose count then, hacking my throat out in the dust. Hailstorms of pebbles sting and cut my head and hands. The barking ack-ack guns are like packs of mastiffs gone berserk.

After an eternity the sirens sound the steady *all clear* — then they suddenly start wailing again. Before we can even lift our heads we're back inside the nightmare universe of thudding and rumbling and flying stones. (When time resumes, I'm stunned to find out the raid lasted nearly two hours.)

Finally it all ends. I slowly sit up. I'm puzzled to see people are still running, through clouds of dust towards the tunnel beneath the railway, to the embankment where the shelters are.

Where the shelters used to be.

Where crumpled figures lie like dirty washing, and people are yelling and digging in heaps of soil, arms and legs protruding here and there. I cannot *comprehend* it.

Pete dashes forward and falls on his knees by a waving arm, and starts pulling a figure half-buried out of the soil. I follow him, simply doing whatever he does, and a woman emerges, bloody and moaning. Men take her away on a stretcher.

'Over there,' I yell to Pete, shoulder moving a few yards away.

We dig down like dogs to free the head, and release an old man, choking and gasping. It takes a while but finally he's free, his grey hair flopping over his eyes.

Pete calls for a stretcher and we help him sit up. There's not much blood, and I pull out my handkerchief and wipe dirt and tears from his face, saying, 'There, there, you're safe now.'

He grasps my arm and whispers, 'Thank you.' Then he stares at me, his eyes wide with shock.

'Tommy, my boy? Tommy, it's me, your *Dad*!'

I feel sick. To quote Billie: fuck, fuck, fuck.

Finally there are no more bodies, living or dead, to be taken away. The shelters took a direct hit and over forty people were killed, and one hundred and sixty wounded.

I still can't comprehend it. So many of those busy, laughing people I saw just hours ago are now dead, while even the lucky ones face a painful convalescence.

Like my father.

Mercifully, Pete doesn't say anything as we drive to my flat, take showers and get changed. Finally we sit down with a stiff whisky each. He rests his head on the back of the lounge chair and says quietly, 'Fuck, fuck, fuck,' just like Billie, and even through my shock and exhaustion I'm mildly amused.

Then I'm not when he says, '*Tommy*, not Toby?'

'Yes.'

'How on earth ...?'

'Oh, dear *God*. I grew up in Southampton.'

'You never said. Why?'

'You saw the old shit. Why do you think?'

'I saw nice Alf Fenn who, incidentally, is one of our best workers.'

'Well, he must have changed utterly since I last saw him.'

'When was that?'

'Ten years ago. When he threw me out of the house for my *unrepentant perversion*.'

'He was pretty glad to see you today.'

'If Hitler had dug him up he'd be glad to see him too.'

'Will you visit him in hospital?'

'Under no circumstances.'

The Spitfire factories survive that dreadful afternoon with little damage, but just two days later they're raided again by eighty bombers and sixty fighters. It goes on for hours and hours, and even from a distance it's obviously carnage.

From the flat I can hear the roar of explosions and see columns of smoke filling the sky. In the evening Pete arrives, exhausted. He showers and I bandage a burn on his arm.

'Fifty-five poor bastards killed today, Toby, a hundred wounded. Bombs and *fucking* machine-guns.' Pete takes a shuddering breath. 'They got both factories this time. Up in flames, only twisted metal left, no roofs, walls collapsed. We had *hundreds* of planes on the go. Now not even one.'

'What will you do?'

'Can't possibly rebuild. Have to move.' He slowly rubs his face. 'We lost all the prototypes, designs, models, test results, archives. Oh, *Jesus*.' After a pause he looks up. 'Right, that's it. Tomorrow we're going to see your father.'

'I'm sorry, what?'

'It can all end in an instant, Toby. I saw two of our people, mother and son, both dead in a bloody *instant*. We're going to see your father. Or I'll go myself and give him your address.'

Next day Pete drives me (silent and sullen) to the hospital. He marches me to the ward and thrusts a paper bag in my hands. 'Grapes for the invalid.'

'*Grapes*? Where the hell did you get them?'

'Your local greengrocer keeps a secret stash for good mates.'

'Well let's just go home and eat them ourselves,' I say brightly.

'No. I'll come and have a word, then go back to the factory.'

'This isn't bloody *fair*, Pete.'

'Third bed on the left. I'll follow you. Got to make certain you don't lose your way, after all.'

The old man is sitting up, staring at the bed cover.

'How are you feeling, Mr Fenn?' says Pete.

'Mr McKee! Goodness. Not bad, doc says I can go home tomorrow. Right as rain soon enough.'

Pete says, 'Look who this is.'

My father focuses on me, dazed. 'Thought I'd imagined it. But it *was* you, Tommy, after all! What on earth were you doing *there*?'

'Just visiting me, Mr Fenn,' says Pete. 'We've known each other for years, but I hadn't the foggiest you were related. Now, I've got to get back to work so I'll leave you to catch up. Hope you're better again as soon as possible.'

I stare in despair as Pete walks away, then turn back to the old monster although, unaccountably, he's so much smaller than he used to be. I clench my jaw, pull up a chair and sit down.

'Mr McKee brought you some grapes.' (I'm certainly not taking credit for them.)

'Goodness, rare as hens' teeth, them.'

He eats a grape then offers me the bag but I shake my head. There's a long silence as he chews. I detest the sight of his moving, white-stubbled jaw. People by the other beds are murmuring and laughing quietly.

'What's the damage, then?' I ask ungraciously.

'Broken arm and rib, bump on the head. Fuss about nothing.' Alf focuses on me again, his greasy, grey hair limp on his forehead. 'Tommy, my lad. Can't get over it.'

'Yes. Odd coincidence.'

'You're a friend of Mr McKee? He's a gentleman him, never raises his voice. Well, well.'

After a pause I say, 'Been working there long?'

'Oh, six months. Good place, good friends. Had to close down the butchery a while ago, the Depression killed it.'

(You mean too many customers getting sick from tainted meat, you careless old fool.)

'And what about *you*, son? Living in London, Maude told me.'

'Yes. She left me her house,' I say. 'You didn't come to the funeral.'

'Oh, we weren't close, Maude and me, only in-laws. So ...' He sighs. 'She said you were a famous writer now. Thought I might embarrass you turning up, so I didn't go.'

'I'm not very famous, and less so every day. But yes, I'm a writer.'

'Your first time back home?'

'No, I've been here often,' I say coldly. 'But I'm still *unrepentant*, so I had to assume you'd prefer I didn't darken your doorstep.'

Alf shakes his head. 'I'm sorry, son. You can't imagine how often I've regretted what I said.'

'Well, I'm sure I'm *so* much the stronger for it. Anyway, I should be going —'

'Maybe we can see more of each other now, lad,' he says. 'I get good money at the factory and I've done up the old house, you wouldn't recognise it.'

'I doubt the good money will continue,' I say, my throat thick with loathing. 'Didn't you hear? The factory burnt down yesterday. Totally. You're out of a job.'

I turn and walk away.

Sitting on the bus back to Bedford Place I want to scream. I hate myself. I hate him. I hate Pete too, pushing me into this charade of reconciliation.

At home I'm agitated, pacing back and forth in the living room. What will I do now? Go back to London? But massive raids are now happening all over the city. They're calling it *blitzkrieg*, lightning war, and it's relentless, day and night.

I think of the other afternoon, the thunder shuddering through the earth, lying in the gutter in a state of terror. I suddenly sit down, arms clasping my belly. At least here the bombs are aimed at factories, docks and railways — not homes.

No, no, I couldn't bear to be in London. I'll just stay put and avoid the horrible old bastard. Keep my head down, keep writing. *Writing?* What a stupid bloody idea. What have *I* got to say?

All I know now is my rage, my gut-clenching rage. Those Nazi warmongering shits! What they've done to my friend Pete, to all those good people — dear *God*, how I'd love to strike back at them! But what on earth could I ...?

Ah. I take a deep breath, put on my coat and walk the half mile to St Mary's fire station, and join the Auxiliary Fire Service.

Over the next few months I fill sandbags, hand-pump water, run up and down ladders, and listen to lectures on gas, bombs and incendiaries. I stand in the back of our truck, clinging on to the tank as we race through the streets, unit chief clanging the bell.

I wear a helmet and boots and a uniform with two rows of brass buttons up the front. (It was too big so I got a tailor to fit it and Pete teases me unmercifully for my vanity.)

The other firefighters are a little stand-offish at first, but over time they accept my willingness to learn from the experienced men — especially about when to stay, when to run and what to watch for.

'Not what to watch for, laddie,' says old George, the unit chief, a Great War veteran. 'What to *listen* for.'

One of the others says, 'Damp timbers squeal when they're alight, but when they're burnt through they're silent, ready to collapse. That's when you run.'

'Aye, and it's the bricks I never forget, that eerie groaning,' says George. 'Only heard it a few times, but it means a wall's coming down.' He laughs harshly. 'And if you're close enough to hear it then you're too bloody close.'

My restless mind revels in the opening up of this new world. Although I've happily put the typewriter away in a cupboard, I jot down events and thoughts in a small journal every night: not for any potential book but simply to keep a record for myself.

And best of all I've stopped worrying about Stefan all the time.

The increasing number of night raids frustrate our fighters, desperately trying to attack firefly targets lit up for an instant by the searchlights. A recent German ploy is to drop incendiaries and use the light for navigation, so we attend a lot of small fires, but since the Supermarine bombings there haven't been any major attacks on Southampton.

Everything changes on 6th November 1940.

That morning, as usual, we wave to a group of cheerful young girls from the Central District school, who always walk past the station on their way to classes at the Civic Centre.

Then at about two-thirty in the afternoon, the sirens start wailing. As we rush to prepare, the planes drop their bombs — only twelve or so but they're big, five-hundred pound buggers, says old George — and we're soon racing towards the plumes of smoke.

When we get there, the entire front of the Civic Centre building has been sliced wide open to the sky above mountains of rubble. A teacher screams, *The children, they're in the shelter, the basement shelter*! I feel a small relief: we may have to dig them out but they should be safe enough there.

We extinguish the few fires. Around us many people are helping, including a group of Canadian soldiers, but the teacher won't stop screaming and, sickeningly, I realise something is very wrong.

The soldiers are trying to hold up a collapsing wall, while others are reaching down, throwing rubble off the basement roof, yelling. We join them, passing bricks and concrete in a chain.

Ambulance men arrive, and through gaps in the roof start pulling limp forms from the chaos. As more of the makeshift bomb-shelter is revealed I see the basement is laced with central heating pipes which were full of boiling water: or they were until the bomb struck.

One by one, fourteen small blistered bodies are lifted out. One girl is wailing in pain and they get her and a couple of others to ambulances, but the others are silent as they're carried to trucks. Mortuary trucks.

I've never known such horror.

We stand there dazed until we're ordered to go to a fire from one of the other bombs. When I get home that night, my throat raw from vomit and smoke, I collapse onto the sofa, my hands over my stinging eyes. The phone rings.

'Toby,' Stefan says, his voice calm. 'Some news — I'm soon being transferred to an airfield about twenty miles from Southampton. Perhaps we'll have a chance to see more of each other again.'

'Good news. I'm glad, Stef.'

But after we hang up I think, am I?

16. Billie: Girl Flyers

Pete rings me up now and then to chat. Tonight I ask, 'Is Toby coming back from Southampton soon? The house is so quiet without him.'

'Unlikely,' says Pete. 'Two reasons. He's doing full-time shifts at the fire station.'

'Does he wear a uniform?'

'Of the utmost elegance.'

I smile. 'I can just imagine. And the other reason?'

'Stef's just been posted to a place called Middle Wallop —'

'Come on, that's not a *place*, it's a punch-line.'

He laughs. 'Nah, that'd have to be Nether Wallop. But Middle Wallop's not too far from Southampton, so the boys'll be able to see each other occasionally. Mind you, Stef's pretty busy flying.'

'Yeah, bet he is, poor bastard. How's the salvage work going, Pete?'

'Still amazes me *anything* survived the bombings, but we've recovered some jigs and machine tools, and we're setting up assembly sites in small workshops around Southampton. Still, it'll be a long time before we can produce anywhere near as many planes as before. What about London? Is it as bad as the papers say?'

'Worse, mate, *much* worse. The papers are censored so the Nazis can't find out how badly they've hit us, but the city's been bombed day and night for months now. We're all in a shambles from lack of sleep. Thousands of poor sods killed and no sign it's ever going to stop.'

'What about you, Billie — holding up?'

'Dunno. You know nothing much scares me, but this is crazy. Boring and terrifying at the same time.'

'You can always come down to the farm for a break sometime, Vivy'd love to see you,' Pete says. 'How are the others going?'

'Charlotte and Otto are fine, haven't been bombed. Charlotte's busy organising everyone in the refugee group with a ruthless efficiency I'd never suspected. Not the efficiency part anyway.'

'I reckon she's happier now than ever,' he says. 'Her energy had no outlet before.'

'She's doing well, Pete, you should be proud. A lot of kids are alive now that might have died without her and Otto and Klara.'

'How's Klara, then?'

'Living on her nerves, doesn't have Charlotte's self-confidence — seems to doubt herself, takes it all terribly to heart. And *bloody* Sofe, head in the clouds and all she can talk about is that Yank cow, Terry. Poor old Klara.'

'Do you reckon Sofia's really in love, or is it just a passing crush?'

'Don't think it's a crush, she's so happy and creative at the same time.' I laugh shortly. 'Jesus, I've only ever felt like that once in my life. It's pretty damned rare.'

'Yeah, Wilf was a great bloke,' Pete says.

After a pause I say, 'Rare for you too?'

'Nah, I'm like that whenever I fall for someone,' he says. 'Only later I wonder what the hell it is I've let myself in for.'

That stings too and I can't say anything for a moment. Pete seems to realise he's put his foot in it and changes the subject.

'You thought any more about the Air Transport Auxiliary, Billie?'

'What, Pauline Gower's mob? Hundreds of women have applied, but they're only taking a few. In any case — well, I've been meaning to mention it, but the fact is ...'

'What?'

'Fact is, Pete, I don't want to fly any more.'

'You don't want to *fly* any more?'

'That's what I said.'

'But surely you're over all that now?'

'All what?'

'You know ... Wilf, Spain.'

'Doubt I'll ever be over it.'

'Maybe not. But you'd have the chance to pilot a *Spitfire*, Billie, for God's sake!'

'No I wouldn't. ATA women only deliver training kites like Moths and Magisters. They'd never let a female near a Spitfire.'

I've stopped going out with Raymond the cellist. I knew it wouldn't last. Once he started seeing me, his unobtainable love decided she was suddenly a lot more obtainable, and now they're enjoying a torrid romance while her husband's overseas.

I suppose that's what happens when everyday life is upended. Like mine. I'm working in an office now, taking orders for cardboard boxes. Big joke — all those years when everyone assumed I was the secretary, and now I am.

The phone rings and I answer it with a coldness barely this side of contempt.

'Sweetie, you'll never win employee of the year with *that* tone of voice.'

'Hello, Charlie. What do you want?'

'Or that, either. I want to take you out to lunch tomorrow.'

'Why?'

'Feel like it. I'll pay. How can you refuse?'

'I can't. Where?'

Toby doesn't charge us rent, although we cover the bills. He says it makes him feel like a modern-day Karl Marx, although when he quotes *All for one...* I suspect he's thinking of the Three Musketeers, not the Comintern. But despite his generosity I still don't have a lot of spare dosh. A free meal, even with Charlotte, isn't to be sneered at.

When I arrive next day at the rather nice restaurant she's chosen, she's already sitting there.

'Hullo, sweetie,' she says. 'Whew, just got back in time from Dovercourt Bay.'

'Where?'

'Oh, near Harwich. Only twenty miles but I almost ran out of petrol. I had coupons but couldn't find a garage for ages.'

'So why go there?'

'Billie, you *really* need to find out a bit more about the world.'

'Charlie, if my head wasn't so full of orders for the cardboard boxes that are, without a *doubt*, going to win us this war, I would.'

'Dovercourt Bay is where the *Kindertransport* children live,' she says. 'An old summer camp.'

'But I thought you and Klara had found them all foster homes.'

'These ones can't get sponsors: they're not young enough or winsome enough, or their foster homes weren't suitable — groping old men or harridans who treat them like servants.' Charlotte shakes her head in disgust. 'Anyway, that's not why we're having lunch.'

'Oh, all of a sudden there's a reason?'

She smiles. 'Of course there is. And here she comes.'

A trim, fair woman in a dark blue uniform arrives at our table. She and Charlotte kiss and coo, then she sits beside me.

'Billie, this is Captain Pauline Gower of the Air Transport Auxiliary,' says Charlotte.

'Yeah,' I say.

'How do you do, Miss Quinn?' Pauline Gower says in a cut-glass accent. 'Charlotte's told me so much about you.'

'Call me Billie, for God's sake.'

'I'm Pauline, of course. Naturally I know of you from your teaching days,' she says. 'In fact, the ATA is fortunate enough to have some of your ex-pupils. They're very good.'

'Glad to hear it,' I say grudgingly.

'I used to work in an aerial circus like you, Billie, with Dorothy Spicer — we had *such* fun. Dorothy's working on the Air Ministry's new engines at Farnborough now.'

I unbend a little. 'Wasn't she the first woman to get her D licence, aeronautical engineer?'

Pauline laughs. 'The company that trained her tried to keep it a secret. They were terrified they'd be overwhelmed with hordes of other women demanding to be engineers. How absurd!'

I smile a little. 'Yeah. How's the Auxiliary then? I'm always seeing breathless stories about the ATA-girls in the papers.'

Pauline nods. 'Doing very well, excellent safety record so far. I'm slowly getting them permission to fly all types of planes, even the largest. What's more, I'm determined that one day they'll be paid as much as the male ATA pilots.'

'But women don't get the same rate as men in *any* job,' I say, surprised.

She gives me a level gaze. 'Time they damned well did, then.'

Charlotte looks from me to Pauline, pleased. 'I think I'll have the chicken today. You?'

We eat and chat, then over coffee, Pauline says, 'Billie, we receive more applicants than we have openings, but most are from women with little experience. What do you think?'

'About what?'

'Joining the ATA,' she says.

My throat goes dry. 'Sorry, I haven't been in a plane for two years, and don't want to fly, not ever again. You'll do all right without me.'

I stand up. 'Thanks for lunch, Charlie. I'd better get back to the world of cardboard boxes before they send out a search party.'

A week later I emerge from the Tube, tired and sleepless. The air is thick with the everyday stinks of the Blitz — ashes, shit, ancient rot, and something disgustingly like cooked meat. I stop, startled, at the gap where my office building used to be.

The dingy lino and dirty windows and files of invoices are all gone, and firemen are hosing arched streams of water onto heaps of smoking bricks and timbers.

I notice a familiar-looking file lying on the ground and grind it savagely into the mud with my heel. Then I go home to bed.

I have a few hours of sleep and feel substantially better by lunchtime. As usual I go down to Klara and Sofia's flat — it has a nice kitchen and we all like the company — and find Klara sitting at the old wooden table with a cup of tea and a cigarette.

'Didn't know you'd taken up smoking,' I say, putting the kettle on.

Klara stares at the burning end for a moment and says, 'I was trying it, Billie, but it makes me dizzy. I do not know why so many people say they love it.'

'Doesn't help, simply makes you think it does. Tea's just as good.'

'I am glad to hear that.' She stubs out the cigarette and sips her tea.

'How are you, anyway, Klara? Haven't seen you much lately.'

'I have been staying at Dovercourt Bay.'

'Oh, I know where that is now,' I say. 'Charlotte told me last week.'

'Soon it will be winter and there is much to be done to make it more comfortable.'

'Many kids still there?'

'Perhaps three thousand.'

'Jeez, that's a lot. Can't you find homes for them?'

'Now, in the middle of war, it is much harder.' Klara sighs. 'Their spirits are good, although of course they are sad. And when the war ends they will be sadder still.'

'But won't they be glad to go home?'

She looks up at me, surprised. 'They are unlikely to have homes to go to or parents still alive. I think they will be very unhappy.'

I pour my own tea and sit down. 'But we're not bombing Germany *that* much.'

'Not us, Billie. The Nazis are systematically murdering the Jews in extermination camps.'

'But isn't that just one of those rumours, Klara? I can't believe —'

She shakes her head. 'Not rumours. We have proof of *thousands* of people who have already been killed. They are sent to those camps from the occupied countries too. The Germans have a plan to kill every Jew in Europe.'

'But how could they possibly — I can't — *really*, Klara?'

'Yes, Billie, really. London is burning, the Jews are burning too. Why is it so difficult to believe the Nazis would find one job easy and the other hard? They are very efficient.'

I take her cold hand. 'Perhaps you're living too much with this, Klara.'

'But, Billie, you lived with it too in Spain. I thought you, of all people, would believe me.'

'Spain was a nightmare, but now you're talking — *Christ* — the bottomless pits of Hell.'

'And now I know Hell truly exists,' says Klara. 'I used to think so little of Charlotte yet she does so much for the *Kinder*, for her the task is everything. For me, my heart dies a little every day. There is no comfort anywhere.'

'So it's not really Sofia making you sad then,' I say.

Klara shrugs. 'Perhaps one day she will love me again, perhaps she never will. She is happy in a way I cannot give her. It does not matter.'

She gets up, lights the stove and puts the kettle on again. 'Why are you at home in the daytime, Billie, and not at your job? Are you sick?'

'No, the Germans burnt my office down last night so I don't have a job any more. But I couldn't have stuck it out much longer anyway.'

'What will you do?'

'Maybe go to Southampton, Pete's farm. A rest from the Blitz would be good. But now Sofe's away touring with the orchestra I don't like leaving you here by yourself.'

'I will stay with Otto and Charlotte — it is closer to work and they have not yet been bombed.'

Drizzle trickles down the window outside and the comfortable kitchen looks harsh in the cold light. 'Remember when people were always here?' I say. 'Such a happy place.'

Vivy is asleep on the sofa beside me, her head on my lap, breathing quietly, her face hidden by waves of chestnut hair. 'I should put her to bed,' I say to Pete, 'but I'm so full of Mrs Spencer's amazing dinner I can hardly move.'

'I'll take her up. She's out like a light — what did you do today?'

'She had a ride on her pony in the morning, then we took the dog for a walk over the hills. I now know more about the flora and fauna of Hampshire than I'd ever imagined was possible. She sang for me too. She's got a good voice for a kid, Pete, she ought to have lessons.'

'Yeah, I've been thinking about that. Next year, once she's going to school.'

He gets up from his armchair, lifts the little girl and carries her upstairs. Ten minutes later he comes down again and says, 'Want a brandy?'

'Small one, thanks.'

We sit quietly by the fire for a time. It's cold outside — autumn is ending and winter almost upon us, so the fire is more than usually welcome.

'Saw an old mate of yours today,' says Pete. 'Dennis Fraser.'

'Frazer ... oh, yeah, taught him at Hamble, 1935. Wasn't too bad, not like most of the other public-school types.'

'Ah, there's your colonial chip-on-the-shoulder coming out, Billie.'

'You've got one too.'

'Nah, mine's more a screwed-up-my-entire-life chip,' he says.

I laugh. 'Not your entire life, mate — Vivy's okay.'

'Yeah,' he says, pleased. 'Anyway, Dennis said if you want to have a look at the new planes he'd be delighted to show you. He's one of our test pilots. Makes sure we haven't forgotten any rivets before the Hamble ATA flies them to the fit-out airfields.'

'Didn't know there was an ATA pool at Hamble.'

'Started just a couple of months ago — male pilots, though, not your mates. The women are based in London at Hatfield.'

'Not my mates,' I say, watching the flames through my glass of brandy. 'Pauline Gower's mates.'

There's a silence.

'Why the bloody hell *not*, Billie? Female pilots are already flying Ansons and Oxfords, and I hear they'll even be allowed in Spits and Hurricanes soon. They *desperately* need people like you. Every Transport pilot frees up an RAF lad to go out and fight those bastards. Even Toby's doing his bit in the Fire Service.'

'Good for Toby.'

Pete scowls. 'You wouldn't be so bloody *blithe* if you'd gone through what we did.'

I'm surprised. Pete has been run ragged lately, helping to set up small Spitfire assemblies in old sheds and factories around the town, but he's never been a bad-tempered man.

He clears his throat. 'Hear about the raid here, early November?'

'Pretty small, wasn't it? Compared to the East End, anyway.'

'Yeah. Except they hit the Civic Centre. A kid's class was sheltered in the basement, but the bomb — just *one* bomb — went straight through. They were *little girls*, Billie, thirteen years old. Went along that day to do a fucking needlework lesson.'

'You're thinking about Vivy.'

'Of *course* I am, all the time! And so should you. We should do everything we *can* —'

His voice breaks and he puts his hands over his eyes.

I've known Pete for ten years; as a wide-eyed youth, a swaggering flyer, a passionate lover, a trampler of my dreams. And more recently as Charlotte's besotted husband, Vivy's loving father, Supermarine's careworn manager.

I've seen him cry once — the day he thought I'd died   but never again until tonight.

In the kitchen next morning, at the sink with his back to me, Pete says, 'Look, I'm really sorry. Bit overwrought, too much on lately.'

I butter toast for Vivy and me, the butter (and milk and eggs) a bonus of the country life.

'Nah, don't apologise,' I say. 'You were right.'

He laughs a little. 'Don't think I've ever heard you say *that* before.'

'Even a stopped clock's right twice a day, mate. Don't let it go to your head.'

He turns around and although he's only thirty, I see for the first time how much he's aged.

My throat aches. 'Dennis Frazer's over at Eastleigh airfield, isn't he?'

Pete nods.

'Your old Moth still stored there?'

He nods again.

'Guess I could have a chat to Dennis, see one of your new babies.'

He's grinning now, dear old Pete again. 'You'll *love* the Spit, Billie. My God, it's a great plane.'

'Not promising to rush off and join any bunch of do-gooder girl flyers though.'

17. Izabel: The Doll

'Let's do it *now*,' says Eliza. 'Jump on a ship for Perth and see the family at last. Harry can't take the time off, but I'd love a change of scenery.'

'What about your job?' I say.

'Oh, not much to do at the moment.'

Felix is always complaining he's rushed off his feet, but from snide comments he's dropped lately I think he's forcing Eliza to work as a typist, despite her analyst role in London. I've no idea why, but since security's involved I can't ask.

We quickly make plans, and in September 1940 Eliza, Nancy and I board the *Centaur* for Fremantle. I'm not nervous. A small steamer on the Western Australian coast is probably about as safe as anything can be. Still, we attend lifeboat drills and observe the blackout, stars glimmering in the tropical air.

We pass through islands of the Dutch East Indies, which don't much interest me, then approach the Australian coast, which does.

Twenty-one years — could it really be that long?

I remember sailing from Fremantle as a heartbroken nineteen-year-old, running away to England the year after the Great War. The man I'd loved had died in the influenza epidemic and I'd had the *procedure* Felix had mocked me with: I didn't realise it would mean I'd never carry a child to term.

At least I've known a mother's lot. *Thank you, Laurence.*

We steam along the wild Kimberley coastline for hours, then past the scarlet cliffs of Gantheaume Point, and into Roebuck Bay.

Eliza says, 'That rust-red is so *intense*, it always takes me by surprise.'

'Like embers, Aunt Eliza,' says Nancy. 'And the water's turquoise too, like my mala.'

Eliza takes a deep breath. 'My God, I love this place. Look at the sky, Izabel, it's almost *violet* against that jade sea. Dear old Broome.'

Centaur approaches the long curved jetty I remember so well. Apart from holidays I only lived here for a few years, but it still seems vividly real to me. More real than anywhere else. Except Hong Kong of course.

The ship ties up and we take the steam tram to the shore. Only a few people are disembarking so we pass quickly through the tiny Customs shed, then catch a taxi. *Centaur* will stay for half a day to unload cargo, and we only have a short time to visit Eliza's aunt and uncle.

The taxi stops outside a white bungalow with latticework on the veranda, where Lucy and Danny are waiting for us. Eliza hugs them, but I hold back a little and shake their hands, then introduce Nancy.

'Come and sit down,' says Lucy, leading us into the living room. 'Oh, darling Eliza, it's been so long since I saw you! And Izabel too — how *well* you look. Now, who wants tea — Nancy, would you like some cordial?'

Lucy's being kind, but she always was, although I didn't appreciate it when I was young. She's looking well herself. Slim, her posture straight (she's from the generation of girls who grew up firmly corseted) and the streaks of silver in her brown hair suit her.

'How are your children going, Lucy?' I ask.

'Mike's still at university in Melbourne, and Anna's doing a secretarial course in Perth. They're both too far away from home, Izabel — you're very lucky to have a chick in the nest. Enjoy these days with Nancy while you can.'

'Oh, I do,' I say, and a glance passes between us. Lucy knows what happened to me so long ago.

'Do you like reading, Nancy?' she asks. 'Here, I've a book for you.'

'Thank you,' says my daughter politely as she opens the package, then, 'Oh, *thank* you!' It's the *Girls' Own Annual*, which she loves.

'What a sight, our Lizzie Lee all grown up,' says Danny, in his soft Irish accent. 'But we shan't be meeting your young fellow Harry it seems? There's a pity.'

'He wanted to come, Danny, but the hospital couldn't spare him,' says Eliza. 'Next time, he promises. How's your business going?'

He shrugs, spreading his large tanned hands. 'Nobody wants new luggers nowadays, but I still get work rebuilding the old boats. It's not all gloom and doom. We're doing all right.'

Nancy murmurs to herself, 'Weer doin' oll royt.' She looks up from her book and smiles at Danny. 'I like your accent, although it's not as easy as it sounds at first.'

He laughs. 'Another actress in the family, I see.'

'My chameleon child, Danny,' I say.

Nancy looks up again. '*Ah-me,* how am I related to Lucy and Danny?'

I can tell she's feeling comfortable here: in stratified Singapore she's always very careful to call me Mummy.

'Well, my half-brother Sam was Eliza's father, Rosa's her mother and Lucy is Rosa's sister. But that doesn't explain your relationship to Lucy and Danny. In fact I'm not even sure if there *are* terms for a half-uncle's sister-in-law and her husband, at least not in English.'

Nancy asks, puzzled, 'But why do I call Eliza aunt then, if she's really a cousin?'

'Well, in Chinese she's actually *maternal elder female cousin.* What do you think she'd prefer?'

Nancy and Eliza look at each other and laugh.

The massive tides of Roebuck Bay determine every ship's schedule and *Centaur* must sail that night. When we leave, Nancy hugs Lucy and Danny, and now I do too, although earlier I'd felt foolishly constrained. Lucy was kind to me in my childhood, but there was a time I hated her. I'm glad it's over.

After dinner we sit on deck and watch the stars, then I say to Nancy, 'Bed, young lady.'

'*Ah-me,* why didn't you hug Lucy when we went to their house, but afterwards you did?'

Eliza murmurs, 'Your chameleon child notices *everything,* Izabel.'

'Oh, sweetheart. A long time ago I thought Lucy had done me a great wrong. I was mistaken but I wasn't sure if she'd want me to hug her now.'

'What did you think she'd done?' says Nancy.

'Well ... someone I loved died. She was the nurse and I was angry with her. But he died of influenza, so it wasn't her fault.'

'Do you still love that man?'

I smile. 'Thank God, no. I only love Laurence, your father.'

Nancy says quietly, 'But he is gone, *Ah-ba* is gone. One day you should love someone else.'

'Oh, darling. There'll never be anyone else for me.' My eyes sting.

She takes my hand. 'Don't cry, Ah-me.'

'I won't. Now go and wash and I'll come down soon and tuck you in.'

After she leaves Eliza laughs softly. 'She's like a small human radio receiver.'

'She was always that sensitive, even before Shanghai. I hope it's never a burden to her.'

'Does she know what really happened to her father?'

I nod. 'I worried about telling her but did in the end, very carefully. Death should be honoured with the truth. She should know it was human agency that overturned her life, not random misfortune.'

'That's a good way to think of it, Izabel. And *have* you forgiven Lucy?'

I gaze at Eliza. 'God, yes. Since Laurence, no other man is worth a moment's thought.'

'But Nancy's right. Laurence is gone. You *should* love again.'

'Perhaps, but I doubt I will. In any case, have you forgotten I'm still Mrs Felix Malory?'

'No, and hardly likely to, either.'

'Oh, Eliza. That *stupid* man. He's blocking you from work, isn't he?'

She looks at me, surprised. 'How did you know?'

'We've been married for quite a while, darling. Harry used to say Felix was irrational because of shellshock from the Great War, but I think he just likes being a complete swine.'

Our next stop is red, dusty Port Hedland. We stay on board, relaxing in a cool part of the deck while Nancy reads her *Girls' Own Annual*.

Eliza gazes seawards, shading her eyes. 'I can see the sandbar out there. I heard *Koombana* forded it easily, so she probably wasn't in ballast.'

I'm feeling lazy. 'Sorry, darling, you'll have to translate.'

'The crew would have emptied the ballast tanks, planning to fill them at sea.'

'You're still being wilfully obscure, Eliza.'

'Well, without that ballast *Koombana* didn't stand a chance in the cyclone.'

'Oh, the *cyclone*!' I sigh. 'Sorry, I'm an idiot.'

'Why are you an idiot, *Ah-me*?'

There's a silence, then Eliza says, 'When I was much smaller than you, Nancy, my father Sam died when the ship *Koombana* was lost in a cyclone.'

'Your *father* died?' asks Nancy, blinking. 'So neither you nor I have fathers.'

'That's odd, your mother doesn't either.' Eliza looks up at me. 'Oh dear, have I put my foot in it?'

'No, no,' I say, recovering. 'I haven't actually mentioned it before. Ancient history.'

'*Tell* me,' says Nancy, her eyes large. I take her onto my lap and hold her tense body.

'It's true, sweetheart,' I say. 'My father died of a fever when I was two. But I didn't know him, not the way you knew *Ah-ba*. All I had of him was a porcelain-faced doll he gave me. I used to pretend I could remember him, but of course I couldn't. I only knew his face from a photograph.'

'What did he look like, *Ah-me*?'

'Oh, he had a high forehead, noble dark eyes, a big, *fierce* moustache.' Nancy smiles a little. 'He was Portuguese and he married your grandmother Min-lu and had my sister Filipa and me.'

'What was his name?'

'Leo. Leo Peres.'

'Leo? That means *lion* doesn't it? And Singapore is the Lion City.'

I'm charmed by her butterfly mind. 'Yes, that's so.'

'What happened to your doll, *Ah-me*?'

'My sister threw it in the fire — I was very cross with her.'

'Are you still cross?'

'Not quite sure, darling. Anyway, you'll meet Filipa in Perth. She's rather fond of horses.'

'I like horses too, so we might be friends.'

'I hope so. Filipa is — complicated.' Eliza and I exchange smiles.

'Perhaps one day Aunt Eliza will have a little baby and she can call *him* Leo,' says Nancy, her body relaxed again, curved against my heart.

I hear the faintest intake of breath from Eliza.

Nancy sits up, anxious again. 'I'm sorry. What did I say?'

Eliza shakes her head. 'No, no, darling. It was nothing you said, truly. Please don't ... I'm just tired. I'll see you both in the morning.'

Going south, the small brown ports become greener. Soon we're sailing past familiar sandhills, long Rottnest Island out on the horizon, and into Fremantle port. I think, my goodness, how many times have I sailed in and out of this harbour?

I feel an odd pressure in my chest. I'm surprised to realise it's almost happiness. On the wharf below is Eliza's mother, pretty Rosa, and her husband (third, I think), white-bearded, kindly Anton, an artist as single-minded as Rosa herself.

Beside them is the small dear figure of my mother, and a couple I don't recognise. Then I do: Filipa's husband Eric Barratt, leaning on a stick and — I can hardly believe my eyes — my older sister Filipa.

It's been twenty-one years. Perhaps I've changed as much too.

After Customs, luggage and greetings, we squeeze into Eric and Filipa's car and drive to Victoria Park; to the house I've known since childhood, since my mother and Rosa bought it together before the Great War.

It's not far from the Swan River and overlooks a green reserve, shady beneath great Moreton Bay figs. Light gleams through coloured glass around the doors and lace curtains billow in the breeze.

I know Eliza and Pete love the old house — it's where they grew up, playing in boats on the river (Eliza) and dreaming of Sopwith Camels (Pete) — but I carelessly left it behind for the glamour of London without a glance. What a fool I was.

We arrange to have dinner this evening with Filipa and Eric, then they leave. Rosa and Anton return to their studio, Nancy takes a nap, and Eliza and I sit down to tea with Min-lu. I'd thought my mother unchanged when we met, but now I see her hair is completely white, her back no longer straight — soon she'll be eighty.

Then I'm pleased to discover her mind is as sharp as ever. 'I suppose, on the ship, you didn't hear about the Tripartite Pact?' she says.

Eliza's cup and saucer rattle slightly as she puts it down. 'Oh dear God, it's happened.'

'Tri —?' I say.

'The alliance — Germany, Italy and Japan,' Eliza says. 'We've been expecting it for ages.'

My mother nods. 'Quite an eventful time lately. French Indochina has fallen too.'

'*Fallen?*' says Eliza.

'The Japanese invaded, claiming they had to prevent arms getting to China via the Hanoi railway. The French government acquiesced within days.'

'Damned Vichy collaborators,' says Eliza. 'Of *course* they would.'

'Now the Japanese can station their soldiers anywhere in Indochina, do whatever they like.'

'So they've taken a few steps closer to Singapore,' Eliza says. 'And bloody *Felix* ...'

'What *has* that awful man done now?' says Min-lu.

I say, 'He's blocking Eliza from doing any serious work at the Bureau. You know.'

Through her old friendships my mother does indeed know rather a lot about the work Felix and Eliza do.

'That silly, *obstructive* ...' Min-lu sighs, and we nod.

I'd assumed Filipa's rural life would have turned her into a meat-and-two-veg sort of cook but she surprises me, and I compliment her Chinese banquet.

She's been sharp-tongued with me all evening, and now says, 'We may not be as *sophisticated* as the places you grace with your presence, Izabel, but I still know how to do a fine Hakka meal. Mummy always made certain of that.'

My mother's smile is a little strained. 'Perhaps Eric should get credit too — he loves good food.'

'Certainly do,' says Eric. He pats his belly, smiling.

He and his wife are far from overweight but they're well-padded, and I'm still finding it difficult to reconcile Filipa with my memories.

Once she was the essence of beauty, but now her porcelain cheeks are leathery, her face bitter, her raven curls cropped and grey.

As she sets out the coffee-cups she says, 'And where's that husband of yours, the dashing *barrister beau*? I was so looking forward to meeting the famous Felix at last.'

'Dear God, Filipa, no one's called him that for years,' I say, taken aback.

She shrugs. 'Sorry. I suppose we're just not in the know like you society folk.'

'He's busy,' I say awkwardly. 'Not much interested in relatives and horse-farms and the like.'

'This is a nationally-famous *racing stud*, Izabel,' says Filipa, her lips tight. 'And I expect it brings in a prettier penny than — oh, I don't know — an out-of-work *actress* might ever see.'

Eliza asks quickly, 'Have you had many foals born so far this spring?'

'Oh yeah, some nice ones,' says Eric. 'You like foals, Nancy?'

'Yes,' she says, her head down.

'I'm not trying to be an actress any more, Filipa,' I say. 'I teach children —'

'Oh, *indeed*. Speaking of children, Izabel,' my sister says, her nostrils white, 'your little girl is a little older than I expected. Born *before* the marriage, was she, and conveniently covered up? Not much like your English husband either, is she?'

'She's not Felix's daughter.' I manage to stop my voice shaking.

'*Slut*,' says Filipa, her arms over her belly. 'You'd do *anything* to get a child, wouldn't you, even foist your bastard on your husband?'

'Filipa, stop this *immediately*!' says my mother.

'But you know I adopted Nancy,' I say, bewildered. 'Her father died, with our uncle, remember?'

'*Adopted*? Mysterious car crash? What codswallop! I never believed a word of it.' Filipa turns to Min-lu. 'I don't care what you say, Mummy, it's a pack of lies. Do you know how I know? Because Izabel's a liar, she always *has* been!'

Nancy suddenly stands, her chair clattering to the floor, and shrieks, 'She's *not* a liar! And you threw her *doll* in the fire! How *could* you?'

Later, lying in bed, I furiously think of the taunts I could have flung back at Filipa, but suddenly I feel pity too.

In Asia the Eurasians have their own grudgingly respected social group. There they have each other, but here Filipa has always stood alone, confronting that cold-eyed Australian racism that sees only her Chinese heritage and dismisses it. And her.

Eric's wealthy pastoralist family were bitterly opposed to them marrying, and afterwards they pressured him not to bring a part-Asian child into their 'respectable' lives. I don't know how this has affected their marriage, but my sister has certainly never had the children she always yearned for.

And when she speaks of Nancy her voice is ragged with loss and her eyes dark with longing.

Next day Filipa visits me when the others have gone for a walk: I assume they've colluded but I'm too tired after a restless night to care.

My sister sniffs. 'Just wanted to say … ah, sorry. Probably a bit too much to drink.'

'You only had one glass.'

Silence.

Wondering how honest she'll be, I ask, 'Why didn't you ever have a child yourself, Filipa?'

'Me? Oh, much too busy. Time passes, and then …'

More silence.

Her mouth is a harsh line. 'Actually, we knew it'd cause more trouble than it was worth with Eric's family.'

'And you regret it?'

'A little.' She laughs shortly. 'Well, rather more than a little.'

I say, 'Last night — you know perfectly well I can't have children because of a miscarriage. *Within* my marriage to Felix, I might add.'

She nods. 'I know. I was only being … horrible.' She gazes at me. 'And I do understand you need to be discreet about Bao-lim and China, especially nowadays.'

I nod. 'He died. Nancy's father died, which is all that matters. Out of that I was granted the gift of Nancy, but dear *God*, what I'd give for it not to have happened.'

'You realise I envy you the child. I suppose you could see how much.'

'Yes. Once I cooled down.'

'Sorry. Again.' After a moment she says, 'But what on earth was Nancy saying about a doll?'

'I told her you'd thrown my doll in the fire. Which you did.'

'*Did* I?'

'The one Papa gave me before he died.'

'Oh, *that* stupid thing. Look Izabel, all your life you've said you remember Papa, but it's *me* that remembers him, not you. You've *always* told lies like that and I hate it.'

'You're right. I only wanted to believe I could.'

She stares at me in surprise.

'But you were such a *bully* to me, Filipa, all those years. It hurt terribly and I've never been able to forget that, either.'

There is a long silence.

Filipa says haltingly, 'You cannot imagine how bitterly — ashamed — I've felt for the way I treated you.' Her head is down. 'And you see, Izabel, given I was so unkind to you as a child, I wouldn't have made a very good mother in any case.'

Her cheeks are mottled, her hands clenched white. My heart twists with pity.

'Oh, *Fili* — you'd have made a *wonderful* mother! Everyone says how devoted you are to your animals.'

After a long time she whispers, 'I was so jealous, Bella, you see. He was *my* Papa until you came along, then I wasn't the baby any more. And he gave you that doll, that beautiful doll, and then he was dead and he never left me a doll. He never left me anything.'

'But Fili, it was so sudden! Of *course* Papa would have left you something if he'd been able to.'

'Do you really think that?' she says, her eyes hopeless.

'Without a doubt, darling.'

Another long silence.

Filipa rubs her cheeks quickly and says, 'Perhaps, ah, Nancy might want to have a look over the farm? She said she likes foals.'

'I'm sure she'd love nothing better.'

Filipa clears her throat. 'Mummy says you're very fond of our uncle's house in Hong Kong.' She shrugs. 'I've got no use for my half. Do you want to buy it?'

'I would, very much. I'm going back there one day.'

She sniffs. 'Good luck with that — the Japs may have other ideas. Full market price, of course.'

'Of course.' I hide my joy.

18. Toby: Every Pair of Hands

With Stefan posted to nearby Middle Wallop I hope we'll have a chance to repair our relationship. I also hope he'll have less flying to do than in London, but unfortunately the Southampton skies suddenly seem to be full of enemy planes and our few defenders.

But at last he gets a weekend off at the end of November 1940. It's noon and I've been busy buying food (as far as my ration book and the kinder shopkeepers will allow) and running around tidying the flat, when I hear the door open.

Stefan sets down a small bag and his blue cap, and stands there, smiling a little. 'Hullo, Toby. Good to see you.'

'Welcome home, Stef. Well, it's your place really, I'm just a visitor.' I'm foolishly nervous.

He gazes around. 'You've made it comfortable. Wouldn't have a cup of tea going by any chance?'

'Tea? I've secured a fine bottle of gin, and the tonic is chilled. Wouldn't you prefer that?'

'God, yes,' he says, grinning, and comes towards me. 'Toby.'

'My dear.' I meet him and take his hands, and we hug. His arms are thin and hard, like metal cables, and I can feel a tremor in them. 'Come and sit down. You look tired.'

'Ahh,' he says, relaxing on the sofa. 'Yes I am. It's only twenty miles, but it's a bloody slow bus from Middle Wallop.'

'Let me just ...' I go to the kitchen and pour us drinks, my hand shaking, then sit beside him. 'There. To your health, Stef. It's — extraordinary seeing you again.'

'And you, Toby. It's been such a long time. Good to see you're still the same, not changed like everything else in the world.'

'No, I'd never change, not where you're concerned.'

My throat tightens a little. Have I changed? Of course I have. As for him: well, *unfamiliar* barely comes near it. His hair is as dark, his eyes as green, his nose as straight as ever, but his brow is furrowed and the skin beneath his eyes is bruised. His mouth, bracketed by harsh lines, has a bitter twist I've never seen before.

'Oh God, Toby, it's all right, I know what I look like. We all look like this now.' Stef gulps his gin and puts down the glass. 'Can we go to bed? I have so little time and I've dreamt of this moment for a long time.' He shrugs. 'Well, imagined. Try not to dream, of course.'

In the bedroom I undress, hoping things will be fine — I'm probably just uncertain after so long apart — and we embrace. We lie down and kiss, but he becomes rough with me in a way I've never known before.

He's almost in a rage and suddenly he's hurting me, and I gasp in pain. He falters despite his frenzy, and lies back with a groan, covering his face with his hands.

I move away, staring in shock. He's weeping but I don't turn and hold him. After a time he starts to lightly snore and I get up. I dress and sit at the kitchen table drinking tea in the cold afternoon.

I touch the small half-healed burns on my hands and wonder what the night will bring.

In mid-November, two weeks ago, the town of Coventry suffered a devastating attack, and the famous old cathedral and thousands of homes were obliterated in a firestorm of incendiaries and explosives.

After that the Germans threatened to 'Coventrate' the whole country and, along with every other fireman in Britain, I feel afraid. Still, the locals know what to do when the sirens sound; the blackout has become familiar, no longer a hindrance.

For some it's even an opportunity — the propositions I've had in the dark from randy men in uniform would amaze the service chiefs, convinced their chaps would never do something so *unmanly*. Absurd really, queer sex is about as manly as you can get.

Years ago Stef and I agreed that physical monogamy wasn't as important as spiritual fidelity in our relationship. 'The flesh is so delightfully weak,' Stef would say, smiling.

I've actually had no difficulty with temptation lately, but that may be because of my other concerns. It's our turn again in the series of raids the Germans have named *Moonlight Sonata*.

The locals call it the Southampton Blitz.

It began on the evening of 17th November and continued relentlessly until dawn. It was a Sunday so everyone was at home, which would have been a good thing except the bombs missed the docks and destroyed the residential districts.

Birmingham took the brunt for the next few days, then a week ago, on Saturday night, the bombers returned to us. People were enjoying a few moments of leisure in the pubs and dance-halls and cinemas, when fire began falling from the sky.

The bombers came over in waves — Berlin radio said two hundred and fifty planes. The first lot dropped flares, oil bombs and thousands of incendiaries, and the night turned blood-red.

Then came the high explosives. They destroyed the water mains so we had to pump from the back-up tanks. When they were empty, we pumped from puddles in the craters left by previous bombs.

After that, we had to stand by helplessly and watch as flames consumed swathes of the town. The Germans boasted the fire-glow could be seen from France, and that was easy to believe.

That raid stopped at midnight. Dressing our injuries back at the station, stumbling with exhaustion, there was a final blow: five of our firemen were 'missing' — two of them men I knew well. Next day the papers said, as one voice:

> Enemy planes were almost constantly above a locality on the south coast for some hours last night. Three waves flew over a town and damaged houses, two schools, a cycle store, a doctor's surgery and a furniture store.

A cycle store, a *locality*! Censorship in action: we had to listen to Berlin to find out what had really happened.

Other towns were also left in states of chaos that could hardly go unnoticed and, after much criticism, the censors admitted 'the provincial towns bombed in England were Birmingham, Bristol and Southampton. Extensive damage was done.'

Indeed it was. Seventy-seven people died here that night, and three hundred are in hospital. Others are still missing, one of them a disabled boy who couldn't get out of bed. I don't know why, but that seems particularly cruel.

Now it's Saturday again and the Germans are creatures of habit.

I hear Stef getting dressed. He comes out to the kitchen in his shirtsleeves, puts the kettle on, then stands at the window with his back to me.

'I'm sorry, Toby,' he says. 'I don't know what happened, why I did that. I have no idea, actually, why I do anything now.'

He makes a pot of tea and sits at the table, then silence falls.

Stef takes a deep breath. 'Toby, I fell in love.'

I stare at him, astonished. I have no idea what I'd expected, but certainly not that.

'She was working in the radio section —'

'*She*?'

He shrugs. 'You know I've always been attracted to both —'

'I know *that* well enough. But love?' I gasp in a wave of anguish.

'I don't know how, you're everything to me, Toby. But I've been ...' He rubs his eye-sockets. 'Trying not to notice friends haven't returned. Pretending to be unconcerned. The lads say "tally-ho, old chaps". Tally-fucking-*ho*?' He half-sobs. 'The concentration, the terror. When I have a kill my heart almost bursts and I'm a shambles afterwards.'

'Yes. I've come to appreciate perfectly well what fear can do, Stef.' I'm trying to keep the bitterness out of my voice. 'You needed a fuck.'

He shakes his head slightly. 'No. It was love.'

'Don't give me that bullshit.' My voice is shaking. '*Love*? With some little tottie?'

'She was so gentle. Her brother had been killed, she was devastated, and yesterday I heard —'

'Spare me the *details*, for God's sake.' I stand up, the chair screeching on the floor. 'I have to get to the fire station. Tonight's probably —'

Outside the warning sirens start their eerie rising moan, and I grab my coat and scarf.

'Let me come too,' Stef says.

'*No*, damn you!'
He pulls on his coat and follows me through the door.

Is there a limit to what one can comprehend? Or not so much comprehend, as be forced to face before going mad? I suppose I'll find out, one way or the other.

Despite the horrors I'm now seeing on a regular basis, I'm oddly haunted by the scalded Civic Centre girls and the missing disabled boy. Is it because they were children?

I'm hardly sentimental and certainly don't yearn for some golden infancy — quite the opposite in fact — but perhaps it's something primeval in us to care most for the smallest, the weakest.

And — I'm ashamed to admit — it's only recently I've realised that everyone is an "I" to themselves, the still centre of their own world. Well, of course I knew that, it's stupidly obvious, but I never *knew* it before, I never felt it as a stark, vital reality.

It hit me late one night. I was sitting on a bench at the fire station, my eyes stinging from smoke, watching the others hang up their helmets, wrestle off their boots, wearily pull on their jackets.

Some would sit down at even that small effort, their heads in their hands, and for a moment it was as if I knew them utterly, I became them, I *was* them. And then I wasn't.

It was just an instant's understanding, and I've tried and tried to grasp it again but it's an elusive thing: a knowing that can't be comprehended. Why should I be *this* "I", why shouldn't I be *that* one opening the cupboard, or that one putting on his shoes?

It reminds me of the way stories are usually told from a single point of view, the protagonist the teller of the tale and everyone else the Greek chorus around them. And of course, we always trust the protagonist will remain safe within a story. That's the convention, a compact with the reader.

But for every "I" who is quickly or slowly obliterated — by fire or water or illness or missile from the sky — there is no convention, no tidy salvation. No matter what each and every being yearns to create, or love, or witness, there is only the termination. The full stop.

If I ever write again, which at the moment I cannot quite imagine, I may try to express this. But I'd have to understand it in the first place, and that understanding eludes me like quicksilver.

Stef and I run along the dark streets, jumping through the rubble. The ack-ack guns are deafening and already flames are rising from the docks to the south. At the station Stef is welcome — anyone who can help is welcome.

Dispatch clerk Mavis tells us where we're needed, and we throw on our boots and helmets and fire-coats, jump onto the tanker and race towards the docks, thumping over broken roads, the bell clanging.

We stop halfway down a street where flames are roaring through the windows and roof of a warehouse. Old George, our unit leader, gives Stef a helmet and says, 'Don't get in anyone's way, laddie, and do what you're told.'

My heart is pounding madly but I probably seem as calm as everyone else, despite the heat and searing flames. George tells us where to set up, and quickly, efficiently, we unroll the coils of canvas-covered hose and couple the sections together.

The man at the rear of the tank truck waits for a signal then turns the hand-wheel, and water starts wriggling towards the nozzle, where two men are waiting for the kick of the high-pressure stream.

Sometimes we're lucky enough to have a railing or beam to tie the nozzle to — keeping it trained at the right spot against that pounding pressure is exhausting — but more often it has to be held, hour after aching hour. That's if the water holds out, of course.

The good thing about fire at the docks is the proximity of the harbour for our pumps, and the presence of fireboats that can work their hoses from a safe distance. The bad thing about fire at the docks is the many, many ships loaded with munitions, here at the largest wartime port in Britain.

Wave after wave of planes pass overhead, and the crump of explosions near and far rises above the raging of the fire. Christ, this is worse than last week. I wipe my face and taste soot and salt, and just keep going.

After an hour or so we seem to be getting the upper hand, and George tells Stef to run to the unit in the next street to see how they're coping. Stef dashes back, leaping rubble and broken glass, and yells they need us there urgently.

We pack up and move, and work all night long. At dawn, reinforcements arrive from Portsmouth and Winchester, so we wearily decouple and roll up the hoses, and climb onto the tanker.

We're damp and chilled through from hose leaks and spray and sweat. The truck takes slow detours past bomb craters to get us back to the station, then George tells us to go home for a rest.

Stef and I trudge through the early morning streets, our eyes stinging, the air foggy with smoke. The sheer tonnage of explosives dropped last night beggars belief.

Glass crunches underfoot and I'm only slightly surprised to see that buildings which were whole yesterday are smouldering ruins, while the half-destroyed Civic Centre is now completely flattened.

At home I send Stef to have a shower while I sit, my mind jangling and empty. As I take my own shower he makes us breakfast.

'Sorry you came with me now?' I say as we eat. 'It was a rough night.'

'Not sorry, but God, I'm tired,' says Stef. 'Flying's hard too, but at least you breathe fresh air and you only get burnt if you're unlucky.'

'Speaking of which …' I go to the sideboard and open my first aid kit. 'Show me the damage.'

I put salve on his superficial burns and notice he also has a small, deep wound on the side of his hand. I dab it with iodine and dress it with plaster.

'Ow. Didn't bloody hurt till you started mucking about with it.'

'That's because it's a serious burn, Stef. If it doesn't hurt it means the nerves are damaged.'

'But it's so small. Hit it on a burning splinter when I was running to the next street.'

'Thank God it's small,' I say. 'Hands can't take much damage.'

'I'll wear gloves next time.'

'There won't be a next time. You'll be back at Middle Wallop.'

There's a silence, then he says, 'Toby, can we start all over again?'

'I expect your signals hussy might rather object to that.'

He slowly shakes his head. 'Not really. You see, she died. Poor girl tripped in the blackout and hit her head, a pathetic, fucking *accident*. They told me when I landed yesterday. No, yesterday was the fire, wasn't it? Day before ... maybe that's why I was so stupid ... Sorry.'

He can hardly speak for tiredness.

'Come on, we need rest,' I say. 'I'm back on duty soon.'

We lie in bed clothed, too tired to undress and too wary of what undressing might mean. After a few moments I sigh and turn to him, and put my arms around him. He sobs for a few moments, then sleep takes us both.

We wake at noon nestled warmly together. I feel content and Stef's face is eased. Over tea I say, 'Look — while we're in the mood for confessions there's something I should tell you.'

'A randy bosun in the blackout? Wouldn't blame you in the slightest, my dear.'

I smile. 'Sadly, no. Something I should have told you ages ago. Can hardly even recall why it used to matter, but it's always been there. A lie in our relationship.'

He gazes curiously at me.

'Remember at school I'd say I was an orphan? That my only relatives were Aunt Maude and her posh banker husband?'

Stef laughs. 'You mean he wasn't posh, a banker or her husband?'

'No, the fact is ... I wasn't an orphan. Yes, my mother died when I was small, but my father was not the deceased barrister, Alfred Fenn of Lincoln's Inn — he was the all-too-alive butcher, Chopper Fenn of Northam.'

'Good God, *Northam*? You mean you're a local lad and you've never said a word? Why?'

'You know why. A slum butcher's son would have been cast out at school. Your parents wouldn't have wanted me around you either.'

He shrugs. 'My mother always adored you, but you're right about school, they were utter shits. Still, I don't understand why you didn't tell *me*, Toby. I'd have understood.'

That stings. 'Really? All those years you were fucking every other boy — *and* girl — we knew? I mattered that much?'

'No. I was a fool then. It took me too long to realise I loved you —'

'Until some signals floozy came your way.'

'It was the comfort, Toby. We spoke the same language. Every day she'd be on the radio to some boy in a crippled plane, talking him home. Or not. It was a brutal job.'

'We all do brutal jobs now, Stef.'

He's silent for a time. 'Why tell me after so long?'

'Bloody Pete found out, and now he frogmarches me over to Northam every fortnight to see the old sod and his lady-friend Edie.'

'Is that so bad? We all need our families.'

'I don't need some ignorant bigot, thank you very much. My father not only hates queers, he used to be a Jew-hating Moseley supporter too. Whenever I'm there I think of harassed, hardworking Klara and just want to punch him in the nose.'

'All right, perhaps not family like that.' Stef puts our cups in the sink, then turns. 'I still want to try, Toby. I still want you. When all this is over we can be happy, I'm certain.'

After I time I say, 'Perhaps. Day by day, the great wartime cliché.' I stand up. 'Look, I must get back to the station. Lately they've started returning the night after a bombing to finish the job once and for all — *doppelgänger* raids.'

I stand up and pull on my coat. 'Remember our Classics teacher who'd go into ecstasies over the sheer beauty of the German language? The culture, the philosophy? The fucking *civilisation*?'

Stef laughs. 'I'll come, don't have to report back till late tomorrow.'

'All right,' I say. 'Every pair of hands helps.'

After a long night, as we're rolling up the hoses in the early hours, a girl dispatch rider halts her motorcycle with a screech and passes a message to old George.

We're ordered to another fire. I've never seen anything like it, as we join the other units desperately trying to stop it spreading. At dawn, clouds of smoke are still roiling in the heat-shimmered air, and I wearily notice our reinforcements turning up, this lot from London.

Then I hear a noise, an eerie groan, distinct above the usual crashings and grindings and screechings. I remember old George saying something like that could mean bricks are coming down. I glance around but I'm safe, as safe as any of us ever are.

But Stef? Where's Stef — oh Christ, *behind* —

'*Watch out!*' Old George grabs Stef's arm.

They run and stumble and fall, as a solid inferno bulges and opens and descends around them. I dash with the others and we grab them and drag them away from the glowing rubble.

Slowly, they both sit up and I think, Dear God, he's all right.

George coughs. 'Enough, lads, we're fine.'

He gingerly stands and offers his hand to Stef, who laughs ruefully. 'Better not. Lost my gloves. Bit of a mess.'

Someone lifts him onto his feet from behind. Stef is holding out his arms and I see the shock kick in and he starts to shake. Or perhaps it's me that's shaking.

In the carbon black and seeping red of his palms I can see the whiteness of bone.

Every pair of hands helps.

'Don't worry, Toby,' he says, slurring. 'Doesn't hurt.'

19. Billie: Initiation

I first met Stef when we were both flying at Hamble. He's a fine pilot, and to think of him disabled in such a freak accident is horrible. Poor Toby can't forgive himself for letting him go along that night, but Stef always says, 'You couldn't have stopped me, my dear.'

He's in the burns unit at the plastic surgery hospital at East Grinstead. Most of the other patients in his ward are pilots too, and Stef sometimes laughs and calls himself a complete fraud for having been injured on the ground.

When he can laugh, that is. He's been through dozens of operations over the last six months. He's regained some use of his left hand, but his right is a pink-scarred claw.

At least it's not amputated, as was possible at one stage. He jokes about one day flying a mahogany Spitfire for the RAF — a desk — but even a penpusher's job will be beyond him for a long time yet.

The hospital is about thirty miles south of London, so Toby moved there and now works for the local Fire Service. He's not as busy as he was in Southampton because suddenly, in the middle of 1941, the Luftwaffe attacks have eased. No one knows why.

Despite the pause we still need planes, and every new machine must be ferried by the Air Transport Auxiliary to a maintenance airfield, for fit-out with radios, navigation instruments and weaponry.

The ATA pilots themselves don't have any such luxuries, they simply deliver planes through fog and storm and snow from one end of the country to the other, with little more than an old roadmap on their knees for guidance.

The ATA doesn't just use women pilots, of course. There are perhaps seven times as many men, mainly those unable to join the RAF because of age or disability: famously there are several one-armed male flyers.

And me? Of course I couldn't keep my head in the sand any longer, not after Stef, so earlier this year I applied to join the Air Transport

Auxiliary. Despite Pauline Gower's encouragement it was hardly a done deal and, like all applicants, I had to be assessed at headquarters, White Waltham.

The first time I went up — the first time since Spain, more than three years ago — it was in an old training Moth, a plane as familiar as my own body. Still, I could hardly breathe and on landing I braked too quickly and nearly flipped over: a neophyte mistake.

I sat sweating in shame but the instructor just told me to go up again. The second time was better, and after a week or so most of my old skills returned.

I'm in the women's unit, Ferry Pilot Pool no. 5 at Hatfield, north of London. We're billeted in the town in spartan conditions, but I'm used to that. I'm less used to the required discipline, but I keep my head down and do what I'm told (which amazes Pete).

I even make friends among the other women pilots, something I didn't expect. We joke that ATA means *Ancient and Tattered Airmen* or *Always Terrified Airwomen*, but really, *Anything To Anywhere* just about sums it up.

I spend my early months of service delivering a variety of small training planes to sites all over the country, and enjoy it despite the hard work and long days.

After a couple of months some of us are sent to the RAF Central Flying School for conversion to advanced trainers, like the twin-engined Airspeed Oxford. The Oxford first flew while I was in Spain so it's new to me, but it's still a lot of fun.

One summer evening, after ferrying a Leopard Moth to a unit near Birmingham, I return to Hatfield with five other pilots in the Anson we use as a taxi. When we land we hear the amazing news: a group of senior women were tested on Hurricanes today and they all passed.

Operational kites at last!

And with that barrier breached, our training accelerates on all types of planes. It's just a matter of weeks before some of our pilots are delivering Spitfires, and when they speak of it their eyes shine and their lips part as if they're thinking of a lover.

On 22 June 1941 we discover why the Luftwaffe has been easing back on the Blitz. The Nazis have turned their forces east to attack the Russians, despite the pact between them that triggered this vile war.

Perhaps the Germans believe the Soviets will be beaten easily because tiny Finland held them off for so long, but whether the move is guile or madness, at least the pressure is off us for now.

The Finns themselves have just signed their own pact with the Nazis, hoping to get back the lands they lost to the Russians. Poor Klara is broken-hearted. Her 'gallant little Finland' has joined the Fascist Axis, and Sophia tells us that orchestras now refuse to play the rousing anthem of *Finlandia*.

Because of work I don't see much of them both, but I spend time with Stef when I can, despite the long slow train ride to East Grinstead. That's odd, because our friendship was always based more upon his flying skills, not his sterling personal qualities.

When my friend Lizzie became involved with Stef in the beautiful summer of 1935, I was as taken with his extraordinary charm as anyone else. But then I noticed the charm was more akin to wholesale flirting and wasn't very surprised when he dumped poor Lizzie and turned to Toby, who'd adored him hopelessly for years.

I didn't like Stef much then, but now I'm touched by his courage and love for Toby, who's distraught with guilt. One day, while Stef recovers from a harrowing procedure in the saline baths, Toby whispers in anguish, 'Of course I wanted him not to be flying, Billie, but not like *this*. It's all my fault.'

'Christ, Toby — you preferring Stef to be on solid ground didn't make the Nazis bomb Southampton.'

'But we'd just had an *argument*, you see, and perhaps he wasn't concentrating.'

'It was simple rotten bad luck, mate, as it is for all the poor bastards wounded in this stinking war,' I say. 'Come on, we're meeting Pete in half an hour. Chin up.'

'Chin *up*? My God, such upper-class cant from my wild colonial lass.'

'Well, most of the other ATA girls are horribly posh — they're practically royalty, or Daddy's a millionaire, or he runs the government, or all three.'

'What about famous Amy Johnson? She's working class.'

'But poor Amy's dead. She died bailing out over the Channel, ages before I joined the ATA.'

'Really?' Toby says. 'I *do* need to keep up with current affairs.'

I think for a moment. 'No, I'm being unfair — lately our pilots are all sorts and come from everywhere. Anna and Stefania are Polish, Jackie's from South Africa, Maureen from Argentina, and there's a bunch of Yanks and Canadians, a few Kiwis and a couple of other Australians.'

'Suppose it makes sense that the first lot were posh,' says Toby. 'You had to be rich to fly before the war. But that didn't seem to stop you. Little town outside Perth, wasn't it?'

'Yeah. Surprised you remember that.'

'Despite my tenuous grasp on current affairs, Miss Billie, I still study people, although I'm constantly reminded of how poorly I understand anyone.'

'Your famous *human condition*?'

He laughs. 'God, I used to be so pretentious. And don't you dare say I still am.'

'No, you're just a hardworking fireman in a fabulously well-fitting uniform. Come on, let's go, Pete's waiting for us at the pub.'

Whenever I can get leave for a couple of days I stay at the cottage Toby rents, halfway between the village and the hospital. He has two bicycles so I use his spare one to get around. I think he hopes Stef will ride it beside him one day.

The hospital's chief, Archibald McIndoe, is famous for his advances in burns surgery. He gets his patients living normally, and encourages the locals to perceive the brave people behind their deformities.

So I'm used to the pub regulars by now, with their false eyes and livid scars and missing digits, and those strange tubes of flesh called pedicles which carry blood from healthy tissue to new grafts.

As we enter the lounge I see Pete across the room and wave. It's odd: nearly seven years have passed since we parted, but my heart always seems to clench with some indefinable emotion whenever we meet.

Sometimes I wonder what it means: suppose it's just regret at lost hopes or wasted chances. But would we have been any happier if Pete hadn't got himself expelled from Hamble, if we'd set up our flying school together as we'd planned?

In that case he wouldn't have fallen for Charlotte or fathered Vivian, and it's hard to imagine a world without that small wise presence. I wouldn't have joined the aerial circus and met Wilf and gone to Spain. Or lost Wilf because of Spain.

Of course Pete might still have ended up building Spitfires and I might still have joined the ATA, but yet I puzzle: where would we be, *who* would we be, without that long-ago rift between us?

'Got you both pints,' says Pete as we reach his table and sit down.

'Pete, I've told you I *never* —' says Toby. 'Oh, you cheeky sod.'

'You're such a sophisticate, Toby. Here you are, gin and tonic. Billie, on the other hand —'

'I'm a sophisticate too, you bastard.'

'Don't want this very nice whisky then?'

I laugh. 'Hand it over. How are you, anyway? Easy drive up?'

'Not too bad. Hard to get fuel, but after seeing Stef tomorrow I'm going to some meetings in London, so it all worked out. How's our boy doing?'

Toby takes a slug of his drink. 'Don't know. Two steps forward and then — well.'

'Come on, you old pessimist,' I say. 'He's made great progress lately.'

'Of course,' says Toby. 'But still so far to go, and then what? The prospect of leaving the RAF is breaking his heart.'

Pete says bleakly, 'Well, hearts are breaking on a daily basis everywhere, old mate.'

Toby raises an eyebrow. 'You all right, Farmer Pete?'

'Yeah. Tired, that's all.'

'How's the lovely Mrs McKee?' Toby says. 'I suppose you'll have a chance to take her out to dinner in London tomorrow.'

Pete nods briefly, and finishes his drink. 'Another?'

'Why not?' I say. 'We can all totter merrily back to the cottage later.'

But the air raid sirens start up and Toby has to rush to the fire station, saying he'll see us at home. Eventually the warning turns out to be a false alarm: we hear the droning of planes but they pass, and the silence in the pub becomes a babble of relief.

'Heard something interesting the other day,' says Pete over our next drink. 'Completely confidential though, Billie.'

'Okay. What?'

'Of course you know we need to get the new Spits away from the factories as fast as possible, they're too vulnerable on the ground. So Hamble's being expanded to help out — they're going to relocate the men and start up a new *women's* ferry pool.'

'At Hamble.'

'Yeah. It's already a major repair centre — remember the big hangar? Full of shot-up Spits being fixed by Air Services Training now.'

'I remember the hangar,' I say. 'Vividly. So?'

'Well — doesn't the idea of Hamble interest you?'

'Not much. Anyway, I'm not trained for Spits, and God knows when that'll happen.'

He laughs. 'They won't waste you. You'll be flying them soon enough. And then?'

'Look, Pete, I'll go where they tell me to go. If it's Hamble —' I shrug. 'Don't have to like it.'

He's quiet for a time, then says, 'You're still *that* bitter?'

'Bitter? I'm not ... Christ, it's ancient history.'

'How often must I *apologise*, Billie? Wasn't just your dreams came a cropper, and you've still had a flying career. It all ended for me, right there and then.'

'An aerial circus? A fucking civil war? A *career*? Jesus, Pete, we had one chance to set up the flying school, and if you'd drawn up a blueprint you couldn't have screwed me over more.'

'Billie, I've bloody *paid*.' His nostrils are white. 'At least you've still got your self-respect. If there's a single area of my life I haven't fucked up I'd be interested to know what it is.'

I realise he's serious, and bite back whatever I was going to say next. A few heads have turned our way and I say, 'Look, we can't talk here, let's get back to Toby's. He's probably home by now and wondering where we are.'

I push the bike and we walk in silence along the road. It's a summer evening, the twilight dusty-rose on the horizon. Stars appear and I stop to gaze. After a time I sigh.

'Shouldn't argue like this, mate. Of course we've suffered, but it doesn't compare for a moment with what's happened to people like Stef and Toby.'

'Yeah. Look, Billie, I'm sorry.'

I shake my head. 'Don't say that. Maybe we were just going different ways in any case — you wanted marriage and kids, and you knew quite well I didn't.'

'You married Wilf.'

'On his *death-bed*, you drongo.'

After a pause Pete says, 'So do you call yourself Mrs Bettany, then?'

'Never have. Technically my name, though I doubt anyone remembers.' I stop, exhausted, my shoulders slumped. 'I don't *want* this, Pete. Don't want to fight. Makes me feel sick.'

To my horror my eyes fill with helpless tears and I cover my face with my hands and — of course — let go of the bike and it falls over. I rub my face and Pete helps pick it up and the stupid moment of weakness passes. We carry on.

I clear my throat. 'You haven't made a mess of young Vivy, at least. And Charlotte's almost human nowadays — surely you can take credit for that.'

He laughs. 'Nah, she came into her own once she left me.'

'*Has* she left you?'

'Pretty much. Certainly haven't been lovers since the miscarriage. Now she tells me she's going to have surgery so she can't ever get pregnant again. Most doctors won't do that for a married woman, but she's heard of someone.'

'Oh, Pete. And you wanted more kids.'

'Yeah, but it doesn't seem very important any more.'

We're almost at Toby's house, but it looks as if he's not home yet. There's just enough twilight to find the key under the mat and unlock the door. I pull down the blinds and switch on the lights while Pete stokes the embers of the small fire.

'Tea?' I call out from the kitchen. I put the kettle on the stove and gaze at the blue flame, my mind empty and calm.

Pete comes into the room, the rather small room, and stands just behind me. Sensing him there, my thighs flare with pleasure and I hear his breathing catch.

He moves closer and touches my shoulders and his face is close to mine and I'm weak with desire. I half-turn, yearning, and oh, the scent of his *skin* —

'Kettle on?' Toby calls out from the front door. 'Yes, *please*. Nothing happening tonight after all.' He comes into the kitchen. 'Here, I've got fresh milk in the larder. Goodness, it's lovely to be home with friends.'

After Pete visits Stef next morning, he drives me to London to get the train back to Hatfield. We chat politely all the way, then he stops to let me out.

'Right,' I say. 'Thanks for the lift. Have fun at your meetings.'

He puts his hand on mine. 'Billie?'

'No, Pete. You can't just slot me back into your life now Charlotte's not there.'

'That's not what — *Billie!*' I've half-opened the door.

'Come on, mate,' I say, feeling hopeless. 'Of course there's still something between us, but there's too much pain as well. It'd be a disaster. Look, you're a stubborn bastard, stuck in your ways, and we both know that'll never change. Sorry. Got to go.'

'What do you mean *stubborn*?'

'Oh, Christ. You're asking me that now?'

'Yeah. Spit it out, Billie.'

I turn back to him. 'Okay. You know the reason, the *real* reason you bombed out at Hamble? You cannot bear instruction. You cannot *bear* someone explaining what you should do or how you should do it.'

'You mean that mechanics instructor I had the blow-up with? He was an idiot.'

'No he wasn't, and nor was the navigation tutor either. You *have* got a chip on your shoulder and it makes you bloody inflexible.'

'Inflexible? Exactly *how*? Come on. Do enlighten me.'

'Well, putting aside the many instances of highly-trained professionals you consider fools, here's something really trivial. As long as you've known me, Pete, what do I love doing most?'

'Covers a lot of territory, honey.'

'I'm serious. No idea? Dancing, Pete. *Dancing*. On the ship coming to England, what did you do? You sat and glared at anyone who danced with me. Did you ever ask me yourself?'

'Once or twice.'

'*Once*. And you couldn't stand it. You ran away as soon as you could.'

He shrugs. 'Don't like it, that's all.'

'Why? Too revealing? Too enjoyable?'

'Dunno. Usually feels like everyone's laughing at me and I don't get the joke.'

'The joke is on you for losing something we could have had together, Pete, not wanting to share what I love. But I wasn't enough for you.'

'I was faithful! I didn't get involved with Charlotte till after we'd broken up.'

'Yeah. Perhaps it was more how we broke up. Flying a plane — *drunk* — you weren't even *qualified* for?'

He closes his eyes. 'It happened. But my feelings never changed, Billie. I still —'

'No you bloody *don't*.'

I jump out and grab my case from the back seat. Pete gazes at me, then puts the car into gear and drives away.

When I get back to Hatfield, Pauline Gower calls me into her office.

'Hello, Billie. You look well, the weekend seems to have agreed with you.' (She must be mad.) 'Now, it's time we started using you properly. No more Moths, you're off to White Waltham next week with some of the girls. Conversion course to Class Two, single-engined fighters. Barracudas, Hurricanes —'

'Spitfires?' I say.

'Of course. And then you'll be going to our new women's unit at Hamble — Ferry Pool 15, with Margot Gore as Commander. They'll be flying everything, even Fortresses and Halifaxes, so a few of the senior women are already converting to Class Five.'

Back to bloody Hamble, but good news at least about Margot, we get on well. Dark-haired and funny, like me she laboured at odd jobs to pay for her flying lessons. But Class *Five*, four-engined heavy bombers? Holy hell.

I turn up at White Waltham, aware of how much I need to learn, and find out that the Class Two planes aren't so much a leap of knowledge as an entirely new world of experience. The first time I take off in a Spitfire I'm distractedly tense, but at least I don't come to grief.

Then they send me up again and this time I understand.

The small cockpit, cosy and intimate, wraps around me. The raw power of the Merlin engine intoxicates me, the controls are like my own hands, and the swooping responsiveness leaves me astonished. The Spit is everything people have said and more.

But they don't often say what it *feels* like: and to me it's as fierce, dark and sensual as a tango. I think of Wilf's beloved *inscape*, the beauty born of something that's uniquely, essentially itself, and I know he'd sit beside me if he could and laugh in sheer delight.

After the sixth circuit and bump I hand the plane over to another pilot for her own initiation. I walk to the pilots' sitting room and think for a long time. Then I go to the phone booth and ring Pete.

'Look, I'm sorry we argued. You were right. The Spit's magnificent. It's simply beyond — I have no words.'

He says quietly, 'I'll be in London tomorrow, Billie. Let's go out to dinner and talk. Properly.'

My body is tingling. It's been a year since Raymond-the-cellist, a year since I last bedded a man. Pete and I both know how much our argument revealed, how much we *must* leave behind us.

'Sorry, mate, can't,' I say. 'Another time.'

That evening I put on a dress and go to a bar in London. I pick up a naval commander, a nice married man, and we dance together for hours. Afterwards, at his hotel, we fuck each other into oblivion.

I leave at dawn, and gaze up at the pearlshell sky and smile.

I'll be flying a Spitfire again today.

20. Eliza: The Fall

The voyage to Perth did us all good. To everyone's amazement, Izabel and Filipa came to a truce after a lifetime of sniping — well, the sniping didn't stop, but it became better-humoured — and Filipa sold her share of their uncle's house to her sister.

It seems to mean a lot to Izabel, although I wonder when, or if, she'll ever return to Hong Kong. A most satisfactory excursion, I tell Harry the night we return.

He says he's just pleased to have me home: six weeks was far too long to be apart. I nod in contentment, my head against his warm, Harry-scented shoulder, and then we make love. Again.

I return to work in November 1940, and Felix says coldly, 'Word from Denniston. Seems to think you're up to the job. All hands on deck, I suppose.'

On my desk is a pleasingly large pile of files and the letter from Mr Denniston confirming my promotion to Senior Assistant, with Felix's angrily scrawled initials at the bottom.

Soon I'm immersed in analysis again. Among the stream of reports we receive of shipping losses, I feel a pang of sadness to read of *Killoran*'s sinking.

One of Gustaf Erikson's three-masters, she was carrying corn and sugar from Argentina to the Canary Islands when stopped by the disguised raider *Widder*. Although *Killoran* was from a neutral country, the Germans set time-bombs and blew up the forty-year old barque.

Through an intelligence contact I hear that an officer on *Widder* was making a propaganda film and wanted her destroyed for a dramatic ending. Poor *Killoran*. At least the crew were taken off safely, but they still had to spend time in a German prison camp.

That Christmas the celebrations in Singapore have a frenetic air. People seem to get drunk too quickly and their laughter has an edge of hysteria. Then early in the new year of 1941 we receive the terrible news from England of Stefan's accident. Harry says he'll get the best possible treatment at the East Grinstead burns unit, but it's sad being so far away from my friends at such a time.

Oddly, I haven't made many friends here, although I've got to know my workmates Quentin Baxter and Mr Kingsley much better than in London.

I like Izabel's neighbour Barbara well enough, but can't understand what she sees in Felix (despite the charm he displays when he wants to), especially after meeting her perfectly nice naval husband, Fred.

Izabel's calm acceptance of the affair between Felix and Barbara also puzzles me, but I know she fears for Nancy's future without Felix's protection; and witnessing the treatment of some of the Singapore Eurasians I can appreciate her caution. At least she's content in her work, and her acting studio, The Peres Academy, is very popular.

By February I've been in Singapore for over a year and consider myself acclimatised, so I'm surprised one day to realise how sick I feel. After an eternity of pain and sweating Harry diagnoses dengue fever, and I discover for myself why *breakbone* is so feared.

I don't remember much from that hallucinatory time except Harry's kindness. He nurses me, his sensitive, square hands wiping my face with a damp cloth, or easing my pillow, or loosening my sheets.

One evening I wake from a doze to see him sitting beneath the lamp, working through a pile of hospital documents, light glinting from his spectacles.

The dear man looks up and smiles, and I feel utter peace, knowing the contentment of loving and being loved.

Even when I recover from the dengue fever I'm still not strong. Since Harry is owed some leave we decide to take the opportunity to visit his family in Newcastle, NSW. It's an exciting prospect because I've never flown in an aeroplane before.

In April, we take off from Singapore Harbour in a big Empire flying boat that's been stripped down from its pre-war luxury. I'm nervous at first, then fascinated by the earth passing below.

We stop at a dozen places, sleeping overnight in Darwin and Brisbane. By the time we land on Sydney Harbour I feel like an old aviation hand, and can't wait to write to Billie about it.

At Sydney's Central Station we catch the train to Newcastle, one hundred miles north. We cross the broad green Hawksbury River and stop at all the little bush towns, and in the afternoon we steam into Newcastle Station, where Harry's mother Jessie and sister Tina are waiting for us.

We last met in England five years ago. Jessie was once a teacher, wry and observant, while Tina is a chatty young woman with strawberry blonde curls. They live in an old terrace house close to the beaches where Harry spent his youth.

Our room is comfortable and I quickly fall asleep in the mild evenings. After just a few days I feel stronger and Jessie takes us for walks on a long beach which leads out to a headland looming over the mouth of Newcastle's harbour.

'There's Nobbys Head,' she says in her soft Scottish accent. 'An island, but years ago they built a causeway out to it for the lighthouse. Now you cannot go to it, of course — they've put gun enclosures on the channel side to protect the steelworks.'

On the western horizon is a line of low blue mountains, and the town itself straggles over a steep hill, falling away to the harbour where ships in wartime grey are berthed in rows.

'I loved growing up here,' says Harry. 'The square-riggers would moor along those wharves loading coal for Chile or North America, and I used to wag school to go and see them.'

'You'd have been in hot water, my lad, if I'd known,' says Jessie, and turns to me. 'He got away with rather a lot — seems to have made good despite it all, I suppose.'

Harry hugs his mother, laughing. 'I didn't get away with much, Mum, and you know it.'

At dinner that night Tina says, 'I've just finished at typing school, Eliza. Honestly, it was *hell*. But I don't want to take shorthand — I want to *live*!'

'On air presumably, lass, without a job,' says Jessie.

'That nice man I met on the train said I could be an actress in Sydney.'

'That nice man wasn't precisely offering you work.'

'Don't disillusion me, Mum. I know! I could be a spy like Eliza!'

'I'm not a spy,' I say. 'Just a civil servant.'

Tina laughs. '*Just* what a spy would say.'

'And a non-spy,' says Harry. 'More vegetables?'

'Actually I know all about Eliza's job because of you,' says Tina, spearing a roast potato.

'Me?' Harry says. 'I've said nothing on the matter.'

'Silly, *that*'s how I know it must be secret. You're in signals, aren't you, Eliza? You let slip some jargon the other day when we were chatting about tuning the radio.'

'I'm surprised you noticed,' I say.

'A lot of people are surprised at what I notice,' Tina says happily. 'That's why I'd be a good spy.'

I laugh. 'Spying is just the very slow, *very* boring gathering of snippets of information. It's certainly not trenchcoats or Hollywood glamour.'

'I know that, Eliza, really.' Tina's merry face stills. 'But I want to learn signals. Have you heard of Violet McKenzie in Sydney? She's an electrical engineer who set up the Women's Emergency Signalling Corps, and she teaches wireless telegraphy to women.'

'And what's wireless telegraphy when it's at home?' says Jessie.

'Sending and receiving Morse code,' Tina and I say at the same time. We gaze at each other.

I say, 'You'd like to go to Sydney to train with Violet McKenzie?'

'Yes!' says Tina. 'And I could do typing to support myself. Then — well, there's the Australian Women's Army Service or the Women's Auxiliary Australian Air Force.'

Jessie says softly, 'You're too young, lass.'

'I'm twenty-two, and the services don't post women overseas, so I'd be all right. Harry and Eliza are in more danger in Singapore, and do they look worried?'

Jessie glances at Harry, then quickly away.

He takes her hand. 'I'm not a soldier, Mum. If war comes to Singapore, we'll be evacuated. We're as safe as anyone can be today.'

'Not much comfort, my lad,' Jessie says, swallowing.

That evening she gives me an old photo of my husband as a boy of ten, slight and fair, grinning and holding a puppy: it's almost unbearably moving.

Far too soon our holiday is over and, when we return to Sydney, Tina comes with us and lodges with a family friend. We leave money to help support her and she gleefully begins her telegraphy course. On the flight home I think, there'll be a lot of young women like her soon. I hope they don't have to use their skills in a real war.

When green Singapore emerges from the haze ahead, I sigh, all too aware that as we wake and sleep, the plans of the Japanese Imperial General Headquarters are being argued, refined and manoeuvred quietly into place.

And, back at work, there's yet another small blow among the daily parade of tragedies. Gustaf Erikson's barque *Penang* went missing a few months ago on a passage from Australia to England.

I once met *Penang*'s sailmaker, Winifred Lloyd, a small adventurous woman in her forties, who'd had a life on square-riggers longer than most ships' officers.

Now the Germans report that one of their submarines sank the old windjammer off the Irish coast, and everyone on board was drowned.

'Napoleon? What's *he* got to do with it?' says Quentin Baxter in our office at the Naval Base.

'Dear God, what *do* they teach in schools nowadays?' says Mr Kingsley. 'Eighteen-twelve, dear boy, Napoleon attacked Russia. Got all the way to Moscow, the Russians retreating tantalisingly before him, then winter descended. More than two-thirds of his army died.'

'And you hope this will happen to Hitler?' I ask. 'But the Nazi forces are overwhelming.'

'I'm quietly optimistic,' says Mr Kingsley. 'The Russians are a hardy folk and winter there is always waiting in the wings.'

'But a Nazi defeat won't stop the Japanese,' I say. 'We know they started planning for war in April, a good three months back.'

'*We* may know, Mrs Bell,' says Mr Kingsley. 'But our masters refuse to admit of the possibility.'

Quentin sighs. 'I met such a lovely WREN from Kranji the other night, Joanie. Appalling to think what might happen if we're invaded.'

'We'll be all right,' says Mr Kingsley. 'They'll get the intercept operators and radio boffins and the likes of us out of here quick smart if the Japanese start knocking on the door.'

'But the rest?' I say. 'The Chinese, who are the only group doing civil defence? The Malays, who just want to be left in peace? The Indians who support Britain? The traders, the nurses, the doctors ...'

'Quite so,' says Mr Kingsley. 'Probably not much cheer for them.' He gazes at us. 'Better get back to trying to persuade our masters the fat is very nearly in the fire then.'

In fact our masters are horrifyingly relaxed about Singapore's situation. A new Commander-in-Chief for the Far East, Sir Robert Brooke-Popham, arrived some months ago, but says he's convinced that Japan is too overstretched in China and Russia to be of any real threat to us.

The service headquarters are also worryingly scattered about. The Army's administrative centre of Fort Canning is in Singapore City, yet oddly, Brooke-Popham has made himself comfortable at the Naval Base, a full twenty miles away.

Even more oddly, the head of the Army himself, Lieutenant-General Percival, prefers to spend his days at the Air Force headquarters. Percival is a pleasant man, diffident in the English manner, and if our lives did not depend so much upon his competence he'd be almost endearing.

But few would call the head of the Australian forces endearing. Lieutenant-General Gordon Bennett is a red-faced little man who picks quarrels with everyone.

Bennett is close friends with the much-married, high-living Sultan of Johore and even closer friends (it's rumoured) with the most recent Sultana, a beautiful Romanian.

That may be par for the course in steamy Singapore, but Johore is the strategically vital state on the Strait which separates Singapore from Malaya, and the Sultan is even-handed in his political friendships. He famously gave visiting Lady Diana Cooper a gift of a fine parrot which could speak only Japanese.

A few months ago, Felix decided his talents were going unappreciated by his rivals at the Bureau, and jumped at the chance to recommission into the army. Now he's got a new position as a Major with the intelligence unit at Fort Canning.

'He waves his revolver around as if he plans to hold off the whole Japanese army with it,' says Izabel. 'And he's besotted with his uniform. Couldn't be vainer if it came with a peacock's tail.'

We're taking high tea at Raffles Hotel. The waiters bring us dainty cakes and little sandwiches and tea in fragile porcelain cups. The fans high above move the air slowly around, while outside the palm trees shimmer in the hot breeze.

'I fear he's not much missed by his colleagues in the Bureau,' I say. 'One man said he was ready to punch Felix in the nose, but I told him he'd have to wait in line.'

Izabel laughs as she used to, lightly and openly.

I say, 'You know, since our trip to Perth you don't have that air of remoteness any more.'

She nods. 'I'm still sad at losing Laurence, but at least I'm not swamped with misery.'

'Is it the same for Nancy?'

'Yes, thankfully. But — well — I'm actually a little worried about what she's learning at her convent school.'

'Didn't she do well in her exams?'

Izabel sits back and taking out a cigarette. (A waiter rushes over to light it.) 'Not that sort of learning. No, she and Tessie have become obsessed with martyrs, determined little virgins being persecuted for their faith. Christians are far too fond of the torture of women at the best of times but, *honestly*, the travails of saints Agnes, Euphemia, Cecilia, Agatha and the rest!'

'But don't lots of young girls go through a phase like that?'

'*I* certainly didn't,' says Izabel. 'Min-lu would never let anyone fill my head with that sort of rubbish. It doesn't help that there's a Saint Barbara either, Tessie's favourite — and Tessie herself has some very odd ideas about what's actually involved in matters of sin.'

I laugh. 'I'm sure they'll get over it.'

Izabel leans forward. 'Nancy's only eleven, but I've told her something of the facts of life. I don't want her to imagine innocence will save her from *anything*, not in bawdy Singapore — and certainly not if the Japanese ...' She sighs. 'God, I really shouldn't be so gloomy. The Royal Navy will come dashing to our rescue if we need them.'

'I'm not so certain, Izabel,' I say. 'They're a little preoccupied in Europe after all.'

'The Royal Air Force then?'

I shrug. 'The service chiefs calculated we need six hundred planes to protect Malaya and Burma.'

'Do we have them?'

I shake my head. 'Fewer than ninety obsolete bombers and no fighters at all.'

'Oh my,' says Izabel. 'Still, we've got Felix and his revolver.'

As well as six hundred planes, Singapore needs forty-eight battalions of infantry and two tank regiments. Yet we have a quarter of those troops and not a single tank: Brooke-Popham has decided tanks would be useless in Malaya. Unlike the Japanese, he overlooks the rather good road network.

Lately the RAF has been bolstered by a couple of squadrons of Buffalo fighters, but their inexperienced pilots are having a lot of accidents. Sadly too, some of them think the Japanese can't see in the dark or shoot straight because of their 'slit eyes.'

What's even worse, London's War Office holds firmly to the opinion that any Asian soldiers may be easily dealt with — *three at a time* — by a single strapping British lad.

By the middle of 1941 our intelligence is predicting Japan's next move will be the setting up of bases to attack Malaya by sea. Precisely on cue, the Japanese occupy several important harbours in south Indochina in late August, and start building up a massive presence.

Desperate for raw materials, they speak openly of South-East Asia as their *Southern Resource Area*. We have reports from Thailand and Malaya of hundreds of Japanese 'tourists' blatantly measuring the dimensions of bridges and roads.

In October, the few moderates left in the Japanese government are brutally ejected. The War Minister becomes the Prime Minister, while every single day trains carry soldiers and armaments from occupied Saigon to the Cambodian and Thai borders.

By now even the optimists in the War Office have accepted that invasion is looming. Not so Sir Robert Brooke-Popham.

'Why won't he *see* what's going on?' I say.

'Remember when Duff Cooper was here?' says Quentin. 'He told Churchill that Brooke-Popham was damn near gaga. Brooke-Popham's being replaced so he's furious, digging in deeper. He wouldn't change his mind now if the Japanese gave him their plans in writing.'

'They practically are, with all the transmissions we're intercepting.'

'I'll be more worried when they stop,' says Quentin.

I nod. 'Silence before an attack? Too late by then.'

On 19th November 1941 we'd intercepted the 'winds' message sent to all Japanese diplomatic and military bases.

It said that if Tokyo broadcasts certain phrases then war is imminent: cipher machines must be destroyed, codebooks burnt and diplomatic relations severed.

'But severed with whom?' says Quentin. 'The Americans, *east wind rain*? The Russians, *north wind cloudy*? Or us — *west wind clear*?'

In early December our spies report the destruction of cipher machines at the Japanese embassies in London and Washington. Something is clearly about to happen.

'It's most likely to be us, they need British and Dutch raw materials,' I say. 'Surely they wouldn't be foolish enough to take on the Americans as well, not at the same time.'

'Agreed. I doubt they've got resources for a widespread attack, anyway,' says Quentin.

'But they've got will and desperation.' Despite the heat I shiver.

A few days later we peer from the office window at the ships just berthed at the Naval Base.

'*Force Z*?' says Quentin. 'For Zorro? Perhaps the wee Admiral imagines he's Douglas Fairbanks.'

'That's not fair,' I say. 'They have to call it something after all.'

'Not much of a force. What happened to the aircraft carrier that was supposed to be with them?'

'Ran aground in Jamaica.'

'Jamaica?' He chuckles. 'Surely she went of her own accord.'

'Quentin.'

'All right. So apart from four dear little destroyers, Force Z is comprised of a battleship and an ancient battlecruiser?'

'HMS *Prince of Wales* is very up-to-date. Unfortunately *HMS Repulse* is a Great War relic.'

'God help us. Did you see the papers are calling *Prince of Wales* the "HMS Unsinkable"?'

'That's what they called the *Titanic* too.' I sit down at my desk. 'What worries me most is Admiral Phillips keeps saying aircraft aren't a threat to a properly armed battleship.'

'The man clearly has never heard of torpedo-planes,' says Quentin.

'Here's this morning's report,' I say, passing it over. 'As we expected, the Japanese have just changed their fleet code. Could be weeks before the cryptographers break the new one.'

'The diplomatic traffic has dried up too, so *something's* about to happen, and we're sitting here blind and stupid,' says Quentin bitterly. 'And Brooke-Popham's not even allowed to move unless the Japanese attack first.'

'But he's got to be ready to *respond*, and right now he won't even station troops where we're telling him they'll almost certainly land!' I sigh. 'At least he'll soon be replaced. Perhaps General Wavell will have a better grasp on reality.'

'Reality? Would that be *HMS Reality*, last seen going down with all flags flying?' says Quentin.

We laugh bleakly and carry on working. Every day we wait for a 'winds' message that doesn't come. Are we missing it in the torrent of signals? Was it simply a ploy to confuse us?

Yet even without that warning we *know* the Japanese have amassed a fleet in Indochinese waters that could strike Malaya in a day. Dear God, we even know the names of the vessels themselves!

But Brooke-Popham insists we can't possibly be attacked now: the rainy season has begun.

As well as the ominous build-up near Malaya, six aircraft carriers left Japan a few weeks ago and are steaming east into the Pacific. They are accompanied by a massive flotilla of battleships, cruisers, destroyers, tankers and submarines, as well as four hundred warplanes lined up on their launching decks.

And suddenly the chatter of Kana morse stops.

In the early hours, Harry breathing quietly beside me, I come awake, my heart suddenly pounding. The moon is bright in the clear night sky and, as usual, brilliant Singapore City around us is unsleeping — the cool before dawn is a busy time for breakfast at the chophouses.

At first just a pressure against my eardrums, then growing louder, I hear the throbbing of planes. They must be ours, of course. Precautions may be imperfect but they certainly exist — the air-raid wardens, for instance, can extinguish the city lights from a central control box.

But the sirens are silent, the city lit up like a party.

It's only later I discover the Governor won't let the sirens be sounded without his permission, and he can't be found. And the warden who could turn off the lights has gone home with the key in his pocket.

But that's later.

And in the end the winds blow from every quarter.

PART III. SOMETHING SO HOPEFUL

21. Toby: The Diamant Twins

Will I ever be enough for you, Stef?

I turn to the right, wide awake. Stef has to have my side of the bed so he doesn't lie on on his most damaged hand, but I can't get used to it. I wriggle onto my back and stare at the ceiling.

He's finally been discharged from East Grinstead and we're in my house in London. I'd hoped it would be a homecoming, but we've slept apart for too long. That doesn't seem to bother him though, and after a quick hug he fell deeply asleep.

Stop fooling yourself. It's not the bloody bed keeping you awake.

Again: will I ever be enough for you, Stef?

Yes, we'd agreed long ago that physical monogamy wasn't our priority. But we'd agreed — I thought — a certain emotional fidelity, so I was unprepared for the pain when he told me he'd fallen in love with someone else. It still hurts too, despite the year that's passed since.

When I picked Stef up from the hospital today, I noticed the young nurse's hands lingering on his body as she helped him out of bed. She brushed her fingertips against his cheek when she thought I couldn't see. Just a crush? Who knows?

But Stef smiled, heavy-eyed and complacent.

And the orderly who dressed him so tenderly — poor fellow, he wasn't pretty enough to seduce, but in any case it was obvious he'd have followed Stef through the gates of Hell. Dear God, given a moment's encouragement, I suspect even the distinguished doctor would have dropped his trousers there and then.

Despite his scars Stef is a charming, seductive man. So for that matter am I, but I don't feel the need to ruthlessly attract every mortal soul that crosses my path. And if I did, would expressions of my devotion to one soul among so many have any meaning at all?

Bombing in the provinces has eased but the capital still needs plenty of firemen, so I'm starting a job soon at a large London fire station. I'll be a unit leader, like old George in Southampton. He died last year in a raid. I find it hard to grieve; for him or for the other dead men I once knew. Perhaps there'll be time to mourn after the war.

The lease on Stef's flat in Southampton has almost expired, so I catch the train down to pack our belongings. Of course Stef's hands prevent him helping, but Pete will drive me back to London with our things in his farm truck when I'm done.

It's December 1941 and bitterly cold on the train. The newspaper headlines are all about what's happening in the East, although I imagine the Americans will sort the Japanese out pretty smartly.

I hope Eliza and Harry will be all right, but I don't expect they call the place 'Fortress Singapore' for nothing. I remember Eliza told me her glorious aunt Izabel lives there too. Wonder if she's gone back to making films yet?

The draught makes me shiver. Passing through Northam, I see my father's horrible old butcher-shop is gone and only a pile of rubble remains. A year ago the sight would have pleased me, but now it leaves me unmoved. Just a building, destroyed like so many others in this loathsome war.

I suppose I'll have to go and see the old bastard. He didn't live at the shop, so sadly I can't hope he went up with it. While I've been at East Grinstead I've managed to evade my filial obligations, but I'm sure Pete will drag me over there one last time before I leave.

'Get that scowl off your face,' says Pete, changing gears as we approach my father's place. 'And look, something I should warn you about. Didn't want to mention it while you were so busy with Stef, but you need to know. Alf's not too well.'

'*Alf*? Great chums now by the sound of it.'

'Of course he's a cranky old sod, but he was a good man on the factory floor. Anyway, he's not at Supermarine any more.'

'Did you fire him?'

Pete stops the car with a screech and turns to me.

'No, I didn't bloody *fire* him.' He takes a breath. 'He's sick. Dying.'

'Oh, spare me, for God's sake. Do you expect me to rush to his bedside in a grand scene of reconciliation? That's not going happen.'

Pete is silent. After a time he says, 'No. But have a little kindness, Toby. Haven't seen that side of you for a while and I miss it.'

That hurts. 'You may notice I've had a bit to deal with lately. And given the mayhem that descends upon us on a nightly basis, I don't see much in the way of kindness around me.'

'Then a bit more in the mix wouldn't go astray, old mate, would it?'

Pete starts the car again, and after a couple of minutes of strained silence we stop outside a row of terraces. Alf's lady friend (Edith? Elsie?) answers the bell. She's a small fluffy thing I've never paid much attention to, but she seems a lot less giggly than I remember.

'I'll just get the tea,' she says, opening the living room door for us.

Pete had warned me but it's still a shock. Alf is on the couch in a dressing-gown, blanket pulled up to his armpits. He's essentially a living skeleton.

'Tommy,' he whispers. 'Good to see you, son.'

'How are you?' I say, then want to kick myself. It's obvious how he is.

'Oh, not too bad. Edie's been a tower of strength. Soon be back at work, I hope. Mr McKee tells me they're doing some enhancements to the Mark V — love to have a shufti.'

'Suppose you need to take it one day at a time,' I say, hating every stupid word.

'That's what they tell me. Ah, here she is, nice cup of tea for everyone. Apple cake too, Edie? You shouldn't have.'

He doesn't eat any cake: he can barely swallow. He sips once or twice from the teacup Edie holds to his lips, but it's purely a formality.

'A growth in my gut, the doc says. He operated but it's taking a while to heal. Got to be patient.'

'Expect so.' I can barely swallow either.

'You've been around hospitals a lot lately, Mr McKee tells me. Your friend with the burnt hands getting any better?'

'Slowly.'

'Hope he'll be all right, son, and you too. Never said how proud i am of you being a fireman —'

'Just a job. We've all got to pitch in.'

He breathes painfully. 'Something I want to talk to you about, but I'm a bit weary right now ...'

'Of course. Perhaps when you're feeling better you can come to London and see Maude's house, and we'll have a nice chat then.'

He closes his eyes. 'Sorry, must rest. Thanks for coming, Tommy. You're a good boy.'

'Take care of yourself,' I say as we're leaving, and his hand lifts in a small wave, though he doesn't open his eyes.

'A lot brighter today,' Edie murmurs at the door. 'Fingers crossed.'

'Oh, absolutely. Fingers crossed.'

Pete doesn't say anything as we drive back to Bedford Square in the cold evening dusk, and I'm incapable of speech. He parks outside Ye Red Lion Hotel and says, 'Come on. Drink and dinner.'

After my first gin I lean back and sigh. 'You warned me. How long, do you think?'

Pete shakes his head. 'No idea. You'll pop down again soon though, won't you?'

'Suppose I will. *Jesus.* I've seen plenty of dying people, Pete. Thought I was hardened to it.'

'Well at least we had no grand scene of reconciliation, mate. Wouldn't want that, would we?'

'Bastard.'

Stef's rented flat came furnished, so I don't have any beds or cupboards to deal with, just our belongings. I find my old notebooks and typewriter, and sit gazing at them for a time. After Stef was hurt I still kept my journal, but lately I haven't even jotted down a word.

I rouse myself and pack them, and keep going. I clean the place and hand the keys back to the landlady, Miss Mathison, who gives me a shy hug and sends her best wishes to Stef.

Pete drives us to London with the boxes in the back of the truck. He's staying overnight on the third floor in what we jokingly call our visitor's suite. It's evening when we arrive at Whitfield Street and we carry everything into the house. Finally we're done, and I hear a burst of laughter from the reception room.

'Oh yes, Stef's having some people over,' I say. 'But we can't go in, we're too scruffy.'

'I'm scruffy,' says Pete, opening the door. 'You're debonair. Come on, let's say hello.'

Eight people are seated around the fireplace, the room cosy after the cool night air.

'*There* you are,' says Stef, from his armchair. 'I was wondering when you'd be back. I suppose you've done the usual sterling job?'

He now wears a tan suede glove to protect his scarred right hand, and Pete goes over and very gently takes it, then pats him affectionately on the shoulder.

'Course we have, you old shirker. Sipping cocktails while we've been sweating our guts out? You owe us a few.'

'The tray's over there, help yourself. But first, do you know everyone? Mama, Aunt Danika, this is our old friend Pete — we've often mentioned him. And of course you know Toby.'

Pete and I shake hands with Stef's mother Gabriela and his aunt Danika, Sofia's mother. When they arrived from Poland at the turn of the century they were sooty-eyed chorus girls, the Naughty Diamant Twins, but they soon married into respectability.

They must be approaching sixty now but they're still stunning: perfectly groomed Danika is as elegant as a ballerina, while glamorous Gabriela ties her raven hair back with a long silk scarf.

Charlotte is eyeing them thoughtfully, then deliberately crosses her legs with an enticing slither of silk. I smile and she gives me a tiny wink. We'll never be close, but we amuse each other.

Two young men I don't know are seated on another sofa. One of them manages to stop looking at Charlotte's legs and gets up, saying, 'We bring seats, you come here.' Pete has poured us cocktails, so he hands me one and we sit on the newly vacated sofa. He doesn't go over to his wife but simply waves, and Charlotte waves lightly back.

As the young men return with chairs, she says, 'Now — Pete, Toby, these are two of our *Kindertransport* lads from Poland, all grown up of course. Tadeusz and Alfons are joining the RAF soon, so Klara and I are pressing Stef to give them some intensive English tutoring.'

'Haven't got much on my dance-card for now,' says Stef. 'Might keep me out of mischief while you're at work — what do you think, Toby?'

'Wonderful idea.' They're good-looking kids — seventeen? Fair, blue-eyed, high cheekbones. But even *he* wouldn't ... he's thirty-three, like me, nearly twice their age. Of course he wouldn't.

'How's the Northam butcher, then?' says Stef.

I flinch, though I told my housemates my foolish secret months ago. Once Stef knew, there was no reason to keep it quiet. Of course no one gives a damn, but his casual words still sting.

'Not so good, actually,' I say. 'He's just had an operation — matter of wait and see.'

'I'm sorry, my dear, simply playing the fool,' says Stef. 'You must be rather shaken.'

'A little.'

'The Northam butcher, *kochanie*?' asks Stef's mother affectionately.

'Long story, Gabriela. My father, as it happens. I kept quiet about him at boarding school for obvious reasons.'

'Indeed, the little snobs.' We smile. Gabriela and I have always liked each other.

'Do remind me, Toby, was he related to Aunt Maude?' says Sofia, sounding bored. Klara's face is drawn and she's sitting further from Sofia than usual.

'No, blossom. Maude was my mother's sister.'

'Ah, dear Maude ... still I miss her so,' says Gabriela. 'But tell me — above the fireplace, her portrait — it is simply *beautiful*, Toby. Where did you get it?'

'She left it here for me in the back of a cupboard.'

'Oh! I *remember* it being painted,' says Danika. 'Do you not, Gaby?'

'Of course! The artist was Paul — something.' Gabriela smiles. 'Handsome devil.'

Klara stands and peers at the painting. 'Yes, it is signed Paul, but I cannot read the surname.'

'*O mój Boże.*' Danika sighs. 'Forty years ago.'

Stef is puzzled. 'Do you mean you two knew Maude *before* Toby and I met at school?'

Danika glances at Gabriela. 'Ah. I think perhaps, yes, we knew each other before.'

Gabriela shakes her head. 'But I cannot remember where. Dany?'

'No, no, I cannot either. May I get you another cocktail?'

'Thank you, *kochanie*. Anyone else?'

Charlotte smiles and Stef raises his eyebrow at their surprisingly inept performance. Maude's laughing blue eyes gaze down at us, her blonde hair loose and her wrap revealing a fine décolletage.

Did my aunt have a racy past like her friends, the Naughty Diamant Twins? I do hope so.

A fortnight later I go back for the day to Southampton. I realise I'm not angry with my father any more. In wartime, and after Stef's ordeal, it seems pointless. I can hardly even remember why he used to fill me with rage.

There were reasons of course — when I was young he was brutally bad-tempered, although that was par for the course for Northam men. Sometimes he'd beat me but, thanks to Maude, boarding school put an end to that.

My mother was long gone by then. She died when I was six, and all I remember is a sad, remote presence. Alf disappeared from my life at that time as well. I vaguely recall a succession of 'aunties' who cared for me. A few were kind.

Then my father reappeared when I was nine, in 1917. Good God, had he been away fighting in the Great War? That might account for his absence — but if so, why did he never talk about it?

'Embarrassed, that's why,' he says.

Amazingly, Alf has rallied a little. He's still skeletal but there's a flush of life in his cheeks.

'Embarrassed?' I say.

'See this?' He holds up his hand with the half-amputated fingers.

'You were *wounded*?' I say. 'You mean you didn't chop them off yourself by accident?'

'I'd have been a God-awful butcher to do that, son, and I wasn't. No, I joined the army but I was stationed in London, assigned to some General as his soldier-servant, his batman.'

'So how were you wounded?'

He laughs and shakes his head. 'Windy night, door slammed on my fingers. Didn't heal up properly, had to be cut off. So I was discharged, sent home. On our street there were men without legs, neighbours who'd lost their sons. I wasn't going to boast about my bloody war service!'

Edie brings us the mandatory tea and cake on a tray. 'What's so funny?' she asks.

Later I say, 'I've been wondering — what was my mother like? I don't even have a picture of her.'

'Ivy? Ah, she was a lovely woman. People said Maude was the prettier one, but for me it was always Ivy. The gossips said she could have done better, and they were probably right.' He chuckles. 'Ivy took a risk marrying me, but she wasn't as ambitious as her sister — nor as wild either, thank heavens.'

'I don't recall anything, except ... she wouldn't touch me.' I swallow. 'I remember wanting her to pick me up and cuddle me like the other mothers, but she never did.'

'Oh, son. Ivy was *protecting* you.'

'Protecting me? How?'

'She got consumption, Tommy. Didn't want to infect you. She loved you, I know she did, but she wasn't allowed to hold you.' He clears his throat. 'I joined up after she died, and when I came home I thought you'd forgotten her, so I never said anything. Truth was, I missed her so badly, couldn't talk about her. Took it out on everyone, you especially. Can't tell you how sorry —'

'No. No, it's all in the past,' I say. 'But it's a relief to know there was a reason for it.'

He takes a long breath. 'Well, son, there's something else I need to tell you, too.'

He struggles to sit up and I plump his pillows, second nature after a year of caring for Stef.

'Should have said before, but we had that big argument, and now, who knows —' he shrugs. 'We loved you, lad, but you weren't born Ivy's son. We adopted you. Well, not legally, but we took you in. Maude would've been ruined otherwise. Still all in the family, though.'

I stare at him and suddenly everything makes sense.

Klara is especially delighted for me. 'I *knew* Maude was looking after us!' she says. 'Oh, Toby. Are you happy to have discovered your real mother?'

'Not so much happy, but — more anchored, perhaps. Everything has changed, although nothing really has. The world just seems comprehensible in a different way.'

I lean forward. 'Klara, I think I might be able to write again. About people and choices and not knowing and becoming. Something like that.' I laugh at myself.

She smiles. 'The human condition, Toby?'

'Yes, the bloody human condition. But not — not simply observing. *Being*, perhaps. Somehow. Oh, heavens, woman, I don't *know*!'

'You simply begin with your first words. That is how it was for me.'

'Are you writing anything at all now, Klara?'

'No.' She gazes out the window. 'Poetry has no meaning in a world like this.'

'Perhaps poetry is what it needs, poppet.'

She sighs. 'The fascinating Terry is coming back. Her husband is conducting a program they call *Women in Wartime*, which will have music by Sofia and Terry. Apart from touring the provinces, however, I do not think either has actually known much of wartime.'

'Oh, Klara. I thought you and Sofia were back together.'

She laugh, a little bitterly. 'Toby, no one ever has the full attention of a child of one of the Diamant Twins.'

I shrug. 'They're certainly elusive.'

'Ah, I am pitying myself,' says Klara. 'But I must look to the future. I have been thinking much about children and, with or without Sofia, one day I shall have a baby.'

'But wouldn't a baby require the presence of a man in your life?'

'It would require a man, certainly, but men pass like ships in the night.'

'Yes, but Klara, darling — aren't you forgetting you're a lesbian?'

She smiles. 'I was married once, Toby. I could cope with what is required if it would bring me such happiness.'

'Goodness,' I say in admiration. 'You *are* a pragmatic little Nordic pixie, aren't you?'

My father's rally does not last very long. One cold morning Pete rings to tell me that Alf has died, suddenly in the night. Of course I was expecting the news but it still leaves me horribly shaken.

Charlotte has the use of a car for ferrying around *Kindertransport* children, and says she'll drive us to Southampton for the funeral — me, Stef and Klara. Lately she's been bringing Tadeusz and Alfons over for English lessons with Stef, and they're much more fluent now.

They're nice lads and I'm ashamed of my earlier suspicion that Stef might try to seduce them. Instead he's protective and a little envious.

'So *young*, flying is everything to them,' he says in bed. 'I can hardly believe I was ever that naive.'

'You were never naive, Stef,' I say, stroking his hair. It's taken time, but recently we became lovers again and it feels like our early, passionate days together.

He smiles. 'No, suppose not. Anyway, sleep, my dear. We have an early start tomorrow.'

I don't get much rest, and at dawn Charlotte arrives with the car. As we motor along the highway it's an appropriately gloomy day. I gaze through the raindrops on the glass and say, 'It's odd. They're all gone now — Ivy, Maude, Alf. My whole family is gone.'

'We'll be your family now, Toby,' says Charlotte, her blue eyes kind in the rear-view mirror.

It's a sombre drive, and not just because of Alf. The headlines seem to be all about Singapore: the situation has apparently turned into a debacle. God knows how Eliza and Harry are going. I haven't had mail from either for weeks but, coming by sea, it's often delayed. I hope their bosses have got them out to safety by now.

The drizzle continues at the cemetery. I've been to too many funerals in recent years to take any comfort from the rites. Billie is standing with Pete, looking dashing in her pilot's uniform — she's working at nearby Hamble airfield now.

Of course Alf's Edie is there too, and invites us all back for a spread at her place and won't take no for an answer. At Edie's we eat and drink and talk. I'm greeted with kindness by old friends from St Mary's fire station, and boys I haven't met since school, and wrinkled ancients who used to be large, hearty neighbours.

A little later Pete draws me aside and says, 'Toby, I was with Alf the evening before he died. He wasn't in pain, just drifting, quite lucid at times. He insisted I was to tell you that he loved you and you'd made his life complete.'

On a day of such emotion that's simply too much, and I retreat to a bedroom to sit for a time. Then I wipe my eyes and stand, exhausted, at the doorway.

Across the room, Klara is smiling at copper-haired Billie, who's waving her arms as if coming in for a dodgy landing. Edie emerges from the kitchen and nudges Pete, giving him a tray of sandwiches.

Pete offers them around to my London friends, and the firemen with tanned hands, and two boys from school who are now respectable chaps, a banker and a civil servant. I wonder if many others here realise they're a couple, like me and Stef. Probably not.

Over to one side, their backs to me, Stef himself is chatting to Charlotte. They look good together: Stef's dark intensity complements Charlotte's golden warmth.

If you didn't notice the glove on my love's right hand you'd never know he'd been hurt. His left is almost completely healed too, and lately he's even taught himself to write with it.

But he's not writing now.

He's caressing Charlotte's wrist and fingers and the sensuous cup of her palm. He's smiling into her eyes and she's slowly smiling back.

Toby, no one ever has the full attention of a child of one of the Diamant Twins.

22. Izabel: Shattered Glass

Nancy creeps into my room and snuggles beside me despite the heat. (Felix has his own bedroom, of course, far away in the other wing.)

'A nightmare, darling?' I murmur.

She shakes her head against my shoulder. 'What will we do when the Japanese come, *Ah-me*?'

'Oh. Well, we'll be evacuated long before that.'

'Tessie too?'

'Yes. Everyone we know will be sent away before — if — the Japanese come.'

'What's that noise?'

'What noise?'

'The humming.'

'I can't — oh, yes. Probably the new lot of aeroplanes Aunt Eliza said were soon arriving. Buffaloes or something.'

'Not the Japanese?'

'There'd be air-raid sirens if it were them. No, sweetheart, everything's —'

Bursts of light flicker on the ceiling, then distant booming followed by thudding. Artillery? We sit up. More flashes, more booms, and we rush to the window and stare at Singapore City, four miles away.

Explosions are lighting up the harbour and Chinatown, where Eliza and Harry live. Where flames are leaping into the sky. I grab the phone and ring Eliza, my heart thumping. No answer. I go back to the window.

The flames are high and — far too late — the air-raid sirens start up. The explosions become fewer, then stop. The drone of aircraft fades away, and the sky beyond the city turns pink with dawn.

I hurry to Felix's room. He's asleep, half-drunk I expect. I shake him, yelling.

'God, Izzy, what's the bloody time? Don't *do* that. What?'

'I said Singapore's being *bombed*!'

He sits up, holding his head, and sighs deeply. 'All right. I'd better ...' He stares at nothing for a few moments, then slowly stands. 'Send the boy with some hot water, will you?'

'There's no time to shave, Felix. They've bombed Chinatown and I can't get through to Eliza!'

'Bigger things to worry about than that silly chit. Must get to Fort Canning, find out what's happening. Ah, there you are, Cho-lin. Hot water, best uniform, chop-chop.'

He's gone by the time I've dressed, but I've got a little car and drive Nancy down the road to Tessie's house. Her mother Barbara, her eyes anxious, meets me at the door.

'Fred rang from the Naval Base,' she says. 'The *Prince of Wales* and *Repulse* tried to shoot them down, but stupid Brooke-Popham wouldn't let the planes scramble to attack. Fred says they think the Japanese have landed in northern Malaya. And they've bombed Hawaii!'

'Oh, dear God,' I say. 'I *must* go into the city and find out what's happened to Eliza and Harry. Please, Barbara, would you mind Nancy for a few hours?'

'Of course. Come in, Nancy.'

'You're a darling, Barbara, thank you.'

There's a lot of military traffic on the road into Singapore, but I get through to Chinatown. The damage doesn't seem as bad as I'd feared and the fires are mostly out.

But then in the crowded eating district I see crushed buildings and shattered glass, and bodies in pools of red on the footpath. Ambulance workers are loading stretchers onto the back of a truck and people are standing dazed, crying and staring around them.

Finally I reach Eliza's place, and sob with relief to see the building is undamaged. I bang on the door but no one answers. I turn at the sound of footsteps. Eliza hurries towards me and we hug.

'I've been helping out at the hospital,' she says. 'Now I've got to get to Sembawang, to the Naval Base. What about you? They didn't bomb Tanglin, did they?'

'No, we're fine. But I heard they've landed in northern Malaya!'

'*Exactly* where we said they would,' says Eliza bitterly. She takes a breath. 'Don't worry, Izabel. That's a long way away and a lot of good men are going to try to stop them. And if worst comes to worst, we'll be evacuated.'

'But it's too dangerous for you to be *here*, right in the middle of the city! Eliza, come and stay with us. Harry can still get to the hospital easily and you'd be closer to the Naval Base.'

She hesitates, then says, 'That's a good idea. Our staff too?'

'Of course. Give me some bags, darling, and tell me what things you want and I'll pack while you go off to work.'

When I pick Nancy up that afternoon Barbara says, 'Fred rang again. I know he shouldn't have, stupid security and all that, but he's been trying to patch things up with us.'

'He's a good man, Barbara, you could do worse. In fact I'd suggest, with Felix, you are.'

She goes red, as we normally never allude to my husband. She clears her throat. 'Anyway, Force Z is sailing this evening, and Fred's been ordered to join *Prince of Wales*.'

'Don't worry, Eliza says it's a fine, modern ship. I'm sure the Japanese will be very sorry they ever came into British waters.'

She nods. 'But it's all suddenly so *real*.' She looks up. 'And you probably haven't heard yet — I'm so sorry, Izabel. They attacked Hong Kong this morning, too.'

The pain that never quite leaves me flares for a moment. The house half-way up a mountain; *my* house. The carved front door where Bao-lim and I would greet each other, the elegant sitting room where I met Laurence Kuan, the papers written in my love's calligraphy, wrapped in silk and carefully stored away.

Will my beautiful house survive?

Two days after the first attack, Eliza rings me. 'Izabel, I think you should go over and see Barbara as soon as possible. She's about to receive some very bad news. We all are.'

But by the time I'm there Barbara has already heard. Swarming torpedo-planes have destroyed the great ships of Force Z; and eight hundred and forty men from *Repulse* and *Prince of Wales* have drowned. Soon it's confirmed that one of them is Fred, Barbara's husband.

Christmas 1941 is grim. I do my best, but food and gifts are necessarily limited. Every day the news is bad. Attacks, invasions, Pearl Harbor, Hong Kong, Thailand, Guam, the Philippines.

And of course, our own Malay Peninsula and the nightmare of the implacable Japanese advance. Barbara and Tessie stay with us sometimes, deep in mourning. Felix offers platitudes to Tessie and God knows what to Barbara.

On Christmas Day, we hear Hong Kong has been forced to surrender. Dear God, I hope Mrs Lau is safe. Felix says glumly it's the first time a British Crown Colony has fallen to invasion, and refills his glass.

On the social circuit I've met some of Singapore's most influential Chinese. Our discussions have moved from lighthearted gossip to, lately, clear-eyed exchanges on our dire situation.

At last the local Chinese are being organised into a defence unit, Dalforce. They're in two sections, one for Kuomintang supporters, the other for Communists, but they still share a common purpose.

Sometimes I see them jogging past — handsome, idealistic young men — and remember Laurence and my uncles, and sigh. If the Japanese prevail, the best and brightest among us are doomed.

Yet our optimistic commanders say the Japanese will not prevail. Battlefronts may be collapsing like dominoes the length and breadth of the Malay peninsular, but we're told the reversals are temporary.

But on New Year's Eve the bombers return to ravage us. They do so every night for a week, and soon start coming by day as well.

Unfortunately, Nancy and I are still stuck in Singapore.

It turns out that Felix misjudged the benefits of jumping from the Far East Combined Bureau to the army. Apparently (Eliza tells me), army intelligence focuses upon battles, so of course the intelligence unit — and Felix — must remain *here*.

But the Bureau's cryptographers, analysts and intercept operators are so precious they must be taken away, as far and as soon as possible, and in early January 1942 the Bureau staff board a ship for Ceylon.

Eliza refuses to go with them: she won't leave Harry. She works beside him, helping with the broken bodies arriving in a stream at the hospital in rickshaws, carts and military ambulances.

The European wives and children are being politely encouraged to depart, but most don't take it seriously: the Japanese threat has been downplayed for so long.

People still watch movies in the air-conditioned Cathay Cinema, sip cocktails at Raffles and hold dinner dances in formal dress, even as our troops are being overrun in Malaya by the tanks of the under-estimated enemy.

Am I as complacent as the rest? For years I've dreaded the Japanese, especially after Shanghai and Nanking, but now a kind of paralysis has set in. Like most I find it impossible to believe this is *happening*.

Of course we've had setbacks in Malaya, but fresh soldiers are arriving all the time, and they outnumber the invaders by far. It's a blow when Kuala Lumpur falls, but a week later there's a victory at the Muar River and we feel hopeful again.

Singapore must simply hold on until ... until? We're *told*, over and over again, that relief, rescue, reinforcements are on the way. Felix has managed to overcome his pique at not slipping safely off with the Bureau and, echoing the generals, is loudly positive we'll prevail.

He tells me (hush-hush) that fifty Hurricane fighters packed in crates have arrived. They'll soon be assembled and up in the air, and *then* those bloody Zeros will see what's what. He pats his revolver and winks when he says that, which is so often my clenched jaw aches.

But the threat of crated-up Hurricanes doesn't seem to bother the Japanese. Day after day they fly overhead and bomb us from their elegant formations, three groups of nine planes each.

And still we dress for dinner.

In late January 1942 the time of complacency ends and the time of panic begins. Felix comes home, pours himself a stiff drink and sits down in his armchair. Nothing new about that of course, but he's pale under his tan and his hands are shaking.

'Johore. It's ... they've taken it. The Japs have taken Johore Bahru.'

My knees are suddenly weak and I sit down too. 'But it's just across the Causeway, and the Strait's not even four miles wide.'

'Found out today, Christ, bloody General Percival wouldn't let engineers build fortifications in Malaya. In Johore. On our own coast! Said it'd be bad for morale. *Morale?* The incompetent *ninny*. And now the Japs are here.'

'What will we *do?*'

He takes a deep breath. 'Mustn't panic. Look, we've still got three divisions — British, Australian and whatever's left of the Indians, poor bastards. Even if they get through it'll take them weeks, *months*. And we're going to be evacuated on the next available ships.'

He puts his head in his hands. 'But Christ, Izzy — all those troops who've just arrived? Just green untrained boys!' He looks up at me. 'I'll protect you and Nancy, I *swear* it.'

I say, 'And Barbara and Tessie, too.'

He laughs, shamefaced. 'Suppose they're our responsibility, too. Barbara's a widow, after all.'

'She's also our friend, Felix,' I say drily.

'God, you're a *brick*, Izzy.' He sighs in relief. 'I adore you, you know, though I haven't treated you as well as I should have. Don't understand why I'm such a fool sometimes.'

'Nor do the rest of us, darling. But we've just got to get through this.'

'Absolutely.' He pats his revolver with less conviction than usual.

But I feel a tiny sense of disquiet. Whenever Felix becomes overcome with sentiment about what a *brick* I am, it often seems to accompany some act, small or large, of betrayal.

To the brave skirl of bagpipes, the last troops retreat from Malaya to Singapore at dawn on 31st January, 1942. Then the engineers blow a hole in the Causeway. Unfortunately it's not a very big hole, and within days the Japanese repair it.

Most of our planes have withdrawn now to the Netherlands East Indies. The Japanese have complete mastery of the sky and they don't let us forget it.

Dozens of ships arrive to evacuate people to Batavia, Australia or India. In the first week of February thousands of people get away, but thousands more are left queuing for tickets.

The Japanese shell the Naval Base. Before they abandon it, sailors flood the famous great dry dock and set the oil tanks on fire. Smoke from the bombings has covered the city for weeks, and now a new curtain of burning fuel hangs in the hot northern sky, dropping soot everywhere like black snow.

General Percival stations his best soldiers on a part of the coast he decides will be the invasion point, despite furious counter-arguments. On 9th February the Japanese land somewhere else entirely, and crush the few raw recruits in the way.

Within days, their troops are a third of the way across the island.

Most of the non-essential staff from Fort Canning, including Felix, are given orders to get away by any means possible. Our house at Tanglin is no longer safe so we move, in dazed disbelief, to my academy on Orchard Road, with Eliza, Harry, Barbara and Tessie.

We give the servants what we can and they go to be with their families. The power is out, although we still have candles and a cooking fire in the kitchen.

Water is rationed — and since the Japanese have taken the reservoirs it will probably soon stop altogether. Life is incomprehensible, and every day is more terrifying than the one before.

Then at last a final convoy arrives in port, dodging bullets and bombs, and Felix comes home triumphant with tickets for us all.

We're to sail on 11th February aboard the liner *Empire Star*.

'I *can't*, Izabel.' Eliza is distraught. 'I can't go without him, and he won't leave the hospital.'

'Even if he stays, Harry will be all right. Felix says the Japs do prisoner swaps with civilians. If worst comes to worst he'd be free again quickly. Look at all the couples we know, Eliza, the wife leaving, the man staying — they must, we're at *war*. And how can Harry work while he's worrying about you? Have you thought of that?'

'Of course I have! *Christ*, we were briefed about Hong Kong. Did you know the Japanese raped every woman at St Stephen's College hospital, then slaughtered them all — doctors, nurses, patients?'

'My God. Why wasn't that front-page news?'

Eliza sighs. 'It was supposed to be confidential, Izabel. White women violated *en masse*? British prestige might suffer, you see.'

'But that's even more reason to go — and Harry's *begging* you to.'

'And I'm begging him in return. I'm furious Izabel, he promised we'd always stay together.'

'Then give him some peace of mind at least, darling. You know Harry won't get on the ship with us.'

On the day of our escape, Felix suggests we leave for *Empire Star* in two groups. He'll take Barbara and Tessie and most of the luggage in the big car, while a little later I'll take Nancy, Eliza and a few bags in my small car.

We're in no danger of missing the ship, it's not sailing until this evening, and Eliza wants to go to the hospital one last time to see Harry and beg him to come with us.

Before they leave, Barbara comes to me and grasps my hands. 'Isabel, I just wanted to thank you for everything. And *now* — oh, how extraordinarily *kind* you are —'

She has tears in her eyes and we hug, then wave them goodbye, Tessie sitting wide-eyed in the rear seat amid a pile of suitcases. She and Nancy are still firm friends, although I've noticed that Tessie, a year older, is developing rather quickly.

Nancy has grown up in the last few months too, emotionally as well as physically, and like Tessie she won't be a child much longer. I feel a pang of fear. It's wartime: not a good idea to appear too womanly. Oh God, don't even *think* ...

Just before midday, Eliza returns in a rickshaw. Her eyes are swollen, but she straightens her shoulders and says, 'He won't leave. Let's go.'

We drive along Orchard Road, dodging the bomb-holes and trucks and rickshaws. I'm surprised to see so many of our soldiers ambling along in gangs, or lying around smoking and drinking.

Hillocks of glass glitter beside the bond stores, because their stocks were destroyed to stop drunken Japanese running riot — yet the soldiers still seem to have found rather a lot of intact bottles. Why aren't they off fighting the invaders?

Concentrate, Izabel, drive. Or not. We become entangled in a traffic jam and sit there for ten minutes, the sun beating down, the air thick with the stinks of sewage and burnt rubber and rotting bodies lying unclaimed beneath the rubble.

People are yelling and honking their horns. A couple ahead of us move their car to one side and march off, dragging their luggage. Eliza and I look at each other. We've only got handbags and one suitcase each, and we're just half a mile from the dock.

I park the car, and we set out.

We've only gone a short way when I hear screaming. Down a lane a group of soldiers — *British* soldiers — surround a young Chinese woman, and one of the men is tearing her cheongsam apart.

I yell, 'What are you *doing*! How *dare* you!'

One of the soldiers turns and points a gun. 'Bugger off, bint, or you'll be next.'

Eliza drags me away from the lane. 'We can't do anything, Izabel. We *must* keep going.'

Nancy says in a small voice, 'Are they making a baby with her even though they're not married?'

Eliza says gently, 'They're just cranky, drunken men, darling.'

'But Tessie says that's *sinful* —'

'I'm not much interested in Tessie's opinion right now,' I say.

Ahead is large No. 4 Wharf, but it's hidden by a crowd of people yelling and milling about. Eliza and I take Nancy's hands and push our way through. Discarded limousines clutter one end of the wharf and suitcases lie everywhere, open and plundered.

The ship is crammed with people. Stretchers with wounded men are being carried aboard, army nurses with them. At the gangway, harried stewards are checking papers. Above the hubbub I hear my name and see Felix, Barbara and Tessie waving from the deck, their faces anxious.

Air raid sirens suddenly start howling. A distant hum becomes a roar as Japanese planes approach. There's no cover anywhere so we drop to our knees and cling together. The planes thunder over us, everyone screams, and percussion and heat and light pummel us.

The planes are gone. We stand carefully, ears throbbing, and check each other for wounds: a few scrapes. Someone is wailing. I see blood, broken bodies, a woman, children.

'Come *on*,' I say, and drag Nancy and Eliza towards the gangway. We're there, I'm holding out our tickets, when someone shoves me. I fall over, Nancy with me.

Dozens of soldiers — to my astonishment they're *Australian* soldiers — are yelling and pushing through the crowd on the gangway, waving guns at anyone who doesn't move aside. Some turn and point their revolvers at us, and I try to cover Nancy with my body.

'Fuck off, Pommy bastards,' says one man, laughing drunkenly. '*Our* bloody boat now.'

At the top of the gangway I see the captain arguing with the gun-wielding soldiers, then he gives an order, his face furious. The lines are cast off, the engines throb. The ship moves away then stops a few hundred yards offshore and ties up to a buoy.

I suppose the captain is trying to stop more deserters boarding, but some of the soldiers on the wharf jump and swim and try to clamber up the mooring lines. A guard on the dock shoot one man. He falls into the water and doesn't come up.

We wait there in the exhausting heat all afternoon. At dusk *Empire Star* moves further offshore and lets down an anchor. Crackling fires are raging from the rubber warehouses all along the river, and another flight of planes drops bombs in the east towards Changi.

'We're not getting on the ship today,' says Nancy quietly.

'No, sweetheart, looks like it,' I say. 'We'll just have to try tomorrow. Let's go home for now.'

We trudge back to the car and drive to the studio. Eliza goes to set the cooking fire in the kitchen, while Nancy and I carry our bags inside and lock the large glass doors onto the street.

We sit with cups of tea in the kitchen, too tired to speak. The candles flicker and my mind is blank with shock and despair. What in God's name will we do now?

Glass *shatters*.

I hear drunken guffaws and heavy footsteps in the studio. A whining voice. 'I did see them coming in here, I fucking did. Bitch with big tits and a tidy little bint.'

The hair on my scalp crawls. Eliza and I stare wide-eyed at each other and I whisper, 'Take Nancy, hide in the laundry cupboard out the back. And whatever you hear, whatever you think, do *not* come out, do you hear me, Eliza? Protect Nancy with your life. *Do not come out.*'

They go and I close the door quietly after them. My throat is dry and I gulp a mouthful of tea. I stare into a small mirror on the wall. Think, Izabel, *think*. If you resist it'll be worse and if they find Nancy ... You've got to disarm them. Please them.

You know what you have to do.

I get out my reddest lipstick and, hand shaking, make my mouth voluptuous. I wipe my tears and put on high heels, loosen my hair and undo the top buttons of my dress.

As I walk down the hall to the studio I can hear raucous laughter and a bottle smashing, and I try not to whimper. I take a breath and push open the door.

Dazzling torches suddenly turn on me, and I pretend I'm under a small spotlight (most flattering angle, *please*, darling).

I pose, hands on hips: confident, amusing, sensuous.

Welcoming.

23. Eliza: Scheherazade

Silent tears run down my face but I'm not sure if I'm crying for Izabel or Harry or my own helpless self. The cupboard has just enough space for me to sit at one end, Nancy the other. She's also weeping quietly.

I'm grateful for the doors between us and the studio. The cupboard door, the laundry door, the kitchen door, the hallway door: the doors than prevent us knowing what is happening to Izabel.

After a long, long time I'm cramped and the only thing I can hear is the distant thudding of shells. Suddenly there are footsteps and the light of a candle through the cracks.

The door opens and my heart jumps.

'Izabel! Are you all *right*?' I can't see her face for the candle.

'Of course. They're gone. Sorry it took so ...' Her voice trails away. She takes a breath. 'Come on. You must be uncomfortable.' Nancy scrambles out and clings to her mother. Izabel strokes her hair and murmurs, 'Darling, oh, darling. Let's ...'

In the kitchen she puts the kettle on the cooking fire. 'Could do with a cuppa,' she says, then sits down suddenly. 'Sorry. Tired.'

'No wonder. It's been a long day,' I say as evenly as I can. Izabel has changed her dress. The old one is lying crumpled on the floor. Is it torn, stained? I try not to stare in case Nancy notices.

'Your lip's bleeding, *Ah-me*,' says Nancy. 'Did those men hurt you?'

'Oh, they yelled and pushed me around, like soldiers do, but when I showed them we didn't have any beer they went away.'

'It took ever such a long time. Aunt Eliza and I were very worried.'

'They wanted to tell me stories about fighting the Japanese, but they did go on and on. *Ghastly* bores. Now visit the bathroom, sweetheart, and wash your face and hands, then come back.'

As soon as Nancy's out of the room I say, 'Izabel, what *happened*?'

'Oh, it wasn't that bad. I've had worse reviews on Broadway.'

'*Izabel.*'

'Dear God, Eliza.' She rubs her face. 'Remember all those marvellous parts I used to play? How do you think I got them? Sheer, fabulous, scintillating talent?'

'Well — yes. You're a wonderful actress.'

'My God, you're as innocent as Nancy. I fucked them, the directors, the producers, the choreographers, fucked them all.' She shrugs. 'Well, not all, but enough. Enough to be able to get through tonight and keep a smile plastered on my face.'

'Izabel, that's — oh Christ, that's *dreadful*.'

'The sex wasn't as dreadful as the sheer bloody terror,' she says, gazing distantly. 'They were deserters, sick with shame, desperate to tell me their self-pitying tales of woe. If I'd hit the wrong note they'd have beaten me to death from raw humiliation.'

'But did they *hurt* you?'

'I played the movie star swayed by their manly charms,' she says wearily. 'Strung them along like Scheherazade, and when they mounted me all cocksure, well, lads are wire-trigger sensitive. I brought them off in seconds and sent them away believing I'd loved it.'

Nancy comes back and touches Izabel's face. 'Are you all right now?'

'Actually, sweetheart, I think I am.' She looks at me. 'Those men said two naval ships are coming in tonight at No. 10 Wharf, probably the last ones out of here. We're going back to the harbour.'

Izabel is *not* all right, not in the slightest. She asks me to drive her car, saying she's tired, but her hands are trembling. I avoid the main street, jammed with abandoned vehicles, and get close to the port through the laneways.

We leave the car and carry our bags along the footpath, stopping every now and then to rest in the stinking, humid night. Finally No. 10 Wharf is ahead.

The air is thick with the oily smoke that leaves a disgusting taste in my throat. The islands offshore are on fire and distant guns are shelling constantly, although I've no idea what they're trying to hit.

The warehouses along the river have been burning for days, their skeleton rafters outlined by flames, roaring, crackling and collapsing now and then.

Standing in the eerie flickering light is a silent crowd of men, mainly RAF ground crew.

There are no ships waiting.

Someone bumps into Izabel and she gasps and presses against me. 'Sorry,' she murmurs. 'The sight of brawny chaps in uniform isn't quite the reassurance it used to be.'

I squeeze her hand, and we push slowly through the crowd. I recognise a neat, clever woman standing with a couple of RAF officers, the Governor's cipher clerk. We'd meet up on the social circuit and used to chat whenever I took briefing documents to her office.

'Molly!'

'Heavens — Eliza, how *are* you?'

'Had better days. Are there really ships coming in tonight?'

'That's what they tell me. Oh, hello, Mrs Malory — I'm surprised you're all still stuck here.'

'As am I, Mrs Reilly,' says Izabel, drawing on a cigarette.

'We were supposed to join *Empire Star* today,' I say, 'but deserters rushed the ship and we couldn't board.'

Molly nods. 'Stay with me. The Air Commodore promised my husband he'd make sure I got away.' She pauses, gazing out to sea. 'We didn't have a chance to say goodbye, you know.' After another silence she takes a breath and says, 'And where's your lovely Harry?'

'Staying behind at the hospital.'

'Oh, Eliza, I'm *so* sorry.'

The heartbreak I've contained over this long day almost overwhelms me, but an offshore island — a fuel depot? — explodes into a sky-high inferno. It silhouettes two vessels approaching in the orange light.

A murmur rustles through the crowd then the strange silence descends once more, and even as the warships come alongside and tie up there's barely a sound.

HMS *Durban* and HMS *Kedah* are an odd pair. *Durban* is a Royal Navy light cruiser, twice the size of small *Kedah*, a requisitioned island ferry. A bosun calls, 'Lively, lads,' and with unexpected discipline the men around us form lines and quietly file aboard both vessels.

We follow Molly onto *Kedah*. She murmurs, 'We used to sail on this very ship to the race meetings in Penang. Such happy times.'

In the early hours of the morning, as silently as she arrived, *Kedah* glides away from No. 10 Wharf. I watch the cinders of Singapore flaring behind us, and think, heart-broken, of a line of poetry Billie sometimes recites:

And blue-bleak embers, ah my dear, fall, gall themselves, and gash gold-vermillion.

Ah, my dear.

As part of the Governor's staff Molly receives an officer's berth, but she manages to get the three of us a tiny cabin on the next deck and I almost weep with gratitude at the sight of the bunks. Izabel and Nancy fall asleep quickly, but then I lie awake, my head throbbing.

Damn you, Harry. All civilians were told to get away, yet you were so certain your duty was to stay with your patients. What about your duty to *me*?

You might save one or two more lives, I'd argued furiously, but will the Japanese then treat you, or your patients, or your nurses, any better than those poor souls at St Stephen's College?

Still my husband shook his head. He gave me a briefcase full of documents, the distillation of his years of research, and asked me to make certain his latest paper reached the editor of *Nature.*

He smiled gently, his lean, intelligent face dearer to me than anything in the world. We wept and held each other for a long time, then Harry said, 'Go, my love. Please go.'

I went. How could I refuse him that peace of mind? But what about *my* peace of mind? People have been telling me fairy stories about 'prisoner exchanges' for weeks.

Dear God, I know exactly what happens in war — and in defeat — and it isn't civilised prisoner exchanges. That our Singapore adventure came to this! Oh, *Harry*, how could you let us part?

My anguish ebbs and flows, and finally I sleep.

Next morning I emerge blearily on deck. A soldier tells me we didn't get far last night because the ship had to wait for dawn to navigate a minefield. But now we're moving briskly along in convoy with HMS *Durban* and, surprisingly, *Empire Star*, which must also have been held up by the minefield. I wonder how Felix, Barbara and Tessie are coping. Hundreds of men are crammed into every corner of *Kedah*, and there must be thousands packed aboard *Empire Star*.

The morning is beautiful, cloudless and blue. Suddenly loudspeakers crackle and the captain announces we're coming under air attack, civilians should go below.

Back in our cabin I hear the roar of planes, shells exploding, bullets clanging. Small *Kedah* vibrates as her engines go to maximum, and she heels one way then the other, cleverly zig-zagging.

The cacophony stops and my ears are ringing. Izabel has scrounged a little food — hard biscuits, canned beef and some black tea — and we eat in the cabin. Just as we've finished the alarm starts again, Japanese planes attack again, and the gun crews fight them off again.

I fall asleep for a few blessed hours, then the alarm sounds once more. I go up the stairs and peer out at the deck. High above is a droning flight of bombers. The ship's guns start thudding and silvery objects fall from the planes.

Kedah heels over and I grab for a handhold. Bombs strike the sea where we were just an instant ago, and solid geysers of water thud against the hull. We manoeuvre again and again.

Finally the bombers leave. Silence falls and I gaze around. We may be safe, but clouds of smoke are billowing from *Durban* and *Empire Star*.

Two days later we watch from the deck as *Kedah* motors into Tanjung Priok, Batavia's port; moving slowly because we've had engine trouble. Thankfully, despite the damage they suffered, *Empire Star* and *Durban* are already there at the wharves.

'The first officer told me *Empire Star*'s crew managed to put out the fires,' Molly says. 'But people were packed like sardines and dozens died. God, nurses were protecting patients with their own *bodies*.' She sighs. 'I wonder what's happening in Singapore. I hope —'

'I'm sure they'll be all right,' I say quickly.

She says quietly, 'The captain wants us women off first. They're going to try to deal with the deserters on *Empire Star* and he's worried there might be shooting. But there's a Dutch vessel a few berths over.

They have showers and food, I'm told.'

'Wonderful,' says Izabel. 'It's been days and I feel ... grubby. Come on, Nancy, we'll find out if Tessie's all right, I'm sure she is.'

She is. We meet Barbara and Tessie at the showers on the Dutch ship. Nancy and Tessie squeal in delight to see each other again, while Barbara bursts into tears. 'Izabel! I was terrified we'd never see you again. What did you *do*?'

'Caught the next bus,' says Izabel. 'How's Felix?'

'Gyppy tummy, but all right. He's going to try to eat some breakfast.'

The showers are indeed wonderful. We walk to the mess room afterwards, my hair pleasingly damp on my neck, and see the deserters, over one hundred men, being humbly marched away by a detachment of marines.

'Good riddance,' says Izabel, expressionless. 'Not very fond of deserters myself.'

'Heavens, who is!' says Barbara. 'The word's going round that if the Australians had only had a little more *backbone* we'd have managed to hold Singapore.'

'We might have held bloody *Singapore*, Barbara,' I say, suddenly furious, 'with some serious defence planning, or capital ships, or modern planes. Or if Brooke-Popham had *listened* when we said where the Japanese would land — you think that might have helped too?'

'My goodness Eliza, well, absolutely. Look, here's Felix —'

Felix half stands, and for a man with a gyppy tummy he's got an inadvisably large breakfast on his plate. Perhaps it's the indigestion turning him so pale.

'*Izabel*. How on earth ...?'

Like you, Felix. Caught a ship.'

'But I didn't think there *were* any —' He sits again, slowly. 'Well, well. That *is* good news.' He looks around. 'Breakfast's over there, no table service I'm afraid.'

Nancy and Tessie run to get food and Izabel gazes at her husband for a long moment. She turns and says, 'Tell me, Barbara, why did you thank me that morning before you left?'

' Felix said we might soon be free to marry. I — I thought you'd agreed to a divorce.'

'Ah, of course!' says Izabel, sitting down, staring hard at Felix. 'You knew if we came along later that day we probably wouldn't get aboard *Empire Star*, and then the Japanese would finish me off. Did you leave word of my Chinese family too, just to be sure, Felix?'

He goes red. 'What kind of a monster do you think I am?'

'I have no idea if you planned it or simply hoped it might happen, Felix, but understand this. I am *not* divorcing you — and by God, I'll give you no excuse to divorce me. Awfully sorry, Barbara.'

The damaged ships receive fast, makeshift repairs. Some of the men from Singapore are staying here to fight, others (and Molly) are sailing on *Kedah* to join the forces in Ceylon.

But we're bound for Fremantle, and on 16th February we depart aboard *Empire Star*. Once we're out of port the captain gives us the news we've all been dreading: last night, 'Fortress Singapore' was surrendered to the Japanese.

I feel as if I've been punched in the chest. I was still hoping a miracle might save Harry, save everyone. I tell myself to remain strong for damaged Izabel and confused Nancy, but all I can feel is sorrow.

Is Harry still alive? Would I know it, would I *feel* it, if he weren't?

At night we sleep on the cool deck and the mercifully overcast skies hide us from enemy planes. The ship stops briefly at Broome, where we get the news of the terrible bombing of Darwin, but in my dazed state it doesn't quite register.

We reach Fremantle on 23rd February. Barbara and Tessie go to stay with friends, and I ring my mother Rosa. She lives with her husband Anton and my grandmother Min-lu, and now aunt Lucy and uncle Danny, recently evacuated from Broome.

Mama picks us up from the ship. At the house Felix is allocated a narrow cot on the back veranda and I share my childhood bedroom with Izabel and Nancy.

At dinner I feel remote. How can I be *here*? How can Harry be *there*? At the table my mother is the same as ever, but white-haired Min-lu seems frailer than our last meeting eighteen months ago. The ground rocks beneath my feet after days on the ship and I'm desperately tired.

Next day the sun rises, birds sing, the morning is fresh, and none of it makes any sense. Uncle Danny brings me the paper, and I open it to the war news:

> *NEW YORK, Feb. 24. The Tokio radio today said that 4,600 wounded British soldiers are in the Cathay Hotel at Singapore under the care of the Japanese; also, that 1,282 British civilians, including 92 women, remained in Singapore. Lack of water, incessant bombing and greatly superior numbers compelled surrender. Two hospitals at the time of the surrender had only enough water for 24 hours.*

My throat tightens at the word 'hospitals.' I scan the other columns, but they're reports on Java and the war in Europe. I turn the pages, but that's all there is on Singapore.

'Where's the rest? It's hardly been ten days since the surrender!'

'Ah, the fall of Singapore's already old news,' says Danny. 'I'm sorry, Lizzie Lee.'

Worse than old news, I'm forced to read stories about people who miraculously got away (none of them Harry). Even the Australian leader, Gordon Bennett — that nasty little man — turns up with his own tale of daring escape: sampan, junk, privileged army launch and easy plane flight home.

His aide shamelessly reports, 'The General's bravery has been rarely equalled. It was more striking because, with his rank, he would have been assured of good quarters in which to live in safety until the end of the war, had he surrendered.'

Good quarters? Is he insane?

Another item: *The estimate of 73,000 Allied prisoners, including 17,000 Australians, taken by the Japanese in the fall of Singapore is accepted as accurate by the army authorities.*

Seventy-three thousand prisoners! What 'good quarters' will they — will Harry — receive?

The days of agony pass slowly, one by one. On 3rd March, Broome is bombed. Dozens of planes go up in flames, many of them flying-boats full of refugees, and Lucy weeps: for years she and Danny have lived, worked and raised their children in Broome.

'It's not just because it's home,' she says. 'It's Mike too. He joined the army three months ago. I suppose every mother feels like this, but I don't know if I can bear it.'

'He's training with some Independent Company in Victoria,' says Danny. 'I hear one of those units is doing it rough in Timor.' He sighs and puts his arm around Lucy.

The agony lengthens into weeks, and then months. The Japanese flatly refuse to tell the British the names of their many captives, civilian or military. In late April 1942, I read:

> LONDON. A representative of the Red Cross War Prisoners' Department said that the Japanese had not allowed the International Red Cross delegates to visit any prisoners' camp outside of Japan. 'It seems that they want to clean up all the occupied territory before allowing the Red Cross in,' he remarked.

I doubt it's territory they're cleaning up before the world is allowed to see what they've been doing.

In early June, I'm shocked to read that Harry's home town of Newcastle has just been shelled by Japanese submarines, aiming for the dockyards and steelworks on the harbour.

I quickly write to his mother Jessie, who tells me by return post she is safe, and that Tina is working with a signals section somewhere in Queensland.

I cannot bear to think of how Jessie must feel, with her daughter away and the utter lack of news about her son.

And me? I send Harry's research paper to the editor of *Nature*, who says it's a fine piece of work and will be published as soon as war shortages permit: a small comfort.

Otherwise, all I can do is read the news and worry about Nancy and Izabel. Barbara and Tessie are staying nearby, and Nancy unwisely tells Tessie how Izabel saved us in Singapore by talking for a long time with some deserters.

More worldly Tessie guesses the truth and goads Nancy with her moralising, so now the confused girl won't shut up about sin and saintliness.

Izabel is lost far away in some tense, foggy state, trying to pretend to everyone else she's all right. I try to engage her but it's difficult. One day in the lounge-room, as she stares at nothing, I say, 'Here's an interesting story,' and read out the newspaper snippet.

A CHINESE AMAZON: Thirteen Japanese Killed.

Wei Chin, a 16-year-old Chinese guerrilla girl who fought through the Malayan campaign armed with a rifle and knife with which she killed 13 Japanese, has arrived in Colombo after escaping from Singapore.'

'Thirteen Japanese! Oh, how brave,' says Nancy, looking up from her tattered copy of Girl's Own Annual. 'I'd like to be a guerrilla girl one day and fight soldiers.'

Izabel turns in shock. 'Nancy, *never* say a thing like that again. Have you lost your *mind*?'

Nancy, tears in her eyes, hugs her book to her chest. 'Well, Tessie says *you* should have died as a martyr before letting —'

Izabel slaps her face, and abruptly leaves the room.

Min-lu, on the sofa beside me, sighs and closes her sewing-box.

'This is the last time I will ask, Eliza. What happened to Izabel in Singapore?'

Nancy bursts out angrily, 'She was hurt by soldiers, Nanna. Tessie says it's called rape and soldiers do that a lot, that's why they like being soldiers. So she's been *defiled*, and she won't feel better till she goes to church and repents of her *sin*.'

'It means nothing of the kind, child,' says Min-lu crisply. 'Don't so be foolish.'

Nancy runs crying out of the room. I stare after her and Min-lu stares at me.

'Izabel made me promise not to mention it, not to anyone,' I say helplessly. 'She says she's almost forgotten.'

'*Rape*? Rather difficult to forget, Eliza.'

I take her hand, grateful to be able to speak at last.

'Oh, *Nanna*, it was the night we escaped. Poor Izabel used herself as a decoy, and saved Nancy and me. She *sacrificed* herself for us.'

Brave, beguiling Scheherazade.

I'm suddenly sobbing, and as so often my grandmother gathers me into her arms and comforts me.

For some reason Barbara and Felix quarrel. She organises passages home to Britain for herself and Tessie, but Felix isn't obviously bothered. Nancy is sad when they leave, but both girls make extravagant plans to meet up again one day.

Felix doesn't want to return to the Far East Combined Bureau, now working in Kenya, so he pulls strings to get himself a position in London with its parent body, the Government Code and Cipher School. I suppose they must be short-handed.

While Felix is organising a service evacuation to Britain he starts making himself surprisingly useful around the place. He's puzzlingly solicitous towards Izabel and even kind to Nancy.

Then one day Izabel comes in, smiling drily.

'Felix has just let slip why he's being so civilised. Turns out that GC&CS wants him back because of *me*, his Eurasian wife. After some Indian forces went over to the Japanese they want to understand the Singapore Chinese better — so they're hiring me. Delicious isn't it?'

I laugh. 'It is. What would you be doing there?'

'Who cares? I'm simply *charmed* at how put out Felix is.' Izabel leans forward. 'So what do you think, Eliza? You should come with us, you know — your old section wants you back, and you can clearly do more in London for the war effort.'

'Of course I'd love to work with them again, and be home in our own flat,' I say. 'But London is such a long way from Singapore.'

'Oh, darling. Where you live won't make any difference to Harry. We can only hope for the best for him and do whatever we can.'

Izabel is correct. Five long months after the invasion, the Japanese are still refusing to release the names of their captives, civilian or military; alive, wounded or dead.

The time has come to return to the only job I can do that might help defeat them.

In July 1942 I kiss my relatives goodbye and climb the gangway of a passenger ship at Fremantle, together with Izabel, Nancy and Felix. We set off for London in convoy with merchant vessels, minesweepers and destroyers.

The last letter I'd had from my shipbroker, Mr Weatherall, told me that after Finland joined the Fascists the Allies confiscated three of the Finnish square-riggers, while my dear *Inverley* and four others are laid-up at anchor in Mariehamn harbour: they will not be going to sea again for a very long time.

I stand at the rail and gaze at the hazy blue horizon, and feel nothing of the joy of my old sailing days.

24. Billie: Closed Doors

Eliza's coming home. Thank Christ, somebody sane to talk to at last! Still, she'll find us all very changed from the old days. The avant-garde gang is now split in two, Sofia siding with her cousin Stef, Klara stoutly defending Toby.

Pete and I try to keep the balance, but it's hard. And it's particularly hard to forgive Stef and Charlotte for their blatant faithlessness.

Today Toby and I are waiting at the London docks to meet Eliza, the same place she and Harry sailed from in late 1939. That was in the middle of the Phoney War, when the city was still unbombed and people thought the greatest inconvenience in their lives was carrying gas masks.

Now it's August 1942, half a year since the fall of Singapore, and London itself probably looks something like Singapore did in its death throes. The autumn is mild but there's a chill off the water so I'm glad of my ATA uniform — deep blue belted jacket, white shirt, black tie and best of all, warm, tailored trousers.

After a struggle with some officials who wanted us always dressed in skirts, we were finally allowed trousers for flying. But they're so comfortable we wear them whenever we like. Well, I do, anyway.

The passengers are starting to emerge now from Customs to cries of welcome. I see Eliza's dark head, and beside her is Izabel, thinner and browner than I remember, and a girl with them who's nearly as tall as Eliza, with plaits and shy eyes. Must be the famous Nancy.

But where's Felix? I only met him once but he was unforgettable — black hair, intense blue eyes, charm to burn. There's a man with them, but he's grey, mean-faced and round-shouldered, snapping at the porter. Wait a minute: that's Felix after all! Suppose the tropics are hard on some people.

They don't seem to have taken a toll on Lizzie though — she's still her usual neat, pretty self. Then she hugs me fiercely and I realise, despite her smile, she isn't.

'Oh, *Billie*, Toby too!' She turns. 'Izabel, you've met Billie, I think —'

'You probably won't remember,' I say.

'Hello, darling,' says Izabel. 'Of course I remember. I stole your magnificent air of concentration for a part in a play. My daughter, Nancy, and I believe you've met Felix before.'

'And this is Toby Fenn, the author,' I say.

'More recently the fireman,' says Toby, stepping forward to shake her hand. 'What a pleasure to meet you, Mrs Malory. How was your voyage?'

'Not very enjoyable,' says Felix. 'Can we go?'

Eliza glances at him coolly. 'Where are the taxis, Billie? Everything's changed so much.'

She's right. I've become so used to the sight of barbed wire and sandbags and guardhouses I forget how confusing everything must look to newcomers.

'This way,' says Toby. 'Eliza, you'll be charmed to hear we've *finally* cleaned up the third floor. It's a sight to behold, and you're all welcome to use it for as long as you need. I've spoken to the tenants of your flat too. They'll be moving out in six weeks, so it'll soon be ready for you again.'

'*Dear* Toby, thank you,' says Eliza. 'How good to see you both.'

The absence of Harry is shocking, unnatural. I can't grasp that he's not there beside her.

'Has there been any word?' Toby murmurs to Eliza.

She shakes her head and says brightly, 'Well, how *is* everyone? I suppose Stef's much better now. Has Klara published anything lately? And Sofia! I'm so looking forward to hearing her play with a real orchestra. There was nothing like that in Singapore even before — before ...'

'We'll tell you all the news later,' I say. 'Come on, let's get you home.'

Eliza puts down her teacup with a clatter. 'Stef and *Charlotte*? My God. How's Pete taking it?'

'He's okay. He and Charlotte actually separated a while ago without telling anyone.'

'I suppose in a way that's good,' she says. 'Is Vivy all right?'

'I think so. She's always been close to Mrs Spencer, the housekeeper. She talks to Charlotte on the phone quite often, but hasn't seen a lot of her in the last few years.'

'So it's probably Toby who's been hit the hardest.'

I nod. 'Reckon so, but he says he wasn't all that surprised. Stef's always had a wandering eye — but *Charlotte* the one to catch it? There's the real surprise.'

'Maybe not. Both of them have always needed a constant stream of new conquests.'

'Still, Toby's become more *substantial* too, somehow,' I say. 'I'll tell you more later, but he found out that Aunt Maude was his *real* mother.'

'Aunt Maude! Heavens. But first, what did you say about Klara — she's not *writing*?'

'No. She's lonely and working too hard.'

'But where's *Sofia*?' says Eliza. 'Why isn't she looking after her?'

'Ah. Good old Sofe fell in love with a vixen named Terry. She's now back in New York, and Sofe's been invited to go over there to play with Terry's husband's orchestra.'

'What?'

'I know, all sounds crazy,' I say. 'But even if Sofe stays here, she supports Stef in the Charlotte debacle. And since Toby's one of Klara's closest friends, that makes her doubly furious at Sofe.'

Eliza sighs. 'What a mess.'

'See what happens when you leave us by ourselves?' I say. 'Should never have gone away.'

'Can't argue with you there, darling Bill.'

'Oh, Lizzie. I'm so sorry. Stupid thing to say.'

'True, though. And no need to tell me he'll be all right. I've no idea if he will and nor has anyone else, so please don't say it.' Eliza takes a breath. 'Has anything *good* happened recently?'

'Oh — I'm flying Spits. That's pretty good.'

She laughs and holds out her arms and I hug her.

Our schedule of aircraft deliveries never ends and we don't get much leave, just four days a month, so I'm up early to return to Hamble as soon as possible. Because Eliza and Izabel's family have taken over the third floor (where I usually stay), last night I slept in the spare room in Sofia and Klara's flat.

While I'm yawning over a cup of tea at the kitchen table, Sofia enters, wearing a crimson dressing-gown that suits her dramatic dark looks. She takes a cup and saucer and sits down.

'Enough for another?' she says.

I pour her the last of the pot. 'How've you been, Sofe? Made the big decision yet?'

She pushes her dark curls back from her forehead. 'Still wrestling, dear one. Such a marvellous opportunity, but I do know if I go it means the end of my life here.'

'Doesn't have to be — you can always come back.'

'Not quite that easy,' Sofia says, stirring her tea.

'Why do you think Terry will leave her husband for you, anyway?'

'Heavens, I don't think that at all,' she says. 'In fact I know she won't, and really, I think you're rather oversimplifying the situation. I'm not going because of Terry.'

'Yeah?'

'Oh, Billie, you know I can't get work as a cellist here, *real* work! The orchestra'll toss me out on my ear as soon as the war ends. But in America I could have a future as a musician and composer.'

'But Klara won't be with you,' I say.

'No. She says she'll never leave London, her spiritual home.' Sofia lips are tight. 'Frankly, I wish she were a touch less spiritual.'

'Toby always calls her pragmatic.'

'Toby.' Sofia sighs. 'Look, I'm not taking sides, but it's obvious he and Stef have been going their different ways since the war began.'

'You could say that about everyone separated by events. Jeez, look at poor Eliza and Harry.'

'But don't you see this could be *marvellous* for Stef?' she says. 'His parents are desperate for him to marry and have an heir. Of course, what he does after that would be his own business, but children are obviously not on the cards while he's with Toby.'

I'm vaguely reminded of something, but I'm too annoyed with her to think. '*Honestly*, Sofe, Toby's done everything possible to support him since the accident. How can Stef leave him now?'

She shrugs. 'I fear you have a rather rigid view of relationships, Billie. Even when people decide a particular door is closed to them forever, it's not necessarily so. And sometimes they can try and try and it's *never* going to open. So they should part.'

'Toby and Stef?'

'Yes.'

'Klara and Sofia?'

'I wish I knew.'

But I'm pretty sure she does.

At Waterloo station I discover my train to Southampton has been cancelled but another leaves in an hour. I go to the tea-room to see if they've got what's laughingly referred to as a sandwich. I don't mind the wartime rough-milled bread, it's the slice of stuff they call meat inside that's the worry.

I'm surprised to notice Charlotte sitting in a corner, chin on hand, gazing at nothing. She looks up as I approach.

'Goodness, Billie, didn't see you there. Have a seat.'

'Hi, Charlie. Where are you off to so early?'

'Oh, Guildford. Gabriela and Roger have invited us to the estate for a few days, but Stefan had to go into work suddenly this morning. He'll come down later instead.'

'How's his new job going?'

'Doing well at the Ministry, though naturally he'd rather be flying. I assume you're still happy as a pig in mud?'

'Absolutely. On my way back to Hamble now.' I unwrap my sandwich, then think better of eating it and wrap it up again. 'How do you get on with Stef's parents, then?'

'Gabriela and I amuse each other. Roger treats me kindly, rather as he might a brood mare.'

I laugh. 'Are you and Stef still in the honeymoon phase? It's been six months already, surely the gloss has worn thin by now.'

She runs a lock of golden hair through her fingers, her eyes amused. 'No, I adore him.'

'He's good at being adored. Wafting just out of reach, but close enough so his lovers believe they've got a chance. Maybe he'll waft out of your reach too.'

'Never, sweetie Stefan adores me. That sensible liaison with Eliza? The schoolboy crush with Toby?' She laughs. 'No comparison. We're getting married once my divorce comes through.'

'Given Stef's posh parents, I don't suppose you're going for a quickie adultery divorce, so it'll have to be desertion — but that takes a few years. You'll be a bit long in the tooth by then.'

'Actually, no. Gabriela and Roger have very progressive views,' Charlotte says. 'Pete has agreed I can sue him for adultery, so Stefan and I will soon be free to marry and have a family.'

Pete's name suddenly reminds me of what slipped my mind when talking to Sofia earlier.

'Hold on, Charlie — weren't you going to get your *tubes* tied? Pete said you were planning to.'

'How very indiscreet of him.' She shakes her head. 'No. Couldn't find a surgeon to do it without my husband's written consent, the fusty old dinosaurs. But all to the better really — now I can give Stefan everything he desires.'

She lights a cigarette and smiles, her cornflower blue eyes wryly confident. I wonder, then, why her fingers have the tiniest of tremors.

Pete rings me at Hamble a few weeks later, and I'm not surprised to hear Sofia has left for America.

'Eliza's going to bring Klara down to the farm for a few days, Izabel and Nancy too,' Pete says. 'Take her mind off things.'

'Eliza or Klara?'

'Both, I expect. Actually, Eliza asked if you'd dine with us tomorrow.'

'Oh. Well, yes. Lovely.'

'Fine, then. Seven o'clock.'

I still go out to the farm to see Vivy, but now Pete and I have a polite, sensible friendship, just as I wanted. Almost a year has passed since that foolish surge of desire at Toby's cottage, and I think we both realise we're better off with that door well and truly closed.

I don't know if Pete's seeing another woman — I expect so, given the impending divorce from Charlotte. As for me, after days of aircraft deliveries I don't have the energy to think about flings, although sometimes I'm aware of a new and unfamiliar sense of loneliness.

I mostly spend my few free hours in the mess at Hamble, reading or listening to the gramophone. That Friday night, tired after three delivery flights, I'm contemplating going to my digs when I'm called to the phone. To my surprise it's Pete again.

'Change of plans for tomorrow?' I ask.

'Ah, no. But I just got a telegram from my mother. Some bad news.'

'Not *Harry*?'

'No, thank God. But it's Min-lu, my grandmother. She's *died*, Billie. From pneumonia, very suddenly. Never expected — haven't seen her for years, but I always thought ... I can't ... '

He takes a ragged breath.

'That's awful. Do Izabel and Lizzie know?'

'Mama doesn't have their address, so she wrote to me. But I can't tell them on the phone, it'll have to be tomorrow after they arrive. *Jesus*.'

'I'm so sorry, Pete.'

After a pause he says, 'Remember Min-lu always wore those gold combs in her hair? When I was little, stupid really, I thought it meant she was an empress.'

'Makes sense. Always carried herself like royalty, didn't she?'

'Backbone of our family, Billie. Mama was always so busy, but when Nanna visited — she took me seriously when everyone else ...' He swallows. 'Just such a shock. Needed to talk to someone about it.'

'Yeah — not many others round here who knew her. And Min-lu was a pretty amazing woman, years ahead of her time.'

A long silence.

'Will we call off dinner, Pete?'

He clears his throat. 'No, Eliza'll still want to see you.'

'Okay. Well, see you tomorrow, then. Take care of yourself, mate.'

We hang up.

Poor old Pete. Poor Izabel, and poor Lizzie too.

I sit for a while in a quiet corner of the deserted mess, then a woman comes in and puts a record on the gramophone. She's from the latest intake, Yvonne something. Tallish, mousy, wispy-haired, early twenties like most of the other pilots. I'm one of the ATA ancients and some days I really feel it too

She settles herself and the record starts. Thank God it's not *Boogie Woogie Bugle Boy* for the hundredth time, but a classical piece, something I've heard before.

Light, slow, thoughtful — suits my mood. I'm drifting away with it, then suddenly realise it's one of Sofia's compositions. Odd. The record ends and the woman leans forward and lifts the needle.

'That was nice,' I say. 'Where did you get it?'

She looks around, surprised. 'Sorry, didn't realise ... Oh, a concert a while ago — they'd pressed some copies to raise money for charity. You won't have heard of the composer, though.'

'Bet I have. Sofia Graham.'

'Goodness, yes. Do you like her music?'

'Very much. She's an old friend.'

'*Is* she? Heavens, lucky you.'

'Yeah. Pity, though, she's just gone away to New York.'

'She'll come back, won't she?'

'Who knows? It's a bit rough on ... her mates.' No need to discuss Sofia's private life. I change the subject. 'You've just started here?'

She nods. 'Had my A licence already, but the training's a big help. I love it, but — I don't know. Some of the others aren't very welcoming.'

'You need to show you're sticking around,' I say. 'Quite a few society dames have come along for a week or two, then dropped out. Better to get to know new people slowly.'

I don't mention the occasional shocking accident that leave us all cautious of becoming too fond of each other. Fear — or sorrow — can slow your reflexes.

'Makes sense. I'm Yvonne, by the way. Yvonne Watters.'

'Billie Quinn.' I get up. 'Hope you find your feet soon, kid.'

She smiles, and it suits her. 'Thanks, Billie. I will.'

Dinner at the farm isn't a conspicuous success. Eliza's eyes are swollen, Klara is subdued and Pete silent. Izabel, Min-lu's daughter, is struggling too. She tries, but now and then her gaze becomes far-away, her face still.

Nancy makes friends with six-year-old Vivy, who takes her upstairs after dinner to meet her dolls. Everything's quiet once they're gone, so I say, 'When will you be moving back to your old flat, Lizzie?'

She laughs bitterly. 'I won't now, Bill. The other night it was badly damaged by a bomb, and finding anyone to do repairs is impossible. On top of the news about Nanna —' She rubs her face. 'Anyway, I'm going to stay with Klara for a while.'

'What rotten luck, Lizzie. And ... still no word?'

She shakes her head.

I try again. 'Izabel, have you found a place?'

'Oh, sorry — what was that, darling?'

'Have you found somewhere to live yet?'

'Sadly, no,' she says. 'Impossible to rent a thing. We're going to stay on at Toby's as well. Felix worries that it's all too bohemian for a sensible chappie like him, but I just ignore him.'

Pause. Oh dear. Work?

'Have you started in your old job, Lizzie?' I say.

She nods. 'My department was out at Bletchley for a while, but now it's moved back to London. Pretty convenient for Toby's place too.'

Klara says suddenly, 'Toby's house is certainly very convenient, more than Otto and Charlotte's, where I stayed for a time — Billie, do you remember? But Charlotte, my God she is a lazy cow. I could not bear to live with her. And Stefan is lazy too — lazy with his feelings — so perhaps they will suit each other.'

Eliza touches her hand. 'Klara love, Toby will be all right. You don't have to dislike Stef and Charlotte on his behalf.'

'Not on his behalf, Eliza. No, I had become fond of Charlotte because of her *Kindertransport* work, and now I feel betrayed. And of course I do not need to be told I am angry with Stef because he reminds me so much of Sofia. How heartless they are, the two of them.'

'Sofia will come back, Klara,' I say. 'It'll be okay again one day.'

'Billie, it will never be okay again. However, here is something very interesting. Since Sofia went away I have once more started writing poetry, and I think it is not too bad. That, of course, is one good thing about emotional pain. It is useful if you are a writer.'

Izabel laughs lightly. 'Perhaps we should all be writers then.'

Everyone else retires early, but Klara and I sit by the fire while I have coffee before driving back to Hamble. Klara shows me several of her new poems and I like them very much. They're not easy, the rhythms are subtle, but her eerie images are a delight. (I've learnt a bit since Wilf used to quote Gerard Manley Hopkins to me in Spain.)

'Are you going to publish these, Klara? People have been waiting ages for a new book from you.'

'I would, except my old printing press no longer works and I cannot fix it. Nor, apparently, can anyone else in London.' She sighs.

'You've had a rough trot lately, mate. Don't give up.'

'I will not. But I am lonely, Billie, because Sofia was leaving me for a long time. I am not a kind person perhaps, but it makes me bitter to see people like her and Stef and Charlotte go their own careless ways in the world, without a thought for the grief they cause others.'

'Yeah. Nothing seems to touch them.' I gaze at the red-gold fire. 'Then again, perhaps they do have the odd vulnerability. I saw Charlotte a few weeks ago and she told me she and Stef want to marry and have a family.'

'Why is that a vulnerability?'

'Remember her miscarriage and how afraid she was of becoming pregnant again? Pete mentioned to me she was going to get herself sterilised. I asked her and she said she hadn't gone ahead, but I'm pretty sure she was lying. The scar's not too different from an appendix operation either, so she could probably get away with it.'

'She plans to marry Stef and not tell him?' Klara laughs shortly. 'Perhaps I am a kind person after all. In such circumstances I would feel sorry for them both.'

'Didn't know you were turning lezzo, Billie,' says Daphne in the next armchair in the mess, doing something complicated with her knitting.

'Didn't know I was either.'

'Keep hanging around with Yvonne, you never know what'll happen.'

'Well, according to the world we're all lezzos in the women's ATA.'

'Good God, is that what they say? Of course we're not. But she is.'

I close Klara's book with a small sigh. 'And how do you know that, Daph? Personal experience?'

'Billie, *honestly*. Of course not. Someone from training told me.'

'Oh, based on their personal experience, then.'

'Just mentioning it, for heaven's sake. She seems very *fond* of you.'

'You're only jealous because she's a better pilot than you.'

Daphne's lips tighten. 'That is certainly not the case.'

'Being jealous? Or a better pilot?'

'*Neither.*' She waves a knitting needle at my book. 'And you don't do yourself any favours flaunting your friendship with that — that Sapphic poetess, either.'

'I'm just reading, Daph. Doubt it's going to turn me off men for life.'

'You simply don't take *anything* seriously, Billie.'

Daphne thrusts her needles into the ball of wool and rolls up her knitting. 'And *look* at you — hair like a street urchin, thin as a boy, language that'd make a trooper blush. Is it any wonder no one knows quite what you are?'

She picks up her bag and walks off, and I'm suddenly sick of the place. I close my eyes. I'm tired too, four deliveries today. Nearly got caught too when some barrage balloons were raised unexpectedly, and only some fast manoeuvring saved the plane.

I once saw a Junker fly into a cluster of balloons. A cable took off a wing and it spiralled into the ground. Actually, Daph, I do take things like that pretty damned seriously.

Despite Daph's misgivings I wouldn't mind Yvonne being around this evening. I'd really like some music. Anyway, time to go home, I need a bath. I'm almost at the door when Yvonne comes in.

'Night, Yvie,' I say. 'Need some kip.'

'Me too. But thought I'd sit down for a moment, bit shaken up — almost got caught in the barrage balloons on the flight corridor. They mustn't have got the signal someone was landing.'

'Wasn't just me they nearly did for, then?' I say. 'Christ, that's dangerous. I'll get Margot to make a complaint tomorrow.'

'Thanks, Billie.' She notices the book I'm carrying. 'Is that something new? I've already waded through everything on our one-shelf library.'

'You can borrow it, but mightn't be to your taste. Poetry, fairly surreal stuff.'

She takes it. 'Klara Virtanen? I love her work, but haven't seen this.'

'A small print run before the war. She stopped writing for a while, but now she's started again. Maybe another volume's on the way.'

'Wow. From a flatbed press, and hand-made paper, too — you don't see work like this very often.' Yvonne looks up smiling. 'My father was a printer, the old-fashioned sort. Taught me a lot.'

She turns the title page and stares at Klara's dedication to me written in her even loops.

'You know her?'

'She's a friend.'

'And Sofia Graham's a friend too.' She's puzzled. 'But you're not —'

'How can you be so sure?'

She smiles. 'Trust me, I'd know.'

I laugh. 'Well, everyone else round here seems to have a pretty firm opinion on the matter.'

'Don't they just!' She shrugs. 'What am I supposed to do? Just got to fly as well as I can and mind my own business.' She waves the book at me. 'Thanks. See you tomorrow.'

I turn to leave, then say, 'Yvie — you wouldn't happen to know anything about fixing old hand-printing presses, by any chance?'

'Growing up I was my Dad's mechanic. Loved working on the machines. Why?'

'Would you like to meet Klara Virtanen?'

As I'm leaving, the public phone rings. I lift the handpiece. 'Mess. No one here.'

'Billie?'

'Lizzie! How'd you know it was me?'

She laughs breathlessly. 'Your phone manner's fairly distinctive.'

'You all right?'

'Oh, yes, yes! News at last — the Red Cross finally got a list of the prisoners at Singapore. Harry's there, Harry's *alive!*'

I'm still smiling, my eyes foolishly moist, as I wheel my bicycle from the shelter, dry leaves rustling beneath the wheels. Such good news. Of course poor old Harry's still not safe, but at least Lizzie can dream they'll be together again one day.

I gaze up at the sky, stars dotted through the haze. Winter will be here soon, another bone-aching frigid winter. Must say, England would be a hell of a lot easier to bear with a nice warm man in my bed.

Lately I find myself yearning more and more for the heat of home, the country town of my childhood, the gurgle of magpies, the scent of eucalyptus in the drowsy noon. The blue, blue skies.

I sigh, and hop on the bike and pedal away, nodding goodnight to the old bloke on duty at the gate. It's not far to my digs.

My landlady is nice enough, but she likes an early night and the house is dark and quiet. I park the bike and open the door to the cold, dim hallway.

You're so sure of everything, Daph. Tell me: how long must I endure this loneliness?

25. Izabel: One More Chance

How *tired* we all are of this war. The rationing, the bombing, the scantiness of human comforts — it never seems to end. Even hot water has become such a luxury, everyone on the street seems grubbier and greyer. But perhaps that's just my perception, enduring these cheerless days in this gloomy city.

Eight months have passed since my mother Min-lu died and I still cannot believe she has gone. I suppose — as with Laurence — the long, long silence will itself be the proof.

Min-lu was buried in Perth with Christian rites: she paid lip service to the Western faith. But I know she would have wanted Buddhist prayers recited for her, just as we did for Bao-lim and Laurence.

One day, when Nancy and I return to Hong Kong, we will travel to First Cousin's house and mourn my mother properly at our family shrine. She left her beautiful gold hair-combs to me and I wear them often: in time they will go to Nancy.

Yet my grief at the loss of Min-lu is tempered a little by what followed so quickly afterwards, the news that would have made her laugh aloud with joy.

Eliza's Harry is *alive*, a civilian prisoner in Singapore. We send him parcels of food and clothing through the Red Cross, and receive occasional postcards in return. Dear Harry *lives*.

There are other good tidings: the brutal Russian winter of early 1943 turned the German blitzkrieg into a icy stalemate, and now the Red Army is balefully, implacably, fighting its way back towards Germany.

The Allies won the campaigns in North Africa, while much of the Imperial Navy is rusting at the bottom of the Pacific. The Japanese themselves are retreating island to island, the Americans and Australians pursuing them without mercy.

Within a year — even sooner — the Allies will free occupied Europe.

If only my mother were here to witness it.

Although Toby jokes the house is simply a vulgar Victorian, I like living at Whitfield Street. People are always coming and going, which helps distracts me from all the things I'd rather not think about.

The ground floor has two comfortable reception rooms, and the first floor is Toby's handsome flat, all leather sofas and antique prints. Eliza shares with Klara on the second floor, while we're on the third. Felix and I have separate bedrooms, of course.

I don't know if it's by accident or design, but Barbara and Tessie have come to live just three streets away. Barbara's no fool: rather than be conscripted into war work she found herself a nice job with some Ministry big-wig. I think she and Felix are seeing each other again (he's called me a *brick* a few times).

Tessie goes to the same school as Nancy. Thank heavens it's not a church school, and at last they seem to be getting over their silly religious prurience. They're still good friends, though. I suppose their common Singapore experience created a bond between them, just as it did for Eliza and me.

Singapore.

Of course I haven't forgotten what happened, despite what I tell Eliza. How could I? But it might have been so much worse, I chide myself, as it was for thousands of women then, and for millions of others throughout history.

I wasn't murdered. Really, I got off lightly. Why then can't I forget?

It goes around and around in my mind, especially in the early hours. One soldier had a broken tooth that cut my mouth. One had nauseating breath. One giggled and boasted incoherently until another hit him. One was young and terrified, but that didn't stop you for an instant, did it, sonny?

The last — the worst — had a crucifix glinting at his throat, probably stolen, and for a terrible instant I thought of the gold chain I gave Laurence so long ago.

That last one snarled over and over, grunting on top of me, I'll fuck you with my revolver when I'm done, bitch, and finish you off once and for all. But my graphic promises of future delight persuaded the others to disarm him, and they all finally staggered away.

Indeed, I gave the best performance of my life in Singapore — to my rapists, and later to Nancy and Eliza. And now I never, *never* want to act again.

But I *lived*, I tell myself. I lived, and a year and a half has passed since It happened. I developed no diseases, the cells of my body have renewed themselves, my cycles have returned to their rhythms.

I'm ten thousand miles away from the glitter of shattered glass, the humiliating torch-beams, the crude, *spiteful* violations.

Time has marched on.

Oddly, I now no longer believe Felix split up our group to stop me getting away on *Empire Star*. The chaos that day was certainly a given, but the rush of deserters who stopped us boarding was not. Still, I'm certain he hoped, privately, something like that might happen. Does it make him culpable?

No, but it makes him despicable.

I lived, but still I fear the sound of men's voices in the distance. I cannot stop myself flinching if Felix moves suddenly, and I can't bear the noise of him eating or coughing or even breathing.

He's such a fool too, strutting about in his uniform. Thankfully, now we're in London his revolver is safely locked away. The thought of any gun makes me shiver. *I'll finish you off once and for all, bitch.*

I lived, but my relationship with Nancy has suffered. I feel her gaze, her head full of nonsense about sex and sin and defilement. Does she think it was somehow my *choice* to suffer what happened?

Then, in a way, it was.

I expect many, many women throughout history have done exactly what I did to protect their beloved children. At least my wits saved me, and I didn't die in anguish for the titillation of those monsters.

To them I had no kinship to their sisters, their mothers, their friends, I was a *thing*. A thing in the hands of beings who felt only joy at their untrammelled power to violate me in every possible way.

Am I mad to find this extraordinary?

One day Felix is out, probably at Barbara's, and the others have gone to the park. I hear a knock at the front door, and Billie and Yvonne are on the doorstep, laden with boxes and bags.

Billie says, 'Quick, Izzy, grab that one before I drop it.'

I catch the small box. 'Eggs! Marvellous, everyone hates the powdered stuff. Come in.'

'We've got carrots, potatoes and ham,' says Yvonne. 'And Mrs Spencer's sent a cake.'

We go upstairs and I take them into Klara's kitchen, where we put everything away. 'Hope it wasn't too hard bringing all this from Southampton,' I say.

Yvonne says, 'Billie flirted with some soldiers on the train, so they carried most of it.'

'Nah, we just impressed them with our uniforms,' says Billie.

'Not surprising, you're both most impressive,' I say. 'Let's have some cake and tea. Klara should be back soon. They've just gone for a walk.'

Yvonne smiles and goes pink. She and Klara have been so happy since they met.

'How are things at Hamble?' I ask, handing around teacups.

'Billie's been flying four-engined heavy *bombers* — Halifaxes and Lancasters!' says Yvonne. 'They only let the best pilots near them.'

'But they're enormous!' I say. 'How on earth do you do it, Billie?'

'They carry us, Izzy, we don't have to carry them. They're only planes. We have flight engineers to help too.'

'Female flight engineers?'

'Yeah, some.'

'Because they cost less?'

'Not any more,' say Billie with a satisfied grin. 'Pauline Gower finally got the Air Ministry to start paying us the same rates as men.'

'Are you there, Izabel?' calls Toby. 'I've come to perform my landlordly duties, armed with spanner and wrench and some very nice coffee from the spiv on the corner.'

'Lovely. I'll put the kettle on.'

Toby gives me the black-market tin of American coffee and goes into the bathroom. For a time I hear clanks and clunks and gushing water, then he emerges smiling.

'All fixed. Who'd have imagined such a thing a few years ago, when I hardly knew one end of a hammer from the other.'

'Advantages of being a fireman, I suppose,' I say, setting the coffee cups on the table.

'Not many other benefits I fear, but at least I've made a fascinating set of new acquaintances.'

I pour the coffee. 'Might come in handy when you write your magnum opus about the war.'

'I'm starting to doubt I'll ever write anything again.' Toby sighs. 'My ideas just don't work. In any case, no one will read books about the war when it's over, they'll just want to forget.'

'Perhaps do something that *isn't* about the war?' I say.

'But the war's become *everything*.' He shrugs. 'No, it's youngsters like Nancy who'll write the great novels of the future. She seems to perceive a great deal.'

'She always did, her father once said —' I stop.

Toby gazes at me. 'He was a writer?'

'An academic but, yes, he wrote beautifully. His papers are stored at my house in Hong Kong. I hope they're safe. It's been so long since I've heard from my caretaker. God knows how she is, either.' I sigh.

'Everything will be fine, Izabel, don't worry. Still, shouldn't you be thinking about your own future? A triumphant return to the stage, perhaps?'

'Who'd hire a middle-aged lady with — what did the papers say? Half-Caste Roots?'

Toby laughs. 'Me, I was charmed by your Lewd Oriental Attractions. Though the papers never quite explained what they were, or what the Opium-Besotted Lovers thought about it, either.'

I shake my head. 'What an absurd time that was.'

'But it was *ages* ago. You'd be welcomed back to the stage now.'

'Thank you, Toby, but no, I don't want to act again. Not ever.'

'What a loss! My God, I've never forgotten that lingering profile shot in *The Royal Exile*. The intensity, the depth, the sensitivity. Don't you realise how famous that made you?'

'That shot?' I laugh. 'I hadn't eaten for a week to fit into my corset and all I could think about food — fish and chips, steak with baked potato. I was so hungry!'

'Well you certainly personified hunger of the spiritual sort, my lamb, which is no mean task.'

'Oh, roast lamb too!' I say. 'Doesn't it seem forever since we've eaten like that?'

'Now you're making *me* hungry, Izabel, and I'm almost out of ration coupons. But wasn't there something you wanted fixed in your wardrobe? Better get to that before I go a-queuing.'

'We've got some bacon from Pete's farm you can have,' I say. 'But yes, the railing's come loose.'

We go my bedroom and I open the doors to the wardrobe and start removing coathangers, piling the clothes on my bed. There aren't many, some sensible blouses and suits for the office and my winter coat. On the top I spread out my two precious evening gowns.

'See there, Toby, the bracket's broken.'

But he's not looking at the wardrobe. He strokes the fabric of the gowns and says, 'Paris originals? Magnificent. How on earth did you get hold of these in wartime?'

'I took them with me when I went to Hong Kong, and I've kept them ever since.'

'You saved such fragile things throughout all those disasters? They must mean a great deal.'

'They do,' I say. 'I was wearing the russet silk the first time I met Nancy's father.'

'And the emerald?'

'The last.'

'Ah.'

Eliza has blossomed since we heard the news of Harry's survival. We take the Tube together to work each day, and she's so much happier.

When we returned to Britain she was promoted to a good position in the Commercial Section of GC&CS, while I became a lowly clerk in the small Chinese Section. (Felix is an administrator in a different building, which suits both of us.)

I'd never imagined myself working in an office, but I'm enjoying it enormously. And while my job is lowly, it's far from dull.

To help our agents keep in contact with the most influential Singapore Chinese, I compiled reports on the people I used to know when I first arrived. Some of them are imprisoned, but others are still free, barely surviving.

As I'd feared, many thousands were massacred after the surrender: pure revenge, the Japanese shamelessly boasted, for the resistance of China itself.

As seems mandatory for anything to do with that complicated country, my fellow analysts fall into two factions. The old hands are devoted to the repressive Kuomintang regime, while the younger realists understand why so many yearn for change with the Communists.

The former see me as a Red Jezebel (is there such a thing?) and the latter are people I can actually talk to.

I help with translations and leaflets, working with people who understand a great deal about Asia, and as time goes by I feel at home in a way I haven't experienced since Hong Kong.

Despite the anxieties that sometimes still crowd in on me at night, a year passes in the Chinese Section in a state of near contentment.

But slowly, with a possible end to the war glimmering in the distance, the atmosphere at work changes, and jostling for future influence between the opposing factions takes a vicious turn. Sadly, the conservative British are more sympathetic to the right-wing Kuomintang supporters than the idealistic Reds.

So those of us who dream that Chinese people might have a say in post-war Singapore, or who support a China itself free of dictatorship, are being pushed out of their positions, one by one.

That includes even someone as insignificant as me. With this political realignment my usefulness to the department is over, and after a few months of uncertainty, I'm "let go."

It happens just before Christmas 1943, and I'm left in despair.

What will I do now? A grasp of Chinese politics doesn't leave me very employable at this stage of the war, and jobs are scarce now with so much American wealth, expertise and personnel flooding the country.

I've been secretly saving a little money in the hope of one day making a break from Felix, but without a job it's not nearly enough.

More importantly, I only have British residency through my marriage to Felix and, even worse, Nancy's legal status has never been regularised.

On New Year's Eve I share a drink with the others at Toby's house, and even Felix deigns to accept a sherry. I watch him expound his views on the situation in Hong Kong (he's quite wrong), and think bitterly, Nancy and I are *still* dependent upon this unreliable man's good graces.

Nancy and Tessie often drop by each others' places to do homework together. Felix sometimes walks the few streets over with Nancy to 'protect' her, despite the quiet neighbourhood. Perhaps it's his idea of being discreet about Barbara.

One Sunday afternoon Nancy comes home from Tessie's by herself and I hear her sniffle. When she comes into the sitting room I say, 'Come by the fire, love. Are you getting a cold?'

She shakes her head and I realise she's been crying.

I hold out my hand and she sits beside me. We watch the flames, then she sobs suddenly, 'Tessie doesn't want to be my *friend* any more. She says I get on her *goat*. I don't even know what that means, but I know it's not very nice.'

'Oh, darling. I'm so sorry. Why on earth would she say that?'

Nancy wipes her eyes. 'She thought Felix was going to marry her mother and then she'd have a daddy again. She says you won't divorce Felix because of *me*, so it's all *my* fault.'

I smile. 'I think she's a long way off the mark there, sweetheart.'

'But I wish Felix *was* her father and didn't live with us!' says Nancy. 'He doesn't like me at all, but he's always tickling Tessie and giving her sweets and holding her on his lap.'

'Heavens. Isn't she getting too big to be sitting on anyone's lap?'

'That's *just* what I said, but then she got cross at me and said she was going to tell Felix you were damaged goods and he should *leave* you.'

'What?'

'You know. Those soldiers in Singapore. Tessie says you're a fallen woman. When she was my friend she'd say we should keep quiet to protect your reputation, but now she says she's going to tell *everyone*.'

'Don't worry about it, darling.' I sigh. 'It was so long ago, and really, what does it matter?'

Felix comes home that evening after Nancy is in bed. He pours two whiskeys and hands me one, then sits in his favourite armchair, and clears his throat.

'Izabel, tonight I heard something rather disturbing.'

I put aside the novel I'm reading. 'What's that, Felix?'

'Tessie has informed me of something ... well, I'm astounded, you've never said a word to me. She said you were — *violated* — in Singapore. Surely that can't be true?'

'Actually, it is. A lot of ugly things happened to a lot of people then, including me.'

'But, dear God, Izabel, why on earth didn't you *say* something?'

'Suppose I was in shock. Talking would have made it too real.'

He swallows. 'Of course, at last I understand. That's why you haven't wanted me in your bed for so long.'

He's silent, then looks up at me.

'My dear, what have we *become* to each other? How can I tell you how sorry I am? It's *my* fault. I should have protected you. You think poorly of me I know, but you cannot imagine what I felt seeing you stranded on that wharf.'

I'm amazed to see tears in his eyes. 'It was rather horrid at my end too, darling. But it's all in the past.'

'I have to say ... oh, look, Izzy, I'm so damned *ashamed*. This playing around with Barbara. But you don't want me, and that's hard for a man to take. I know I've been stupidly unfair to both of you. And — well — the fact is, I don't really want to *marry* the woman.'

'Oh?' I sip my whiskey. 'She thinks you do.'

He reddens. 'We all say stupid things in the heat of the moment, but I want to be with *you*, Izzy. I've never stopped loving you, *never* forgotten those early days, remember? You had my heart from the instant we met. That glorious night, your silver dress, the orchid in your hair — dear God, you were lovely.'

I laugh sadly. 'Of course I remember, Felix. You were extraordinary, too. I'd never felt … not like that. You meant everything to me.'

He shakes his head. 'I'm an utter fool. Must be the shellshock. You know I don't speak of Arras, but it's been twenty-five years and *still* the old terror never leaves me. It's so *humiliating*. God knows I'm not entirely rational but — oh my dear, can't we try again? I can be the man you once loved, I swear it.'

Felix rarely mentions his dreadful experiences in the Great War, and he's never before been so open with me.

I take a breath. 'Still, I wonder if we might be happier apart —'

He says quietly, 'But, Izabel, I'm not sure I could survive. Could you give me … just one year, perhaps? And I'll *show* you how much you and Nancy mean to me.'

'A year?'

'Remember that makeshift identity pass the Hong Kong governor issued for the child?'

I nod.

'After the war there'll be literally *millions* of refugees, and the government will start cracking down on irregular documents. But through my connections I can get Nancy her own British passport. Then she couldn't possibly be separated from us.'

'My God, Felix, you don't *seriously* think—?'

He nods sadly. 'It will be a new world then, Izabel, with an unyielding bureaucracy. Yes, even mere children could be sent away from their families.'

I cover my mouth in horror.

Felix clears his throat. 'Also, I am aware you have, at times, felt constrained by your own situation should the question of divorce ever arise.' He bites his lip. 'I'll make sure you get a British passport too.'

He gazes at me, raw and heartfelt. 'One year more? You'd be free then, my love, to choose a life with or without me.'

26. Toby: The Pale Blue Dawn

'But London must be *crawling* with men willing to take advantage of you, poppet. How can you possibly say you can't find anyone?'

As our train steams towards Guildford, Klara gazes at the countryside where patches of blue-shadowed snow lie beneath the trees. She sighs as she turns to me.

'Toby, it is more difficult than I expected to find the right man to impregnate me. Even after many drinks I cannot find that Nordic pragmatism you tease me about.'

'Oh, darling. I only say that because you're really so other-worldly. But is it because of Yvonne? You're a very different person with her.'

'I did not realise that I always knew in my heart Sofia would leave me. But now with Yvonne, I am certain —' she smiles. 'Oh, Toby, I am *certain*. And I cannot bear the thought of anyone touching me but her, even to make the child we want so much.'

'Well that's a pickle. What will you do?'

'There are other ways, such as those farmers use for animals, or Swiss clinics use for people. Pregnancy is a simple matter of transferring sperm, whatever the method.'

'But you've still got to find someone to supply the raw material, Klara, and they might feel very different when a child is born. You could be stuck with a stranger in your life forever.'

'Yes. That is why Yvonne and I would like to ask a favour of you, Toby. Would you supply us with what we need to make our child?'

'*Me*? That's absurd. I don't want to be a father, not by any means. You'll have to try someone else. As I say, London is crawling with potential papas, but not me, darling.'

'We would not expect anything more. Perhaps only for you to be like a godfather.'

I shake my head. 'Klara, you *know* I'm ambivalent about families at the best of times. And now, on this fraught expedition — regarding parentage, you may recall — you ask me something so unnerving?'

'Oh. I am sorry, Toby. I thought perhaps it would make you happy.'

'Happy? What might make me *happy*, blossom, is knowing the truth about my past, or writing something readable. But pulling myself off into a glass jar for your nefarious purposes? I doubt it.'

Klara turns to look out the window and there's a long silence.

I shiver in the draught. January is a horrible time of year to be travelling, but my curiosity has finally outweighed my shock. (My friends seem to think I've handled Stef's betrayal terribly well: they have no idea of the grief that still thickens my throat.)

I sigh. 'I'm sorry, Klara, love. I'm being a brute.'

'It was a foolish idea. I see I will have to become more pragmatic after all.' She gives me a quick smile and I take her hand.

'I really am sorry, my lamb. I'm just terribly nervous.'

'You know, Toby, I have never heard you admit to being nervous before?'

'Well, I've never *done* anything like this before.'

'But are you not good friends with Stefan's mother?'

'I thought so, yet she hasn't contacted me since Stef left. Perhaps it's the war and she's just too busy. But I'm *certain* Gabriela knows something about Maude — and about the man who painted her portrait, that Paul somebody.'

'When Yvonne came to mend my printing press I asked her to try to decipher his signature on the canvas because she has much experience with old manuscripts.'

'I doubt that's *all* you asked her, my dear.'

'No, Toby, I was restrained, although I found her most attractive. But after she worked on the press all night she was covered in grease and ink. I simply offered to help her wash it off.'

'And then?'

She smiles. 'You know perfectly well.'

'So once the poor seduced girl had a chance to look at the signature, what did she think?'

'Only that it begins with *C* and ends in *ll*.'

'Could be anything. Carroll, Cornwall, Cardwell — what else?'

Klara shakes her head. The train whistle toots and the conductor walks through the carriage, calling, 'Guildford, next stop. Guildford.'

The taxi drives away past the sculpture fountain, the frosty lawns and the picturesque, winter-bare trees. I used to stay here during school holidays with Stef, but that was long ago and I'd forgotten how enormous the place was.

Many of the great houses of Britain are now hospitals and military depots, but not the Sadler estate. Stef's father Roger is extremely well connected.

Gabriela stands at the grand entrance with a lackey at her elbow who looks at us disapprovingly. I'm tidy enough, but Klara's hair is boyish and her dress sense is best described as bohemian.

'Happy New Year, Gaby,' I say, and kiss Gabriela's cheek.

'Happy New Year, *kochanie*. And this is —?'

'Klara. You met her the night you and Danika visited us, two years ago, remember?'

'Of course, Sofia's little friend. Welcome, *kochanie*. Do come in.'

'What does 'kohanya' mean?' says Klara politely.

Gabriela laughs. 'It's *darling* in Polish. I suppose most young people today are unacquainted with the major European languages.'

'Yes. I am afraid I know only Finnish, Swedish, German, French and English,' says Klara evenly. I don't think she likes being called anyone's 'little friend'.

Gabriela ignores her and leads us into a beautifully decorated drawing room. 'Tea, please,' she says and the lackey disappears.

'Now, let me *look* at you, Toby. Goodness, you have become rather a muscular fellow, have you not? All that running up and down ladders, I suppose. It must keep you very healthy.'

'It's certainly very different from my pre-war life, Gaby. Are you and Roger well?'

'Marvellous, but so *busy*, a wedding does not plan itself, you know.'

'Oh. So Stef and —'

'In August. The roses on the western lawn will be a glorious setting for dear Charlotte.'

'You too, Gaby. I'm sure you'll look wonderful.'

Her dark hair (a shade too dark?) is tied back with a silk scarf, her makeup impeccable, her skin a miracle of the surgeon's art.

'Dearest Toby, always so charming. I am very much anticipating the children to come, although they will make of me a grandmother *far* before my time.' She smiles. 'Roger is very happy too. He must have an heir, of course.'

Klara glances quickly at Gabriela, but says nothing.

The lackey returns with a tea-tray and for a time we're busy with the formalities. Then Gabriela says, 'Now, Toby, you must tell me why you have come so far. Your letter was *most* mysterious.'

'I want to know about Maude, Gaby. How you met, what she was like. What happened.'

'Heavens, we know what *happened*. They were wonderful days, you understand — laughing, champagne, handsome men.' She sighs. 'But of course, sometimes there were consequences. Maude made a mistake, that is all. How we met? Backstage, a theatrical revue. As you know, my sister and I were the Naughty Diamant Twins —'

'Yes,' says Klara. She's still watching Gaby with an odd intensity.

'Maude played the socialite, the little French maid, that sort of thing. She was pretty and very good at it. She had a lightness, a wit most of the other girls lacked. We became close friends.'

'Then tell me — *who* was my father, Gaby?'

'Are you certain you wish to know this, Toby? If you hold hopes of a man of good birth or influence you will be sadly disappointed.'

'I don't have any hopes. I just want to know.'

She shrugs. 'It was that painter, of course, the one who did her portrait. Paul Cornell.'

'*Cornell.* Ah. What happened, Gaby?'

'He was too poor, Maude was too young. She gave the baby — you — to her sister, then came back to the theatre. All the girls were looking for husbands and Maude finally found hers, a banker.' She smiles. 'Of course my sister and I married purely for love, you understand.'

'Of course,' says Klara.

'But what happened to Paul Cornell?' I ask.

'The Great War began and he —' she waves her hand dismissively. 'Well, I was hardly surprised, I knew he lacked backbone.'

'Gaby?'

'I said you may not wish to hear this, Toby, but you insist. *So*. He claimed he was a conscientious objector, but everyone in our set thought he was simply a coward. He was disgraced and gaoled. I do not know what happened then.'

'That's all?'

She nods. 'Poor Maude. I think she always loved him, but it was obvious he would behave badly. They all did. He might have been fair and blue-eyed but he could not escape what he was.'

I carefully put down my teacup. 'And what was that, Gabriela?'

I feel sick because I know what she's going to say. I heard her when I was young, but didn't understand then.

She laughs prettily. 'A *Jew*, of course. Why would you expect civilised behaviour of a Jew?'

Klara becomes very still. After a pause she says, 'You are aware that your future daughter-in-law Charlotte has a Jewish father?'

Gaby shrugs. 'It is the mother that matters in these things, and hers was a purebred Aryan, the best kind of German. And unlike so many girls today, Charlotte appreciates the value of *Kinder, Küche, Kirche*.'

She looks mockingly at Klara. 'You understand that, don't you, little invert, with your fine grasp of European languages?'

'*Children, kitchen, church*. Yes, I understand.' Klara is pale.

'Of course, the Nazis now control my country and no Pole could be happy about that.' Gaby sips her tea. 'Yet their ideals will outlast this foolish conflict. Cleansing Europe of degenerates is a good beginning.'

'But the Nazis would call Stefan a sexual pervert,' says Klara, 'and put him in a camp and work him to death. Your own *son*.'

'Utter nonsense! The camps are simply re-education facilities. Still, if a degenerate will not cease his revolting behaviour what kindness does he deserve? Or *her*, for that matter.'

Gabriela glances thin-lipped at Klara. 'No, my darling boy was merely led astray, but now he has found *true* love. Naturally, there is no such thing as true love between the perverted.'

'Right then,' I say. 'I think we'll be off. May I call a taxi?'

'Of course, *kochanie*. It's been such a pleasure to see you.'

'That bitch, that fucking bitch,' says Klara, beside me on the train back to London. I've never heard her swear before.

I shake my head. 'It seems there's still a swathe of the upper class thinks the Nazis have some simply spiffing ideas. Christ. How could *anyone* say such things?'

'There are many who will never give up the vile comfort of their hatreds,' says Klara. 'I cannot understand it, but they are there, they always will be.'

'Not always. We'll beat them this time.' I squeeze her shoulder. 'Are you all right, poppet?'

'When she said *there is no such thing as true love between the perverted*— I almost wept, Toby, you are a man who is *made* for true love, it runs deeply inside you. And Yvonne and I, we will raise our baby within our true love, too.'

'Do you ... do you really believe that about me, Klara?'

'Of course. You are a good man, Toby.'

Years of agony clench in my chest and twist. Slowly I breathe, blinded by tears, and hide behind my handkerchief.

I finally whisper, 'You see, I thought Stef was wise to leave me. I always thought something was fundamentally wrong with me.'

'No, *no*, Toby. You are honest and kind, always. It is Stefan who will be unhappy forever, because he can never love anyone.'

'My goodness, how true that is. What callous stock he springs from, how callous he is himself.' I wipe my eyes and take a deep breath. 'But suddenly I don't *care* any more about bloody Stefan. Isn't that absurd? I don't care and I feel as if I've dropped a twenty-ton weight. Oh you little Nordic pixie, I'm so *glad* you were with me today.'

'I am glad too, but it was certainly difficult to restrain myself with Gabriela.'

I put my handkerchief away. 'And I did like what you said about raising your baby within true love, Klara. Only problem is, of course, you haven't got a baby.'

She nods and sighs.

'Well, I suppose I can find a clean glass jar *somewhere*.'

Spring 1944 arrives, and everything takes on a sense of great purpose. We pretend we don't notice the hordes of fresh soldiers, the docks full of ships, the flocks of thrumming planes overhead, the meetings between generals, the signing of great treaties.

The sense of breathless expectancy.

There are fewer raids now because the RAF is ruthlessly attacking Germany, and enemy fighters must stay to protect their own cities. Still our work never ends — when we're not firefighting we labour with the Heavy Rescue teams and the Bomb Disposal units. I'm sick to my heart of pain and fear and obliteration in the long dark nights.

But it's also a spring of great purpose for me: I'm writing again. Something loosened after the confrontation with Gabriela, and this time, this time — *ah*.

Whatever else I'm doing, some part of me is aware of the meander of the story, the swirl of the characters, the reversals, the clashes, the ebb and flow of connection.

And after yet another night of tragedy comes a glorious dawn.

Against the familiar scenery of folding hoses, gathering tools and murmuring men, I look up to the translucent sky, and it's the crystal blue of Klara's eyes, her beautiful eyes when when she told me she was certain she was pregnant.

We wept and laughed with Yvonne, and made foolish jokes about names and schools and nappies. I don't know Yvonne very well yet, but still I love her for the happiness she's brought Klara, and that Klara has brought me.

This war has created lots of puffed-up little men who imagine a uniform turns them into big men. Specifically Felix Malory, who often scurries past me on the stairs with his mouth pinched, as if it's me he'd love to shoot in lieu of any actual Germans.

I have no idea why Izabel stays with him. (Yes, I call the great actress Izabel and she calls me Toby. If I'm dreaming, please don't wake me.)

Before I have a well-deserved rest I pop up to Izabel's flat — there's something wrong again with her water heater. As I get to the landing Felix emerges and nods curtly at me. I say elegantly, 'Oh, good *morning*,

Major Malory,' and he grunts. I think he suspects I'm not fond of him.

'In the kitchen, Toby,' calls Izabel. She's seated at the table with Eliza, who's dressed for the office. Izabel isn't, because she, poor thing, was fired due to some kind of political shenanigans in her office a few months ago. Not that I'm supposed to know what kind of an office it is, and that goes doubly for Eliza.

I say, 'Off to your glamorous job again, Eliza, I see.'

She laughs. 'Toby, it's so mundane. Just yesterday I was reading some order for sailors' vests.'

'Ah, but sailors of which particular adversary? And for what extreme of climate?'

She smiles. 'Now that's where we draw the veil of discretion. Want tea? Izabel's just made a pot.'

'Thank you. Sorry about all the soot, I haven't had a bath yet. Have you seen Klara?'

'No, Yvonne was catching the first train, so they left early for the station,' says Eliza. 'Oh! Does this mean you've got *news*, Toby?'

'I have indeed, and marvellous news, too.'

'How lovely! When?' asks Izabel.

'Mid-October, we think. An autumn baby.'

'My goodness.' Eliza blinks back tears, her hand over her mouth.

'Oh, darling, don't cry,' I say. 'It's *got* to happen to you one day. When dear old Harry's back you can go at it like rabbits and I'm sure all that pent-up passion will work wonders.'

'Not quite sure that's how it works, Toby.' She wipes her eyes. 'And it would be *if*, not when.'

'Eliza, don't even *think* that,' I say sternly.

'They've sent thousands of soldiers to build a railway in Burma, and we hear —' she stops.

'But Harry's a *civilian*.'

'Being a civilian doesn't keep you safe from typhus, malaria, beri-beri, starvation.' She takes a deep breath. 'Sorry. Must dash.'

After Eliza leaves I say, 'What a fool I am. Of course Klara's good news just reminds her of what she can't have.'

'Nothing to be done, Toby,' says Izabel gently. 'Of course she's happy for your baby.'

'Well, it's Klara and Yvonne's baby, I'm just the less-than-innocent bystander.'

'You may be surprised.' She smiles. 'Babies are intriguing.'

'In fact, the baby I most care about right now is my manuscript. It's going very well, thanks to your idea.'

'My idea?'

'To do a novel that isn't about the war. Well, not *this* one. It's the Great War and the objectors who refused to fight. Ordinary people faced with impossible choices, what they felt, what happens. Actually, I'm *terrible* at saying what a book's about. If I could do it in a hundred words I wouldn't need to write thousands.'

'Is it because of your father, Paul Cornell?' Izabel asks.

'Not because of, but it germinated when I started researching his life. Unfortunately that's hit a brick wall right now — I think the ghastly Gabriela has told all her friends to give me the cold shoulder. Still, I'll keep digging. But what about you, Izabel? Any prospects?'

'Not for work,' she says. 'What *can* I do — file papers in Chinese? Rather limited talents, really. And in any case you see, Felix prefers to be the sole provider.'

'Do you *want* him to be the sole provider?'

'I enjoyed having my own money, but he's well paid so we're comfortable. I suppose I do it to bolster him, to show I believe in him.'

'Do you?'

'Well he's stopped seeing Barbara and he's being kinder to Nancy.'

'So he damned well should be.'

'And, thank God, he's sorting out our passport situation at last. He's being so much nicer too, Toby. Finally willing to talk about his hopes and fears, and even his shellshock — he never would before, it's a remarkable change.'

She smiles sadly. 'I loved him once. I must give him another chance.'

My old publisher Alastair Jenkins crawls out from under whatever rock he and his Associates have been skulking beneath for the last few years, and after reading some of my chapters he offers me a most satisfactory contract. My manuscript grows and grows.

One day Klara, rounded and content, says, 'I have a request, Toby. Please sit down.'

'What is it, my dear?'

'I would like us to be married.'

'*Married*? Why?'

'I want to take your name,' she says. 'It will protect the child.'

I laugh. 'I won't ask you to go down on one knee.'

'That is fortunate, Toby, as I might have difficulty getting up again.'

'I'm quite flustered,' I say. 'I don't know, Klara — are you *sure*?'

'Yes, I am sure.'

'I suppose it's not nearly the oddest thing you've ever asked of me, poppet.' I shrug. 'And so much has changed in my life lately, why not throw my cautious bachelorhood to the winds too?'

'Yvonne and I will be very happy.'

'Sounds as if I even get two wives as well! I'll have to call you both Mrs Fenn, at least until the joke wears unbearably thin.' I stop and think. 'Klara, this is really rather a good idea. If anything happens to me, then you and the baby would get my fireman's pension.'

'So for the sake of the child we must *both* be pragmatic?'

I laugh. 'Yes, fiancée mine.'

So another extraordinary thing takes place in this spring of great purpose, when Yvonne and Pete stand as our witnesses at the registry office. Pete drives up from Southampton for the day and brings young Vivy and Billie, elegant in her uniform. I'm stupidly happy.

Eliza, Izabel, Nancy and Felix attend as well and I overhear Felix grumble, 'It's absurd, Izabel, he's a *fruit*,' but choose not to notice. I simply smile when he gets dreadful indigestion after our celebration at a restaurant.

On 6th June 1944, all that pent-up purpose explodes into D-Day and the re-taking of Europe begins. Far overhead, squadrons of planes fly paratroopers to France, while steel armadas depart from every harbour with weapons-laden men and trucks and tanks. They return for doctors and nurses and more soldiers, over and over: Operation Overlord.

Almost immediately the Nazis launch rocket bombs in retaliation, each carrying almost a ton of explosives, and up to one hundred a day descend upon Britain. The enemy calls them vengeance weapons: *Vergeltungswaffe-1*, but soon we just call them V-1s.

Some V-1s are stopped by artillery, or pilots flipping them with the windflow from wings, but they keep coming, their engines clattering like cheap motorcycles. Then they cut out and, spiralling silently, plummet and explode.

Because of the V-1s I insist Klara move her papers downstairs from the vulnerable attic, and on the occasions I'm not working it's very pleasant to sit and chat with her about books and poetry and babies.

My manuscript grows. I'm close, so close to the end, but then hit a logical and emotional roadblock I can't seem to resolve. Klara and I talk about it — I trust her understanding of my characters and narrative completely — but I still can't quite resolve the story.

Between writing and fire-fighting I don't have time to be lonely, but the contentment that Klara and Yvonne share does make me a little envious.

This sunny morning in late June I'm walking the few streets from my house to University College. While researching conscientious objectors of the Great War I'd had a pleasant chat on the phone some months ago with an historian.

He rang me again last night. He said he'd found a report I might like to see, an interview with someone who actually knew Paul Cornell.

I knock on the door marked *Dr Nichols* and a man of my own age opens it and shakes my hand. He's brown-haired and slim, with a limp that becomes obvious as he sits down at his desk with a small grunt.

'Sorry,' he says. 'Playing up a bit today. Got me off the front line but sometimes in academic circles I'd still rather be facing the Germans.'

I smile. 'Thank you so much for this, Dr Nichols.'

'Please do call me Jim.'

'I'm Toby, of course. Where did this report come from?'

'A colleague did these interviews twenty years ago, but objectors were so despised then he chose to work on something that had safer career prospects. Fortunately he archived the documents.'

'And what *have* you found?'

He picks up a paper. His slim hands are well-formed and, absurdly, I feel myself flushing.

'I'll give you a carbon-copy, but briefly, the interviewee and Paul Cornell were friends, both with long-held pacifist ideals. They had excellent grounds to object, but the tribunal still assessed them as suitable for combat. They refused, were gaoled, and suffered hard labour and solitary confinement. Brutal treatment.'

'Did my father survive?'

'Yes, despite three years in prison. It didn't end there, either. Objectors were kept locked up for an extra six months after the war ended, then no one would hire them. Still, I think your father, as an artist, was able to cope better than most.'

Jim smiles and I like the shape of his eyes. 'You're mentioned, too, Toby.' He reads aloud:

> Paul had an illegitimate boy, Toby, who lived with the mother's sister. The mother, Maude, married up, didn't see Paul or the kid for years, she thought it was best. Broke Paul's heart, poor sod. After the war they met again and decided to run away, take the kid, have a family life together after all those years they'd lost. Might have worked out too, but Paul always had rotten luck. Stepped in front of an omnibus on the Mile End Road. I heard the mother went back to her posh husband. Christ knows what happened to the boy.

'They were going to run away together, then he *died*?' I say. 'Oh, dear God, how tragic. Poor Maude.'

'You said she took an interest in you after the war. After Paul died.'

'Yes. She must have been so unhappy herself, but still she got me out of a miserable home into a good school, never said a word. And then she left me with a final gift, a house that's been a refuge for years. It's changed my life.'

'Well, here's something else, Toby. I asked an art dealer friend about Paul Cornell and he actually has a painting of his from 1919. He sent me a photo — here you are. It's called *Maude, Once More*. Apparently the gossip was that her husband commissioned Cornell to paint her portrait, but couldn't stand the result. Suspected something was going on between them.'

'And now we know it was! Look, Jim — Maude's eyes are so *happy*.' I shake my head. 'She must have thought her life was about to open up. Then Paul died and she had to stay in that awful marriage.'

'But she'd started to know you better by then, Toby. That must have been satisfying, at least.'

'Yes, we became very close in later years. Maude always mattered to me, but oh, God, I wish I'd known how much! Why didn't she *tell* me?'

'People of that era were reserved,' Jim says gently. 'After a lifetime of hiding her secret she probably couldn't talk about it. But I imagine her leaving you the portrait of her younger self, painted by your father, was meant to be a clue.'

I sit back and sigh. 'That's a comforting thought. It feels significant — *extraordinary* really — to have discovered this. Thank you, Jim.'

He smiles. 'History can be rather dry sometimes, so it's it's pleasing to see the human side come to life.'

I say, suddenly daring, 'You know, I owe you for this. Might I buy you a drink one night?'

Jim becomes a little flushed himself. 'I know a nice pub near Goodge Street, if that suits.'

'Definitely. Perhaps something to eat afterwards too, if you felt like it.' My heart is thumping.

He gazes at me with those very nice eyes. 'Not a bad idea. Tomorrow, perhaps?'

I walk out in a cloud of happiness, with the address of the pub and a carbon-copy of the interview, thinking, Well, *that* was the last bloody thing I ever expected!

I take a breath and look up to the sunny sky. What a day. And out of the blue, ideas are racing through my head and threads of my novel are coming together and a perfect resolution assembles itself as if it's simply been waiting for this moment to manifest.

Yes, yes, that's *it*!

Suddenly I hear the ragged clatter of a motorcycle engine and my heart thuds. No, relax, just a dispatch rider. Another horrible thing the V-1s have done to us is make such everyday noises sinister. Probably a ploy by some German psychological warfare unit, but I am *not* going to let anyone spoil this glorious moment.

At home I call out, 'Mrs Fenn?' and Klara yells, 'In the attic, Toby.'

I dash upstairs (well, not exactly dashing after the third flight).

'Klara! What on earth are you doing up here? It's much safer to work in your flat.'

'I am just getting some of my books. Toby, when can we move all of them downstairs?'

'Next time Pete visits,' I say. 'Those bookcases are very heavy.'

'And my big desk, too.'

'Yes, yes, we'll move everything soon, I promise. But listen, Klara, I've had the most astonishing morning. I've met a man, a *lovely* man, and I've found out about Paul and Maude, and I've even realised how to finish off my novel — oh, such a sweet twist!'

As she makes piles of books, I tell her about my meeting with Jim, and my even more wonderful resolution, grinning like a fool.

'He certainly sounds like a very nice man, Toby. And I *do* like your new ending very much. It concludes the story but does not leave it too neat and tidy.'

'I *know*! I'm bedazzled by my own genius. Or perhaps my muse has turned up at last.'

Klara laughs. 'Your muse has always been with you, but maybe she has been asleep for a time. Now, you take this pile and I'll —' She looks up. 'What is that?'

'Just a stupid motorcycle, poppet. Made me jump earlier too.'

'No, Toby, listen.' She stands, her arms full of books.

It's not a motorcycle and it's clattering high overhead. And suddenly everything is silent.

'Klara, *down*!'

I leap and grab her and shove her under the desk and fling myself alongside to shield her. Klara stares at me, wide-eyed.

Her gaze is so blue in the pale blue dawn, so *blue* —

27. Billie: We Are Diminished

Pete drives Yvonne and me to London. We leave Vivy with Mrs Spencer, she's a bit too young for all this. In the back seat Yvie is in tears. I would be too if I weren't holding myself together so intensely.

I rub my face. Just a week ago Yvie and I attended the funeral of one of the other ATA women — my officious mate Daphne, who wasn't that bad a pilot, despite my jibes. She was bringing a shot-up plane back to Hamble for repairs and the propeller failed. Poor old Daph.

Poor old us.

Whitfield Street is still full of rubble so we park a distance from the house. As we walk to the front door Pete and I glance at each other. Two hundred yards away is the V-1's crater at the rear of a police station. Unbelievably, only one person there died, a female constable. Poor cow. Welcome to the modern girl's working world.

Still, Toby's house looks almost intact. On the phone Eliza said the attic roof suffered the only damage, the other floors are all right. That seems amazing. The house next door lost its top two storeys, and the one beyond that, closest to the crater, is basically a pile of bricks.

Eliza answers our knock, and hugs Pete and me tightly at the same time. 'Pete, Billie. You got here.' She lets us go and turns to Yvie, and hugs her too. 'Come in,' she says. 'Almost ready to leave.'

We greet Izabel and Nancy, waiting in the sitting room. Felix (who's terrified of me) nods with the lofty air of somebody plotting an advance through Normandy.

I hear footsteps coming downstairs and turn. 'Oh, *God*,' says Yvie, and runs to hug Klara, murmuring incoherently.

When they join us I see Klara is pale and bruised. She's wearing a black dress that must date from the Great War, a high-waisted style that suits her round belly. I kiss the top of her head, avoiding the line of stitches beneath an adhesive plaster in her silvery hair.

Felix has borrowed a car from an army motor pool today, and is going to drive Eliza, Izabel and Nancy. Klara joins Yvie and me in Pete's car, and we make our way to Hampstead, to to the churchyard where Aunt Maude is buried.

I'm so sick of funerals. Same icy churches, same hard pews, same hollow words, same weak light through blast-taped windows, same coffins up the front.

But this one is different. This one holds Toby.

Of course I cry, how can I not? There's a limit, and today I think we all reach it. I crack when I realise there's not a soul left alive from Toby's family. Not his adopted parents or his birth parents, not a sister or brother or aunt or uncle. No one.

We bury our friend among the dark yews, weeping willows, Gothic memorials and ranks of severe wartime headstones. Men in firefighter uniforms stand with us, as well as a few of Toby's old friends from Southampton.

I notice the well-known face of his publisher Alastair Jenkins. He's looking glum, probably because of the money he'll miss out on from the never-to-be-completed manuscript. Toby let me read some of his early chapters and I think the book would have made him famous.

Otto Fischer stands across from me and we smile regretfully at each other. Another loss. Otto has battled the forces of destruction since the days of the Spanish civil war, and now his beard is white and his burly frame stooped.

Beside him is his daughter Charlotte, glamorous in the black that makes the rest of us look anaemic, and her fiancé Stefan, Toby's faithless love. One of the Diamant Twins has made her appearance too. Stef's mother Gabriela dabs daintily at her eyes with a lace handkerchief, although I see no evidence of tears.

We endure the comfortless words, the muffled sobs, the thud of soil on the coffin. At last, thank God, it's over and I walk with Klara and Yvie towards the cars.

Yvie has her arm around Klara, who's close to collapse. By horrible mischance we meet Stefan, Charlotte and Gabriela on the pathway.

'Oh, *Stef.*' Klara halts, anguished. She whispers, '*Why couldn't you have loved him better?*'

Gabriela looks at her with contempt. 'A bastard in your belly, a pervert in your bed — what does your sort know of love?'

Klara closes her eyes for a moment, then says steadily, 'At least, Gabriela, my parents will one day have a grandchild. Your future daughter-in-law may offer you *Küche* and *Kirche*, but sadly, no *Kinder*. Charlotte has been sterilised. Oh? This is news to you? Still, I am quite certain the love, the non-*perverted* love, of Stefan and Charlotte will overcome all obstacles.'

Straight-backed, Klara walks to the car with Yvie, while Gabriela grabs Stef by the arm and pulls him away, muttering at him furiously in Polish.

Only Charlotte and I are left. She looks at me and shakes her head in exasperation. She gets out her cigarettes, lights one and takes a deep drag, and after a time says, 'Klara's quite the little firecracker beneath all that fairy floss, isn't she?'

'Sorry, Charlie. Probably all my fault,' I say, exhausted. 'I told her once I suspected the situation. She'd never have said anything though, except for ... all this.'

'You must be more perceptive than I gave you credit for, Billie. I thought I'd lied rather well.' Charlotte sighs. 'But I fear there'll be no getting this particular cat back in the bag. Anyway, I was getting a little tired of Gaby's Fascist rants.'

'But don't you and Stef *adore* each other?' I say. 'Surely your breeding potential can't compare to that.'

'Most amusing, dear. No, I rather think the wedding is off.' She drops her cigarette and grinds it out with her heel. 'I'm sorry about Toby, though. He was a nice man.'

'Yeah, he was. Look, I'd better go. See you at the wake, Charlie.'

'Doubt I'll be coming, sweetie. Touch awkward.'

She squares her shoulders and walks unflinching past Gaby, still muttering malevolently, and Stef, who stares cravenly at the ground as she passes.

I can't cope with the crowd still milling about, so I go back to the grave for a moment.

Christ, Toby. Bet you didn't expect *that*, did you?

I look past the fresh mound of earth to the elegant tombstone beside. I knew Toby was being buried next to his mother, Aunt Maude, but beyond her grave is another, a simple stone that says *Paul Cornell 1884-1920*, and my eyes fill once more with helpless tears.

Oh, mate. You're with your parents at last.

We hold the wake at Whitfield Street. It's not really a solemn affair, because reminiscences of Toby invariably recall his wit, so small gusts of laughter rise here and there between groups of old friends, and those of us who had the privilege of living with him here in Aunt Maude's house.

I notice a man standing by himself, and go over to say hullo and offer him a sandwich. Turns out he's an academic who discovered something interesting about Toby's family, and told him about it on the morning of the bomb.

'We were meeting the following evening for a drink,' he says, 'but Toby stood me up, or I thought he did. Still, I took my pride in my hands and rang him here, only to find out —' He clears his throat. 'I liked him very much.'

He smiles sadly and limps away, and I want to bang my head on the wall in sheer misery. I turn and Otto is there. He hands me a glass of wine and says, 'A most interesting scene at the cemetery, Billie.'

I take a swig. 'Oh God, it affects you too, doesn't it? Were you hoping Charlie would give you more grandchildren?'

'I hope for nothing these days, Billie, thus I am rarely disappointed. I am sad for my daughter of course, but Vivian is treasure enough.' He sighs. 'I wish I could see more of the child, but there have been so many reasons to be busy, so many causes. Lost causes.'

'Not *lost*, Otto. We're beating the bastards back at last.'

He pauses. 'You are a realistic woman, and Klara has told you something of what we expect to find in Europe. I pray every night it will not be true, but I know I am wasting my breath. We may beat them this time, certainly. But humanity itself will never recover from so profound an evil. So *shameless* an evil.'

That evening we sit together in Klara's kitchen and eat leftovers from the wake and drink wine. At one point, a little pissed, I say, 'Reckon it hit me hardest when I realised all of Toby's family is gone, completely gone. There's something so terribly bleak about that.'

'No, Billie,' says Klara. 'There is still *one* left — when Toby saved me he saved his own child.'

'Dear God, that really was a miracle,' says Yvie, taking Klara's hand.

Izabel shivers. 'No, darling. It's marvellous, but not a miracle. A miracle would be Toby alive and living the life he deserved, and not just Toby, all those good people who've had their lives ripped away from them and discarded like *rubbish*.'

She stares at the wall and everyone is silent.

'All of them. Miracle after sweet beloved *miracle*, wiped out by monsters with nothing but emptiness in their own ugly souls.'

She puts her hands over her face and sobs. Eliza and Nancy exchange glances, and Eliza strokes Izabel's back, saying, 'Think we'd all better get some rest now.'

Everyone retreats. Klara and Yvie to their room, Eliza to hers, and Izabel, Nancy and Felix to their flat upstairs. In the past Pete and I would usually stay (separately) in Toby's spare room, so we go down to the first floor. Eliza has tidied it up and put away Toby's clothes and belongings, but it's still his place, completely his.

Pete and I sit in the familiar leather armchairs and stare silently at the fire. We haven't had a moment to talk all day.

I say, 'How're you going, Pete?'

He takes a deep breath. 'I've got friends, Billie, good men. But I never realised before what Toby meant to me. How he looked after me.' He shakes his head. 'Remember when we separated and I was a useless fool? Toby took me in. My truest friend, then and always. Haven't the foggiest what I'll do without him.'

I nod, my eyes aching. 'Same for me.'

Pete sighs. 'Anyway. Got to sleep, I'm buggered.' He pauses. 'Not in Toby's bed though, wouldn't be right. Look, you have the spare room and I'll be all right here on the sofa.'

I laugh sadly. 'Oh, Pete, remember, years ago? When I was beaten up by that little shit and you stayed in my cottage in case he came back?'

He smiles. 'Yeah. I was going to kip on the couch but you let me sleep in your bed — fully clad though. It was still pretty amazing.'

'You were twenty-one, kid, and totally single-minded. It was hard to battle you off.'

'Come on, crazy lady, it was years before you even let me touch you.'

'Yeah. And it still needed a plane crash to change my mind.'

'Perhaps we'd have never ...' He stops. 'Do you ever wonder, Billie? If that crash hadn't brought us together?'

'I do wonder, sometimes. I don't regret it, Pete. Still, it was hard when we separated.'

'But I *begged* you to take me back.'

I shake my head. 'Impossible. You were well off the tracks by then.'

'Till Toby saved me.'

'Till Toby.' I sigh.

'Suppose it left you free for Wilf, though,' says Pete. 'Love of your life and all that.'

'Wilf?'

'The guy you married.'

'On his bloody death-bed, drongo. No, I thought the world of Wilf, but he wasn't the love of my life.'

'So you've never —?'

'Look, Pete, we're both stupid with exhaustion. Come on, we can share the spare room.'

'Clothes on?'

'Absolutely.'

We go to bed. Although nine years have passed since we last lay side by side, there's no awkwardness between us and we both fall easily into welcome unconsciousness.

In the early hours Pete comes awake, sobbing. I hold him and he fits into my arms as if the bones themselves remember him.

'I keep forgetting where we are, Billie, why we're *here*,' he whispers. 'And then I remember and I just feel terrified, for you and me and Vivy, for our own helpless, *pathetic* mortality.'

'There, mate, there. Yeah, me too.'

I nuzzle Pete's hair and his eyes and his damp cheeks, and the familiar scent of him makes me ache with loss and longing. He reaches his hand to my head and pulls my face to his and kisses my mouth.

I don't move for a moment, then I kiss him back slowly, and whimper: not from pain. We stretch against each other in yearning and desire. In mutual and untolding desire.

It's been nine years since we parted, nine years of moulding ourselves to other bodies, but nothing between us is forgotten. We discard those pointless layers of clothing until only skin remains and then it seems not even that can separate us.

Afterwards, still joined, I lie on top of him, his arms about my waist, his thighs snug between mine. With my face against his neck and my breathing slow, I feel a relaxation so profound I doubt I'll ever want to move again. We fall asleep.

Some time later I come awake with a deep breath. Pete does too.

'Sorry, I've dribbled on your neck,' I say.

He laughs quietly. 'I've done worse to you.'

'Still the schoolboy humour.'

'It helps.'

'Yeah.' I move to the side and our hips slowly part.

'Ow. If we'd stayed like that much longer we'd be glued together for life,' he says. 'Bit inconvenient. Nice though.'

I smile and turn over, and we spoon together.

He kisses the back of my neck and says, 'I love you, Billie. Always.'

'You too, Pete. Always.'

The Allied armies slowly advance. In July 1944 the Soviets free the first extermination camp, Majdanek in Poland. It's beside the city of Lublin where, almost in plain view, the Nazis murdered tens of thousands of people and left them in a helter-skelter hillock of skulls and bones.

So profound an evil. So shameless an evil.

It's possible then to hope that's as bad as it gets. Of course it's not.

Paris is liberated in August and Brussels in September, and by mid-October most of France and Belgium is free. Five years of blackouts become dim-outs as the threat of night bombings recedes. But a new V-2 revenge weapon, a rocket that arrives silently at any time, becomes the latest burden Londoners have to bear.

ATA pilots finally get approval to ferry planes directly to Europe, male pilots at least: females are excluded because of high-level prejudice. Several ATA women resign then, including Yvie, and she leaves to live in London with Klara.

At Hamble we're busy delivering aircraft to the two invasion centres, White Waltham and Aston Down, then bringing back beaten-up old birds, usually to be scrapped.

It's unrelenting work by day, but in the evenings there's Pete and Vivy and the peace of the farm; and at night there's Pete and the sweet warmth of our bed.

In October we get the wonderful news: Klara and Yvie (and Toby) have had their child, a girl they'll call Claire Maude Fenn. We visit them and find Klara flourishing and the baby as fair as an angel.

With the child at her breast, Klara looks up. 'I thought I knew what poetry was, Billie, but I did not have the slightest idea.'

Vivy leans over the baby, enchanted. 'Perhaps Billie and Daddy will have a baby, and I'll have a sister then.'

Nancy says teasingly, 'You said I could be your sister.'

'You are, Nancy. But I want a *little* sister. You're grown up now.'

Nancy has certainly blossomed. Just fourteen, she's slim and lovely, although there's an odd restraint in her eyes. Still, she has to live with the tedious Felix.

Eliza is there too, pale and quiet. Her joy at Harry's survival has passed and I think she knows more, and worse than we imagine, about the life he must endure.

She says, almost to herself, 'When the war ends it will be the season of children. The only thing possible to ease such loss.'

Klara puts the sleeping baby in the cradle beside her chair and says, 'Now you are all here, I have something to tell you. We have another reason to celebrate.'

Pete says, 'Beyond little Claire?'

'Indeed,' says Klara. 'About Toby. You see, he and I would often talk about his novel. He worried because he could not resolve the ending, but on the day of the rocket he was very happy because he had finally worked it out. He told me his idea, and even among the noise and blood, I forced myself to remember.'

She looks up at us. 'I put my arms around him and I *promised* him I would remember. He could not hear me, but I knew it mattered to him more to him than anything else in the world.'

She smiles. 'So I have completed his novel just as he wanted. His publisher is happy, and the book will soon appear. Toby and I have produced two beautiful things, and we should celebrate for him.'

That night in bed I wriggle into the comfort of Pete's arms but he doesn't slip his hand beneath my nightgown. (The only reason I wear it is for the pleasure of having him remove it.)

'Billie, I was thinking.'

'Really, *now*?'

'What Vivy said about us giving her a sister. I know you don't have much time for marriage, and I know it's not the right moment, but perhaps one day — what do you say?'

'You romantic devil.'

'Billie, I'm serious.'

There's a silence. 'Pete, I need to tell you something. Now we're back together have you noticed I don't seem to bother much about avoiding pregnancy?'

'Oh, yeah, now you mention it. You always used to mess about with rubber things and making me use frenchies,' he says. 'What's changed? You're not an old crone yet.'

'Thanks a lot. Well. After we separated I decided to forget any possibility of having kids.'

He laughs. 'Forget? How? A lot of women would like to know that little trick.'

'Like Charlotte. I think that's why I knew she was lying about it.'

He leans up on an elbow. 'Are you saying you've had your tubes tied?'

'Yup.'

'But why don't you have scars?'

'You remember that mark I said was from appendicitis?'

'Oh.' He lies down. 'I always was pretty gullible. But both my wives getting themselves sterilised? What does that say about me, mate?'

'I'm not your wife, mate.'

'My women, then.'

'Not that either.'

'No. You're the cat who walks by herself, aren't you Billie?'

I sigh. 'We seem to have taken rather a dark turn here, Pete.'

He sighs too. 'Yeah. Sorry. Bit of self-pity. But I've never wanted you for your child-bearing hips, you know that. I just want you for you.'

'I'm here. You've got me.'

Next morning I'm up early and making a pot of tea when I hear the doorbell. To my surprise it's Charlotte, awkwardly holding several packages.

'Hello, Billie. Won't keep you. I thought Klara might be able to use these. Some very expensive bits and pieces Gabriela bestowed on me when she still had hopes for a litter of grandchildren.'

She turns to leave.

'Don't go, Charlie, have a cup of tea. No one else is around.'

She pauses and sighs, then follows me upstairs to what we still call 'Toby's flat', although the house itself has passed to Klara. We sit by the fire and I pour the tea. Charlotte seems unusually subdued.

'How're you going, Charlie?'

'Oh, this and that. Living with my father, working with the *Kindertransport* children again. It's going to be complex getting them home again once Germany's defeated. Lot of issues to consider.'

She takes a sip of tea.

'No, come on, what the hell made you think you'd get away with not telling Stef?'

'My God, Billie. Don't you have the slightest tact at all?'

I consider. 'Not with you. For someone who tells lies all the time you're brutally honest.'

She smiles a little. 'Oh, Christ, I don't *know*. I was madly in love with him. I just wanted — I thought somehow it wouldn't —' She shrugs. 'I loved him. How could babies compare to that?'

'Did to Gabriela.'

'That bitch. No, Klara certainly did me a favour there.' She hesitates. 'The worst of it, Billie, and I can't get *over* it — at the cemetery Stef wouldn't even look at me. I loved him so much, he was so brave. Nobody knows what agony his hands caused him every single day.'

'Yeah? Reckon Toby did.'

Charlotte gasps and tears come to her eyes.

'Oh, hell, Charlie. Didn't mean to rub it in.'

She shakes her head and wipes her face. 'No, you're right. In some ways Toby knew Stef better than I ever could.' She clears her throat. 'Anyway, I'll be back on my feet again soon. Might find myself a nice American general with aspirations in politics. I'd make a good Washington hostess, don't you think? Or ambassador's wife?'

'Probably,' I say, smiling. 'But what about Vivy? I know you don't see each other much, but you talk on the phone fairly often. Hard to do that if you're in America.'

'I thought *you* were — you know — her step-mother now.'

'Me? Nah. Love the kid dearly, but Pete's been both mother and father. Mrs Spencer too, of course. Vivy's probably closest to her out of everyone — calls her Spencie.'

'Spencie? I didn't know.'

'She calls *you* Charlie.'

'Heavens, can't imagine where she learnt that charming bit of insolence.' Charlotte clears her throat. 'Still, it sounds as if she'll be fine, she doesn't need me around.'

'Jesus, how stupid *are* you? Of course Vivy needs you, whether you live together or not. I know you had a crazy mother, but not having one at all would have been worse.'

Charlotte shrugs helplessly. 'To be honest, I don't really want to go *anywhere*, Billie, certainly not away from Vivy. I just thought everyone would be delighted to see the back of me.'

'You're a fucking idiot, Charlie.'

She throws her head back and laughs.

Pete, at the door, says, 'What's the joke, then?'

'Hello sweetie,' says Charlotte. 'Just ... this and that. How are you?'

He kisses her lightly. 'Extremely well. Have you brought gifts for Klara's baby?'

'Yes, but you give them to her later. She won't want to see me.'

'Klara's feeling guilty about you more than anything,' says Pete.

'Everyone cheered when she went for Gabriela, but she's embarrassed you got caught in the crossfire.'

'I've come to the view she did me a favour,' says Charlotte. 'And I think the world of her.'

'Just go and see her,' I say.

'Oh, I don't —'

Vivy dashes into the living room, her hair-ribbon askew. '*Charlie!*' She kisses her mother. 'Have you brought *presents* for Claire?'

'Let me fix your hair, sweetie.' Charlotte ties a neat bow, then sighs. 'Is the baby's name Claire? I do have some presents for her. Perhaps you could help me carry them upstairs.'

In January 1945 female ATA pilots are at last allowed to ferry planes to Europe. It feels strange landing at aerodromes that were once names in atlases, then tragic battlegrounds, and once again are now simply farmers' fields. Every flight is tinged with nostalgia — the days of the ATA are coming to an end.

The war-front edges closer to Germany. The Soviets liberate more extermination camps, including a vast one in Poland called Auschwitz, where only a few skeletal beings are left alive to be freed. The horror mounts, the joy of conquest grows.

By April, victory is a certainty.

In May I receive a letter from my father in Perth, addressed to Miss Wilhelmina Quinn (only my parents use my real name). After a period of estrangement twelve years ago, just before Pete and I came to England, they decided to forgive their only daughter for becoming an aviator.

And I decided to forgive them for being my pig-headed parents. We've gotten along nicely ever since.

Dearest Wilhelmina,

I am sorry to tell you that your mother is unwell and in hospital. She is in no immediate danger but I fear her time in the not too distant future may start to run out.

She would never ask this of you herself but, perhaps when convenient, if you could find your way back to see us once more I believe it would make her content.

You might also be interested to know there are major avenues in the aviation field opening up in this state. If you were of a mind to establish another flying school you would have both the business opportunity and, if you would accept it, my own financial support to make certain your plans had a solid footing.

With all our love, Dad.

I sit on the side of the bed, staring at the rolling green fields of the farm, the trees hazy with spring growth. Is Mum in pain? Is she dying? Is Dad is begging me to come home despite the restraint?

Home. After yet another brutal English winter I yearn for light and warmth. Perhaps I could go home. Would it be so absurd? Everything is changing.

The ATA will soon be closing down and there'll be nothing like that for me again. All the post-war flying jobs are going to ex-RAF pilots. My friends are scattering too.

Once Harry is free, Eliza will go back to Australia to live with him in Newcastle. Izabel wants to return to Hong Kong (although Felix frowns if she mentions it), while Klara, Yvonne and baby Claire are off to visit Klara's family in Finland.

Charlotte will be travelling with *Kindertransport* repatriations and Otto plans to go to Germany: to bring justice to the Nazis he says, his voice implacable.

Would Pete and Vivy consider taking up a new life in Australia?

On 8th May 1945, Germany surrenders. It's Victory in Europe Day, and that evening Pete and I sit on the sofa and celebrate with black market brandy.

'Hard to believe it's over,' he says with a sigh. 'The Spitfire factories are being wound up and all our beautiful birds are coming home, just to go on the scrapheap.'

I nod, my head on his shoulder. 'When this is remembered they'll only think of the glamorous fighter pilots. They won't care about people like you, who did all the work behind the scenes.'

'Doesn't matter. All I see is the light at the end of the tunnel — the day I can leave work and be simply Farmer Pete.' He kisses my head. 'Ah, Billie. I was never a real pilot at heart, you know, just a young fool with fantasies. I guess that's the truth of why I botched out — even at Hamble I felt like a fraud, scared witless most of the time.'

I shake my head. 'I had no idea, Pete.'

'No, I doubt you'd be able to imagine it.' He smiles. 'Why I love you.'

I look up at him. 'I'm sorry for saying you were stubborn and couldn't bear anyone explaining things. It's not true.'

'As I recall, you also said I was inflexible. Your rock-solid evidence was that I didn't want to trot round the dance floor with you.'

I laugh. 'Okay, I wouldn't want to stand up and defend that in court.'

'In fact I can prove you wrong, probably for the first and only time.' Pete stands up. 'May I?'

'You want to *dance*?'

'Yeah. Come on.'

He puts a record on the gramophone and holds out his arms. At first I fear for my feet but quickly realise there's no need for concern: he dances very well.

We do the foxtrot and tango, the samba and jitterbug. He changes records again and again and, finally at the end, we waltz together slowly and sweetly.

When the music stops Pete says, 'Enough for you yet, crazy lady?'

'Enough, kid. Let's sit down, sheer amazement is making me dizzy.'

'Nah, that'd be my fabulous technique.'

'But how, *when*?'

He grins. 'I saw a sign in the town centre — a dance studio had just opened. I thought, why not? So I've been sneaking out at lunchtime for lessons.'

'From Spitfires to sambas? Oh, *Pete*. You're pretty good, you know.'

'Not bad. But I had an ulterior motive. I want you to marry me, Billie, and I'll offer you years of wafting around the dance floor if you do.'

I can't reply.

Eventually he says quietly, 'Suppose that's a no. Again.'

'Wait, Pete, not *no*! But what would you think about going back to Perth? My mother's ill, my father wants to set me up in a flying business and, oh God, I just want to go *home*! I want to be warm again and see blue skies and gum trees and sunlight. I'd happily get married there and we could have a good life. Vivy would love it!'

Pete goes to the gramophone. He lifts off the record and put it in its sleeve, his back to me.

'I can't, Billie, you know I can't,' he says in a low voice. 'The farm and Vivy's school and her friends are here. Charlotte and Otto and Mrs Spencer are here. I can't go back to Australia. And I don't really want to. This is my home now.'

'But you always used to talk about the wonderful land east of Perth.'

'Fantasy. This life *here*, now, is reality.' Pete faces me and I see he means every word.

I take an anguished breath. 'But my mother's sick. I have to go.'

'I know.' He sit again, and rubs his face. 'It's how it's always been, though, isn't it? Intangible, elusive Billie, forever out of my reach. I've loved you since we met — Christ, fifteen years ago. And I've never, not for one minute, felt certain you'd be there when I needed you.'

'But I *love* you, Pete. You know I do, I always have.' My chest hurts.

He nods. 'In your own way, and when I was a young fool that was enough. But I'm a father now and Vivy comes first. This farm matters to me too — the work, the plans, the improvements. The farm grounds me, ties me to the earth, and you've never, not *once*, understood that.'

I have to think about breathing in and out because I fear my heart will simply stop if I don't. It's all true. Pete's bond to the land has never made sense to me, and I've only ever been a friendly acquaintance to small Vivy.

I could have done more, understood more, but I didn't.

I couldn't.

I can't.

Tears overflow and I wrap my arms around my aching chest.

Pete says gently, 'I know you must have your freedom, Billie, you'll go mad without testing yourself every day. But it doesn't leave much room for the rest of us. You really are the cat that walks by herself.'

'But I don't *want* to be!' I sob. 'I want us to have a life together, but I don't — I can't —'

Pete sighs. 'It's pretty clear there won't be work for women pilots in Britain after the war. If your father wants to help you set up a flying school in Perth you'd be mad to turn him down. I know you've got to go back, Billie, I really do.'

He puts his arm around me and I weep helplessly.

'Hey, we can visit you, though,' he says gently. 'Vivy's never met my family over there, after all. And before we know it she'll be fleeing the nest and I'll start feeling the cold. That land east of Perth could look pretty welcoming by then.'

I shake my head. 'No, Pete, don't promise me anything. After all, some nice woman who wants to be a farmer's wife could come along for you any day.'

'And some smooth flyboy with his head in the clouds could come along for you, too.'

'Nah,' I say, wiping my eyes. 'I am completely *done* with flyboys.'

'Me too. Another waltz, then? For now.'

28. Izabel: The Honourable Thing

A year has passed and, just as he promised, Felix has been as kind and charming as he was so long ago. He tells me not to worry about anything, he's simply happy we're together.

He's still working on obtaining British passports for Nancy and me, but the obstacles of proof of education, travels, residence, and especially birth certificates, are taking forever. My family documents are difficult to find among Min-lu's vast collection of records, while Nancy's are almost impossible, with both her parents dead in China and her father's papers under Japanese control.

Still, for a time I feel a certain relief, a return to the trust of the past, to the husband I once adored who's trying so hard to help us. But lately I feel a sense of something looming, something ominous.

It's probably just war-weariness, but it's as if I hear a whisper: Look, Izabel, *look*. Look at what?

I work hard to be a good wife and often list Felix's good points to myself. I even tried to let him enter me one night, but my body just closed down. Still, he reassured me it didn't matter. He understood.

And he was so kind to me when Toby died. Toby my friend, whose wisdom and sly wit I still bitterly miss. Klara's baby brought us all joy, but she's taken Yvonne and Claire to Finland for several months. Only Eliza lives here with us now and sometimes the house is so quiet.

Look, Izabel. What am I missing?

The relief of victory in Europe has come and gone, and when the Japanese are defeated we'll all have to come to grips with a world no longer at war. When the rationing, the travel bans, the clothing coupons, all the everyday petty restrictions are lifted, what then?

Dear God, let it be *over* soon so we can go home to Hong Kong.

But can we? Perhaps that's what's nagging at me: lately Felix goes quiet if I mention it. He seems far more interested in relishing all the gossip about political reshuffles at GC&CS; almost as if he expects to be staying here indefinitely.

He's also drinking more than he ever did, and I have the feeling he's seeing Barbara again (she wears a distinctive perfume). I can't blame him after our bedroom debacle, but still it stings a little.

The other day he took our identity documents, mine and Nancy's, to be checked at the Home Office, he said, then stored in a bank vault for safekeeping.

Every day I feel more anxious and confused.

What am I *missing*?

Tonight Felix comes home brandishing a bottle. 'Something to celebrate, Izzy! Glass of champers?'

He's had a few already and pours me one (I want it, though, it eases my anxiety).

'What are we celebrating, darling?'

'*Promotion*,' he says. 'I've been appointed head of a new section!'

'New section? But won't Intelligence be shedding staff once the war's over?'

He laughs. 'Shedding? We're expanding. War with Japan might end, but war with Communism will go on forever.' He takes a swig of champagne. 'Job for life it is, job for bloody *life*. Why we have to stay here in London, you see.'

'Here? But you said we could go home. I *have* to go home, Felix.'

He's silent and I see a flush rising on his neck. I realise he's had more to drink that I thought and feel a jolt of apprehension.

'Home, Izabel? To Hong Kong? To give comfort to the *Reds*?' He laughs. 'I don't think so. Took me a long time and lot of fancy footwork to shake off the taint of those Commie uncles of yours.'

'My *uncles*? But Felix, you *know* China isn't simply a case of communism versus capitalism.'

'Ha! Kind of nonsense those fellow-travellers in your section used to spout. Still, the reports you all did will come in handy when we're clearing out the Reds in Singapore.'

'Clearing out?' I say in horror.

He laughs again. 'Don't assume the worst. Out of power, that's all.'

Is he lying? He's very drunk.

I stand up. 'Might make a cup of tea now, darling. That drink's gone right to my head.'

'Lovely bit of stuff isn't it?' he says, coming close to me, swaying. 'You're a lovely bit of stuff too, Izzy. What say we try having some fun again? Come on.' He clutches at my breast and I can't stop myself.

'*No!*'

He gazes coldly at me, then refills his glass. 'Had your chance then, Izabel. Had your bloody chance. Don't be surprised if I turn my attentions elsewhere.'

'Then *turn* your attentions elsewhere.' I notice his smug face. 'You're seeing Barbara again, aren't you? Oh Felix, *please*, just let Nancy and me go home to Hong Kong.'

'Don't be stupid, that'd put me straight back into the bad books again. What if you got yourself another Commie boyfriend? *Disaster.* No, you're in it for the long haul, my dear. And don't even think about complaining to anyone. Nancy's in a delicate position, you know.'

'But you were sorting that out and getting her a British passport!'

'Taking longer than I expected. But until then, be discreet, Izabel. We don't want our little dear to end up deported, now, do we?'

After Felix leaves for work next day I hear noises downstairs and realise Eliza is still at home. When she answers the door I'm shocked at her drawn face.

'It's nothing, don't worry,' she says. 'Just tired, got a cold. But I couldn't face work today.'

'Oh darling, Harry will be home soon. The Japs don't have a chance.'

Eliza laughs bitterly. 'Perhaps they don't, Izabel, but they're still murdering their prisoners to cover up —' She sighs. 'Come and sit down. You look as awful as me.'

'I've got to tell you or I'll go mad. Felix is threatening me, hinting he might get Nancy *deported*. He's taken our identity documents and says he won't let us leave, because if I go back to Hong Kong it'll be bad for his job. And now we're trapped.'

'No, he's lying, Izabel, he doesn't have that kind of power. But your documents? Do you have any idea where they might be?'

I wipe my eyes. 'He said he put them in a bank vault. Perhaps he meant a safe deposit box, but why not call it that?'

'Sounds more like a lie. Is there anywhere in your flat he might have have hidden them?'

'Mmm ... perhaps. There's the locked drawer in his desk where he keeps his revolver.'

'Really? He should have returned that to the armoury by now,' says Eliza, frowning.

I nod. 'I *know*. He always wants to play the big man.'

'All right, can you get hold of the key to that drawer?'

'When he has a bath,' I say. 'He leaves his things on the dresser.'

Eliza smiles. 'This is absurdly cloak and dagger, but I want you to make a wax impression of the key, and I'll get someone at work to make a copy.'

'Heavens. I thought that only happened in novels. What sort of wax?'

'Just a candle. Press the key into it deeply enough so the locksmith can cut the same profile.'

I nod, then remember something that puzzled me.

'Felix actually mentioned my Commie *uncles*, plural, and my Commie boyfriend. But how could he possibly know Third Uncle was alive and we'd met in Shanghai? Or that Laurence was my lover? You're the only person I've ever told.'

Eliza nods slowly. 'That *is* odd. Years ago I spoke to one of our China specialists about the ambush, and he certainly didn't know. So how does Felix?'

I make a wax impression of Felix's desk key without being caught. A few days later Eliza brings me a copy. 'See if the documents are there,' she says. 'But if they are, just leave them till you decide what to do.'

'Thank you, darling. I can check this evening, he's out until late.'

'I tracked down that China specialist again and we had a chat,' Eliza says. 'In later years he found out about Third Uncle, because Colonel Huang would get drunk and boast about killing the notorious guerrilla, Lee Yun-sen, and his Red poet brother, Lee Bao-lim.'

'Ah. So he *did* know I'd lost two uncles — and he told Felix?'

'Yes, Felix bailed him up fairly recently. The man's his junior, so he had no choice.'

'But did the specialist know about me and Laurence?' I say.

'Now that's the odd bit. I dangled a morsel of misinformation, nudged a little and watched him. He hadn't the faintest idea about Laurence being your lover, so he couldn't have said anything.'

I shrug. 'Perhaps Felix was just taking a pot-shot.'

Eliza nods. 'Probably. But something else the specialist said might give you some satisfaction. Colonel Huang is dead. And he died slowly and painfully.'

'A war wound?'

'Poisoned — by his own men too.'

'Good.' I put the key in my pocket and go upstairs.

That afternoon Nancy comes home from a visit to Tessie's place. They resumed their friendship after last year's argument, but now she rushes to her room. I wonder if she's upset again. She's nearly fifteen and lately there have been one or two swings of adolescent emotion.

I tap on her half-open door and go in. She's sitting on the bed, staring at nothing, running the turquoise beads of her father's mala through her fingers.

'Is everything all right?'

She keeps her head down. 'Don't know.'

I sit beside her. 'What's happened, love?'

'Tessie —' she stops.

'Oh dear. Have you argued again?'

'No, just ... she's worried.'

'About what?'

She shakes her head.

I ask, 'Has she told Barbara?'

'Can't.'

'A boy I suppose,' I say carefully.

'Tessie's such a *hypocrite*,' says Nancy angrily. 'Always going on about sin and purity, but ...'

I say, 'Sometimes the worst sinners are those who most like to preach about sin, darling.'

'I'm starting to see that,' she says sadly.

'It's all right. Tell me.'

'Tessie's afraid,' Nancy sighs. 'Afraid she's going to ... have a baby.'

I'm suddenly alert.

'But she says they haven't — you know — he's just touched her, under her clothes. I *told* her that couldn't make her pregnant but she doesn't believe me. She never believes me about *anything*.'

'Well if she's not careful she will find herself in trouble,' I say as calmly as possible. 'Who is he, anyway? One of your neighbours?'

Nancy shakes her head miserably, crimson to her very ears. 'I can't say,' she whispers.

'Why not, darling?' I take her hand.

She swallows and there's a long silence.

'You must tell me, Nancy. Tessie might be in danger,' I say. 'She may be sixteen but she's still very naive.'

Nancy quickly wipes her eyes. 'But it could change *everything*. For *us*.'

'Us?'

She says in an angry rush, 'Because it's *him*, it's *Felix*! When Barbara isn't around he takes Tessie into another room and then ... he comes out all pleased with himself and Tessie's happy too, but afterwards she's awfully worried. It's *Felix*!'

The hair lifts on my scalp.

Somehow I comfort Nancy. Thankfully she's just young enough to believe that grown-ups are capable of fixing even a disaster like this. I try to spend a normal evening with her, but it's a relief when she finally goes to bed.

I hold my aching head and think, Oh, you shit. You loathsome shit. Just one more year to show how much we *mean* to you? Lying to my face for so long, leading foolish Barbara on as well!

Did you always have designs on her daughter? Dear God, she's just a *child*. You utter swine, Felix.

I stand up suddenly. *Enough*. I cannot bear this life a moment longer. I must find where Felix has hidden our documents and get away as soon as possible. I go to his desk, my hands shaking with rage, and smile with cold satisfaction when Eliza's duplicate key works smoothly in the lock.

On top of the papers in his private drawer are a small box of bullets and his stupid revolver. The sight makes me even angrier. How typical of him to keep it — the war's over, you pompous, *pathetic* little man. I push them aside and lift out a pile of papers.

They're mainly unpaid accounts — drink, tobacco, expensive shirts, a bill for a night at a famously seedy hotel. With whom, I wonder? I find one of Tessie's distinctive hair ribbons, and (my skin crawls) a satin garter, and a card with roses and glitter, saying coyly, *To dearest F, all my love, your own T.* Poor, silly little bitch.

I lift out more papers, then my fingers find the cardboard edges of our documents, and I pull them out in triumph. Yes, *yes!* You bastard, you'll never get these from me again!

I put them in my pocket, go to replace the papers, and notice an ripped-open envelope with Chinese stamps. A flimsy letter protrudes from it, a letter written in an achingly familiar hand.

I stare at it in astonishment and take it out, my hand shaking. Then I must sit down, overwhelmed with shock and despair and love.

September 1939
Beloved,

I do not know when or where or if this will ever find you, but I trust your cousin will do his best to send it on. You will know there was a battle. I had given what I was carrying to a comrade, and your uncle Bao-lim was about to do so, when we were attacked. Both men died immediately, along with three others. Third Uncle Yun-sen dragged me away, badly wounded. I am told the soldiers assumed we were both among the dead.

Brave Yun-sen also died later, and I did not recover for a very long time. To the world I was gone and you, I hoped, had ceased to mourn. I knew if I returned to Hong Kong I was a marked man, one who would lead my loved ones into great danger. I also found myself in the company of revolutionaries, courageous people sacrificing themselves every day. I made the agonising decision to stay and lend them my support.

I feared you would remain in Hong Kong even as it became more dangerous, so I had a comrade tell you all was lost so you would discard any hopes for me. He reports that you and Nancy have now sailed to the security of Singapore, and I may at last face my duty with serenity. I have no words to describe the gratitude I feel, knowing my daughter is safe and in your care.

One day Hong Kong will no longer be under threat and, although I must expect that by then you will have made a new home somewhere else — perhaps with someone else — still I dream you may return. It is unlikely I shall have the same opportunity. But even in the midst of battle, my love, I will always be stronger for the hope we may meet again.

Laurence lived after the ambush, dear God, Laurence *lived!*

I look again at the envelope and hear a soft rustle. At the bottom are a few tiny links he sent from the gold chain I gave him in Shanghai. A memento? A reassurance? A farewell?

Oh my love, my love.

First Cousin had forwarded the letter to me in Singapore, and Felix must have intercepted it and kept it hidden ever since.

I groan in anguish.

Of course, that's why he taunted me: *And who's to say you wouldn't get yourself another Commie boyfriend?*

I look through the drawer but there are no more letters. I check the date, and start to sob helplessly. Laurence sent it six gruelling years ago, and never wrote to me again.

My gentle academic, like so many millions of others, could not possibly have survived the civil war, the epidemics, the accidents, the violence, the genocidal invasion.

Perhaps I mourned for him too soon, but in the end I would still have had to mourn.

I wipe my eyes and hide the precious letter and documents. Despite my anguish, I wait in disciplined calm. *Look*, Izabel. Yes, at last I see what I've been missing for so very long.

At midnight I hear Felix's key in the door. 'Still up?' His voice has the slur of drink.

'Something I wanted to have a chat about, Felix.'

'What?' he says, then notices his desk, the drawer left wide open. 'Have you been going through my papers? How dare you? Private drawer, Izabel.'

'You left it unlocked.'

'Did I? Thought I'd ... in any case you shouldn't have gone riffling through. My revolver's there too. Should be locked away — danger to Nancy you know.'

'Not the only thing that's a danger to Nancy around here, Felix. I fear she's growing up a touch too quickly. Tessie's been telling her some extraordinary tales.'

'Oh? Little minx. Can't believe a word.'

'Ah. But I do, you see. And so, I'm certain, shall your superiors. I fear you left some unfortunate mementos in your drawer, proof of something that started long before the poor girl turned sixteen.'

I'm only guessing at that, but he goes scarlet.

'You *can't*, Izzy! Look it's nothing, a flirtation — just a foolish child.'

'Apparently that child believes she's become *pregnant*.'

At that he goes white. 'But she couldn't be, I was careful!'

'Clearly not careful enough. Still, I'm sure your bosses can discover the truth. They're very good at that in intelligence, aren't they?'

'Izabel, you can't possibly — my God, what if I lose my *job*?'

'Heavens, how does that compare to the security of the realm? We both signed the Official Secrets Act, Felix, we both know this makes you a high-level risk, leaves you open to blackmail.' I shrug. 'Leaves you unemployable.'

'You'd tell them and *shame* me in front of everyone? There'd be nothing left to live for, *nothing*.'

Felix grabs the revolver and box of bullets from the drawer. 'I'll have to end it all, you know, Izabel,' he says, his voice smug and insincere. 'Do the honourable thing.'

He sits down heavily on the sofa and makes a great play of loading the bullets, then looks up, tears of petulance in his eyes.

'Do you bloody-well *hear* me, Izabel? I'll have to kill myself and it'll be all *your* fault. Over a chit crying *innocent*? Little whore. I'm warning you, threaten me like this and I'll put an end to it here and now. By *God*, you'll regret it!'

He holds the gun dramatically to his head.

I think briefly about the mess. I'm wearing an expensive dress and have just had the sofa covered in a rather nice chintz. I sigh and sit down beside him.

'Oh, my darling. Not like *this*.' I rest my hand gently over his.

Felix sobs. 'I knew you wouldn't let me down, Izzy —'

'Like this.'

I press his finger hard on the trigger.

The dress never suited me anyway.

29. Eliza: Fair Winds and Following Seas

After the Americans release the new bomb they call Little Boy over Hiroshima on 6th August 1945, President Truman warns the Japanese to *expect a rain of ruin from the air*. They don't respond, so three days later Fat Man ignites the paper and timber and flesh of Nagasaki.

Japan surrenders.

The Germans bitterly dream of how the war might have gone had their own nuclear research not been curtailed, while the Soviet Union atomic program goes into overdrive. Something certainly ended with those bombs, but it was probably any hope of future peace.

Still, the surrender is signed, and that's all that matters to me.

As an Australian prisoner-of-war Harry will be repatriated to Sydney, so I've started packing and will soon leave my job. It seems as if every ship on earth is being diverted to bring soldiers home, but I pull a few strings and book myself a passage to Australia.

I can pull strings now because I'm head of a small section of GC&CS, a matter not widely known, of course. I've enjoyed it enormously, but the department has become a very different place, and even if I weren't returning to Australia I probably wouldn't stay.

My old boss, dear Mr Denniston, was forced out in an office coup a few years ago, while nice Quentin Baxter has spent the war with his beloved Joanie, working in intelligence in Kenya and Ceylon.

At least Mr Kingsley got back after Singapore, although lately he's been speaking wistfully of retirement — he wants to complete his study on the Taishō poets. One of his translations led to the shooting down of a Japanese Admiral, so mild Mr Kingsley probably saved more lives than the rest of us put together.

GC&CS is expanding, renamed the Government Communication Headquarters, so charmingly innocuous. The intelligence services were wound down after the Great War (hardly a job for gentlemen), but that certainly won't be the case after this one. Not with such glorious careers ahead for all the newly-minted anti-Communists.

I meet Charlotte for a farewell dinner.

'Found myself a General after all, sweetie,' she says, her blue eyes wryly amused. 'French, not American, and not at all interested in politics — or having children, thank God.'

'Is Parisian couture a bonus too?' I say.

She laughs. 'That and the château in Brittany certainly help, but he's kind and sophisticated, and I do like him. Best of all, I won't be far away from Vivy.'

'Well, I'm glad for you and Vivy both,' I say. 'I went down to the farm last week to say goodbye to her and Billie and Pete. Billie says the ATA is closing down soon, then she's going back to Perth.'

Charlotte sips her gin. 'Do you think she'll really leave Pete forever?'

'For now. Forever? That's a word for marriage vows, not real life.'

Charlotte leans forward. 'Speaking of vows, Stef quietly tied the knot last month to an English rose with money, a title and a sad resemblance to a mare. Perfect breeder — in fact the word is she's already incubating, thanks to some cad who dumped her.'

She shrugs. 'So Stef will finally get his heir, then they can go their separate ways. Good luck to them. I'm just glad I'm out of it.'

'Does this mean you're redeemed at last, Charlotte?' I tease.

'Dear God, Eliza, are you mad? I'm not redeemed, I'm just happy.'

Aunt Lucy writes to tell me she and Danny have moved to Fremantle: they can't return to Broome, the town is a half-deserted shambles. Their son Mike survived the war, despite a wound from East Timor, and he's now going back to his old life and finishing his studies.

Will Harry also be able to go back to his old life?

I have no idea how he is. His few letters said he was well but naturally he'd say that, not to worry me. Last year the civilian prisoners were moved from Changi to Sime Road, where conditions apparently weren't as unspeakably vile as in some camps.

But I often wish I didn't know so much about what happens to those who've been abused, body and soul, for a very long time.

And me? Only thirty-seven, but I'm bitter and careworn. There's a grey streak in my pulled-back hair, and my clothes are drab. I'd like to call the creases near my eyes laughter lines, but I've done so little laughing. There are no kind words for the sad downturn of my mouth.

When Harry and I first met, sixteen years ago, we were beautiful with youth and optimism. As friends we worked on the four-master *Inverley*, and for years remained no more than friends. But in the end we found each other, and all that had gone before meant nothing.

Except for *Inverley*, of course, and her sisters.

I remember saying to Harry, 'Isn't there something so *hopeful* about a sailing ship?' But in the chaos of war the square-riggers had as little hope as the rest of us.

Olivebank was shattered by a mine in the North Sea, *Killoran* time-bombed in the Atlantic, *Penang* torpedoed by a submarine off Ireland. The war stole so much from so many.

And now I feel it's taken my love for wind ships and my young, foolish memories too. It's been a hard decision to make, but I've decided to sell my share in *Inverley* to shipowner Gustaf Erikson, just as he always wanted.

Poor man. One of his sons was lost at sea during the war, Maria and Captain Nilsen wrote to tell me. At least they survived on their quiet Ålands farm, but our old friend Artur, brave survivor of *Olivebank*'s sinking, will never sail again. He died during Finland's Winter War.

Inverley has spent the last six years anchored in the harbour at Mariehamn. Perhaps Gusta' will work her again in the grain trade or perhaps he'll simply sell her for scrap. I cannot, must not, let myself care: that part of my life is over.

But I expect Gusta' would swap every vessel in his fleet for the return of his boy.

After the ambulance-men had removed what remained of Felix, and Nancy was comforted and asleep, Izabel told me what really happened.

Her eyes distant, she said, 'You know, I planned never to act again. But I suppose a final encore is required: a modicum of widow's grief.'

The coroner, a busy man, didn't take long to rule Felix's death a suicide. The funeral was sparsely attended. I think young Tessie had a faint air of relief and Izabel wore her mourning convincingly. Only Barbara truly wept for him.

When it was all over I pulled some more strings and managed to secure passages for Izabel and Nancy to Hong Kong. Although Izabel's house had been looted twice, the caretaker Mrs Lau survived (along with a couple of Nancy's pets) and the place is still intact.

The ship leaves tomorrow, and tonight Izabel and I sit together by the fire for the last time.

'The coroner said there's rather a lot of suicide about,' she says, stirring her tea. 'So many soldiers are despondent at the thought of returning to dull civilian life.'

'But surely he noticed your fingerprint near the trigger?' I say.

'Of course he did, darling. We all know I tried desperately to wrestle the gun from Felix.'

I smile. 'Does it worry you at all?'

Izabel hesitates. 'In the instant I thought, not *another* death? But then I thought of the truly guilty, those who take whatever they want, just because they want it. They're *everywhere*, Eliza. They invade countries and they invade bodies, and Felix was as guilty as any of them. No, it doesn't worry me in the slightest.'

I'm not shocked. Not after the experiences we'd shared in Singapore, and the secrets His Majesty expects me to preserve for a lifetime. In fact, nothing shocks me much now, except perhaps the infinite gifts of governments for hypocrisy and violence.

I nod. 'Will you try to find out what happened to Laurence in China?'

'Not yet. As soon as the Japanese surrendered, the Kuomintang turned everything they had on the Reds, so it's full-scale civil war again. But when peace comes, I'll try. Perhaps I'll find out.' She sighs. 'Perhaps I won't. At least Nancy and I will be in our own home again.'

'Harry and I will visit you one day. We'll take a leisurely cruise and see where Min-lu came from, and say a prayer for her in the temple.'

'I'm going to travel too,' says Izabel. 'To Macau, to find out more about my Portuguese father.'

'Do you remember on the *Centaur*, when we were sailing to Perth?' I say. 'And Nancy said if I had a baby I should name him Leo after your father?'

'Oh, dear, yes. She wasn't to know how sad you were about not having children.'

'But I *do* like the name, and if it did happen — if we were to be fortunate beyond measure — I'd call the baby Leo.'

'Lovely.' Izabel laughs. 'But what if it's a girl?'

'Heavens, haven't thought that far ahead. Just a silly fantasy.' I stop. 'Dearest Izabel. Give me a hug, then you'd better finish packing.'

'Well whatever happens, darling, we're *both* going home,' she says. 'I'll unpack those bags in my own house half-way up a mountain, and you and Harry will soon be safely back in Newcastle.'

Safely back? My chest tightens.

Izabel leaves. The fire drifts into embers and I think, of course lives can't be *mended* with babies, but a new generation must surely come along without our burden of memories; one that believes (like ours) it's the first to invent fashion and sex and outrageous art.

And just as we did, those fresh young creatures will barely wonder why their elders are so quiet and regretful and lost in the past.

My trunks have been sent to the docks to be loaded onto the liner and my bags are stacked downstairs. It's a clear dawn in late summer, and I'm sitting at the familiar old wooden table in the kitchen at Whitfield Street, waiting for the taxi to arrive.

This house has been such a refuge over the long, lonely time without Harry, but the heart went out of it for me when Toby died. I'll think I'll always miss him.

He's famous now. His posthumous novel, finished by Klara, has been a great success. I can just hear him saying, 'I'd have had myself blown up years ago, blossom, if only I'd known that's what'd get people to read my books.'

I'm alone and the place is empty. Klara has taken Yvonne and baby Claire to Finland, so I won't be able to say goodbye to that wise, poetic presence: I hope we meet again one day.

The third-floor flat, where Felix met his fate, is ready to be let to people who won't know or care what happened there. (Besides, if fatalities were any impediment to renting a property, half of London would be uninhabitable.)

A car horn beeps, and I run downstairs. The driver loads my bags into the taxi, and I go back inside to leave my key.

I gaze for the last time at the painting above the fireplace, the pretty fair-haired woman, bare-shouldered and laughing. Toby's mother, the guiding spirit of the house.

Thank you, Aunt Maude. Goodbye.

Six weeks later our ship steams through Sydney Harbour, and everyone around me noisily admires the sights. I watch silently and, as always, keep to myself.

Harry won't be back in Australia yet of course: civilians are at the end of the repatriation queue, and soldiers are still arriving home en masse every day.

I sent his mother Jessie my arrival details from London, but heard nothing in return. Like me — like so many — she must be anxiously waiting, waiting.

Still, it's a perfect day and my heart loosens with a feather-touch of hope. Clouds are sailing in the blue sky, the winds are fair and warm, seagulls are mewling and swooping through our wake.

Neat ferries chug from side to side of the choppy harbour, motor launches come and go from the naval bases, and the silhouettes of moored warships lie long and grey in the background.

We're heading for the wharves just beyond the vast steel bridge looming massive and riveted ahead of us. As we pass beneath, I notice something tied up at the shore to one side, something absurdly out of place on these bustling modern waters.

Barely one hundred yards away is *Lawhill*, a four-masted barque.

After Finland joined the Axis she was taken as a war prize by the South Africans and has been carrying cargo 'nobly' to and from Australia for the last few years. (Whenever column space needs filling, editors love to print some guff about the wind ships.)

People are chatting and pointing at the now-rare sight of a four-master. Poor *Lawhill* is scruffy and run down, and Gusta' would be furious to see his handsome old vessel in such a state.

I can only clutch the rail, astonished, my heart thumping, my eyes filling with tears. Perhaps I haven't forgotten my young, foolish memories after all.

But it's not why I'm weeping. There's a figure on the shore near the ship's bow, a figure standing exactly where anyone who knows me would be certain that's where I'd look.

A man is waving his hat, a thin, brown, utterly beautiful man, with light glinting from his glasses.

Laughing, I cry his name aloud and wave back.

Thank You, Readers

Thank you for reading *Embers at Midnight*. If you've enjoyed it, please recommend it to your friends and give it a review or rating on your favourite book site.

This is the second volume of the Tempo trilogy, and follows *Testing the Limits*, set in the 1930s. The foundation novel of the entire trilogy is *Silver Highways*, about Broome in the early twentieth century, and based upon award-winning *Redbill*.

The rear-cover images are drawn from public domain sources. Top: Air Transport Auxiliary pilot, Diana Barnato Walker, 1940s. Middle: the burning Cold Storage Depot in Southampton, August 1940. Bottom: Japanese map of Singapore, 1942. The front cover is from iStock.

http://seabooks.net provides links to all my books, with reviews, extracts, images and background information.

About the Author

I grew up near Lake Macquarie, NSW. My background is in science and technology, but in 2000 I ran across the story of the charmed life of an old Broome pearling lugger, and discovered the joys of historical research and writing.

My first book, *Redbill*, won the Western Australian Premier's Book Award for Non-Fiction in 2004. My second book, *Alan Villiers*, won the Mountbatten Maritime Award in 2009, and my novels include *Testing the Limits*, *Silver Highways, The Turning Tide* and *Atomic Sea*. I live in green South Gippsland.

I post on Twitter as **@katelance6**, and you may also contact me through **http://seabooks.net**, where you will also find extracts and reviews of my books. (Image above by Alex Lance.)

Acknowledgements

As ever, I'd like to thank my friends Alison Shields, Gillian Clarke and Ruth Carson, for their insightful editing and fine company over so many years, and my sons Alex and Joe, for always entertaining discussions.

Fiction by Kate Lance

TESTING THE LIMITS — Kate Lance, Seabooks Press, 2020

The love of the old. The thrill of the new. The turbulence to come.

1930s England: will the sunny days of ships, flying and love ever end?

Eliza McKee sails away to a new life in London, where her glamorous aunt Izabel is a star with a secret to hide. Her brother Pete yearns to fly, but has no idea how much he needs to learn from fierce pilot Billie Quinn.

Eliza's friend Harry loves golden Charlotte, but Charlotte just loves gambling with flyboy Pete's heart. And when a great white barque encounters the coast one foggy night, more than an era of sail finds itself tested to the limits.

SILVER HIGHWAYS — Kate Lance, Seabooks Press, 2018

From pearling to war. Is there any way home?

In 1906, Lucy Fox is sailing to Melbourne with her sister Rosa, when a tragic landfall leaves her life entangled with three seamen: gentle Sam, cynical Danny and beautiful Gideon.

After Rosa's scandalous elopement, trader Min-lu draws Lucy into a new world of silks, spices and the silvery pearlshell of Broome: a place where breaking the rules is a way of life.

The Great War begins and Lucy's beloved must go to sea, where ruthless U-boats stalk the last of the old sailing ships. But with peace comes the influenza pandemic ... and Lucy discovers how cruelly she has been betrayed.

ATOMIC SEA — CM Lance, Seabooks Press, 2016

"Brilliant! Every chapter holds a twist you can't see coming. Fast moving and worth the reading ride."

Chernobyl, the nuclear power station that contaminated Europe. Fukushima, smashed into radioactive rubble by a tsunami. And now ... Broome?

Worm Turning nuclear waste plant is fast-tracked on sacred ground near Broome. A certain Great Power says it'll take all responsibility. Sadly it's lying.

Life ashore becomes surprisingly threatening for scientist Lena and hacker Jessie, and their only refuge is Simon's old lugger. Sadly he's lying too.

An eerie blue boat turns up with a glowing cargo, the grand opening of Worm Turning is just days away, and a cyclone called Cyril is on the move.

And Lena discovers being stuck on a committee isn't her worst nightmare after all.

THE TURNING TIDE — CM Lance, Allen & Unwin, 2014

"It took me about two pages to fall in love with this beautiful Australian book."

Mike Whalen trained as a commando in 1942 at rugged Wilsons Prom and fought in East Timor. Now a widowed academic in his sixties, and more damaged than he realises, he meets Lena, the granddaughter of his glamorous old friends Helen and Johnny.

When Johnny died in the war he left Mike with a burden of secrets, and as Lena draws him back into her family he discovers more secrets existed than he ever imagined. From the Prom to devastated Hiroshima, this is a saga of adventure and passion.

Non-Fiction by Kate Lance

ALAN VILLIERS: VOYAGER OF THE WINDS

2nd Edition, Seabooks Press, 2020. **Mountbatten Maritime Award 2009.** Fully revised and with over 100 photos.

"A delightful warts-and-all biography of one of the world's most notable chroniclers of seafaring life."

When Australian journalist Alan Villiers sailed on the last of the giant merchant windjammers in the 1920s and '30s, his writings and photographs made him famous.

Villiers crewed on beautiful *Herzogin Cecilie* and tragic *Grace Harwar*, took tiny *Joseph Conrad* around the globe, sailed on Arabian dhows, led wartime landing craft, captained *Mayflower* II across the Atlantic, and inspired sail training and ship restoration projects.

Drawn from his personal diaries, this award-winning biography of the author-adventurer reveals both his mythmaking and his achievements. It is a tribute to the greatest sailing ships ever launched—and to the extraordinary man who loved them.

REDBILL: FROM PEARLS TO PEACE

Fremantle Press, 2004.

Western Australian Premier's Award 2004 for Non-Fiction.

"Lance has presented the biography of Redbill with quiet passion and exquisite detail."

Redbill is the true story of a sailing boat's voyage through a century of history. She began life as a Broome pearlshell lugger owned by the buccaneering Captain Gregory, then became naval vessel HMAS *Redbill*, bombed in Darwin during WW2.

After the war *Redbill* went pearling in Papua, then worked for Greenpeace in Tahiti, and raised funds for refugees. *Redbill* also filmed a Bass Strait voyage, *If It Doesn't Kill You* and reunited a young Aboriginal man with his long-lost family.

Finally she took on an epic voyage around the coast of Australia, to return to the North-West to face her greatest challenge yet: Rosita, the most powerful tropical cyclone to strike Broome in ninety years.

Manufactured by Amazon.com.au
Sydney, New South Wales, Australia

10510932R00166